Praise for Kathleen Kent's

THE BURN

"A labyrinth of a police procedural punctuated by nonstop action…
The Burn barely allows the reader to take a breath as believable
twists careen throughout…Kent is just beginning to explore Betty's
many layers."　　　　　　　　　　—Oline Coghill, *Associated Press*

"Deeply satisfying…[Betty is] an obsessive, borderline unstable,
fascinating, Brooklyn-born seeker of truth…With Betty Rhyzyk,
Kathleen Kent brings those mean streets to life as excitingly as
anybody has in years."　　　　　　　—Richard Lipez, *Washington Post*

"Kent's Dallas setting is so meticulously drawn that one can practically smell the streets…All of her characters are memorable,
and not a single one, even the minor characters, is less than three-
dimensional. Kent has a talent for creating real people with a few
succinct sentences…Her plot is complex, and much of the action
is violent as one expects from noir novels."
　　　　　　　　　　　—D. R. Meredith, *New York Journal of Books*

"Kent continues to reinvent and subvert traditional noir expectations with the larger-than-life, damaged, courageous Betty... Action-driven mystery anchored by dynamic, deep characters."

—*Kirkus Reviews* (starred review)

"Betty's struggles with PTSD and challenges to her identity as a cop spark compelling character evolution as she lowers walls to bond with a pair of old souls she meets on the streets. A gripping, powerfully human procedural."

—Christine Tran, *Booklist*

"A great follow-up to *The Dime* ... A suspenseful mystery right up until the end—and an effective exploration of trauma and its ongoing repercussions, not only for survivors but also for those who care about, and for, them."

—Norah Piehl, *Bookreporter*

"The blunt, volatile, and relentlessly brave Betty leaps off the page, and Kent hits her with a frequently terrifying obstacle course of hair-raising scenarios. Readers will clamor for the irresistible Betty's next chapter."

—*Publishers Weekly*

THE BURN

KATHLEEN KENT

MULHOLLAND BOOKS

Little, Brown and Company

New York Boston London

Copyright © 2020 by Kathleen Kent

Mulholland Books / Little, Brown and Company
Hachette Book Group
1290 Avenue of the Americas, New York, NY 10104
mulhollandbooks.com

Originally published in hardcover by Mulholland Books, February 2020
First Mulholland trade paperback edition, February 2021

Mulholland Books is an imprint of Little, Brown and Company, a division of Hachette Book Group, Inc. The Mulholland Books name and logo are trademarks of Hachette Book Group, Inc.

ISBN 978-0-316-45058-4 (hc) / 978-0-316-45057-7 (pb)
LCCN 2019939533

LSC-C

For Alisa, Josh, and Remi

Where the Devil cannot go, he will send a woman.

—Polish proverb

THE BURN

CHAPTER 1

FRIDAY, JANUARY 21, 1999
ALPHABET CITY, MANHATTAN
AVENUE D AND 3RD STREET

My Polish grandmother, to the end of her days, never trusted a man who smiled at the dark or wore white in wintertime. That was because *Kostucha,* the Grim Reaper, appeared at the moment of death, grinning like a dog at a feast and wearing a robe the color of snow.

I had never before that night met my brother's partner, even though he was the subject of endless dinner conversations. My father knew Paul Krasnow, of course, because, like my brother, Paul was a detective at the 94th Precinct in Brooklyn. Paul was older than my brother, Andrew, by a decade, had been in the narcotics division for eight years, four of them undercover, and was rumored to be next in line for sergeant's stripes.

Paul had an unbeatable record in Brooklyn: two dozen arrests of mid- to high-level crack dealers at Christmastime alone, close to half a million dollars in cash recovered, and over twenty fully automatic weapons taken off the streets.

Reluctantly, I had agreed to drive my brother and his partner into Manhattan so they could meet up with their CI to "settle some business." According to Andrew, he had been working an undercover operation for half a year and the CI, who lived in Alphabet City, had something to show them. When I asked him why he couldn't take his own car—or drive into the city in Paul's brand-new Cadillac—he told me with a guilty smile that he had given his car to his girlfriend for the evening, and his partner didn't want his car getting dinged.

"Great," I had said. "So my hard-earned Toyota is the sacrificial lamb."

I reminded Andrew that I had an academy exam in the morning, and that I couldn't stay out all hours. Any of their pub crawling afterward would have to be done back in Brooklyn.

"Betty," he had said, using the wheedling tone he always resorted to when he wanted to flatter or cajole me. "You are more of a man than I'll ever be, and more woman than I'll ever deserve. Do this for me," he winked, "and I'll slip you the answers to the policing ethics exam."

The streets were slick with a frigid rain when the two of us picked up Paul in front of his apartment on Franklin Street. I took the Brooklyn Queens Expressway, crossing over the Williamsburg Bridge to Alphabet City. Despite my cautious driving, it took us less than forty-five minutes to get into Manhattan.

Paul sat in the back, but he might as well have been riding shotgun: he leaned forward the entire time, resting his arms on the front seat, talking constantly over my shoulder, asking nonstop questions about my time at the academy. Was it hard being a woman there? Did I want to get my detective shield? What division did I want to join? These questions seemed designed to make me think he was genuinely interested in my career in law enforcement, but I suspected they were to gain information about me that Paul could use to his advantage.

He never once cracked the inevitable cop-among-cops dirty

joke—usually involving a drunken old lady or an inebriated stripper—so I assumed that Andrew had already given him the caution talk. But whenever I'd catch his reflection in the rearview mirror, his eyes were on mine like drill bits, despite the amiable banter.

I parked on the river side of Avenue D at 3rd Street, directly across from a Puerto Rican bodega. We were kitty-corner from the turn-of-the-century, five-story apartment building where the CI lived, in the heart of what was called, in Spanglish, "Loisaidas," the Hispanic section of the Lower East Side. In the last ten years gentrification had begun transforming the neighborhood into an anglicized bastion of low crime and overpriced apartments and shops. There were still holdouts, though, who insisted on sitting on their stoops well into dark in the summertime, and cooking plantains and garlic with all the windows open.

Paul and Andrew got out of the car, promising me they'd be gone only ten minutes, twenty at most. They crossed Avenue D, pausing once to talk outside the entrance to the building. Undercovers do this thing where they learn to talk with their mouths barely moving, so that anyone watching can't read their lips. I smiled observing my older brother, his arms crossed in front of his chest, dancing from one foot to the other to counter the bitter cold. His face, even at twenty-five, still had some of the round curves of his boyhood. I was four years younger than him but taller, with more sharp angles to my face—and to my personality. But he was still my protector against all threats, foreign and domestic.

I could tell from his impatient gestures what he was trying to say to his partner: *let's get this over with.*

At that moment, Paul's gaze locked onto mine. He was good-looking in a terrifying sort of way, with his jutting cheekbones and hatchet-like chin, wearing a snow-dusted sheepskin coat that would have set me back six months in tips at the restaurant where I worked, along with pale, acid-washed jeans. The corners of his lips curled upward, revealing the strong white teeth of a predator. A fleeting protective instinct made me want to call Andrew back to the car. To tell him to return with me to Brooklyn, leaving his partner to do whatever he was going to do. But Paul had already put a proprietary arm around Andrew's shoulders and was guiding him toward the entrance.

They buzzed someone on the intercom and disappeared into the building.

I turned up the volume on the radio, pulled the heavy academy textbook onto my lap, switched on my penlight, and started reading: *Corruption and Incident Complaints. In this course, students will examine the department's complaint reporting system, the backbone of the COMPSTAT process...*

I reviewed the proper techniques for filing complaints for bias-motivated incidents, threats to witnesses, police impersonation. When I looked at the clock, ten minutes had passed with no sign of Andrew or Paul. The woozy rain had turned to an icy sludge, the droplets on the windshield becoming hardened crystals. For the millionth time that month the radio station started playing "1999" by Prince, so I turned the dial until I caught a Britney Spears song, "Baby One More Time."

My loneliness is killing me... I sang along with the track, my mind on Carla, my fellow cadet. Sweet, sweet Carla, who had "Frisk me" written all over her smile.

It was getting cold in the car. I maxed the heater, tilted the seat back, stared at the building across the street. On the second floor, in a brightly lit apartment closest to the corner, a little girl was standing at the window, the frame a tall, golden rectangle set into the exterior crusted with a century of grime. Her pajamas were yellow, the ebony hair springing in tightly coiled ringlets atop a dewy, round face. She was patting the window gently with both hands, her mouth open with laughter, fascinated by her breath ghosting on the glass. I waved to her, but I was too far away, and the interior of the car was too dark for her to see me.

A full twenty minutes had passed. In all of the information packed into the four hundred pages of the Police Academy textbook, there was nothing about the crushing boredom of the stakeout, the bane of undercovers everywhere.

The little girl in the window had turned her back to me. I could see that she was standing behind sheer curtains. Vague, dark shapes moved beyond the gauzy fabric. Adult-sized shadows were floating through the interior of the apartment, now fast, now slow, as though they were dancing. Someone was pushed toward the window, knocking the child against the glass, and I jerked up in my seat, fearful that the glass would break, cutting her—or, worse, pushing her out into the sky.

Within a moment, all the shapes beyond the curtains had disappeared from view. But the girl had pressed herself against one side of the window frame. She stood motionless, intently watching something inside the room. Her hands were cupped over her mouth in shock, or surprise. Yet it was the utter stillness of her rigid body that set alarm bells clanging in my head. I turned the radio down but heard only erratic traffic noises, buffered by the scrim of slush. I had been waiting in the car for nearly half an hour and my brother and his partner had not reappeared. A dark thought, like the onset of a migraine, tightened the muscles at my temples: *Andrew and Paul were in that apartment.*

Again someone was shoved up against the glass, face forward this time, the gauzy curtain revealing a man's mouth opened in pain, or fear. The little girl crouched down, her arms crossed defensively over her head.

I wanted out of the car. But I was paralyzed with uncertainty. I could guess the CI's apartment number and start ringing buzzers, but any distraction or interference on my part could jeopardize my brother and his partner. The interior of the car wasn't cold anymore. It had become unbearably hot and close.

Then there was movement on the sidewalk below the window; Andrew and Paul hurrying across the street toward the car, my brother's chin lowered into the folds of his coat. Paul's face was a study in granite, expressionless. And it was the deadness, the lack of any animating emotion, that made me fling open the door, ready to propel myself from the car.

"Don't get out," Paul ordered, his voice low and urgent.

It was Andrew who got into the back seat this time. His partner threw himself into the passenger seat.

"Let's go," Paul said, eyes focused on the road ahead.

I checked the rearview mirror and saw Andrew with his head bowed, staring at his hands.

My eyes scanned the second-story window, but the child was no longer there.

"What happened?" I asked, my voice strangled with tension.

"I'll tell you on the way back," Paul snapped.

I hesitated and he turned his eyes to me and I understood that whatever had occurred in that apartment building was something bad. Something, I knew, that would not have happened without Paul's presence.

"What's going on?" I demanded, turning to Andrew.

"*Drive!*" Paul hissed, his face inches from mine. "You're fucking up our entire operation."

I put the car in drive and made a U-turn in front of the bodega, searching the apartment window one last time for a glimpse of the girl in the yellow pajamas. But she was gone, the filmy curtains flowing backward, as though pulled into the room by a strong vacuum.

We'd driven the few blocks to Houston Street, stopped at a red light, when the explosion ripped through the air behind us. I whipped my head around in time to see the street filled with fiery debris. The air was a dust cloud pocked with bricks and hunks of metal signage that rode the updrafts in untethered loops.

Paul's hand wrapped itself like an electric wire around my wrist.

"Keep driving," he said. "Or get out of the car."

We heard the first sirens by the time we got to Delancey Street. A dirty gray plume of smoke rose behind us as we drove east over the bridge to Brooklyn. But we were almost to Franklin Street before Paul Krasnow opened his mouth again. His tone was steady, instructing. The CI had lured him and Andrew, and two other undercovers, to the apartment under false pretenses, he told me. What the CI had wanted was more money in exchange for information. When the cops refused, the CI had threatened to expose them all to the dealers they were setting up. One of the other two undercovers drew his weapon and told Paul and Andrew to leave, that they would deal with the CI.

"And the explosion?" I asked, my hands white-knuckled on the steering wheel.

Paul looked at me dead-eyed and said, "An unhappy accident."

I pulled up in front of Paul's apartment and waited for Andrew to corroborate or refute Paul's story. When I finally summoned the nerve to check the mirror, Andrew's chin was still buried in his chest. He hadn't uttered a word.

"Look, the guy made drugs inside his apartment," Paul said, his hand on the door handle, ready to bolt. "There were enough dangerous chemicals to blow up Chelsea Pier. It was bound to happen sometime."

Before he had finished speaking, I knew the entire story had been pulled out of thin air in the short time it took us to cross the East River. And that he was feeding it to us both.

Paul thrust the door open and got out. But before he shut the door, he said to me, "You say anything about what happened tonight and we're history. And that includes your brother. You got it?"

He waited until I nodded, then said to Andrew, "We good?"

When my brother didn't respond, Paul leaned in over the front seat and asked again, "We good, partner?"

Andrew looked at him and nodded once.

I drove to Greenpoint with Andrew in the back seat, his body hunched, voiceless, a portrait of misery. I parked on the street in front of our parents' house, the house where we both still lived, the engine running, the heater insufficient for the cold. I wanted answers. When had the other two undercovers shown up? Was any part of Paul's story true? But more terrible than not knowing was the possibility of knowing what my brother had done.

I studied him in the mirror, his image as familiar as my own, taking in the new coat, the expensive watch, remembering his girlfriend's new necklace, and it gave me all the answers I needed.

"There was a child in the apartment," I told him, my voice barely above a whisper.

He did not exit the car so much as launch himself from the back seat, and he stumbled up the steps and into the house. I followed close behind, my fear giving way to anger. I banged through the front door in time to see Andrew running up the stairs, taking the risers two at a time. In front of the stairs, my father stood sentinel. As though he had been waiting for us all evening.

"Leave him alone," he barked at me, blocking my way, his eyes bloodshot from Jameson.

I tried to push past him but he shifted deftly like the street fighter he had been, his mouth a thin line of disapproval.

"You don't get to ask what happened," he said, his sour breath in my face. "You're not a cop. Yet. You haven't earned the right to ask the hard questions."

When he was satisfied I wasn't going to follow Andrew up to his room, he shuffled unsteadily back to his recliner, focusing his eyes again on the television screen.

"Until you've walked the walk," he said, drinking from his glass gripped with careless fingers, his face indistinct in the shadows, "you can't possibly know what it means to keep a fellow officer's confidence. When, and if—and that's a big *if*—you earn your badge, you'll find out there is no 'thin blue line.' There is no black or white. There's only a wide gray band the size of Brooklyn that separates us from the perps, and the rest of the clueless civilians."

I remained in the darkened room with him and watched the news reports already coming in about the explosion in Alphabet City. A four-alarm fire had burned the entire building on Avenue D and would have destroyed neighboring structures if it had not been a stand-alone, and if all the rooftops hadn't been so wet. Most of the apartments had been evacuated, but the tenants on the second floor were incinerated.

In the morning, the remains of three adults and one child were recovered, their flesh gone, their bones charred to ash. The explosion had burned hot and fast, helped along by an accelerant. The destroyed apartment had been owned not by some desperate junkie who might have been working as my brother's CI but by a high-level drug dealer named Raphael Trujillo-Sevilla. By the afternoon, it was confirmed that two policemen were among the adults who had perished in the blaze.

There was a formal, citywide investigation after the incident. Rumors of police corruption swirled—officers taking bribes from dealers to look the other way, planting evidence on the players who wouldn't pay up, even orchestrating hits on snitches who threatened to turn state's evidence—but nothing ever came of them. Not one officer was even cautioned, and the streets went back to business as usual. The lone assistant DA who tried to make a name for himself by pressing for further investigation left in disgrace after photos of his tryst with a prostitute were leaked to a prominent city paper.

Of course, there had been witnesses on the street that evening who gave testimony about the circumstances surrounding the explosion. At one point during the inquests, a report surfaced that a red Toyota Corolla, the same make and model as mine, had been spotted leaving the front of the building moments before the explosion. But it was a commonly seen car in Manhattan, and the report went nowhere.

One evening late, two NYPD officers came to our Greenpoint home and disappeared into my father's office—a private, smoke-filled place I'd rarely been allowed to view, let alone visit. After an hour, my father called me into the office and closed the door. The good bottle of aged whiskey was perched on the desk, its contents well diminished. The officer with the lieutenant's badge smiled at me—a thin-lipped, humorless grin—and told me I had nothing to worry about. My impotent rage threatened to erupt from my head like a geyser of blood onto the tobacco-stained walls of the study. I almost told them, the unspoken words like a knotted rope through my tongue, that it had been me who had sent the anonymous note about the Toyota to the ADA's office.

I'd stopped talking to my brother altogether, spending most of my time away from the house, catching only brief glimpses of him as he tried to make his way silently through the hallways, or when I passed him in the kitchen, my body shrinking from any contact with his.

The last time I heard Andrew's voice was when he spoke to me through my closed bedroom door.

"Betty," he had called, rapping softly with his knuckles. "Please…"

I got up only to lock the door and turn up my radio.

Two weeks after the explosion, my brother killed himself. His shirtless body was found on a frigid south Jersey shoreline in early February, with no outward marks of violence to indicate how a strong, seemingly healthy young man could have ended up washed from the Atlantic Ocean, until an autopsy revealed a fatal amount of barbiturates and alcohol in his bloodstream. The coroner's report also noted that he'd had red hair and blue eyes. Almost identical to mine.

I had never asked him the hard questions. I had never asked him anything at all. But in a letter left to me, Andrew told me about the fire. He and Paul Krasnow had been taking protection money from Trujillo-Sevilla. The dealer had tired of paying so much and threatened to expose them. The two undercovers who were killed were also bent, but they were willing to be less greedy. Tempers had flared, guns were drawn, and Andrew shot one of the cops. Paul followed by shooting the second cop and the dealer. From there it had been an easy fix to rig the gas stove to blow: the gas turned on at every burner, a lit candle, drug-making chemicals upended, and a fast retreat. Andrew had no idea a child had been in the apartment. It was this last bit of knowledge that pushed him over the edge. He just couldn't live with the guilt.

I tore up the letter and never revealed to another soul my brother's part in the whole dirty mess.

A year later Paul Krasnow made sergeant. It was his hand that I shook onstage at my cadet-graduation ceremony, welcoming me into the brotherhood of silence, the smile on his wolfish face taunting and smug. Once I became active duty, I followed his every move, right up until the day he was taken out by a bullet to the back of the head by a retaliating cartel enforcer. Or maybe another cop settling a score.

I burned Paul's newspaper obituary while it was still in my father's hands. He'd been reading the paper over his usual breakfast of bitter regret and Jameson, and I'd simply reached forward, lighter in hand, igniting one corner with a pass of the flame. When he dropped the paper, his astonished eyes met mine, and for the first time realized he was looking into the eyes of an honest cop.

CHAPTER 2

MONDAY, DECEMBER 30, 2013
DALLAS, TEXAS

This I've come to know. Avoiding uncomfortable truths about oneself is like putting a threadbare mattress over hard, stony ground. No matter which way you turn, it's going to hurt. Might as well quit stalling and get busy clearing the field.

Yet here I am in a ramshackle dive, facedown on a hard bench, submitting myself to a man holding an implement of torture—in this case, a tattooing gun.

The awkward position causes my right leg to cramp, the leg with the ruptured Achilles tendon, the shredded fibers sewn together with medical sutures strong enough to hold up a suspension bridge. The calf muscle twitches more painfully, and I flex the toes carefully upward to forestall a massive spasm.

It's been a full three months since the reparative surgery, and an agonizingly slow recovery and rehab. Three months and change since a narrow, plastic-coated cable was threaded through an incision in my ankle, forced beneath the major tendon, and passed through to the opposite side. The ends of the cable had been fastened together and attached to a heavy chain, the far end of which was anchored to a large stone upon which my captors had painted *SUBMIT, E 5:21.*

The *E* for *Ephesians,* the number indicating the biblical chapter and verse: "Submit yourselves one to another in the fear of God."

Closing my eyes, I can still hear Evangeline, my captor's voice reciting the passage in her gliding East Texas accent. It was during a long, hard drug investigation that I'd been held prisoner by Evangeline Roy and her two sons, the leaders of a cultlike ring of meth dealers. Several people had died, including a member of my own team, and I'd managed to survive, but just barely. The injury to my leg had curtailed, maybe forever, my ability to run—the key to my sanity. Until my injury I had run faithfully every day of my life, through other hurts, fevers, sprains, burns. I ran to keep the internal destructive forces at bay; the Kali-headed, bile-throated, hatchet-tongued impulses that threatened hourly to overcome every peaceful, balanced, orderly event in my life.

The best thing in my world was my partner, Jackie, the love of my life. But the past three months of sick leave from the Dallas Police Department—limping around our new house looking for something constructive to do, too wired to sleep at night, too mentally exhausted during the day to be truly useful—had come close to bringing my relationship with Jackie to an end. My irritability, the volatile frustration that I couldn't quite keep a lid on, had strained her monumental patience to wilted apathy.

I hear a restless shifting and crane my head over my shoulder to look at the guy standing behind me. He's shirtless, his shaved head glowing dully under the overhead fluorescent lights, bulging pectoral muscles inked with a large skull entwined with snakes, twitching impatiently. I've been told he's a master at what he's about to do.

"I haven't got all day," he warns me, grabbing hold of one of my ankles.

"Yeah," I say. "Just give me one more minute. Please."

I'm pathetic, cowardly.

You and no one else brought yourself to this, I think.

The worst part of not being able to run, though, has been the loss of connection to my uncle Benny—my father's brother, and a respected homicide cop with the 94th Precinct in Brooklyn—the total and absolute evaporation of his voice, his wisdom, his warnings and admonitions from my head. When I run, I hear him as clearly as though he was racing alongside me, breathing into my ear. The fact that he's been dead for several years has not vanquished my certainty that he's out there waiting to talk to me, if only I could unleash my mind to channel him.

Betty, he'd probably tell me in this moment, *you're being an asshole. You've been diminishing the finest thing in your life. You're driving Jackie away, and then you'll be stuck forever in the abyss of your own morass...*

"Hey," the guy barks.

"Okay," I breathe. "I'm ready, you bastard. Do what you have to do."

A metallic, buzzing noise starts up. Holding the now-active tattooing gun, the guy takes a seat next to the bench where I'm lying and begins the long, tedious process of inking in the outlines of the design that he's drawn on my right calf, just above the damaged ankle. The guy, professional name Tiny, was recommended to me by my partner, Seth, who swore to me that he's an artist, the best tattooist in North Texas.

I grab at the Saint Michael medallion hanging from a chain around my neck. Gone is the original medallion, which had been a gift from my mother, making me the third generation to have worn the old emblem, pitted with wear, brought from Poland. It had been taken by Evangeline while I was rendered unconscious, and I had no real hope of regaining it.

Jackie, always thoughtful, had replaced the missing medallion with a new one. It was beautiful in the way that modern copies often are—shiny, a little too hard-edged, a little too perfect—but I wore it every day, even as I mourned the loss of the original.

The tattoo on my leg is slowly taking the shape of the Archangel Michael, the patron saint of cops, wielding a sword, about to skewer a dragon beneath one sandaled foot. The tattoo will be large and lurid.

But the pain is immense, the prickling, punching needle ravaging the already hypersensitive skin around my surgical scar, which will be fashioned into the body of the serpent-devil. It will take hours to complete. Against Tiny's recommendation, I'm doing it all in one sitting. He'd warned me I would rather be shot in the stomach than continue the process past the first thirty minutes. Tiny's been shot several times, so he ought to know.

But I knew it would hurt. It's my penance for being an asshole. For being blunt, impatient, and unkind to the people I care about. For keeping secrets.

Punishment for being me.

When I flinch, Tiny asks, "You wanna stop?"

I tell him to screw off and keep going.

"Atta girl. You won't have to draw your weapon when this one's done. Just pull up your pant leg and scare 'em to death."

CHAPTER 3

On New Year's Day I wake before dawn. Jackie's still sleeping, the blanket pulled up over her head. I slip out of bed, dress, and leave the house without waking her. There's been a drizzling mist for a few days, and the temperature during the night has hovered just above freezing, making the roads treacherous and the Dallas drivers, unused to maneuvering on snow and ice, even more so.

I drive past downtown to Trinity Grove, a former industrial area burgeoning with new restaurants and boutique breweries, and park in the empty lot facing the steep Trinity River embankment. I often come to the long pedestrian bridge, which crosses the river, to run. Or, better said, to try to run.

I make my way across the footbridge from west to east, my breath steaming forcefully in the cold, easing myself into a rapid, gimpy walk. A more taxing pace brings about the inevitable and excruciating muscle lock in my lower right leg. There's not another soul on the pavement who can offer help, who might politely ask if I need assistance crossing the walkway—a crutch, a wheelchair, a stretcher—or who might shout out words of encouragement to not give up, to keep going; clichés designed to brighten my day, but which make me want to body-slam the Good Samaritan into the asphalt, drop-kicking their reusable, eco-friendly water bottles into the muddy banks of the Trinity.

Happy fucking New Year.

I make it to the downtown side of the bridge without incident. On the return trip, however, my muscles seize up and I stop midway and lean over the railing to look into the turgid water below. There are a few ducks floating motionless midstream, and bits of plastic bags snagged on the tips of branches, waving like tattered flags. But there's something larger and more solid lying on the westernmost bank, right at the waterline. It's a man, lying facedown in the mud; shirtless, the torso pale and unmoving.

I look around, but there's not another pedestrian in sight. I hurry to the western end of the bridge and hobble down the stairs to the path edging the river. The man is a stone's throw from the nearest support pile.

The sloping bank is pocked and muddy and I slip trying to negotiate the incline, sliding on my ass down to the water's edge, flopping over onto my side, barely missing him. I come to rest with my head not six inches from him, his face turned in profile toward me. The one eye I can see is lifeless and staring, the iris still a vivid blue, not yet opaque and milky as in one long dead. He's young, maybe in his late teens. His arms lie naturally on either side of his body. There are no signs of violence that I can see anywhere on him, other than the old and numerous track marks made by needles puncturing the skin of his arms. He's wearing jeans, the lower half of his legs still in the water.

I lie next to him, the steam from my breath on his face, and I have the disquieting thought that he might suddenly wake up. But he remains motionless as I work to control the unexpected sting of overwhelming sadness. He's very young, and his shirtless state makes him seem vulnerable, even in death. I push away from the body, crawling on hands and knees back up the embankment to the path. I stand and wipe the muddy frost from my hands, then pull my cell phone from my jacket pocket and dial 911.

A memory takes shape but it's painful, like scratching at concrete with a fingernail that's pulled away from the quick. My brother, on a beach in winter, his skin pale except for the places that have turned mottled and blue from floating in the Atlantic Ocean.

By the time the first patrol car arrives, I've regained my composure. I wait around for the medical response team and then the lone homicide detective who appears at the scene rumpled and unshaven, clearly not happy at being called out early on New Year's Day. He shivers inside his jacket, his dark face pinched and ashen with the cold.

We exchange names; then, puzzled by my insistence on sticking around for the crime scene personnel, he asks, "You know the victim?"

"No," I say. I watch him watching the body lying half-naked in the mud. "He's got track marks on both arms."

"This was somebody's child," he says with surprising bitterness. "You work narcotics, right?" When I nod, he says, "Yeah, I recognized your name."

He closes his jacket tighter across his chest and turns away from the dead man. "I don't envy you your job," he says, before wandering back to the warmth of his car. It is the first time that a homicide cop—someone whose main purpose in life is sorting out dead bodies—has ever expressed sympathy for the job I do.

The med techs give me a blanket and some hot coffee from a thermos to keep me from freezing while we wait.

An hour later, a tech from the medical examiner's office takes a few rapid photos of the dead man in situ. When he's flipped over onto his back, they discover more needle marks gouged into both arms. There's no ID in the man's pockets, no jewelry, no visible tattoos, nothing to give him a name or a home.

"Looks like an OD, hastened by exposure," the tech says.

They bundle the remains into a body bag, place it in the van, and everyone drives away.

I walk back to my car and sit motionless in the driver's seat, staring through the windshield toward the river, my hands clenching the steering wheel. The drizzling rain has started again, whipped sideways by a strengthening wind, the gray clouds peaked and turbulent like vast ocean waves, and I think of my brother, found frozen and lifeless on a deserted stretch of sand.

I then pull from my jacket pocket the coin I always carry with me since being rescued from the Roy family. Some long-lost, discarded dime I had found in my prison room. Through a drug-induced fever, I had dreamed that I used it to call Uncle Benny—or whatever entity he had become while inhabiting the Great Beyond—from an old-fashioned pay phone on a Brooklyn street. And it was his ghost voice, speaking to me through the receiver, that told me what to do with the dime that would make possible my final escape.

There are no more working pay phones in real life, but the dime is the one remaining connection I have with Benny, his essence, his voice. I bring the coin to my lips and smell the salty tang of metal. Or maybe the whiff of the sea as the waves press you under.

CHAPTER 4

I stare at myself in the mirror of my car visor, taking inventory. Both of my eyes are underscored with dark circles, my hair short and choppy, only a few months since my captors roughly cut it with scissors, punishment for not being a cooperative prisoner. My one true vanity had been my long red hair—"hussy red," my mother had called it—a birthright from my Polish grandmothers that was as close to a battle flag as I would ever carry. Jackie had reassured me time and again that it would grow back, and grow it has, but at a glacial pace. The woman staring at me in the reflection still has the overly thin, haunted expression of a rescued wilderness survivor left too long in the brush. Inexplicably, in a moment of rash, proactive defiance while getting dressed, I had taken some of Jackie's makeup—something I'd never done before—and painted dark kohl lines around both eyelids. But it hadn't been to beautify. It was a signal: *keep your distance*.

With my black leather jacket and dark jeans, I could be some Goth girl about to stumble into the police station to file assault charges against my musician boyfriend.

The car engine is still on, the CD player blasting the last of the compilation tracks that Jackie had put together for me: "Brother," by the band the Organ.

Here we go, they're back again. Look alive, warn your friends...

I reach for the key to turn off the engine, but that would mean I would then have to get out of the car, walk up the driveway, and enter the station for my first departmental meeting since the morning of September 23, 2013, when I drove with a fellow detective and team member toward the town of Uncertain, Texas, for the last time.

A recalled flash of red, the spray of blood from a shattered skull, and my mind veers away from thinking about Bob Hoskins. I close my eyes and take a deep breath, drawing in the new-car smell. At Jackie's prompting, I had traded in my perfectly adequate four-door for a newer sports coupe. I think she thought it would jump-start my vacationing libido. It hasn't.

The band on the CD keeps singing about how no one is ever really safe, no matter how many protective walls we surround ourselves with.

And to prove the point, I've got the same old nightmares despite the new house, the new car, the new tattoo.

I had told Jackie that I was going to get inked, but she was stunned into silence when she saw the size of the glowing, sword-wielding Saint Michael on my leg, looking like a mural from a Mexican shrine. For the first few evenings she had insisted on dabbing the antibacterial cream herself, her fingers gentle but her face a mask of disapproval.

I look into the mirror once more. Baring my teeth like a wolf, I think, *Buck up, Betty. This is as good as it gets for a while.*

Flipping up the visor, I see my partner, Seth, standing in front of the car, his arms tightly folded, his brows crowded together with concern. He cocks his head to one side, wondering why I've been growling at myself in the mirror.

In the harsh light of day he looks thinner than I'd remembered him, and worn, with three-day stubble on his chin. For months I'd seen him only after hours, in between his undercover prowling around alleys and beer halls, setting up buy-and-busts in the parts of town where nice white folks would ordinarily never venture. Not unless they were looking to score.

Despite Seth's scruffy appearance, his was the kind of masculine beauty, with an athlete's body and Nordic Viking features, that pulled women in like an industrial-strength magnet, the rough edges of his undercover guise promising a bad boy with good manners. A passerby might never know that a month before my injury he'd been shot in the abdomen, spending his own time on leave from the force. But he'd beaten me back to active duty, and I am grateful for his welcoming committee of one. With a pain that's sharper than the grinding, hobbling ache of my injured leg, I've missed his daily presence in my life. He crooks a finger at me and smiles, and the relief of seeing my strong, capable partner waiting for me—his blond hair artfully spiky, gleaming like platinum wire in the sun—is so intense it's almost erotic.

Seth walks to the window and I roll it down.

"The hell you doing, Riz?" he asks, using the nickname that he alone can use. "You waiting for an engraved invitation?"

"Just taking inventory," I say, cutting the engine. The car interior goes abruptly silent.

I get out and hug my partner. His arms feel good around my back.

"Damn, Riz, you been working out? Your biceps are bigger than mine now."

I look down at my injured leg. "Yeah, well, compensatory displacement."

Daily, I spend hours in the gym: pull-ups, push-ups, leg lifts, the recumbent bike. Just no running. I can walk on the treadmill for short periods of time, sweating and cursing like a Marine—the requirement to pass the departmental physical—but the only fleeing suspects I'm going to catch will be sprightly octogenarians.

"Okay, let me see it," he says.

"What?"

"Jackie told me you got a tattoo that puts the Sistine Chapel to shame."

I dutifully turn around and pull up my pant leg, showing him the Saint Michael emblazoned on my right calf.

"Holy shit," he says. "I don't know whether to run away or kneel down in wonder."

"Yeah, well, you can thank your guy, Tiny, for the special effects."

"Ready to go back to work?" he asks me, grinning.

God, he's so eager for me. Like a lonely kid finding a long-lost friend.

"Sure," I say and follow him into the building, trying to match his pace. Trying not to limp.

I trail Seth down the familiar hallways toward the meeting room, nodding at fellow officers who smile, telling me "Welcome back," waiting for me to get almost out of earshot before muttering about how bad I still look.

But they've heard the stories, and they're all replaying in their heads the reports of my escape from my kidnappers; ramming a shard of glass into one captor's neck, disemboweling another with a Civil War–era bayonet.

One rookie gapes openmouthed at me as I pass; the unruly red hair, my height, my Garb of the Underworld all working to disorient his sense of departmental order.

"Beetlejuice," I bark at him, and he startles.

Half a dozen cops laugh at this and I flash them the victory sign before ducking into the meeting room filled with North Central Division narcotics officers.

The first people I see, waiting for me by the door, are Kevin Ryan and Tom Craddock. Apart from Seth, they are the only remaining members of my original team now that Bob Hoskins is dead. My old sergeant, Verne Taylor, is gone too, a fatal heart attack sustained a few days after my kidnapping.

Ryan shakes my hand, his shy smile warm against the harsh overhead lights of the meeting room. The past few months following my leave from the force have aged him. He now looks twenty instead of eighteen, although in reality he's all of twenty-six. He had worked undercover with me, posing as a high school senior, setting up a bust for a heroin dealer selling his product to minors. I'd also heard that he'd gotten married just before Christmas; a week after that, a close family member had passed away.

"Congratulations on your wedding," I tell him. "I'm just so sorry to hear about your brother-in-law."

Ryan blinks a few times, his eyes averted, nodding his thanks. "Welcome back," he manages to say before being elbowed out of the way by Craddock, who slaps me roughly on the back, then squeezes my shoulders reassuringly, like a coach encouraging a reluctant player right before the big high school game.

"You look good, Betty," he tells me.

"I look like shit." I laugh. I point at his sizable belly. "But it's nice to see that you've been taking care of yourself, Tom. You bring the kolaches this morning?"

"Hell, yeah," he says. "You think I'd forget the return of the

Polish Princess? I did bring the cream-cheese ones you like so much, but, uh…" Here he stops, does an exaggerated sweep of his head, and then whispers, "I ate them already."

He laughs in his weirdly stuttering, good-old-boy way, and I laugh with him. Following a trail of blood leaking from my wounded leg, Craddock and Ryan had tracked me to the place I'd stumbled upon after fleeing my captors' house. Craddock, with his skills as a hunter, had spotted the signs, but it was Ryan who had saved me from my pursuers, taking the shot that dropped Tommy Roy as he rushed at me with a knife.

"Can we get started with the meeting now?" A rumbling baritone from the front of the room.

We all find our places, me next to Seth, and I sit with arms crossed, staring at Marshall Maclin, Verne Taylor's replacement.

"Good morning, Detective Rhyzyk," Maclin says. "Glad to have you back again."

His appraising gaze and mocking tone, however, convey *Nice that the funeral ended in time for you to make it to the meeting.*

"Good to be back." I give him a tight-lipped smile.

Maclin had transferred into the vacant sergeant's position from Homicide. And following the events of the past few months—the pursuit of Mexican cocaine dealers and homegrown meth producers who left mangled bodies across Texas—the leap from the Murder Squad wasn't that extreme.

Both Taylor and Maclin were good, experienced cops. But Verne was rumpled and comfortably capable as sergeant, his door always open to his officers. Maclin's all thrusting ambition, prickly edges, and freshly shined shoes, and the jury's still out on what kind of team leader he'll be.

Verne's burning hatred of the cartels and their dealers fueled a zealous commitment to cleaning up the streets. He took the fallout from the drug wars personally. It's probably what helped kill him in the end. Maclin's approach is purely tactical. The dealers aren't even human. They're just pieces to be taken off the board and out of play. Working homicide too long can do that to a person.

Maclin gestures to the talking points written on the whiteboard behind him. "Last September, Alberto Carrillo Fuentes was arrested by Mexican authorities. Since then, hundreds of heads have rolled."

Fuentes was the leader of the Nuevo Juarez cartel, a serious rival to the larger Sinaloa cartel. I duck my chin, smiling sadly, remembering Bob Hoskins teasing me about Fuentes's nickname, *Betty La Fea:* Ugly Betty.

"Something funny about beheadings, Detective?" Maclin asks, looking at me.

There's a sharp intake of breath from Seth. He knows, and I know that Maclin knows, that I had an up-close-and-personal experience with a disembodied head: one of Fuentes's top dealers, Tomás "El Gitano" (Gypsy) Ruiz.

Written in bright red marker on the whiteboard behind Maclin is a laundry list of the cost, in dollars and lives, of a six-year period in the war on drugs: 60,000 people killed, 26,000 people missing, 6,700 licensed firearms dealers along the U.S.–Mexico border selling guns to Mexican criminals, 70 percent of guns recovered from Mexican activity originating in the United States, 90 percent of cocaine sold in the U.S. transiting Mexico first, $19 billion to $29 billion annual take by cartels, the streets of Mexican border towns littered with bodies and body parts.

"Do I find something funny about beheadings?" I say, repeating Maclin's question. "Not unless there are party favors inside."

There is dark snickering from the cops in the room, and I feel

Craddock, sitting behind me, give me a congratulatory nudge at the small of my back with the tip of his shoe.

It's Maclin's turn to give me a sour-lipped smile. He picks up a stack of papers from a nearby table and hands it to the officers nearest him to pass around.

"Gathered statistics from last year. Most of it stuff we already know, or suspected. The good news first. Cocaine presence is down, but marginally. Now for the bad. There's more heroin coming in from Mexico. A lot more. And for the first time we're seeing labels on the balloons and baggies of black tar and powdered brown: Mud, Dog Food, Ace of Diamonds, and Hearts. They're selling on street corners the way they used to sell crack. And this stuff is strong…"

"…and cheap," Seth says. He gets noises of agreement from the room.

"And we're not seeing overdoses just with the hardened users," Maclin continues. "We're seeing kids, especially high school age."

Maclin unbuttons his jacket and perches on the table at the front of the room.

"And, as most of you already know, meth is now our second-most-frequent problem, exceeded only by marijuana. The liquid P2P meth coming from Mexico is stronger and more addictive than anything we've seen from the local shake-and-bake operations."

From the back of the room a Latino cop named Ortega says, "And you guys think we don't have a good work ethic."

More laughter until Maclin stands up and points to the officer. "That's right, Ortega—we know how hard you can work. That's why I'm assigning you to head the buy-and-bust operations I want set up in North Dallas. The chief has made it absolutely clear that no more black-tar heroin poisons our kids."

"Especially the kids from the private schools," Seth mutters to me.

"You can pick your team, four from this room," Maclin says, addressing Ortega. "We'll be coordinating with DEA and our law-enforcement task force along the border, so we'll know who the players are and when they're coming. I'll give you the particulars in my office at eleven hundred hours."

Ortega nods his head, serious as cancer, and gets a low five from his partner.

Maclin turns to Seth. "Detective Dutton, you'll be lead on the buy-and-bust heroin operations within our central district. You have the field experience, and you have the CIs in place. Craddock and Ryan, you're on the team as well."

Then Maclin makes eye contact with me. "You can pick one more officer from this room."

Seth starts to turn toward me, but before he can say anything, Maclin says, "Not this officer."

The room goes silent.

"I have something special in mind for Detective Rhyzyk."

I feel all eyes on me, but I keep my face a mask. His tone does not suggest anything pleasant, but hope springs eternal, even in my dark little Polish heart. Everyone in the room begins to stir, ready to start the day.

"El Cuchillo," Maclin says, addressing the group, holding us in our seats. "Anyone in this room ever hear of him?"

Maclin looks over the blank expressions.

"The Knife?" Ortega says. "Never heard of him."

Ortega has worked both gangland and narcotics, so if he's never heard of El Cuchillo, the man must be a practiced ghost, expert at covering his tracks.

"A guy was picked up off the streets by EMTs last night,

skinned like a rabbit. He was still alive, barely, when they brought him to Baylor Hospital. Turns out he was a high-level dealer for the Nuevo Juarez cartel. He died, but not before telling a cop it was El Cuchillo who had carved him up. I checked with Don Haslett, special agent in charge at DEA, who got all hot and bothered at the idea El Cuchillo's in the area."

"Who is he?" Seth asks.

"El Cuchillo's real name is believed to be Alfonso Ruiz Zena, but nobody knows for sure. He came up in the ranks of the Sinaloa cartel to head Los Antrax."

The silence in the room deepens from the routine quiet of a group of law-enforcement officers listening to a briefing to the weighted silence of dread. The skin on the back of my neck tightens. Los Antrax is the security force for the Sinaloa cartel leader, Joaquín "El Chapo" Guzmán. In a world of torturers and murderers, Los Antrax ranks next to Pol Pot in barbarity, if not in numbers. Even the Mexican army, filled with first-rate killers, is afraid of them.

Maclin starts to pace, warming to his subject. "Zena has no wife, no children, no other family. He had two brothers, Ismael and Hector, who he reportedly killed with his own hands. He has no long-term lovers, male or female, and can evidently go for days without sleeping. Doesn't drink or do drugs, which makes it hard to find his Achilles heel. No one's really sure how old he is.

"Whenever there's a power play with a rival cartel, El Cuchillo is the fixer. He had five high-level enforcers from two different cartels delivered in pieces to their people. They had been skinned like cattle, while they were still alive. One of the tortured men had a tattoo of a scorpion on his arm. Another had a tattoo on his chest—a skull surrounded by thorns. The tattooed sections of their skin had been removed from the scene, and later it was reported by a DEA agent (who heard it from one of his captured bodyguards) that the Knife had made a pair of boots out of the dead men's skin. Evidently he has several pairs of these boots."

For the briefest of moments I allow myself to hope that maybe Maclin's special project for me involves tracking the Sinaloans.

"Where the Knife goes," Maclin says, "the bodies pile up. And until now, he's never been reported outside Mexico. Catching him would be the next-best thing to capturing El Chapo. Keep your eyes and ears open. You hear anything about this guy, I want to know it."

Maclin walks to the door and opens it. "Detectives Dutton and Ortega, I'll see you both in my office later. The rest of you, except for Detective Rhyzyk, can start your day."

Everyone gets up to leave. Seth gives me a reassuring nod and murmurs, "See you outside."

I stay seated until the room is empty except for me and Maclin.

"Ready to get back to work?" he asks.

"I've been given the go-ahead for duty by Medical," I tell him confidently. "I've met with my peer-support team. I've been weapon requalified, cleared by the DA's office. And my post-incident intervention counselor came back with a sterling report."

"I read the medical assessment," he says. "The Fitness for Duty Report recommended light duty for a minimum of thirty days—"

"I read it too," I interrupt, ignoring Maclin's scowl, "and it didn't 'recommend' anything. It said that I passed all of the physical requirements—strength, range of motion, response time—and needed to be fully reinstated—"

"Oh really? With that bad leg you can't even break into a turkey trot. What are you going to do when your suspect runs? You gonna gimp along behind him, letting your partner do all the heavy lifting?"

Right on cue, my right calf muscle twitches. I breathe in, willing the tension away, trying to tamp down my impatience.

Maclin sits down next to me, crosses his arms, and stares at the whiteboard. He's taken the manspreading pose, his closer thigh almost touching mine. Before he knew better he had asked me out, and after I'd refused him—telling him the reason—he'd attempted to bait and bully me; standing too close, engaging in staring contests, literally breathing down my neck. And when that didn't work, he actually tried coming on to Jackie.

While I was out on medical leave, I had heard that I was being considered for sergeant in Verne Taylor's stead. I had also heard that Maclin, who badly wanted the position, trash-talked me to anyone who would listen.

The truth of it is that he's started with these intimidation tactics on my first day back because I intimidate *him*. I disturb his sense of The Ways Things Should Be. He can't fit me neatly into a box that can be weighed, measured, and compartmentalized, the way I suspect he's done with other females on the force. I talk back, loudly. I question him mercilessly. And his charm, such as it is, does nothing to sway me. He's stuck with having to treat me the way he'd treat his male counterparts.

Uncle Benny would have called his continual female-intimidation tactics "Boors' Head Turkey."

I swivel in my chair, facing him. "I'm ready to go to work."

Maclin adopts a patronizing tone. "Glad to hear that, Detective. Listen, I know you're eager to join the ranks again. But I have to take your safety into consideration, as well as the safety of the other officers. Let's see how the next few days go. Get your desk in order. Catch up on emails. Come see me later today and we'll talk about the best fit for you until you get your sea legs."

He lifts his right hand, and for a moment I think he's going to pat me on the thigh. Reflexively, I pull away. He casually brushes lint from his pant leg.

"You'll be out in the field before you know it," Maclin tells me.

He grins humorlessly, stands, and walks toward the door.

I glance at the board with its devastating statistics, the enormous cost in time and resources spent fighting a war that is without end, that can never be won, the wreckage of countless lives tallied in bloodred scribblings. The efforts of law enforcement failing to affect the numbers in any meaningful way.

Before I can stop myself, I clutch at the strained calf muscle, cramping from sitting too long in one position.

"By the way," Maclin calls from the door. He gives me a pitying look, catching me massaging my leg. Then he circles one eye with a finger. "I'd rethink the vampire look. This isn't Vice."

CHAPTER 5

I perch on one of the few vacant stools, nursing my shot of Jameson, lazily spreading the ring of condensation with the bottom of the glass. Dottie, working behind the bar, picks up a massive bucket of ice and pours it effortlessly into a stainless-steel well. She wipes up the errant pieces of ice with a rag, then flips it over her shoulder and faces me, hands flat on the bar, her bare, skinny arms ropy with muscle earned from a childhood spent on a ranch in El Paso. Dottie is the owner of Slugger Anne's, but she also passes along information about the local drug dealers when the activity around the bar has gone once more into the red zone. Until she got clean and sober, I bailed her out of jail several times when no one else would pick up the tab.

"Want another?" she asks.

I push the glass toward her and she fills it from a bottle that reads PROPERTY OF THE POLISH ARMY. She keeps it for my personal consumption.

She regards me, squinting, pushing back a tuft of graying hair from her forehead. "How'd it go?"

"Great," I say, frowning.

"Uh-oh," she responds, but before she can ask me about the misery of the day I've just had, she's called to the end of the bar by one of the waitresses.

I take a sip of my drink and look around. Slugger Anne's is always busy after dark—weekdays or weekends, it doesn't matter—the all-female customers gathered in groups, or singly, or as couples. Male customers aren't usually encouraged, Seth being the notable exception. My partner's nickname is Riot, as in "One riot, one Ranger," but given the razzings he's received from Dottie, I believe Seth would rather work a biker bust than submit to her cold and disapproving stares. Secretly, I know she's come to like Seth—she's told me so. But it's too much fun to watch him squirm to let him in on the joke.

The black-and-white vintage photographs of cowgirls, lovingly framed and lit with tiny spotlights, are more numerous than ever, and I think that Dottie may have recently bought the entire inventory from some failing Western museum.

I catch the eye of a woman sitting alone at a booth. She is slender, with long black hair and Eurasian features. She smiles at me and shifts with a dancer's grace to offer the arch of her neck, a reflection of light on the soft lunar curve of her face. I give her the ghost of a smile before spinning around on my stool to face the bar again.

Dottie is standing in front of me, smirking. "How's Jackie these days? Jackie, you know, your girlfriend."

I finish my drink and tap the empty vessel with my finger. Dottie gives me the evil eye but fills it again.

"She should attain sainthood status any day now." Cupping the glass with both hands, I say, "No, that's unkind. She's better than I deserve. I tell you, Dottie, I've not been much fun to live with the past few months."

"Oh, and why is that?" she brays, hands on hips. "Just a little kidnapping, near-rape and murder, torture, serious bodily harm…?"

The couple to my left, both of them in gym clothes, have stopped talking. Though they're still looking at each other, I know they're straining to hear more.

"Jesus, Dottie," I say, hunching into my shoulders, gesturing for her to keep it down. "Want to read aloud my last gyno exam as well?"

"I don't know," she says. "Anything good left in that lonely old box we should know about?"

My eruption of laughter, unfettered and loud, causes the couple to snort their drinks through their noses. They quickly turn away, embarrassed but still giggling.

"I do so love you, Dottie," I say, toasting her.

She leans over the bar, resting on her elbows. "No you don't. You just lust after me, that's all."

I stare at the two large, almost life-size paintings hanging on the wall behind Dottie: Annie Oakley and Calamity Jane, two women who often fell outside the bounds of what was deemed acceptable female behavior, breaking barriers, challenging male-dominated fields. The first, however, was the beloved "good" girl, gentle and well-mannered, while the other was considered by most to be the "bad" girl, argumentative, abrasive, but above all unapologetic.

"I've been a certifiable bitch," I tell Dottie.

"Well, we all have our bad days," she says. "But they should be just that. Days. You've been home for how long now?"

"Three months and six days."

"That's a long time for Jackie to put up with your bad temper. Things may get better now that you're back on the job. But you probably have a lot of making up to do. Right?"

I glare at the remainder of my drink.

"Well?" Dottie asks, her face in mine.

I take a breath. "Yeah," I mutter. I look Dottie in the eye. "Yes, I do."

"You know what my NA sponsor used to say to me every time I'd get into my little pity party? She'd say, 'Okay, Dottie, it's time to stop crying in your beer and get into some gratitude.' You have a lover willing to put up with your shit. You've got your job back, and"—she pauses to look at my raggedy hair—"you're only going to look like Johnny Rotten for another couple of months."

The waitress calls to her again and she wags a finger in my face before striding to the end of the bar to make more drinks.

As Dottie just reminded me, I have my job back. But whatever I had imagined about the challenges of reentry paled by comparison with the mind-numbing banality of my first assignment. After reading all my emails and aligning every object on my desk with surgical precision, I was finally called into Maclin's office and told what my first job would be: trolling head shops throughout the Metroplex, taking inventory of which stores were still selling K2—synthetic marijuana—and buying batches for DEA lab testing. The stores market and sell the fake pot as "herbal incense," but they aren't fooling anybody. The packets of dried herbal concoctions are sprayed with a powerful drug that mimics the effect of THC, and they sell for about what a three-gram bag of grass would cost on the street.

As fast as the hallucinogenic compounds can be analyzed and made illegal, however, the drug recipe—the psychotropic element that is sprayed onto the mix of nontoxic herbs—is moderated slightly, therefore staying legit. Recently, though, two of the largest hospitals in Dallas have reported dramatic increases in overdoses, manifesting as severe psychotic episodes and even a few heart attacks among users, mostly high school–aged teenagers.

There were almost sixty head shops within a twenty-mile radius of Dallas alone. I'd be spending weeks collecting, sampling, and doing follow-up paperwork after the drug analysis.

A warm body squeezes between me and the person to my right. It's one of the floor waitresses—a young, downy-skinned woman with wild blond hair, indigo eyes, and a tiny silver nose ring. She's wearing a bright yellow T-shirt that reads SLUGGER ANNE'S, WHEN YOU WANNA...

"Hi," she says, giving me a grin that blinds the wicked and derails the foolish.

"Hi," I say, trying not to breathe in her floral scent as she reaches behind the bar for a cup filled with limes.

"Can I get you something?" she asks. I can smell the lavender mint on her warm breath.

"No," I tell her, a bit too sadly. "I'm good."

"Uh-huh, you are that," she says teasingly, before slipping away to the booths along the far wall.

Dottie is back again, brow raised, pursing her lips at me.

"You still here? You can't mend fences while sitting on your ass in this place," she says.

"Dottie," I tell her, "you're the only person I know who has actually mended fences."

I start to pay my bill and Dottie asks, "How's Seth, by the way?"

"Seth? He's good. Looks a little world-weary these days."

She stands in front of me, arms crossed, gazing at me intently. I know Dottie well enough to know she's debating whether or not to tell me what she wants to tell me.

"What?" I ask.

"You sure about that?"

Something in her tone resurrects the image of a haggard Seth from this morning. "Okay, I'm listening."

"I've heard he's keeping rough company these days."

"He's an undercover cop, Dottie. He's not a middle school teacher."

She shrugs and starts to walk away. I call her back. She's never been one to deal in idle gossip or rumors; her information is always solid.

"All I'm saying is that you might want to have a heart-to-heart with your partner. Make sure he's okay."

"Could you be a little less vague?" I ask, wondering with a jab of uncertainty if Seth's got some new health concern he hasn't told me about.

"In NA we have a saying: 'What's said here stays here.' So a lot of people come into the meetings, sharing some pretty dark things off the streets. Some of it's straight-up bullshit. But some of it's true. You should talk to your partner."

I thank her, shove my change into my pocket, and head for the door.

Dottie calls after me, "Tell Jackie I said hey. Oh, and tell Seth the girls have been asking for him...*Not!*" She snickers and waves before clogging her way to the far end of the bar, her ancient cowboy boots sliding over the wooden floor.

I step outside the bar, tightening my scarf against the wind, my growing concern for Seth leaching away the liquid cheer of the Jamesons. My car is parked close to the curb. On the other side of the street, alone at a bus stop, stands a woman. It's already dark outside and there are no streetlights, but the building behind her is brightly lit and I can see that she's staring at me. She's small in stature, wearing a quilted coat and sensible shoes. She has bright red hair. Like Evangeline Roy's.

I pull up short, every muscle in my body flexed and rigid. My hand, reaching for the car door, pauses in midair, a stop-action ad for a horror flick.

The woman regards me calmly, her head tilted with curiosity at my frozen state. Slowly she reaches up and tugs at the edges of her hair. But it's not her hair she's adjusting. It's a woolly hat, an orangey-rust color, which I've mistaken for red hair. As soon as it registers in my brain as such, I'm confounded that I could have misidentified it as anything other than a winter head covering.

I wave to her awkwardly, swearing under my breath (which is steaming like a factory flue), open the car door, and throw myself in. I can see her through the windshield. She's still watching me, probably thinking I'm either drunk or a lunatic. And it's possible I'm both.

When my hands are steady enough, I start the engine and drive toward home. Halfway there I try calling Seth, but it goes straight to voice mail. On impulse, I decide to stop by his house in case he's on the couch and just not answering his phone. If only to let him know how much I appreciated his support on my first day back, and to tell him about my ridiculous encounter with the woman in the orange hat. He'll laugh along with me, pressure me into drinking one of his awful longneck beers, and send me home to Jackie with a smile on my face.

And…

Dottie has raised a warning flag. I need to look my partner in the eye and make sure that he's good, and that I'm good, and that the world is where it should be. See? No monsters here.

Seth lives on the M Streets in east Dallas, in a small house that was built in the 1920s, when craft was king. There are very few streetlights, narrow driveways, and, this being Texas, everyone over the age of eighteen has their own car, so parking can be a problem. I pull up curbside a house away, turn off the engine, and prepare to get out, when the light on Seth's porch comes on. The door opens and a man walks out and stands talking to Seth, who's perched on the threshold.

The overhead light is strong, and I can clearly see that the man is short and compact, with wide, bullish shoulders—built, in sum, like a brick outhouse. His face is in profile, and I can see the nose smashed almost flat against his face, the cartilage turned to a spongy mass as a result of the many MMA fights he endured before becoming a drug dealer, petty thief, and pimp.

Chuffy Bryant.

He'd been Seth's CI before he'd almost beaten the life out of one of his street girls, and was sent away for two years for assault and battery. The fact that he had gouged, mashed, and mangled his opponents in the ring—blinding a novice fighter in one eye and almost gelding another with successive heel strikes to the groin—seemed to give no one pause until he took his good dope and mad-dog habits to the streets. He got his nickname, Chuffy, from the sound he made whenever he tried to suck air through his puréed sinuses.

Chuffy walks across the darkened lawn to his car, parked opposite Seth's house, and I think he's going to leave. But he opens the trunk, pulls out a small plastic shopping bag, and returns to the porch, handing the bag to my partner. They exchange a few more words, then Chuffy gets in his car and drives away. The light on the porch goes out, as does the lamp in the living room, leaving the house in darkness.

After visiting the hospital and seeing for himself what his CI had done to the prostitute, Seth had sworn he'd never use Chuffy as a source again. But even if he had changed his mind about getting street intel from the ex-fighter, it was unlikely to impossible that Seth would have allowed Chuffy to appear at his door, let alone come inside his house.

I watch the building for a while, my pulse ragged in my throat, leaving only after I get a text from Jackie asking when I'll be home.

CHAPTER 6

JANUARY 6, 2014
THE HOUSE, DALLAS

My car has been parked in the driveway for several minutes, but I haven't been able to bring myself to open the door, walk up the sidewalk, cross the threshold, and greet Jackie. I can see her through the front bay window, walking back and forth from the kitchen to the dining room. She's set the table with good glasses and candles. A celebration for my first day back on the force. Every light in the place must be on, and the house glows like one of those deep-sea bathyspheres, floating in a dark, nameless sea.

I'm still shaken by the encounter with the woman at the bus stop, as well as by seeing Chuffy Bryant skulking out of my partner's house. I want nothing more than a shower and a few more shots of Jameson, with very little accompanying conversation. But, knowing Jackie, she'll want to talk about our day apart.

So I stall by looking out the car window. There are few streetlamps in our neighborhood, and most of our near neighbors are older folks, used to going to bed at eight p.m. One solitary flashlight flares briefly down the street—a neighbor walking their dog, perhaps. I watch the beam of light for a while until it's extinguished, like a candle blown out. The front porch is shrouded in patches of blackness. A perfect place for someone to hide. I make a mental note to add more lights to chase the shadows away. To stave off the troubling thoughts that rob me of a peaceful evening's rest.

I had started sleepwalking as soon as I returned home from the hospital, my unconscious mind trying to escape the nightly dreams of being tangled in sharp wires piercing every limb of my body, dragging me down into a well of fetid, black water. Jackie told me that I would wander around the house, disoriented and mumbling incoherently. Once, coming upon me standing in front of the hall closet, staggering around with eyes closed, she touched my arm and I snapped into full offensive mode. She screamed loud enough to startle me awake, and I was horrified to find my fist drawn back, ready to strike her.

My paranoia of being recaptured leaked into my waking hours as well. I installed extra locks on all the doors, then stashed a handgun in the table next to the bed and another in a drawer in the living room. Jerking reflexively at car backfires, jumping out of my skin and cursing like a Fury over a bottle rocket in the street—all signs that my mind, unlike my leg, was not recovering as it should.

Evangeline Roy was still in the world. Her two sons were dead—one by my hand, the other killed by a member of my team—but she still had a very large extended "family" cult stretching from Louisiana to West Texas, including law enforcement, medical staff, and lawyers, fortified by lots of money and resources to stay hidden. Three months after my ordeal, she still had not been located. I think of the woman at the bus stop and I shudder.

I cup one hand over my mouth and exhale, my nose capturing the pungent tang of Eau de Whiskey. There's no gum in the glove compartment or console, so I swallow a few times and haul myself from the front seat onto the driveway.

The shrill double chirp of the car door locking brings Jackie to the front window. She gives me a tentative smile, and waves. I raise a hand to her in greeting, pocket my car keys, and let myself in the front door.

Jackie meets me in the foyer and gives me a hesitant, one-armed hug, her face uptilted and expectant. Like Seth, she longs for my reemergence into the world to be good enough, to be satisfying enough, at least, to pull me back into a more cheerful semblance of my old self. But like any good swimmer, she's testing the water before diving in.

"You left the front door unlocked," I tell her. Since my kidnapping, I make sure the doors—all the doors—are locked at all times.

"I knew you were on your way home," she says, tensing under my scolding.

She pulls away slightly, giving me a questioning look, her nostrils flaring. "You stop on the way for a drink with Seth?"

I pause a fraction of a second too long and her brows come together.

"No," I say. "I checked in at Dottie's." Another pause. "She just wanted to congratulate me on getting back to the job." I do not want to mention stopping at Seth's and having to explain what I don't yet fully understand.

She unfurrows her brow and takes a breath. I can almost hear the thoughts in her head: *Dangerous rocks ahead. Best steer clear and start over.*

"Okay," she says. "First rule of thumb for the end of the first day back at school. Don't ask how the day went."

She takes hold of my hand and leads me into the dining room.

"Second rule. Supply drinks and plenty of snacks."

Jackie gestures grandly over the table, where she's laid out a bottle of wine in a silver ice bucket, a platter of her famous stuffed mushrooms, a green salad, and a basket of warm bread. She's also set the table with her mother's best china, gifted to us this past Christmas. It's taken nine years, but Jackie's mother, Anne, has finally turned down the burner under her resentment of her daughter's baffling involvement with me.

The candlelight makes everything look coated in butterscotch, smoothing over the remembered rough edges of family hurts, slights, and judgmental attacks.

"It looks beautiful, babe," I tell her.

She pulls out a chair for me to sit and pours some wine into my glass.

"Third rule, don't mention how tired the returning weary traveler looks. Instead," she says, giving me her playful, Etruscan smile and easing onto my lap, "show, rather than tell, your sweetheart how much you love her."

She kisses me and I tug playfully at her hair. The sharp thread of irritation at her likening me to a child returning from day care scrapes at my patience. But I smile. "I think I'll go to work every day if this is what I'll get when I come home."

"Drink your wine," she orders, springing back up and heading for the kitchen. "Dinner is just about out of the oven."

The wine, a Pinot Grigio, is citrusy and tart, and I drain the glass as though it was lemonade. I quickly pour another, hoping Jackie won't notice the declining level of liquid in the bottle. The smells from the kitchen are heady—garlic and spices, with the tang of shellfish—and I know she's made her Spanish zarzuela, a seafood stew, something she would have spent hours preparing. I feel bad for having stopped at Dottie's, worse for staying for several drinks. I assuage my guilt by finishing half of my second glass of wine.

Jackie walks back into the dining room. "Two more minutes," she tells me.

She lifts some salad and mushrooms onto my plate and then hers and, noticing my glass is half empty, pulls the bottle from the bucket. It pauses midair, long enough for me to know that Jackie knows I'm on my second helping. She doesn't say anything, only pours more wine in my glass.

She fills her own glass and sits at the table. "A toast," she says, raising the glass. "To my ferocious woman."

We look at each other for a moment and I realize that she's the one who looks tired, with deepened lines around her eyes, which are certainly not laugh lines. For months she's been my caretaker, shrink, referee, and dartboard. I understand now, more than ever, that we've settled into an accepted routine of my unacceptable behavior. Dottie's right—I have a lot of making up to do. The only thing that has rendered the weeks of pain and boredom bearable has been killer workouts, followed by having a few drinks. It's not like I've been getting drunk every day, but the few beers (or shots of Jameson) have made the waiting around less onerous.

I take another sip and am about to tell Jackie how much I love her, how much I'm willing, and wanting, to change, how different things will be now that I'm back to work, when she tells me, "Slow down a bit, baby. I only bought one bottle of wine."

She says it lightly, but it grates on me. I tighten into defensiveness.

"I can run down the street and get another bottle, if you want." I pull the car keys out of my pocket and place them pointedly on the table. I haven't made a solicitous offer; I've just made a threat of leaving.

She carefully sets her glass on the table. Her face is flushed, her jaw set. "I'll be right back," she says, pushing away from the table. She walks into the kitchen, the glint of tears in her eyes.

I put down my fork and stare at my hands. Jackie's trying so hard, and I'm being exactly what I told Dottie I've been the last few months: a certifiable bitch. She returns a few minutes later with a steaming roasting pan, and she sets it down forcefully in front of me.

"I'm not doing this," she tells me.

"What—?" I say.

There are no tears in her eyes now. Only anger. A cold, steady fury that's been building for weeks.

"I'm not going to be turned into the clichéd, downtrodden cop's wife."

"What are you talking about—?"

"You know exactly what I'm talking about." She moves around to her side and sits down, her clenched hands resting on the table. "Do you know what I had to deal with today? A three-year-old child was brought into the ER with multiple rib fractures. Serious internal injuries. The father—who's a doctor, by the way—tried to sell us the story that the girl had OI type 4."

I shake my head, not understanding.

"Brittle bone disease," she says. "The kid was a mass of bruises. It's a miracle she survived the trauma. The DA is going to prosecute the case based on my medical report confirming that the type of bruising I noted on the girl's torso could only have been formed from the outside in, not the other way around."

Jackie, a pediatric radiologist, and I have often shared the kind of gallows humor common among cops and ER doctors as a way of dealing with the often-gruesome aspects of our careers. An outsider, overhearing the messy details of our respective jobs, might find our lighthearted banter cruel. But Uncle Benny, knowing the restorative value of laughing in the face of death, would have distinguished between dark humor and bully humor. The first, he once said, is like whistling through a graveyard; the second would be like callously kicking over the tombstones.

Jackie is not laughing now.

"You know why I'm telling you this? Because it dawned on me looking at that little girl's chart today that it was like looking into my own body. The way it feels, inside, when *you're* out of control. But I'll tell you something: I'm not going to be your whipping girl. Not now, not ever."

"Jackie, I'm sorry. Truly I am." I reach across the table, covering her fisted hands with mine.

Her hands relax only slightly.

"You have got to go talk to someone," she says.

"I do," I say, trying to smile reassuringly. "I talk to you."

"No, you don't." Her voice sounds flat, despondent. "You manage and misdirect me. You bark and snap at me. But you don't talk to me."

She picks up her glass and finishes the wine in one gulp. "This fear is not going to go away on its own. I'm telling you right now that you've got to get help." She stands and walks from the room. "I'm going to go take a bath."

I limp into the living room, backlit by the candles on the dining-room table, my calf muscles tight and cramping from the tense exchange with Jackie. The room is dark, soft music seeping from the wall speakers. I gaze out the bay window facing the empty street, and a flare of light on the lawn catches my eye. It's the briefest flicker of a flashlight beam, but when I turn toward it, it abruptly vanishes. There is a scuttling movement across the grass, a shadow shaped like a man, blacker than the evening darkness, but no sound. The single front-porch light is on, but it casts only a small circle of illumination. I quickly check the locks on the front door, making sure that Jackie's pistol, a Glock, is still in its place in the drawer in the living room. After five more minutes of staring through the bay window, and seeing no more lights on the lawn, I walk into the kitchen to wash the dishes.

My hands wrist-deep in suds, I try to assemble my scattered thoughts around a cohesive plan to fight the destructive chaos in my head. Uncle Benny, a homicide cop, understood better than most how suppressing dangerous memories could poison the soul. He devised his own method of helping his fellow officers expel those demons. He called it "Reaping the Grim," a combination group-rehab session with primal-scream therapy mixed with voodoo, inappropriate laughter, and large quantities of alcohol. But mostly it was my uncle's empathy and experience with the darker side of human nature—knowing the right thing to say at just the right time—that brought the traumatized cop, sometimes fresh from a murder scene, back to sanity.

Benny was legendary for it. He had the lowest burnout rate for his officers of any division in New York. Now, not able to run, I am incapable of accessing his voice, his wisdom, his peace.

Benny, I breathe. *Tell me what to do.*

I turn off the dining-room lights and check one more time for movement on the lawn. The only motion in front of the house comes from the gentle whiplike motion of some winter-bare trees. I check the front door locks again and close the curtains.

By the time I've made my way to the bedroom, Jackie is in bed on her side, her face turned away from the door. She doesn't answer when I ask her if she's still awake.

I lie for a long time in the bed, my nerves on fire, straining to decipher every house noise, every subtle nocturnal sound outside my window. The last sonar operator in a submarine planted at the bottom of the Mariana Trench.

CHAPTER 7

The owner of the head shop has been eyeing me since I walked into the place. For ten minutes he's watched as I ambled slowly up one aisle and down another, lingering over pipes, lighters, rolling papers. It's the fifth shop I've visited today, each store uniquely different in its décor, ambient lighting, and background music, but all alike in selling paraphernalia to get high. Most of them also sell K2. Packaged and labeled as *incense,* the crumbly, weedlike product is a mixture of dried plant materials sprayed with a strong psychotropic drug. The psychotropic drug keeps changing as law enforcement moves to ban each new concoction.

My first shop of the day had been Al Fakher Smoke Shop, the manically cheerful guy behind the counter greeting me with what sounded like "Welcome to Ole Fucker." I had wasted no time in asking for some K2 and, smiling, he brought a large plastic bin from beneath the counter filled with an assortment of packages labeled *Syn Incense, Burn,* and *Mr. Nice Guy.*

Keeping it friendly, I asked him which brand he preferred.

His upper lip arched and he said, "They're all good."

A skinny white guy wearing a bandana, he had long dreads that were beaded elaborately and smelled strongly of coconut oil. He'd leaned closer to me, elbows on the counter, as if to get cozy, but he had to crane his head up to look at me. At nearly six feet tall, I towered over him, as well as outweighing him by a good thirty pounds.

"You lookin' to dance, or to chill out with your man?"

"Oh, definitely chill out with my man." I met his stare and smiled coyly.

"Then what you want is *Cloud 10.*"

"Maybe I should take several different kinds. Just in case my mood changes."

"Cool." He had nodded with approval. He chose four different packages and bound them together with a rubber band. I paid for the packets with a credit card.

He rang me up and as he was handing back my credit card, he took my hand in both of his. His palms were sweaty, his nails overly long, one pinkie painted black. A stranger's unwanted hands on me, like the undulating pass of a water snake crawling over my skin. For an instant I had a flash of other hands on me, binding my wrists, immobilizing my half-naked body.

I resisted the impulse to head-butt Island Dude and managed to keep smiling.

"I've got some of the real stuff in the back," he said, massaging my fingers. "I could close up the shop for a little while and we could have a smoke in my office."

With my free hand I pulled my badge from my belt, hidden under my coat, and laid it ever so gently on the counter.

"Or," I told him, "you could be my date for the day at *my* office and close up the shop for a good long while."

A cascade of emotions at the revelation—alarm, anger, and

then hurt, as though I had picked up his dog for not wearing a collar—flushed his cheeks scarlet. He quickly withdrew his hands, muttering "Not cool" at my retreating back.

I shook the packages over my shoulder at him as I left the place. He would now get rid of all his current K2 stock. In a few weeks he would have a bin full of new product with a new chemical compound, tweaked just enough to be legal. But I didn't care. Seeing the stricken look on the guy's acne-laden face had been worth it.

The next three shops I visited had been basically a replay of the first, sans the badge reveal. Asking for product and getting it, no questions asked.

This time, however, is different. The owner of the Rebel Yell has somehow nailed me as law enforcement and has firmly denied having any K2 in his store. His displeasure at my presence is all the more heated because he's had to turn away several customers asking for the same thing.

I stop in front of a Bob Marley poster—the musician as a young man, playing his guitar. He looks impossibly vulnerable, holding a spliff in his hand while he fingers a chord. To no one in particular, I say, "This is my favorite of him."

The owner—his business card nestled in a coyote skull reads *Ricky "Bluebeard" Morgan*—is a heavyset man with a full *Duck Dynasty* beard and narrow, untrusting eyes. He stands in front of a large Confederate flag the size of a bedsheet, and I'm wondering if he gets the irony of selling Bob Marley posters, faux Cuban cigars, and Jamaican flag medallions in his store.

I cross back over to the counter and take my time looking at the intricate glass pipes in fanciful colors lining the glass shelves, including one that sits on top of the case. Hideously ugly, the bong is blown from neon-orange glass, tall as a toddler, with a price tag of twelve hundred dollars. I stand and loudly drum my fingers on the countertop just to piss him off. I can feel Ricky burning a hole through the top of my head, but I point to a pipe shaped like a dragon and ask sweetly if I can see it out of the case.

"Look," he says, "stop wasting my time. I don't have any K2 in my store, so why don't you just leave?"

As if on cue, another man comes out from a back office and stands next to Ricky. They're both built like loggers, with full, bushy facial hair. I'm thinking brothers, the newer guy the younger of the two.

Ricky tells me again to go.

Bluebeard the Younger then joins in: "Did you not hear the man? He said you can go now."

"Or what," I say, "you'll call the cops?"

Had it been just one Neanderthal confronting me rather than two, I might have left. But their intimidation tactics—trying to stare me down, leaning aggressively over the counter, crossing their arms like menacing temple djinn—all work like superglue, rooting my size-ten burgundy Doc Martens to the floor.

"Just get the fuck out of my store." Ricky's eyes have gone from squinty to nonexistent, tucked somewhere under his protruding brow and cheek fuzz. His beard actually quivers.

I lean in close enough to smell the nicotine on his breath. "Are you threatening me?"

Finally Bluebeard the Younger says, "How about this threat: Why don't we just lock the front door and rape the shit out of you, you uppity cunt?"

Two things occur to me at the same time. First, Bluebeard the Younger probably doesn't realize I'm a cop; having exited his office late in the game, all he can see is that there's a strident, won't-back-down female in his shop.

And second, it doesn't fucking matter.

I point upward to the nearest corner, where a video camera perches.

"You want to say that again for the camera?" I ask.

"No sound," says a smirking Bluebeard the Younger.

"Oh," I say, "then it'll be anticlimactic when I do *this*."

My arms sweep outward in an operatic gesture, as though I'm about to embrace the Beard Brothers, or make a concession to some brilliant point they've just made. The back of my right hand catches the toddler-sized bong, its swirling orange, hand-blown glass winking under the carefully aimed mini-spotlight. It wobbles, tilts, and falls, crashing with a spectacular explosion, not so much breaking apart as shattering into a thousand beaded pieces that scatter to the far corners of the shop.

"Oops," I say, backing a few feet away from the case. I feel my lips stretch into an ugly grin. "My bad."

Ricky's mouth falls open and it appears for a moment that he might start wailing. Bluebeard the Younger launches himself around the side of the display, his face a mottled red, gobbets of spit on his hairy chin like sequins on a party dress.

I pull my badge and gun at the same time, rapidly backing up, as it appears that Junior will not stop until he's tackled me to the ground.

"Stop—stop right there," I command, and he comes up short, still huffing with anger.

"*You bitch!*" he howls, spraying more spittle onto his chin.

"Yeah, that's me. Park your asses down," I yell. "Both of you. Now sit on your hands and keep quiet."

For a moment it looks as though they are not going to comply, and I'm starting to regret my forced confrontation. I don't want to shoot these guys, so I point my gun at the next-largest object on the counter: an antique hookah. A magnificently ornate brass pipe, inlaid with enamel.

Elder Bluebeard's eyes widen. He says, "Do you know how much that thing costs?"

"Not a whole lot if it's shot to shit," I answer.

The two men lower their bulk into a seated position and two patrol officers arrive within five minutes of my call for backup, placing the Beard Brothers under arrest for attempted assault. A plastic tub under the cash register yields, on a quick count, about three thousand dollars' worth of K2. Elder Bluebeard is yelling about his expensive glassware being intentionally damaged.

"How'd the pipe get broken?" one of the patrolmen asks me.

"I'm Polish," I tell him. "We can't talk without using our hands."

"Tell me about it," the other officer says, pulling an unwilling Bluebeard Jr. out the door. "I'm Italian. But in the case of this creep, the pipe would've leapt from the counter and found its way straight up his ass."

An hour later I'm in Marshall Maclin's office. He's on the phone, but giving me the stink eye. The look that Uncle Benny would have referred to as the Gwanna Gaze. As in *"I'm gwanna give youse the ass-reaming of your life…just as soon as I get off this important call."*

I can tell that Maclin's on the phone with one of his old homicide buddies because his five o'clock shadow has gotten noticeably manlier within the space of a few minutes. He's also doing that thing that homicide cops do when they're figuring out where they're going to meet up later. I'd overhear Benny doing it with his fellow detectives when he was giving directions. It would never be a matter of simply giving out street names, addresses, or intersections. It was always in the context of former cases, as in: "Okay, so you go two blocks past that triple we pulled Christmas Day two years ago. Yeah, up from the pizza place where the Korean guy got stabbed by the Ukrainian midget."

Maclin hangs up and I meet his stare until he's ready to talk.

"What the hell, Detective," he says. "You're not even back an entire week."

I resist saying, *Oh, I'm sorry, Sergeant. I mistook doing my job for a walk in the park.*

"I didn't expect to be bum-rushed, Sergeant," I tell him. "Just doing my job."

"Your job does not include blowing shit up. You're supposed to be undercover. As in quiet in, quiet out."

He stares at me a moment longer, then says, "I'm asking for a review of the Psychological Fitness for Duty Exam. It's my recommendation that you get some counseling. You've got anger issues."

"I thought that's what being active duty was for—"

"Don't be a smart-ass," he snaps. "Right now, you're a liability to the department."

The anger I'm pretending I don't have is crawling its way up my throat. Willing my shoulders to relax, I ask, "Does this mean I'm suspended?"

"I don't know yet what it means."

My lips are dry, heart pounding in my chest. My fingers clench painfully in my lap, and reflexively I look for the red tension balls that Sergeant Taylor always kept close at hand; the ones through which he channeled his frustration and anger. But Sergeant Taylor is gone, and I have to wonder what advice he would have offered me, given the same situation. Surely not to see a shrink. More likely, being an avid rodeo rider, he would have prescribed taking up barrel racing, or calf branding.

"Look, Betty, this is not personal," Maclin says. Because he's used my first name, I know that it is.

"This is not personal," he repeats emphatically. "You and I have butted heads, but I know your worth as a cop. I'm not telling you that you're not up to *my* standards. You're not up to *your own* standards, and you know it.

"You went through something…" He pauses, shaking his head. "Things I can't even imagine. And I don't *want* to imagine them, because then I'd be bugshit crazy, staring at the walls all night. This is not punishment. This is for your survival in this department. I need strong, stable cops on my team.

"For now, you're on desk duty. And I want you to see the department shrink. We'll let him decide when you're ready for street duty again."

I open my mouth to protest, but he cuts me off. "This is not a suggestion, Detective. It's an order." He hands me a card with the shrink's name on it.

"I'm calling him today," he tells me before ordering me out of his office.

CHAPTER 8

T hat sucks, Riz," my partner says. "I hate all those enforced psych evals."

Seth has to lean on the bar and yell in my ear to be heard over the two women singing karaoke on the stage. They're both holding mics, performing a pop tune, something with a rap interlude that clashes with their nicely pressed jeans and matching pink T-shirts. The noise from the speakers is deafening, the stage lights changing from red to yellow to green in rapid, dizzying succession.

I've been trying to read the slogans on the singers' shirts—I can make out only the word *Pokeno*—but their gyrations, bringing loud catcalls and whistles from their dozen or so lady friends seated at a table close to the stage, along with the shifting lights, make it difficult to see.

I've also had three shots of tequila and two beers in less than an hour's time. The question that's burning on my tongue is why the hell was Chuffy Bryant hanging around Seth's house during prime action hours? For the moment, though, even with the red flags waving, the desire to lean in to the relaxed, pre-drunken state with my partner is greater than my desire to go digging.

"What the fuck is Pokeno, anyway?" I ask.

"It's a card game. A Southern thang," he drawls, giving the ladies onstage a friendly wave. Several of the women at the table have turned more than once to smile at him.

"Wow," I say, jabbing him in the ribs. "It's hard to keep focused on the stage with that brilliant light reflecting off all their diamond *wedding* bands."

"That's the great thing about Pokeno," he tells me, grinning. "You play it, it makes you horny."

"Oh really?" I say, raising the beer bottle to my lips, even as the now-woozy voice of reason is telling me to quit before I'm too drunk to walk to the bathroom without pinballing off the tables filled with rowdy customers. "Is there a lesbian version to that game?"

"Yeah," Seth answers. "I think it's called Chutes and Ladders."

I careen off my stool, catching myself one-legged, snorting beer through my nose and choking with laughter.

"You're the best partner a girl ever had, Riot," I say once I've recovered. *Even if you do keep secrets.*

"Yeah, well, as your best partner, I think I should encourage you to slow down."

I push the bottle away. "I guess it would be bad form to show up hungover at my first shrink appointment." The department's psychiatrist has agreed to see me tomorrow. No telling what Maclin said to get the doctor to shoehorn me into his schedule so quickly. Either Dallas police are distressingly sane and don't need therapy, or my sergeant thinks I'm way too close to the edge to let another week go by.

Ever since the circumstances regarding my killing of Curtis Roy and one of his henchmen had been revealed, Craddock told me as I left the station, the cops of North Central Division had taken to using the phrase "to go all Betty" on someone when having to respond with lethal force.

Seth puts one hand over mine. "You just got to hang in there. You had a bad injury."

I make a face, dismissing the concern, but his hand feels good, warm and undemanding.

"I just wish I'd been there to see you knocking over that giant bong," he says, laughing.

There's a spasm in my leg and I reach down to rub at the muscles.

He pulls something out of the top pocket of his jean jacket. "You still in pain from the surgery?"

"Sometimes."

He opens his palm, showing me a white pill. "You want one?"

"What are you still doing with Oxy?"

He shrugs. "Nerve pain. I take one every once in a while."

"Where'd you get that one?"

He looks at me like I'm blockheaded. "Uh, my doctor."

It could be true, but the glibness of his answer rings false.

"You keeping company with Chuffy Bryant these days?" I regret the words as soon as I utter them, but I need Seth's reassurance that the world outside my head isn't as dark as the one inside it. Seth doesn't break eye contact; he just waits.

"I went by your house last night," I say. "Got there in time to see your ex-CI leaving your house."

He pulls back, squinting, as though trying to decipher a foreign road sign. "Why didn't you let me know you were parked out in front of my house? You should have come in."

"You using Chuffy as a CI again?" I try to keep the tone light, without the whiff of accusation, but the escalating noise in the bar makes reasonable conversation difficult.

"No," he says, then takes a slow drink from his beer. "Absolutely not. He had some information he didn't want to give me over the phone, is all."

"He handed you a package from his car." I had leaned in toward him to make myself better heard, but also to look him in the eye.

Seth slowly shakes his head as though disappointed, puffing air through his nose. "The 'package,'" he says, using air quotes, "was a dinner from Chicken Express."

He puts his face closer to mine, then stage-whispers, "And it was fucking awesome." He grins and pops in his mouth the pill he had offered me. He breaks it in two with his teeth and washes it down with a swallow of beer. "You could have had some of it, too, if you hadn't been sitting in your car acting like an amateur dick."

Seth is still smiling but there's an edge to his voice, as though I've hurt his feelings or taken the wrong side of an argument. I look down at my hands on the bar, feeling disloyal. But mainly I don't want him to see the residual doubt on my face that he's gaslighting me. He's an experienced undercover cop. Misdirection is what he does for a living, and he's good at it. But I'm an undercover cop as well, and doubting is my job.

He grabs me by the front of my jacket and shakes me in a non-threatening, theatrical way so I'll meet his gaze. "This is me, Riz, your partner. Remember? And you're back on the force, so relax. Stop being such a fucking nervous Nellie. And a nag." He pokes me gently in the middle of my forehead and drains the rest of his beer.

"I just don't think you should be drinking with the meds," I tell him in my best nagging voice.

"If you've noticed, I've only had one beer. While you, on the other hand—"

"Yeah, well," I say, "good thing I have you to drive me home, then."

Whenever that may be, I think. I haven't yet called Jackie to let her know I'll be home later than usual. I'm not ready to hear the disappointment in her voice, so I put off calling her. Which will only make it worse when I do get home.

Some new customers have entered the bar, blinking at the wall of candy-colored lights, their hair speckled with rain. They look to be Mexican day laborers, their clothes and work boots still heavily grimed. The men make their way toward the bar, shy and awkward in the press of people. They ask the bartender for the cheapest beers on tap. There is something noble and sad about the way they pull loose change from their pockets, counting out the exact amount with hard-worn, probing fingers. They perk up considerably, though, upon noticing the Pokeno ladies shrieking with laughter at the nearby table.

"That's what I love about this place," Seth tells me. "You get bikers, suburban moms, immigrants…"

"We're *all* immigrants, pard," I say, mimicking Craddock's Texas twang.

I catch my reflection in the large mirror behind the bar: a pale wash of skin beneath a halo of untamed hair, a wild Medusa's cap hued magenta under the pinkish strobes. Two alien eyes, mistrusting and restless. The invader among the immigrants.

There's an older woman sitting at a small table by herself. Her mirrored self holds my gaze. She sits primly, looking out of place in the raucous din of the bar. She has lacquered red hair.

I whip around, almost knocking myself off the stool, but the woman is looking at the singers on the stage now. She doesn't have red hair; the lights have tinted it that color.

Seth notices me looking alarmed, staring off into space, and he chucks his chin at me, as if to tell me to crawl out of my own ass and rejoin the celebration.

"You'd tell me if something was wrong, right?" I ask him.

"Riz, you'd be the first to know." My partner's talking to me, but his focus is pulled again to the Pokeno ladies onstage, bumping and grinding in happy abandon.

I check my phone and see that Jackie has tried calling me twice. I slip the phone back into my pocket, not yet ready to leave.

Reaching for my now-warm beer, and eager to turn the conversation normal once more, I bump Seth's shoulder with mine and say, "You know how my day has gone. How was yours?"

"The weirdest thing," he says, turning to face me again. "My downtown snitch has gone dark."

"You mean Wayne?" I ask.

Wayne Rutherford was the informant we had called on last year when we were trying to get answers about the Family. A mostly harmless little meth tweaker, Wayne—nicknamed Flush after two of his fingers were cut off and flushed down a prison toilet—had been Seth's primary CI for years.

"It's like he fell off the planet," Seth tells me. "He didn't have the money to go anywhere—or even to score, for that matter. He was eager to meet with me 'cause I was going to give him fifty bucks to tide him over." He shrugs. "He'll show up when he's desperate enough." He catches the eye of one of the flirtatious blondes sitting at the Pokeno table. He slowly brings his beer to his lips, his tongue seductively piercing the tip of the bottle like a javelin.

"You are shameless." I laugh.

I want to order another beer, but Seth tells me it's time to go home. As we pass the Pokeno table, he bends down and whispers something to the smiling blonde, slipping her his contact card.

In the car I call Jackie, and I can tell from the way she says my name that something's wrong.

"Someone tried to break into the house," she tells me. There is real fright in her voice.

"Are you alone now?" I ask, gesturing to Seth to drive faster.

"No, James is with me."

James Earle is Jackie's great-uncle. A Vietnam war vet and an ex-military cop, he is as close to a replacement for my uncle Benny as I've ever found. Last fall his experience, and an instinctual sense of danger, had led him to make an urgent call to Jackie, telling her that all was not right as I drove toward my captors on that fateful assignment. Hoskins had been murdered, but precious time would have been lost had James not made the call, and I might never have been rescued from my kidnappers.

"Let me talk to him," I say, and I can hear his raspy, cigarette-laden breathing before he even puts the phone to his face.

"Where you been, Red?" he asks.

"I've been with my partner. What's going on?" The woolly fuzz from the tequila has retreated with a surge of adrenaline.

"Jackie said she heard someone prowling around the back of the house, working on the kitchen doorknob."

"Did she see who it was? Did you?"

"By the time I got here, there was nothing in the yard but air."

"We'll be there in twenty."

I'm out of the car before Seth has pulled his truck to a complete stop in my driveway. The light rain has turned to a heavy downpour and my jacket is soaked by the time I walk into the front hallway. James is sitting with Jackie in the living room, Jackie's small pistol in his lap.

She doesn't stand up to hug me, so I peel off my jacket and sit next to her on the couch.

"I was lying here with the lights off," she tells me, "when I saw something like a shadow pass by the window. I thought I heard the bushes out back being disturbed. So I went into the kitchen and was standing at the sink, looking out at the backyard, when I saw the doorknob moving. Someone was trying to get in." Jackie runs one hand through her hair. "I screamed like a banshee and whoever it was took off."

James shakes his head. "They obviously didn't know it's a cop's house, or they wouldn't have tried something so stupid."

Seth, who had followed close behind me, has looked into every room of the house. He signals that he's going to check out the backyard.

"Jackie says you might've seen someone creeping around last night," James says.

"I'm pretty sure it was a man," I say. "I saw the glow of his flashlight. It was too dark to see anything else."

Seth walks back into the living room, his clothes sodden and steaming from the warmth of his body, his cell phone pressed to his ear. When he disconnects, he says to me, "Can I talk to you for a moment in the other room?"

When we're in the kitchen he says, "That was Wayne. He's got something to tell me, but he wants to meet in person downtown."

"Let me come with you," I say. The alcohol I drank earlier has bubbled feverishly to the surface of my skin. The house is overly warm, and I'm feeling painfully cramped and restless, veering toward the claustrophobic.

"What about Jackie?" he asks. "Don't you think you should stay here with her?"

"I'll ask James Earle if he can hang around a little longer."

I see hesitation in his eyes. I'm officially on desk duty, but Jackie doesn't know that yet. I'm also hoping that Seth knows that, like a caged animal, I'll start eating my own if I don't get enough useful deployment.

"I can't be much good to Jackie in my current state of mind," I tell him.

He crosses his arms, thoughtfully pinching at his lower lip. "She still seems a little shaken."

"Come on," I beg. "It'll give me a chance to sober up."

He finally nods, and we walk into the living room together.

"Listen, James, can you stay here for a little bit longer?" I ask. "Something's come up. A confidential informant that we've been tracking just called Seth."

James says, "Sure. I'll stay here all night if you need me to. I'll just camp out on the couch."

"Thanks," I say, gratefully. I sit down next to Jackie again and put my hand over hers. "Will you be all right until I get back?"

I lean in to kiss her, but she pulls away.

"Sure," she says, her tone frosty. Cutting her eyes meaningfully to Seth, she says, "You're driving, right?"

An embarrassed silence fills the room. I stand abruptly, throwing on my coat, and head for the door.

"I'll be back in a few hours," I say over my shoulder, not waiting to see if Seth is following.

In the car, driving, Seth says to me, "She's just looking out for you. You probably should have stayed."

Slumping down in my seat, I watch the road and the rain, taking frequent sips of bottled water to stifle any defensive comebacks. It feels good to be driving with my partner again. Meeting with a CI in a disreputable place, getting my shoes muddy again. The dense barricade of alcohol-related numbness has faded, leaving only elation.

"What are you smiling about?" Seth asks, teasingly.

"If you tell Jackie how much I'm enjoying this right now," I say, grinning back, "I'll split your lip."

We drive south on the freeway, exiting east for downtown, and finally Deep Ellum. Resurrected from run-down, turn-of-the-century houses and abandoned warehouses, it's now lined with refurbished shops and restaurants. But where we're meeting Wayne—at the southern edge of Deep Ellum, under US 75 at Dawson Street—the roads have run out of buildings with fresh paint. The underpass is home to the street people who didn't know they were supposed to be gentrified along with the early cotton-gin factories and automobile plants. Locals call it Tent City or the Jungle. The bunker-like Dallas City Marshal's Office and Detention Center building is only a few blocks away.

Seth drives through a fast-food place, picking up burgers, fries, and a large coffee for Wayne. We park under the highway, next to a battered chain-link fence erected to keep the homeless from setting up housekeeping on public property. Wide openings have been cut in the links every five feet or so, rendering the fence useless.

The downpour has turned to a lashing torrent that floods the gutters, soaking the ground where dozens of tents have been thrown up beyond the flimsy barrier. Two huddled forms sitting against the fence stand, their arms shielding their faces against the car headlights. Seth cuts the engine and turns off the lights. One of the forms approaches.

Seth rolls down his window and waves to his CI to get into the car. The other huddled form appears to be a young woman, heavily pregnant, a blanket thrown over her shoulders.

Wayne quickly gets into the back seat; the smell coming from under his steaming coat is like week-old Chinese food packed inside a poorly sealed trash bag.

"Hey, Wayne," Seth says, rolling down his window. "You're not looking too good. You sick?"

Wayne shakes his head, shivering hard under his thin jacket. "Nah, man. Just running on empty."

Seth hands him the coffee and the bag of food. Wayne immediately pours six packs of sugar into his cup and slurps loudly at his drink while I crack my window as well.

Seth and I both twist around, facing the back seat, and stare at Wayne wolfing down one of the burgers.

He licks the paper wrapper clean of any ketchup left over from the fries and wipes his hands on his pant legs. "Thanks for helping a brother out, man. I'm saving the other burger for my girl." He looks at me. "You got a smoke?"

I shake my head. "Sorry."

"That's okay. Bad for the health anyway." He grins at me with graying, broken teeth, then swallows the rest of the coffee. "The sugar helps with trying to give up the drugs. At least that's what my old lady keeps telling me. One day at a time, though, right?" He stares expectantly into the empty cup as though waiting for it to magically refill.

"What's this about, Wayne?" Seth asks. "You said you had something important to tell me."

Wayne looks out his window for a moment, absentmindedly picking at his teeth with the hand with the two middle fingers missing. "You were the one taken by the Family," he says.

It takes me a second to realize he's talking to me.

"Yeah," he says. "I heard about that. All anybody talked about on the street for weeks." He leans forward, blowing his breath in my face. "Hey, Riot tells me you got a world-class tattoo. Can I see it?"

Giving Seth a dirty look, I press my palm against Wayne's forehead, pushing him back into the seat. "No, you may not."

He laughs good-naturedly; then grows serious. "I heard you killed Tommy and Curtis Roy. You made one big mistake, though."

"Oh yeah?" I ask, not bothering to correct him: I'd killed only Curtis Roy. My team member Kevin Ryan had killed Tommy with his service pistol. "What's my big mistake?"

"You didn't finish off the queen bee. That's going to come back to bite you."

Seth, seeing the look on my face, quickly says, "Hey, Wayne, over here. You called me. What's up?"

He looks at Seth hopefully. "You got my fifty dollars you promised?"

"Sure. Once you tell me what's on your mind."

The *pop* of a car backfiring nearby startles Wayne and he slumps in the seat, away from the window, pulling his cap further down over his forehead. "Let's drive somewhere else."

Seth exhales impatiently. "We're fine here. There's no one around."

My partner's phone buzzes and he takes it out of his pocket, glancing at it before setting it on the dashboard.

"You recording me?" Wayne asks in alarm, his hand on the door handle.

"Goddammit, Wayne. I don't have time for this foolishness. Either tell us what you know or get the hell out of my car."

"There's some new player taking Mexican drug dealers off the streets," Wayne says.

Seth rests both arms over the back of the seat so he can study Wayne's face. "I'm listening."

"You hear about the stiffs down here?" Wayne asks Seth.

"Stiffs?"

"Yeah. Fuckin' dead people in Deep Ellum."

"I don't work homicide, Wayne. And my territory's north of here."

"You don't have your ears to the street, then. Two Mexican dealers were shot dead...*tonight.*" He taps his forehead with one finger. "Bam! The crazy thing is they were from two rival gangs. Latin Kings and MS-13."

"Rivalry gone lethal?" Seth asks.

"Not so sure about that," Wayne says, vigorously shaking his head. "They were both shot up close and personal. Then the shooter just melted away, leaving all their stash and money behind. That don't sound much like gang enforcement. And a rival gang would have been trumpeting that shit."

"Sounds efficient," I tell him.

"Fuckin' A it does," Wayne says. "You know what *was* found on one of them, though?"

"What?" Seth asks.

"A Bible verse!" Wayne looks at me while bobbing his head, signaling *Crazy shit, right?*

Worrisome, desperate thoughts crowd the back of my head like a swarm of angry flies.

Before I can ask him what kind of Bible verse it was, he says, "Written on a piece of paper. Something about flashing swords and vengeance. Old Testament shit."

Now I'm the one looking around at the murky spaces just outside the safety of the car, peering into the shadows, tracking the jolting movements of a street wanderer, the plastic shower curtain thrown over his head and shoulders making his form amorphous and threatening. The Family had sent me just such a message, written on a scrap of paper, before I had been forcefully abducted. Before they had shot a member of my team in the head.

The message was from Deuteronomy: "When I sharpen my flashing sword and my hand grasps it in judgment, I will take vengeance on my adversaries…"

I sense Seth's gaze on me and he slides his hand over the seat to grasp the top of my thigh. It's meant as a gesture of reassurance, but his touch makes me jump.

"How, exactly, is this information useful to us?" Seth asks.

"It was Pico one of the ones got shot," says Wayne.

Pico, a member of MS-13, was a dealer Seth had been tracking for the past few weeks, suspected of supplying both meth and heroin to his downstream dealers in North Dallas. Product that was making its way to some local high schools.

"Well, that just made my caseload lighter," Seth says to me. "I'll bet Maclin will have some news about this tomorrow from his friends in Homicide."

"How'd you know about the Bible verse, Wayne?" I ask.

"There's this guy I used to smoke with. Gary. He was laying low in the alley waiting to score, and he saw some guy talking with Pico, looking like he wanted to make a deal. But then the guy takes out a gun, with a *silencer,* puts it against Pico's head and puts him down. The guy vanishes and Gary starts running, but not before he sees this big-ass white piece of paper with the verse laid over Pico's face like a fuckin' mask."

"Uh-huh," Seth says. "Gary's no doubt reading what's on the paper while he's rifling through Pico's pockets for drugs and money."

"Hey, far be it from me to judge another brother for taking advantage of a golden opportunity. Anyway," Wayne says, rubbing his hands together. "Get this. Gary thinks the shooter may be a cop."

Seth makes a face. "Yeah, right—"

"Why'd he think it was a cop?" I ask.

"The way the guy carried himself. He was clean, not street. No tattoos. The gun was a Sig."

"You don't think a criminal could get ahold of a SIG Sauer?" I ask.

Wayne whispers conspiratorially. "Gary says the guy flashed a badge before he put the bullet in Pico's head. I just thought you should know." He looks out the window, waving to the young woman moving restlessly against the fence.

Seth counts out fifty dollars and hands the cash to Wayne. "I think your friend Gary has an overactive imagination. But if you hear anything else, you let me know, right?"

Wayne smiles sadly. "You know me, man. I'm a fountain of information." He gets out of the car, shielding the bag of food under his coat, and shuffle-walks back to the girl by the fence. He hands her the food and she squats down on her haunches to tear open the bag.

Seth starts the engine, but I tell him, "Just a minute."

I get out of the car and jog over to Wayne and his "old lady," who looks up at me guardedly, as though I'm going to take away the only meal she's probably had all day. She can't be more than eighteen, if that.

"Hey," I say to Wayne. "Where you squatting tonight? You got a tent?"

Wayne shakes his head, jamming his bare hands into his pockets. "Nah, we're going to walk over to Austin Street Shelter. Sometimes they got beds."

I glance over at Seth sitting in the driver's seat. He raises his chin at me, *What gives?*

"Come on," I say to the girl. "Get in the car."

Her face clouds with worry. "You're not spending the night out here tonight," I tell her. "And you don't need to be walking to the shelter in the rain. You too, Wayne. Come with me."

The two of them follow me to the car. Once they're settled in the back seat, I get in and tell Seth to drive the few blocks to the shelter. The place is filled to capacity, but with some begging and pleading a cot is found for the girl, and Wayne is given a blanket and a small corner of space in the men's section. I hand the girl my card and slip her forty dollars. I tell Wayne to get his hands on a tent, and to make sure his girlfriend gets a hot breakfast in the morning.

On the drive back to Jackie's, an uncomfortable silence fills the car for a good five minutes before Seth asks if I'm okay.

"A Mexican drug dealer is found dead," I say, "his face covered with the same Bible verse sent to me last fall by the Roy family. Wayne's drug buddy thinks the shooter could be a cop. And there's a creeper around my house. No, I'm not okay."

"This guy Gary's full of shit. We'll get more out of Maclin tomorrow," Seth says. "You all right to go home now?"

I nod and reach over to turn up the car heater. I'm shivering from the cold, but also from nerves. I'm completely sober now, wondering if I'm going to need to drink more when I return home to get to sleep. Maybe I'll find some forgotten bottle of tequila in one of the kitchen cabinets—hiding, perhaps, behind Jackie's vitamin supplements. I'll want to be in the station early, even though I'm officially on desk duty, on standby to see the departmental shrink. And I don't want to miss any homicide updates on the dealers shot tonight.

Seth stealthily removes another white pill from his jacket pocket and quickly palms it into his mouth. He chews on the pill like it's a breath mint before he senses me staring at him.

"It hurts when it rains, Riz," he says. "Nothing more."

I hold his gaze for the span of one long breath.

"Really," he says, irritation glazing his tone. "Don't go all Mother on me."

When he drops me off at my house, there are no lights left on except the porch light, which means that Jackie and James Earle have gone to bed.

I turn to Seth and ask, "Seriously. What do you think about what Wayne said? About the shooter being a cop?"

Seth makes a face and I say, "Yeah, that's what I think too."

Getting out of the car, I wave to Seth as he pulls away, scanning the street for anyone lurking about. There is no movement except for the trees rustling in the wind. I want to call Seth back, get in his car, and just keep driving until there's enough sun in the sky to beat back the shadows.

CHAPTER 9

I hang around my desk, shuffling papers, until Seth crooks his finger at me and I follow him in to see Maclin, whom we catch checking his teeth in a small mirror that he keeps hidden in a desk drawer. He quickly closes the desk drawer and nods to Seth. When he sees me standing behind my partner, he frowns.

"You know anything about two dead dealers found in Deep Ellum last night, one a Latin King and the other MS-13?" Seth asks.

"And you know this how?" Maclin asks.

"I met with my CI Wayne last night downtown. He told me that Pico, one of the drug operators we've been tracking, was one of the victims."

Maclin's eyes flick from Seth to me. "You need something, Detective?" he asks impatiently.

Apart from being re-upped to active duty, my leg fully healed, my girlfriend's good graces returned, my connection to Uncle Benny restored—as well as having all my doubts about my partner's well-being eradicated—I need to know what's going on with dealers being murdered on the streets.

"I was with Seth last night when he met with Wayne," I say.

Maclin's brows come down in displeasure.

"Hey," I say, "I wasn't officially working. I had to go along. Seth was my ride home."

The sergeant looks back at Seth and says, "Remember Bernard Tate from Homicide?"

Seth nods. Tate had been Maclin's partner for a couple of years: a tough, East Coast transplant, a bantamweight ex-boxer who bounced on his toes when in conversation with both friend and foe, as though every verbal exchange might turn into a boxing match at any given moment.

"He called me this morning to tell me that Pico Guerto and a dealer named Ernesto Patron were both shot dead last night," Maclin says. "Both done with a nine-millimeter handgun. No casings found on the scene. The ME recovered one bullet from each victim's skull."

"Wayne tells me he knows somebody who witnessed Pico's shooting," Seth says.

Maclin sits back, clearly surprised. "Really?"

"Drug bug named Gary."

"You know him?"

Seth shakes his head. "Can't put a face to the name. But I can run him down."

"Where would you start looking?"

"Probably Tent City, downtown with the other drug bugs."

"Would he come in for a statement?"

"Possibly," Seth says. "In return for our help supplying a witness, you think Homicide will keep us in the loop about their progress in tracking down the shooter?"

"And this is important because—?" Maclin asks. "I would think you'd be happy to close the case on Pico. Get further along on your other cases."

Seth looks at me, so I tell Maclin, "The CI also said there was a Bible verse found on Pico. The same one that was delivered to me last fall by the Roy family."

The expression on Maclin's face tells me he already knew about it. "Yeah, Bernard gave me the news."

"There's something else," Seth says.

He pauses for a moment, uncomfortable about sharing the next bit of information.

"Gary told Wayne he thinks the shooter may be a cop. He flashed something that could have been a badge."

Maclin takes a breath and stares at my partner. "You believe him?"

"I think it's more likely it's a competing cartel looking to clear some space for commerce," Seth says.

Maclin doesn't ask me what I think, so I say, "Considering the consequences the last time someone started slinging Bible verses around, I'd like to be kept in the loop."

"It doesn't mean you're in danger," Maclin says. "The rumor of a killer with a badge and Bible verses could be misdirection. Besides, whoever the killer is, he's targeting dealers."

"Could it be the Sinaloans?" I ask, thinking about El Cuchillo's reported presence in Dallas.

"Possibly, although it's not their style," Maclin says. "But I don't want either of you conjecturing about this to anyone else. If you hear something more about it, you come to me—and me alone. And you're still on desk duty, Detective Rhyzyk. No more little alley excursions for you until you've been cleared by the doctor, which I hope will provide you with enough of an incentive to take it as seriously as I do."

Maclin tosses an appointment card across the desk to me. "Name, address, and time. It's up to him when you're returned to active duty, so try not to bite him on your first appointment."

I glance down at the doctor's name, Theo Theodosiou. "So I shouldn't make fun of his name right off the bat, you mean."

"With a last name like *Rhyzyk*," Maclin says, jabbing a finger for Seth and me to get lost, "I wouldn't be throwing stones."

After we leave Maclin's office I catch Seth putting on his coat and walking toward an exit.

"Where're you off to?" I ask.

"Downtown," he says over his shoulder, walking fast in a way that precludes any further conversation. "I'll call you later."

Watching my partner breeze through the door, expectant and energized with a purpose greater than filing reports, makes the muscles in my stomach contract with longing. I feel like a toddler who's been dropped off at day care without her lunch. My personal cell phone in my left pocket rings. I answer the call and hear James Earle's ragged voice box squeezing out a "Hello!"

"Hello yourself," I say. My first thought is that there's been trouble again at the house. "Everything okay?"

"I was actually going to ask you the same thing," he says.

"Yeah, everything's good," I say. I can tell by the silence at the other end that James Earle knows it for the deception that it is.

He takes a long drag on his cigarette, exhales, and says, "I thought maybe we could have lunch today. Things seem a little tense between you and Jackie lately."

"I don't know, James Earle. There's a lot going on right now at work."

Uncle Benny used to have a name for a person who would "take his legs under his belt," as a Pole would say, and skulk away from someone wanting to talk about family business: *tchorz*. Coward.

"Sure," I say, stopping myself. "I'd love to. Want to meet at Norma's Café at twelve thirty?"

"You got it," James Earle says, pleased. "I'll be there."

I disconnect from the call and find Craddock waiting for me at my desk, reading *Antique Gun Collector* magazine. "Reading" is perhaps too weak a word. I'd seen the same transfixed, reverent gaze come over my grandmother's face during Holy Communion. Craddock has only ever admitted to having a dozen collectible weapons—Civil War rifles, handguns from the Second World War, a Prohibition-era Thompson submachine gun—but I suspect he has a few more modern, semiautomatic rifles hidden in the back of his bedroom closet. On my desk is a large box of donuts.

Craddock points to the box and grins like he's at a clown-and-pony birthday party.

"Hey, Tom," I say, gesturing to the magazine. "Does that refer to old guns, or old collectors?"

In answer, he picks up a donut and waves it tauntingly in front of my face.

"Not for me, thanks," I say, staring longingly at the dewy, glazed pastries. In my running days I would have eaten several without hesitation.

Craddock shakes his head in sympathy. "Watching your boyish figure, *Dee*-tective?"

I grind a knuckle playfully into his gut. "I wouldn't talk, Tom. Yours has all but disappeared."

Kevin Ryan arrives just then. Craddock checks his watch and says, "You're late, pard. Again."

Ryan looks unshaven and tired, but he throws his coat over his chair and joins us at my desk. The skin around his fingernails is raw and ragged from being chewed on.

THE BURN • 83

"Seth told me there were a couple of homicides downtown last night," Ryan says. "Two Mexican dealers."

"Yeah," I say. "We heard about it from Seth's CI."

"Any ID on the shooter?" he asks.

I cave in to my desires and pick up a donut. "Not yet. Maclin is checking with Homicide."

The first bite melts on my tongue, the sugar a warm balm to my system.

Craddock, with his own mouth full, says, "Sounds like rival gangs cleaning house."

"You might think that," I say, taking two more bites. "But the killer left the drugs and money behind."

"Makes a stronger message to leave the competition's product on the body," Ryan says.

Shamelessly, I lick the glaze off my fingers. "Maybe. The shooter was careful—used a silencer, then picked up the casings."

Ryan frowns. "A silencer. How do you know that?"

"There was a witness," I tell him. "In the alley where Pico was shot. Seth's CI spoke to the guy. We're going to try and convince him to talk to Homicide."

"We?" Craddock says, picking up a second donut. "I thought you were on desk duty."

"Force of habit," I tell him. "I mean *Seth* is going to bring the guy in for an interview."

"Who's the guy?" Ryan asks.

I shrug. "Somebody named Gary."

Looking around to make sure no one is in earshot, I turn my back on Maclin's office and say quietly to Ryan, "There was something else found at the crime scene. Remember that Bible verse delivered to me by the Roy family?"

"When I sharpen my flashing sword—" Ryan recites.

Craddock looks impressed with Ryan's memory. He wags his finger at me. "Take heed, heathen—religion does pay off sometimes."

"You found that verse on the Aryan power website related to the Roys," I say, ignoring Craddock. "One Nation, One Race, something like that."

Ryan says, "OneNation OneTruth OneRace."

"That's the one," I say. "Can you do a little digging to see if there's been any new activity on the site?"

For a moment Ryan looks at me, expressionless, the skin below his eyes deeply shadowed. And then the ghost of a smile appears.

"Sure," he says. "I'll take a look."

I watch Ryan walking away, then ask Craddock, "He seem okay to you?"

"He's had a hard time since his brother-in-law died," Craddock says, wiping his sticky hands on a napkin. "A damn cop and one of his own family dies from a drug overdose."

"Nobody escapes it," I say.

Craddock has reached for his third helping, but the hand holding the donut pauses when I ask, "What about Seth?"

"What *about* Seth?" he says.

"He's not looking too healthy either."

"He's your partner," Craddock says. "Why don't you ask him about it?"

"Seth's not exactly an open book these days."

Craddock shrugs. "You do this job long enough and there's not enough booze or meds in the world going to fix the slide into ennui."

The way he pronounces the word—*own-wee*—makes me smile. "So you think he's self-medicating?" I ask.

Pointing cheerfully at the donut in my own hand, Craddock asks, "How many grams of high-octane sugar did you just inhale?"

We laugh together, guiltily, like two kids with a found wallet. Anyone looking at Craddock and taking him at face value would assume he's a Texas hick. The kind of overweight cop who eagerly dresses as Fat Elvis for a laugh at every departmental Christmas party. He's what Uncle Benny would have labeled a *yahoo,* molded by the three Gs: guns, grits, and God. But Craddock paid his dues before making detective, working for years on street patrol in some of Houston's worst neighborhoods. With all his ceaseless talk about his hunting exploits and love of NASCAR, this man who stands in for Santa Claus at local charities had walked into the line of fire to rescue a child from his abductor, a known pedophile who'd previously murdered, and then buried, two other boys. And he had assisted, with no small risk to his own personal safety, in my rescue from the Roy family. Apart from Seth, I trusted him more than anyone else on the force.

"Can I ask you something?" I lower my voice so I'm not overheard.

He nods, sensing my need for discretion. "Sure."

"You hear anything on the street about Chuffy Bryant?"

"Chuffy?" he says, surprised. "Not recently. I thought he was in jail. Why?"

"I saw him delivering a package the other night."

"What kind of package?"

"Not sure. But I doubt it was take-out."

"Want me to check into it?" he asks.

"No," I say. Any more conversation about the matter will bring questions about the recipient, or where I was when I spotted Chuffy. "That's okay, I'll do it myself. I'm on desk duty, remember? Lots of time to spend on a computer."

To change the subject, I point at Craddock's ratty jeans and polo shirt. Usually, he's dressed in neatly pressed pants and a sports coat.

"Jeez, Tom," I say. "Whatever happened to pride in the uniform?"

He grins, sugar from the donut coating his mouth. "I'm doing a buy-and-bust today. Got to look the part."

I grab the partially eaten donut out of his hand. "With all due respect, Tom," I tell him, "I hate your ample guts right now."

"Hey," he says, his face growing solemn. "In all seriousness. Can I ask you something? It's kind of important."

"Of course, Tom," I say, thoughts of bad news crowding my head. "What is it?"

He leans in and whispers, "Seth told me you got a badass tattoo. Can I see it?"

"I'm going to kill him," I say, slapping his shoulder hard. "No, you may not."

Craddock walks away laughing. As soon as he's out of earshot, I grab my personal phone and call Dottie. When she answers I ask, "Anybody in those NA meetings of yours talking about Chuffy Bryant?"

"I got to hand it to you, Betty," she tells me after a pause. "You are damn quick on the uptake."

"What's the best way to find him?"

"Romance or finance, sweetheart. But I'd start with romance first."

I thank her, end the call, then dial Seth's friend in Vice, a detective who had given Seth and me vital information for the Roy case.

"Hey, Brant," I say. "If I needed to track down Chuffy Bryant, which lovely lady of the evening would I call on?"

"He in trouble already?"

"Just keeping tabs," I say.

He tells me he needs to make a few calls and he'll get back to me. After twenty minutes my cell rings and Brant says, "Looks like Chuffy's moved in with a street hustler. A trans woman named Pearla Simms. Pearla was overheard bragging about the new man in her life, an ex–MMA champion who's going to be her knight in shining armor."

"Where can I find Pearla?" I ask.

"At ten thirty in the morning?" he says, laughing. "In bed. Apart from that, when she's not picking up tricks, she bartends afternoons at the dance club the Church, on Swiss Avenue. She'll probably be there today."

"Where does she live? I'd like to talk to her as soon as possible."

"Downtown, somewhere near the fairgrounds. You want the address?"

"Thanks," I say, writing down the information. Seth had told me he was going downtown. *Which doesn't necessarily mean anything,* I tell myself. As well as vice in many guises, anything fun or interesting or exotic walked the streets of downtown Dallas.

"Do me a favor?" I say. "You get any word that Chuffy's dealing again, you'll let me know?"

"Be careful with this guy," he warns me and I disconnect the call.

I sit and rustle papers around, wanting to get in my car and go sit on Pearla's doorstep until Chuffy appears, and then I'd...*What?* What would I do? Confront him and ask if he's selling drugs to my partner?

Uncle Benny used to tell me that one of my most potent qualities was my ability to fixate on a problem and run after it until I could sink my teeth into it and pull it to the ground. He also told

me it was my most unattractive quality; that I had to learn the difference between obsessing on a problem and focusing intently on
solving it. That my obsessions would block out the important aspects of my life that gave it purpose and balance...

I glance at the clock on my phone and see that it's nearly twelve
thirty. *Shit.* I'm late for my lunch with James Earle.

CHAPTER 10

Thanks for coming over last night," I say to James after the waitress has taken our order and walked away.

He nods, pouring a torrent of sugar into his coffee. "That's what family's for."

He holds his cup in both hands while he takes a sip, his red-veined eyes over the rim, steadily holding my gaze.

"Still having nightmares?" he asks.

"Sometimes," I say. But I've said it too quickly, too flippantly, and he smiles sadly, carefully setting the cup on the table. He runs a hand through his hair, held off his forehead by an overabundance of hair gel.

"You know," he says, "it took me a good long while to get rid of the worst of the creepy-crawlies after I got back from 'Nam. And I was a whole lot better off than some who spent more time in-country than I did. Now they call it PTSD. Back in the day we just called it PAP—Prolonged Adjustment Period. Night terrors, shortened attention span, an even shorter fuse. My wife took the brunt of it. I was told by my doctor to 'buck up.' Take it like a man. So I did. Started drinking like one, too. Lost my wife, my job—just about everything. I was angry all the time. It took me twenty years to figure out it was because I was so damn scared all the time. And I was just an MP. I fired my service pistol exactly twice, and those were just warning shots."

The waitress returns to our booth with a plate of chicken-fried steak and mashed potatoes drowning in white gravy for me, and a hamburger for James. She stands next to the table, eagle-eyed, absentmindedly probing her mile-high, lacquered hair with a pencil, watching me until I pick up a fork and start eating.

"God loves a good eater," she says before walking away.

I take out Dr. Theodosiou's appointment card and pass it to James.

"I'm seeing him tonight."

"That's good," he says encouragingly.

"Yeah, well, it's the only way I'm going to get back to full engagement. I've been put on desk duty. According to my sergeant, I have some 'anger issues.'" I smirk and put air quotes around the phrase.

"Do *you* think you've got anger issues?" James asks, passing the card back to me.

I take a bite of the steak but it's already losing heat, the gravy morphing into wet cement. Pushing the plate away, I say, "I'm frustrated, James. I need to get back to work, but I'm being blocked at every turn by a boss who's got a bug up his ass about me. I can't run, I can't sleep at night. And I can't do my job sitting at a desk all day." *I'm also imagining that I see Evangeline Roy everywhere I turn.*

James takes another sip of oversugared coffee; he hasn't yet touched his hamburger. "That would be enough to piss me off," he says quietly.

"Everyone tiptoes around me like I'm made of glass."

"Maybe they're afraid of you."

I shake my head. "The people I work with should know I'm all bark and no bite."

"I wasn't talking about the people you work with."

I realize he's talking about Jackie now. My face turns red in recognition of the truth.

And it makes me angry.

I divert my gaze to a sign above the counter: LIFE IS SHORT… START WITH DESSERT. Suddenly I want pie, or a brownie, or a piece of cake—anything sweet to take the bitter taste out of my mouth. I'm searching for the waitress so I can engage her in whatever inane conversation will move the topic away from me and my "anger issues."

James Earle is saying something, but I'm concentrating on the glass confectionery case next to the cash register.

He taps me on the arm until I look at him and he says, "Betty, you killed someone. Two people, in fact. Not from a distance, but up close and personal. And this after you witnessed a partner murdered not three feet away. That changes a person. Poisons them, if they let it. Jackie's worried about you. I'm worried about you."

"Stuck in the abyss of my own morass," I mutter. To James's questioning gaze I say, "Just something Uncle Benny used to say to me. Look, I know that I need to tone down the drinking, stop raging around the house. I'll step up my workout routine, start a yoga class or tai chi or something to release my inner-Zen self. I know I've been a bear to live with, and I'm sorry that Jackie's taken the lion's share of it—"

My work phone in my right jacket pocket buzzes and I answer it.

"Riz." Seth's voice is in my ear, tension thickening his voice. "We've found another ex–drug dealer."

"Dead?" I ask, a little too loudly, and James looks up quickly, brow furrowed.

"As a doornail," Seth says. "Carlos Rivera, another MS-13 member. His body was discovered just east of Stemmons Freeway, right behind the Spearmint Rhino. He's been dead for a couple of hours."

The Spearmint Rhino is a high-end strip club in northwest Dallas, entertainment home to sports heroes and politicians but also to drug dealers and pimps.

"I thought you were headed downtown," I say.

"I was, but got the call from Craddock. Guess what we found on his body?" He asks the question the way a doctor would ask a critically ill patient if she's sure she wants the results of her most recent blood test.

"Holy shit." I know without his telling me that another Bible verse was left at the scene.

"Who discovered him?" I ask, frantically signaling the waitress to bring the check.

"Craddock and Ryan have been tailing him. But Craddock was the one who had set up the buy-and-bust. When he got to the meeting place, he found Rivera shot once in the head."

Poor Craddock. The first time in months that he's worked a buy-and-bust on his own, and he catches a stiff.

The waitress slips the bill under my plate, pouring more coffee into my cup before sauntering away.

"There are patrolmen on-site," Seth says. "Homicide should be here soon."

"Who else is there?" I ask, fishing money out of my pocket.

"Just Craddock and Ryan," he says. "You want to do a look-see before the meat inspectors come?"

"You bet your ass I do. I'll be there in twenty." I put some cash on the table without counting it.

"What's going on?" James asks, worry crimping his forehead.

"A dealer's been shot," I say, standing up. "I'm sorry about this, James, but I've got to go."

"I thought you were on desk duty," he says.

I nod my head impatiently. "That's why I need to get there before Homicide—"

"We didn't finish talking, Betty," he says, reaching for my hand. "This is important."

I give his hand a squeeze and then pull away. "I know it is, James. I'll tell you all about it after my shrink visit."

Rushing through the door, I turn once to see James still seated, staring down at his folded hands, suspended sadly over his untouched meal.

CHAPTER 11

The strip club, a vaguely Italianate building fronted by plaster-of-Paris statuettes of Roman goddesses, sits in a depressingly shabby neighborhood, flanked by a windowless bowling alley, a car-repair shop, and a liquor store. I pull up behind the club, into the large parking lot—now nearly empty, but filled to capacity on weekends—where Seth is waiting for me. Standing nearby are six uniformed patrolmen, who've already strung yellow crime scene tape around several industrial-sized dumpsters. Two of the cops are engaged in a lively conversation with three young, lissome women, dressed almost identically in formfitting jeans and short leather jackets, who are laughing at some joke they've just been told. The kind of smoke-up-your-ass-you're-so-funny giggling that's been used by exotic trade capitalists since the invention of the belly button. One of them hands both cops her club card.

The other patrolmen are keeping a dozen curious club-goers at a distance from the crime scene. When I get out of my car, one of the men, in cowboy boots and a large-brimmed Stetson, yells, "Hey, Red, the show's inside!"

Amazingly, Homicide has not shown up yet.

Craddock and Ryan stand inside the taped perimeter, both of them looking restless. Seth walks with me to the dumpsters.

"Shitty start to the day," I say to Craddock.

"You're telling me," he says. "I've been working for weeks to get this set up. Even so, somebody ought to get a medal for taking out this scumbag."

"Tell her what happened," Seth says to Tom.

"I get here at one o'clock and wait in the back parking lot, like we'd agreed. I see his truck, but no Rivera," Craddock says, gesturing to a large white pickup about a hundred yards away. "So I drive around front, thinking maybe I'd missed him. When I do a second pass-by, I see a pair of feet sticking out from between the dumpsters; that's when I find Rivera, already cold and stiff. Looked like he'd been dead for hours."

"He been moved at all?" I ask.

Craddock shakes his head and shifts out of the way so I can see the body for myself. Rivera is lying on his back between two dumpsters, a neat bullet hole drilled into the middle of his forehead, blood puddled around his head. On his chest is a sheet of white printer paper with writing on it.

I kneel down so I can read the handwritten message: *When I sharpen my flashing sword and my hand grasps it in judgment, I will take vengeance on my adversaries and repay those who hate me.*

Taking a few deep breaths to still the jolt of fear filling my head, I stand and meet Seth's gaze. "It's the same message," I tell him.

A metal door at the back of the strip club clangs opens loudly, startling everyone. A massively overweight man, clearly irritated at his dancers frittering away their time in the parking lot, pleads with them to come back inside. The women ignore him, more interested in the arrival of an unmarked vehicle and another Dallas police patrol car.

I walk back to my own car and lean against the driver's door to steady the tremors in my legs. I know I should leave, but my need for answers is greater than my worries about being further hammered by Maclin for sticking my nose into an active crime scene.

Two plainclothes detectives get out of their car, and Seth, Craddock, and Ryan gather with them at the dumpster to fill them in on finding Rivera. Two of the club dancers try to finesse their way past the uniformed cops to hear what's going on. The third dancer, with the tightly muscled body of an athlete, has been staring in my direction, and now she makes a beeline for me.

The sky is sunny and clear—no trace of the storm from last night—but it's cold, and her breath streams into the air in rapid bands of white vapor. She's waving languidly at me, as though greeting an old friend. The woman has dark glossy hair falling below her shoulders and she glides like a streamlined tank on ball bearings.

"Hey," she calls out.

The dancer positions herself within a few feet of me, one hip against the frame of the car, her back to the men at the dumpster. I want to be irritated with her, to tell her that I'm working and can't talk to a civilian right now. But then she takes off her sunglasses and smiles at me.

"Nice car," she says.

"Thanks."

She has brown eyes flecked with gold.

"You a cop?" she asks.

"On my good days," I tell her.

She tilts her head to one side to get a better look at my gun. "How come *you* didn't ask me any questions?"

"What should I have asked you?"

"What times I work. What time I get off." She hands me a club card, handwritten across the top: *Sheela G gets off work at 4:00 p.m.*

"I work the lunch shift here, but I'm finishing up my chiropractic studies in the evening. I give good adjustment," she says coyly.

In spite of myself, I smile and shake the card like it's caught fire. "I think this tells me everything I need to know."

"Surely not everything," she says, leaning in closer. She has a small mole over her upper lip that just begs to be licked.

"Okay, how about this," I say. "Where were you this morning, a couple of hours ago?"

"In bed, sleeping. Alone," she says, pouting.

"So you wouldn't have seen the gentleman behind the dumpster getting shot, then."

"No. But, uh—" She pauses and looks over her shoulder at the detective who's now squatting down on his haunches to examine Rivera's body. "I did see one of your colleagues take some shit out of the gentleman's jacket."

It takes a few seconds to absorb what she's saying. "Excuse me?"

She points to Seth. "The one with the tight ass and the teeth. He pocketed something he lifted from the dead guy's jacket. Something he didn't want his partners to see. A plastic baggie with some pills inside."

I'm not looking at Sheela G anymore; I'm watching Seth watching one of the detectives searching Rivera's pockets. As if he feels my gaze on him, he turns his head toward me and lifts his chin in his typical "What's up?" gesture. I want to believe that he's been sneaky about lifting something from Rivera's corpse because it's something that he initially wants to share only with me. But my armpits are damp under my T-shirt.

"Look," Sheela G says. "It's no skin off me, but…if you see something, say something, right?"

"Anything else?" I ask her. The fantasy glow has worn off and I'm impatient for her to be gone.

"I guess not," she says, clearly disappointed at the chill in my tone. She turns and glides her way back to the club, passing through the rear door without another glance.

I walk to the dumpster and, while Ryan and Craddock are talking to some of the civilian bystanders, Seth introduces me to one of the homicide detectives, Euell Tilton. Tilton, a black man with a bodybuilder's physique, shakes my hand, smiling at me as though he knows me. There's something familiar about him that I can't place right away. And then it comes to me.

"The Trinity River body," I say.

"What a way to start the new year, right?" he asks.

"Ever find out who the victim was?"

"Yeah, actually I did," he says quietly, but he doesn't elaborate.

"Detective Craddock tells me you're familiar with the message left on our current vic," Tilton says, pointing to the piece of paper on Carlos Rivera's body. Tilton's look of sympathy lets me know that Craddock has also filled him in about my time with the Family.

"Unfortunately, that's true," I tell him. "I guess you know about the two drug dealers found dead last night in Deep Ellum. Pico Guerto and Ernesto Patron. Pico was wearing the same verse."

He nods his head. "As was Ernesto Patron."

"Have you found any bullet casings around Rivera's body?" I ask.

"Not yet," he says.

"According to our sergeant, there were none found at the scene in Deep Ellum either," I say.

"Who's your sergeant?"

"Marshall Maclin."

There is the slightest pause from Tilton before he smiles, and he says under his breath, "Lucky you."

"So you know him?"

"Played poker with him a while back when he was with the Homicide squad. If it's moving, he'll put a bet on it."

"Or try to put the make on it."

The smile gives way to a full grin of delight. "Yeah, that's Mac."

"And just so *you* know," I say, quietly, "I'm not technically supposed to be here. But I have a vested interest in staying in the loop because of—" I point to the Bible verse.

"Okay," he says. "I understand." Tilton hands me his card and asks for mine. "But I'd like to talk to you, when you have the time."

He holds up a set of keys pulled from Rivera's pants pocket and waves for Craddock and Ryan to rejoin him.

"You ready to check out what's inside Rivera's truck?" Tilton asks them.

Craddock says, "I am."

He follows Tilton toward the white pickup, leaving me behind with Ryan and Seth.

Seth says, "As soon as we're finished here, I've got to track down Wayne's friend, Gary. Bernard Tate wants to interview him about Pico's shooter."

"You know Gary by sight?" Ryan asks.

Seth shakes his head. "Never seen him before."

"Where are you going to start looking?"

"Tent City, or Austin Street Shelter," Seth says. "According to Wayne, Gary never strays too far from Deep Ellum."

"So you're definitely going down there today—?"

Seth exhales restlessly. "Give it a rest, Kevin. I said I've got this covered."

Ryan frowns, his jaw clenched at Seth's snappish tone. I put a hand on Ryan's arm. "Could you give Seth and me a minute, please?"

"Sure," Ryan says brusquely. "I'll just go and finish up with Tom."

He walks away, hands in his pockets, clearly miffed. When he gets to Rivera's truck, he keeps glancing at us while searching the interior with Craddock and Tilton. Maybe Sheela G wasn't the only person who'd witnessed Seth snatching crime evidence from a victim's body.

"What crawled up your ass today?" I ask.

"Nothing. I'm just eager to wrap this up."

"You got something else you need to tell me?"

I look steadily at Seth, waiting for him to tell me what he took from Rivera's pocket. He holds my gaze, as though he has nothing to hide. The moment stretches on, but he says nothing.

Finally, he says, "Look, I know this has got to be a shake-up, seeing this Bible verse pop up again like a bad genie."

"I'll be fine," I tell him, but I don't feel fine. Between the growing suspicion that the creeper around my house may be related to the reemergence of a Bible verse–scribbling killer and the four-alarm worry that my partner is in trouble with drugs, I feel nothing but anxious.

"You want to sneak a ride with me to Tent City?" he asks.

I shake my head. "I've got an appointment with the department shrink at five o'clock."

"Oh shit, Riz," he says, stifling his laughter with one hand. "I am so sorry. Not for you, but for the poor bastard who's going to try and get into your head."

"So there's nothing else you have to say to me?" I ask. I want to show a compassionate front, a safe space for him to confide his sins. But the question comes out frosty and steel-tipped.

He looks all wide-eyed and innocent at me. "No. But I'll be sure to let you know what happens when Wayne and I find Gary. I'll call you later. Stay frosty," he says as a goodbye.

Stay frosty? What the hell?

I watch Seth get in his truck and drive off. Some of the by-standers have left the premises as well, bored with the lack of action despite the arrival of a medical examiner's team, or they've gone back into the club to continue enjoying the Rhino's daily buffet-lunch special. The man with the Stetson and boots is still standing on the civilian side of the yellow tape, cracking jokes with a patrolman.

He sees me watching him and waggles his tongue obscenely. "Hey, Red," he yells. "I got some undercover work for you. Ha-ha-ha—"

I wave to Craddock and Ryan and get into my own car to drive back to the station.

Stetson Guy is still talking, his mouth puckered like an anus, making kissing noises. The men standing around him are laughing and elbowing him in sweaty, bro-time camaraderie.

I reduce speed as I pass him, rolling down my window, and he croons, "Come sit on my face, baby."

"No thanks," I say, loud enough for my voice to carry. "I already have a shitcan at home."

CHAPTER 12

I'm on the Tollway, headed north back to the station, when my work phone buzzes. The number is not one I recognize, so I answer it cautiously.

A female voice asks, "Is this Detective Rijack?"

"Close enough," I say, getting ready to cut off a sales call.

"You gave me your card," the female says. She sounds young, and scared.

"Okay…" I wait for a few seconds, but all I hear is breathing.

"This is Mary Grace," she finally says. Another pause. "You took me and Wayne to the shelter last night?"

"Right, right. Everything okay?" I ask.

Then I hear more breathing, ragged and distressed. I take the next exit and pull into a gas station, all the while listening to Mary Grace crying.

I don't know what to say, so I blurt out an incredibly inane question: "Are you in trouble?" Which only makes her cry harder.

Of course she's in trouble, dimwit—she's seven months pregnant and living on the streets.

"Where are you?" I ask.

"I'm still at the shelter," she wails. "But Wayne went off somewhere this morning and he hasn't come back yet and they're telling me they may not have room for me here tonight 'cause I left to go look for Wayne and when I came back they said I had to get to the back of the line again—"

"Hold on, hold on," I say, trying to interrupt the panicked monologue.

She stops midstream, sniffling and hiccupping loudly into the receiver.

"Mary Grace, isn't there a women's shelter you can go to?" I ask.

"They've already called two, and they're filled up. One lady here told me I should go to hospital emergency, tell them I'm having contractions, and they'd give me a bed for a few hours. But they'll give me drugs, and I'm afraid it will hurt my baby—" She's sobbing again.

So I tell her, "Hold on. I'm coming."

I disconnect and immediately call the station. I tell the desk manager, Shania, to tell Maclin that I forgot I had a doctor's appointment for my leg and that I'll be back at the station in a couple of hours.

I make it to the Austin Street Shelter within thirty minutes and spot Mary Grace standing at the curb, looking like a knocked-up fourteen-year-old—which she very well could be—beside the swelling intake line. Every year the line gets longer, the population composed more and more of women with young children.

She gets in my car and we stare at each other for a moment. There's a lot of surface dirt on her face and hands, but it's not the ground-in kind that comes from living on the streets for long periods of time. (Pavement grime eventually discolors the skin like a second-degree burn.) Mary Grace is pretty in a ragged sort of way, and seems to have all of her teeth so far. She can't have been homeless very long.

"How old are you?" I ask her.

"Seventeen," she says, clutching a small cloth bag holding whatever possessions she has left.

"Do you have any family?"

"None that want me." She says it matter-of-factly, as though the least traumatizing aspect of being alone and pregnant is having blood relations who would turn out a young, vulnerable girl.

"You look like you're pretty close to your time," I tell her.

"Maybe another couple of months?" she says uncertainly.

"Have you seen a doctor?" I ask, but she shakes her head before I can finish the question.

I study the long line of homeless people, their faces shell-shocked and rendered vacant through drugs, alcohol, or just plain bad karma, waiting resignedly for some kind of minuscule break in their shitty-luck lives.

"Stay put," I tell the girl. "I think I can help you." I get out of the car and walk a few feet away. I dial Jackie's number at work.

She picks up on the second ring and says, "Is everything all right?"

"We're going to have company tonight," I say.

I tell her about Mary Grace and her predicament.

"Do you know anything about her? Where she comes from?" she asks.

"No and no," I answer. Jackie is the kindest, most compassionate person I have ever met, but she's not crazy, and like most sane people she wants to hold on to her household possessions such as televisions and jewelry.

"It's just for a night or two until we can find a place for her to stay that's safe."

For a moment there's silence on the other end, and I think that maybe she's pulled the receiver away so I can't hear the impatience in her breathing. I turn to peer through the windshield of my car and see Mary Grace staring back at me, her face a pale oval behind the glass, her posture rigid, as though I might change my mind about helping her.

"Jackie? You still there?"

"Yes. I'm here."

"I have that shrink appointment at five, so I'll ask James Earle to sit with her until you get home. Is that all right?"

"Yes, that's fine. And Betty, I'm really glad that you're going to be talking to someone."

"Yeah, well, I'm glad you're glad," I say. "Hey, who knows where this will lead? First it's rescuing orphans and beginning therapy. Next it could be adopting kittens and taking ballet lessons."

That gets a laugh, and it feels good. It's been a while.

"I'll see you later," she says and disconnects.

I get back in my car and tell Mary Grace she'll be spending the night at my house.

She smiles, ducks her head, and then looks out the window, her eyes misting with relief.

I call James Earle when I'm back on the Tollway headed north, and I don't have to ask twice for him to stay with our foundling for a few hours until Jackie gets off work. His old Crown Vic is in the driveway by the time I make it home. I take Mary Grace inside and she stands shyly in the entrance hall studying her frayed sneakers, as though afraid to track dirt on the carpet. She's startled at first by the appearance of James, walking from the kitchen wearing an apron, holding a spatula in one hand and a frying pan in the other.

He nods to me and says to Mary Grace, in a courtly, almost formal way, "Welcome."

"Hello," she says uncertainly, eyeing with suspicion the frilly, cotton apron that once belonged to Jackie's mother. James is also wearing faded jeans, a work shirt, and mountain boots, his weatherworn face looking like fifty miles of unpaved roads.

"You like grilled-cheese sandwiches?" he growls.

She nods and he says, "That's good. I often find the best people like grilled-cheese sandwiches." He gestures with his spatula for her to follow him into the kitchen. And just like that—no preamble and no introductions, after only a welcome and a promise of food—he has taken Mary Grace into his care. She drops her cloth bag on the floor and follows him into the kitchen.

I put fresh towels in the guest bathroom, then turn down the blanket in the guest bedroom. The room is used most frequently by Jackie's mom, Anne, but lately she's chosen not to stay the night when she comes for dinner because of the increasing tensions in the house. Tensions caused by me.

I sit on the bed for a moment, brooding over Seth's actions, his taking what were probably drugs from the dealer's pocket. Sheela G had no reason to make up the story. Downing a few Oxys recreationally is cause for worry enough, but stealing them from a stiff is a whole other level of bad. I've never known Seth to lie to me. And I would have counted almost anybody else in my life as dishonest before suspecting Seth of dealing dirty. But there's a saying that's as true as anything can be in Narco Land: *How do you know an addict's lying to you? His lips are moving.*

I try calling Seth on my personal cell phone, but it goes straight to message.

My partner was on his way downtown to look for Gary. If I were to find Gary first, it might win me some points with Maclin.

The thought of going back to the station, sitting at my desk, and listening to other cops talking about their busy days out on the streets fills me with a swelling sense of *own-wee,* as Craddock would say.

I walk quickly into my bedroom and change into a shapeless pair of baggy pants, my tactical, lace-up boots, and an old T-shirt. From the hall closet I pull out a ski cap, which I jam on my head, covering my forehead and ears. Slipping into an old camo hunting jacket originally belonging to Jackie's grandfather—one we keep around for those few icy mornings when we need to work outside—I grab a pair of large aviator sunglasses and walk into the kitchen. In my pockets I carry, as I usually do, my badge and two cell phones: personal cell in my left pocket, work cell in my right. Clipped to my waist, under the jacket, is the SIG Sauer.

Mary Grace is sitting at the small table, a patch of sunlight illuminating her face, which is turned in rapt attention to James Earle, who is telling her a story. She's holding the remnants of a grilled-cheese sandwich in both hands, another whole sandwich on her plate.

"Hey, James," I say. "Can I borrow your car? I'll bring it back in a few hours."

He looks at me puzzled, taking in my lumpy attire. "You join the Ukrainian army?" he asks.

"I need to go somewhere," I say, "and I don't want my car recognized."

"This more desk duty?" he asks, catching and holding my gaze.

"Look, I just need to check on my partner," I tell him. "It may be important."

James frowns, but throws me his keys. "Just be back by six." He winks at Mary Grace. "I've got my pottery class tonight."

Mary Grace giggles, eagerly picking up her second sandwich.

"There're clean towels in the guest bathroom," I tell her. "And the bed is ready for you. Why don't you rest a bit after you've eaten? Jackie will be home later; until then, James Earle will keep you safe."

James gives me an exaggerated salute, and Mary Grace laughs again.

The Crown Vic takes a little coaxing to start but finally roars to life, and I back out of the driveway like I'm pulling a small Chris-Craft from its mooring. As soon as I'm on the highway, I call Dr. Theodosiou's office and tell them I'm going to have to cancel my five o'clock appointment. I've come down with the flu and I'll have to call them back to reschedule. I'm already in the shit with Maclin, and I'm fully prepared to do an extra set of mea culpas tomorrow.

Traffic has already started backing up northbound, but the southbound exit to downtown is clear. I park next to Tent City on Dawson Street, praying that I'll come back to an undamaged car. There are always extra cigarettes in James Earle's glove compartment. I find two packs and stuff them into my jacket pockets. Pulling the cap down as far as it will go and still allow me to see, I lock up the car and slip through the nearest gaping hole in the chain-link fence surrounding the homeless area. Adopting a slow shuffle, I make my way toward a group of tattered, mud-spackled tents, covered by bits of drying clothing and empty plastic bags, looking like long-abandoned Sherpa dwellings. A lot of the street citizens sleep their days away in their tents, but a few are sitting on flattened cardboard boxes or ratty lawn chairs smoking, talking, or staring off into space in the manner of the patient poor.

A few of them make eye contact but most pointedly ignore me, even when I stand next to one group playing a slow-motion game of poker, the players seated on an old picnic blanket, using empty pistachio shells for chips.

"Hey, I'm looking for Gary," I say, taking out a pack of cigarettes.

I squat down next to the nearest player, a woman with frizzy hair and a faded tattoo on her hand of a heart pierced with flowers. She's wearing a quilted purple ski jacket, mended in places with duct tape. I shake the pack so that a few cigarettes are easy to grab and offer one to her. "Anyone here seen him today?"

The woman gives me a withering look but takes two of the cigarettes. I offer the pack to the man sitting beside her, but he leans away from me as though from a toxic cloud. There's no question they've already made me for what I am, but maybe I can still get someone to talk to me.

"What about Wayne? Anybody seen him today?"

"Anybody seen Wayne today?" The woman with the tattoo mimics the question in a cartoony, high-pitched voice.

I plop myself down next to the woman, sitting cross-legged in the dirt, rubbing my hands together. "Well, I guess that means I'll just have to park it here for a while until somebody remembers where Gary is."

The card-playing man sitting farthest from me asks, "You got a hundred dollars?" He takes off his battered ball cap and holds it out to me like an offering plate.

"No," I say. "Afraid not."

"Then fuck off," he says, putting the hat back on his head.

The group snickers loudly and goes on playing. When it's clear that I'm not about to go away, the group stands in weary unison and moves away, leaving the scattered pistachio shells and the picnic blanket behind.

I hear derisive laughter, low-pitched and resonant, coming

from behind me. I look over my shoulder and see an older black man—dreadlocks halfway down his back, haunches overflowing a large wooden deck chair, paperback novels piled in his lap—regarding me. There is no word to describe him but *massive*.

"You looking for something?" he asks me.

There's a pitying grin on his face, as though he's discovered my most embarrassing secrets.

"Looking for a friend," I say, standing, brushing the dirt from my backside.

"Ah, a friend," he says, his smile broadening. The book at the top of the pile is *The Scarlet Letter*. He glides his fingers over the cover like he's stroking a cat.

I move closer, holding out the pack of cigarettes. "Want one?"

He studies my outstretched fingers, then my jacket, and finally my face. He reaches carefully, almost delicately, for the entire pack, and it disappears into an inside coat pocket.

"Thank you," he says, graciously, as though I've just given him a box seat at the opera.

"You know a guy named Wayne? He goes by Flush as well."

"You going to arrest him?" the man asks.

"What makes you think I'm going to arrest him?"

"Because people come down here for only two reasons," he tells me. "To crack a Bible, or to crack a skull. I don't see you with no Bible, snow princess."

"I just want to talk to him."

"I haven't seen him today."

"Do you know Gary?"

He shifts slightly in his chair, bringing one hand up to count off on his fingers. "I know a lot of Garys. There's Big Gary, Little Gary, Tattoo Gary, Short-Eyes Gary—" He stops for a moment, frowning. *Short-eyes* is prison slang for child molester.

"But Short-Eyes Gary didn't last too long down here. We chased him off."

"Let's call this one Drug Bug Gary. He was a smoking buddy of Wayne's. I don't want to arrest him. I just want to talk to him."

My skin itches under the wool cap; knowing that everyone here has figured out I'm a cop, I pull the cap off my head, scratch my scalp, and say, "There were several shootings down here last night. Wayne's friend may be an important witness to at least one of the killings."

The man has been staring at my hair, now untamed and spiky. He says, "You're the one that took Mary Grace to the shelter last night. But I heard she left this morning with a redheaded Amazon driving a fancy car." He tilts his head, studying me. His eyes go half-mast—the Caterpillar studying Alice before the revelation of the mushrooms.

"Yeah, well, she's staying with me for a bit until we can figure something out," I tell him.

"Bunsen Gary," he tells me after a pause. "He's who you're looking for."

He sets his books down on the ground and stands with surprising grace, his girth barely squeezing free of the two armrests, threatening to lift the heavy chair off the ground. He's tall—at least six feet five—and weighs well over four hundred pounds.

"I think I know where we can find him. Come with me," he commands and he sets off in a southerly direction, toward Hickory Street.

He holds out a hand for me to shake. "I'm Mountain."

"I'm Betty," I tell him.

"Red Betty, Red Betty—" Mountain riffs in a singsong way, matching his words to the beat of our steps.

We turn left at Hickory, walking until we get halfway to Orleans Street. Mountain then stops as though hitting a glass wall.

"I can't go any farther," he says, slightly out of breath. He's too distant from the protective shadow of the underpass that umbrellas Tent City. He squints painfully against the last of the day's sunlight. He points east, to the end of Hickory Street. "Past the old meatpacking plant, just before you get to Malcolm X, there's a dope house. Red birdbath in the front. That's where you'll probably find Bunsen Gary."

He turns to face me, his back to the ruins of a once-vibrant neighborhood.

"You carry a gun?" he asks.

I pat my right hip.

"Good," he says. "This place used to be run by a code. But those days are gone. As dangerous as Tent City has become, out there is worse."

He grimaces and bends down to rub one knee.

"Old sports injury?" I ask.

"*Sports?*" he asks in response, an edge to his voice. Mountain draws himself up, looking down at me with disdain. "Black people don't all play ball, stretch. Until last year I was a librarian."

I wince to show him I deserved the dunk, but thank him for his help and hand him the other pack of cigarettes. I watch him for a while, slowly making his way back to his throne.

My work phone rings. It's Maclin. I don't answer the call. When I replay the message he's left, his voice is pinched with anger. He says Theodosiou's office called him, and I'd better be deathbed sick to have canceled my psych appointment. If I don't call him back within an hour, he's putting me on suspension. I try calling Seth again, but the call goes straight to voice mail. I've never known him not to answer when he sees I'm trying to reach him.

There are no cars on Hickory or Orleans, even though it's five thirty and the traffic is humming loudly on the freeway behind me, and only a few pedestrians walk listlessly in the direction of the soup-kitchen food trucks. A man pushes a rumbling shopping cart filled with found treasure; he crashes it over the curb, then disappears into the lengthening shadows of the underpass.

I walk east on Hickory where the street becomes a shadowed canyon, sandwiched between two large warehouses, now closed for the day. A chain-link fence surrounds a parking lot to my right, where out-of-service vans have been stripped of everything but their rust.

Pulling my cap over my hair again, I quicken my pace. Sunset is only a few minutes away and the temperature has gotten dramatically colder, despite the clear weather. The street ahead is deserted but I glance over my shoulder a few times, making sure no one is behind me. I look for any signs of trap stars—local slang for drug users—dealers, or their lookouts, posted on the corners at the far end of Hickory near the dope house. But the area feels as empty as a vacant film set right up to the point where the pavement is swallowed under the gray support beams of the Malcolm X overpass. On the other side of Malcolm X are more warehouses; weedy, overgrown lots; and weather-beaten, shuttered houses built fifty years or more ago.

At the end of the warehouse to my right is a stout metal cage housing the building's electrical system. It would take a blowtorch and the Jaws of Life to pry through the thick metal mesh to get to any of the valuable copper wires within. Next to the cage is the dope house. In the 1920s it would have been a cozy family home, but now the single coat of paint applied a decade ago has all but peeled away from the spongy wood; the peaked roof, high enough to be seen from the overpass, is shedding roof shingles like a dog with mange. Most of the windows have been broken and repaired with cardboard or plywood. Nestled in the front yard is a tiny birdbath, painted fire-engine red.

The place looks deserted. No sound comes from inside the house. I wait for a few minutes, propped against the metal cage, my eyes scanning the road for new arrivals looking to score. There is ambient illumination from the tall security lights on the back side of the warehouse and a lone streetlamp in the middle of the block. The Dallas city lights are only a few miles to the east, but it might as well be full-on night at this end of the street.

I stand in front of the door and press my ear against the wood. There's the slight rustling noise of old wood settling. When I test the doorknob, it rattles against the cylinder but seems to be locked.

An inspection of the side of the house closest to the overpass reveals more boarded-up windows and a high wooden privacy fence. The panels are sagging and loose, but it's too dark to see what, if anything, is in the yard. Some barely perceived sound coming from the cavernous mouth of the underpass behind me makes me turn, my hand reflexively feeling its way under the hem of my jacket to the SIG Sauer in its holster. I squint into the blackness, the muscles in my thighs tensed to hunker down, but nothing of substance materializes until a fluid shadow close to the ground slinks its way along the curb. A cat, I realize, and I finish exhaling.

Careful not to trip over the trash in the yard, my imagination conjuring unpleasant images of loose needles and discarded condoms, I make my way back to the front of the house. It's too dark—and too dangerous—to keep stumbling around a known drug house, and my determination to track down Bunsen Gary, along with my partner, is being eroded by the sense that I'm out of my mind to be lingering around this area past sunset. Most of the serious users will not be found with guns; they would have pawned them sooner or later to buy drugs. But the suppliers *will* be armed—and more than willing to shoot first and ask questions later. Even my overarching need to know who left the Bible verses on the dead drug dealers is fast taking a back seat to a healthy fear. I also need to return Maclin's call, assuring him that I'm home sick in bed, before he can make good on his threat to suspend me.

A circlet of light from a cigarette flares briefly under the overpass, the blinking red eye of a nocturnal creature roughly the height of a tall man. I freeze, trying to make myself invisible in the shadows. The cigarette is then extinguished, followed by the unmistakable sound of a woman's high heels hard-striking the pavement. A murky figure emerges from under the freeway— wide-shouldered, with thick, muscular legs, bare atop gravity-defying platform shoes—moving onto the sidewalk opposite me. Hips moving in an exaggerated swing, long, wavy hair the color of molten lava too thick to be anything other than a wig, the woman is fully illuminated briefly under the streetlight, wearing a short fur coat, her hand thrust inside a large handbag. She dips her chin at me, and throws me the look: *I see you, motherfucker, and my hand ain't reachin' for my lipstick.* She pauses briefly, facing me in a wide-legged stance for better balance, taking the measure of me. Then she turns and continues walking rapidly toward Orleans Street.

I've decided to take her lead, walking back to Tent City and to James Earle's car. But, not wanting to startle her, I linger for a moment by the front of the house. I glance at the door.

Previously closed and locked, it's now slightly ajar, with about six inches of disquieting blackness between door and frame.

* * *

Someone inside the house—Bunsen Gary?—has opened the door. Either he saw me and decided not to bolt, which means he's still inside, or he snuck out when I was on the far side of the house.

I press myself against the outside wall, setting loose a cascade of fracturing paint chips. Again there's no sound, but the skin on my forehead tightens with the thought that someone has been watching me from inside the house.

I pull my gun from the holster. "Dallas Police," I say. "Come on out."

Nothing. Not even a creaking of wood.

"I'm not going to ask you again to come out. Look, I'm not going to arrest you, I just need to see you don't have a weapon."

I inch closer to the open space, pressing my cheek against the frame. I want to do a quick look-see, but it's too dark to observe anything inside. I take my cell phone from my pocket and power up the screen to flashlight mode. I point the light into the void; just inside the door is a sneakered foot attached to the leg of someone lying on the bare wooden floor. I direct the light upward to the torso of the motionless man, his head haloed by blood. Beyond him are other bodies.

I do a rapid sweep of the interior, looking for any movement, but there are only motionless forms. Kicking at the door, I scramble into the room, crouched low, trying to throw light into every corner of the room at once. My breathing is hoarse and loud; there's no movement in the room except the arc of my gun hand braced over the other hand holding the phone and its beam of blinding LED light.

There are perhaps five people in the room, lying facedown or faceup, one slumped figure seated against a chair, his head falling over his outstretched legs. Fresh blood, looking like chocolate syrup in the depth of the shadows, spatters the floor.

"Hey," I whisper to the closest man, shaking his leg. He's still warm, his flesh supple beneath my grasp. He hasn't been dead long, but any shots fired would have been heard a block away, especially half a dozen rounds fired inside a thin-walled house. I've been in close proximity to the house for fifteen minutes and heard nothing. These people have been dead less than half an hour.

I shine the light on the next-closest body, a woman whose staring eyes catch the beam, but there is no remaining consciousness there. When I lean over her face, her pupils remain fixed and dilated. I position the phone so I can call for assistance.

A shifting shadow, a rushing movement, and I pivot on my heels. The seated man slumped behind me has reanimated, the hood of his jacket pulled over his head and face, and he's on top of me before I can raise my gun, knocking the phone and the gun from my hands. He's not big, but he's wiry with muscle, and strong. A glancing weight crashes heavily off the side of my head and I fall facedown on top of the dead woman.

Another blow connects with the back of my head. The sharp pain carries me into a floating blankness.

When I come to, I'm lying on top of something soft, a damp and acrid cushion; the tang of cigarettes and sweat is sharp in my nose. My hands are raised over my head, and when I flex my fingers, they feel uncomfortably sticky. Chocolate syrup, I think, immediately followed by the recalled image of the blood pooling and spattered across the floor. In a wave of nausea, I realize that the cushion I'm on is the body of the dead woman. Once more, I'm caught in the wavering, jagged-edged hole of forgetting.

I hear voices, two men whispering loudly, and the sensation of hands turning me over onto my back. When I open my eyes, I'm confused to see that it's a man and a woman leaning in close enough for me to feel, and smell, their breath on my face, the woman's long hair tickling my cheek. The hair is impossibly red. Like the hair of Evangeline Roy.

I flail outward with my hands, pushing them backward. Both of their faces—weirdly underlit by my retrieved cell phone, the flashlight app still going strong—crimp with fright and they retreat into the shadows. The woman makes comforting, cooing noises, waving her palms at me in the universal signal of "no harm." Bringing both my hands to my savaged cranium, I realize that my hat has been knocked completely off my head.

"You okay?" the man asks.

Blinking and squinting, I recognize the man as Seth's CI, Wayne.

The woman gives Wayne a withering glance. "She look okay to you? Honey, you just relax," she tells me, patting my arm. "Help is on the way."

The woman, I see now, is the bewigged person I had observed earlier, sashaying her way up Hickory.

With their help I sit up, my head threatening to crack apart like an egg. At the back of my neck, something wet. I gingerly touch the wound at the base of my skull, and I'm startled to find my fingers caked with dried blood from the dead drug addict.

"What happened?" I ask.

"Somebody rang your bell," the figure in the red wig says. "I was on my way back to Tent City when I ran into Wayne, who'd been looking for you all over the place. He described this tall, female undercover, and I remembered seeing you—and, honey, I made you for a cop the minute I saw you sniffing around the house. Girl, you can*not* be out here alone after dark with these trap stars.

"Just as me and Wayne got halfway down the block we seen this man break from the house, running back under Malcolm X like a bitch with his hair on fire. Except for these Betty Grable come-fuck-me pumps, I would have gone after his punk ass, because I just knew he was up to no good, and then coming in here and seeing all these poor dead junkies—"

"Did you get a good look at him?" I ask, interrupting the avalanche of words.

"It was a man, that's all I know," she answers. "And I couldn't tell you if he was black, white, or in between."

I turn my head to face Wayne, every muscle in my neck starting to spasm. "Where's Seth?" I demand. "He was supposed to meet up with you."

Wayne looks shaken, uneasy. "Uh," he says uncertainly, his eyes flitting around the room.

From blocks away comes the sound of approaching sirens.

"Take me out of here," I tell the pair. They help me up, my arms around their shoulders, carefully guiding me around the bodies and out the door. They gently lower me onto the curb, where I sit, my throbbing head between my knees, my stomach threatening to eject itself onto the pavement.

Wayne sits beside me, his body rocking in agitation, his arms wrapped protectively across his chest. I ask him again, "Where's Seth?"

We watch as three patrol cars turn off Orleans onto Hickory, lights flashing, sirens blaring, my muscular savior in a dress standing in the middle of the road waving to the oncoming cars like a welcoming game-show model.

Wayne looks at me, his face barely discernible in the dark, and says, "Someplace he shouldn't be."

CHAPTER 13

I'm sitting on a hospital bed, my bare feet dangling over the edge, inches from the ice-cold floor, being examined by the emergency-room doctor. He presses a little too hard on the fleshy lump at the back of my skull, like a produce shopper fingering an avocado. I pull at the neck of my scratchy hospital gown and grimace.

"That hurt?" the doctor asks.

"Oh no," I say, giving him the thousand-yard stare. "It feels great."

"The CT scan shows you have a mild concussion from the blow to the back of the head, but no cranial damage at the left temple. Only bruising. No stitches needed, just the few Steri-Strips we've already applied. I don't think it's anything we need to worry about," he tells me.

"Well, I'm glad *we're* not going to worry."

The doctor is young, his medical diploma newly minted. Apparently he missed the classes in treating sarcasm.

"My throat hurts," I say. "Feels like it's closing up."

He tells me to open my mouth, stares down into my throat,

probes my neck quickly, and shrugs. "I would recommend a few days' rest," he says, brusquely. "Your blood pressure's a little high. Come back to the ER if you get nauseous, light-headed, or if you have difficulty in swallowing. If any headaches persist, tell your GP about it. You should see him within the next few days for a follow-up anyway. The nurse will be in soon to discharge you."

He pulls back the curtain, ready to make his escape. During my five-minute exam, two gunshot victims have been brought in by ambulance, Baylor being the hospital of choice for gangbangers in Big D. He tosses off a "Good luck" and vanishes.

"My GP's a woman, by the way," I call after him, but he's already out of earshot, the privacy curtains still billowing in his wake.

Maclin appears at my bedside like the Angel of Death, smiling a winning *Kostucha* smile and wearing white in the form of a crisply starched shirt, rolled rakishly at the sleeves. Solicitous and sympathetic at first—he heard the "Officer down" call and raced to the hospital, arriving even before Jackie—his mood changes as soon as he realizes the bane of his existence is going to live.

"I'm going to initiate proceedings for two weeks' suspension without pay," he says angrily. "The only way you'll get back on duty is to be cleared by Dr. Theo." He holds up three fingers. "No fewer than three office visits—you hear me, Rhyzyk?"

I make a face and he asks in a savage whisper, "What the fuck is wrong with you?"

I'm tempted to be a smart-ass: *Besides a mild concussion and some lacerations, I'm aces.* But I've screwed up royally by putting myself in jeopardy—chasing after my partner on suspicions I concealed from my superiors, defying Maclin's lockdown, canceling a mandated psych eval, walking into a dope house knowing that a killer had shot three dealers within a twenty-four-hour period. And that's only the stuff Maclin knows about.

"I want to see you tomorrow morning, ten o'clock, an incident report on my desk," he says. "We've got four junkies shot dead, one of whom may have been a witness to the death of Pico Guerto. And we almost had an ex-cop." He looks at me carefully. "Did you get a look at your attacker?"

I shake my head.

At that moment Bernard Tate, Maclin's old Homicide partner, pokes his head into the examining room.

Tate says, "Christ, Rhyzyk, you got quite a shiner started there." *Quite a shinah stahted theyah.*

Maclin and Tate give each other friendly nods and Maclin says, "Take her, please. She's all yours."

He leaves in a huff, and Tate asks me what I remember about the attack.

I tell him as much as I know, except for my growing suspicions about Seth. "I was following a lead to find the witness to the shootings in Deep Ellum," I say.

"Gee, Rhyzyk," Tate says. "Homicide really appreciates your help with doing our job. What with your experience in investigating murders and all."

"Always happy to help," I say, defensively crossing my arms. But it's hard to look tough when you're mostly naked, wearing a powder-blue beddy-bye hospital wrap.

We glare at each other while he pulls from his pocket a plastic evidence bag with a piece of paper inside. "Did you see this when you were crawling over the bodies?"

It's another Bible verse.

"No, I guess you didn't," he says, taking in my rigid posture. "You feel well enough right now to talk to my guys?"

I nod and Tate starts to leave. Then he turns suddenly, as though he's just thought of something important. "By the way," he says, "great tattoo. You give out popcorn with that show?" He snickers unpleasantly and walks away.

Tate's detectives take my statement, and afterward I lie on the hospital bed waiting to be discharged, the mattress nearly vibrating with my tension. I've brought myself to a near disaster over worry for my partner, impatience with my physical limitations, and a growing need to deny those limitations with dangerous behavior. Just like the good old days in New York. A few years after joining the NYPD I was usually the first officer into a condemned building, and the last one to leave following a drug bust.

Jackie comes into the room and stands by my bed. She takes my hand, kisses it, and asks, in all seriousness, "Are you out of your mind?"

"Looks that way," I say. "I'm on suspension for a few weeks."

The relief on Jackie's face makes me pull my hand from hers. "Don't look so pleased about it."

She stares at me sadly while handing me my pants. "Don't think for a minute I don't know who'll get the worst end of that deal."

"What do you mean?" I ask, knowing exactly what she means.

"I'll wait for you outside."

She turns to go and I grab her arm and pull her to me, embracing her in a tight hug. I smell her hair—soft floral notes drowning out the smell of alcohol swabs and industrial disinfectant—and am relieved to tears when her arms go around my waist.

"We're going to get this sorted out," I tell her.

She pulls back and looks at me, her hands on either side of my face. I imagine she adopts the same kind of sympathetic yet hopeful expression when informing her patients they have a cancerous but treatable tumor.

"Betty, you can't sort this out like a junk drawer. I know you.

You think you can compartmentalize everything into neat little piles, then blur the rough edges with enough Jameson. And you can't bludgeon your fear into submission by putting yourself at risk, either."

"You do recall that I'm a cop, right?"

She smiles. "Yeah, a *cop*. Not a paratrooper, Baghdad Betty."

Jackie puts her fingers gently over my carotid pulse. I feel it beating strong and fast under her touch.

"What's your diagnosis, Doc?" I ask, smiling.

"That you're afraid," she says softly. "All the time."

My body stiffens reflexively, but she refuses to let me pull away. She holds my gaze, as though willing me to see what she's seen so clearly. What I hadn't wanted to fully admit to myself, or to anyone, until this moment: that the suffocating feeling gnawing at the back of my throat, the discomfort I had told the doctor about, was terror, pure and simple. Terror that finding Bible verses at murder scenes meant that Evangeline Roy, or what was left of the Family, was having a little fun with me while getting rid of the drug competition.

"You're not in this by yourself," Jackie says. "Remember, I'm a farm girl, and we can be pretty tough too."

"I'll bet you did drive a mean pickup truck," I say while kissing her neck.

"You should've seen me driving a combine. Now *that* was scary."

We laugh and a discharge nurse comes in, smiling over our antics.

She stage-whispers, "My partner and I just celebrated twenty years together. She's a nurse too!"

The nurse then goes over all the discharge instructions: make sure I take it easy, no heavy lifting, no driving, no bending over, no sleeping alone tonight, and a prescription for pain medication, to be taken only after twenty-four hours of noncomatose behavior.

No way, I think, grateful for that bit of oblivion. *I'm taking one of those puppies as soon as the drugstore delivers them.*

Seeing the script for Oxy makes me think of Seth—who, Jackie has told me, is sitting outside in the waiting room, along with a battery of fellow cops, friends, and newfound acquaintances: Craddock, Ryan, James Earle, Mary Grace, and Wayne (the last of whom asked unsuccessfully to be treated with narcotics—for his own shock, of course). The tall trans woman, whose name turns out to be Dusty Rose, is also there, giving her initial witness statement to the detectives and flirting with every male nurse or EMT who comes her way.

I get dressed and walk stiffly from my cubicle to the waiting room. The lights had been dimmed in the examination room, so the overhead neon illumination in the public areas stabs at my eyes.

Everyone in the waiting room stands, uncertain how to greet me. They've all heard about the four people in the trap house—two women and two men, all shot in the head—and about my close encounter with the probable killer. I catch Seth's gaze, but his smile falters when he catches my expression. I crook my finger at Craddock and we step into the hallway.

"Did you find anything on Carlos Rivera's body when you searched him today, other than the Bible verse?" I ask. My intensity makes him take a step backward. "Any drugs?"

Craddock looks at me strangely, possibly thinking the blow to my head has left me addled. But he says, "No."

I thank him and tell him I'll see him tomorrow, at least for the short time it will take me to write the report for Maclin, gather my things, and do the walk of shame out of the station.

"Maclin says you're off the clock for a couple of weeks," Craddock says.

"Yeah, well, I have no one to blame but myself for that one."

"You gonna be all right?" he asks, one hand on my arm.

Craddock stands in his ill-fitting jacket, his belly stretching the buttons at his waist, his barely disguised orthopedic shoes already crushed at the arches, nothing but empathy on his sagging face, and what I want right now more than anything is for him to hug me and tell me everything will be fine. But I'd rather die than admit how weak I feel in this moment.

Instead I assure him that no permanent damage has been done, that I just need some time to heal, and then I stick my head back into the waiting room, gesturing to Jackie that I'm ready to leave. "Thank you all for hanging around," I say. "But I need to get home now."

James Earle approaches and gives me an awkward hug.

"Oh God, James," I say. "Your car's still in Tent City."

He shrugs. "Don't worry about it, Red. I'll deal with it later."

"Look, I'll talk to someone about giving you a lift to Tent City."

Ignoring Seth's attempt to catch my eye, I let Jackie take one arm and Mary Grace the other, and they help me limp out of the emergency room and into the crowded parking lot, Dusty Rose and Wayne following close behind.

Ryan catches up with us and helps Jackie ease me into the car. He leans in, fussing with the seat belt when I can't seem to maneuver the strap across my chest. His face is inches from mine, giving me searching glances, and I wonder if I've still got blood on my face.

"Did you get a look at the guy who attacked you?" he asks. His brows are furrowed, his face pale with exhaustion. The skin under one eye pulsates in nervous rebellion.

I shake my head, which seems to cause tiny bits of my brain to melt into my sinuses.

"You're sure?"

"Yes, Kevin, I'm sure. It was really dark—and the bastard hit me from behind."

"Is there anything more I can do for you?" he asks.

Without being invited, Dusty Rose has slithered into the back seat with Mary Grace, leaving Wayne standing forlorn on the pavement next to Ryan.

"Will you help Wayne get settled somewhere? Mary Grace will be staying with us for the night—"

Dusty pipes up, "And I *know* y'all don't want to show ingratitude after my saving your life tonight by leaving *me* out in the cold."

I dig James Earle's car keys out of my pants pocket and hand them to Ryan. "Can you also find a ride for James to go retrieve his car?" I tell him where I'd parked the car at Tent City, and he nods and gently closes the car door. I pull down the visor mirror, the first time I've had a chance to inspect the damage myself, and see that there is, in fact, a smear of blood, in a pale wash of pink, just below the hairline at my left temple, above my black eye.

Jackie is saying something to me.

"What?" I snap, my entire body on fire with nerves, and head pain, and the residue of fear.

She places her hand over mine. The sensible thing for her to do would be to get really furious with me—for putting myself at risk, for the growing number of waifs who seem to be inserting themselves into the sanctuary of our home, for the aching distance that seems to grow daily between us—but she's smiling. It's a sad, pale expression of mirth, but a smile nonetheless.

"Should I break out the good china?" she asks.

"God, I love you," I tell her.

As Jackie pulls away, Ryan watches us leave. He was all concern when he was buckling me in, eager to be of assistance. But there is a stiffness to his posture, his arms rigid at his sides, his fists clenched as though ready for a bare-knuckle fight. Wayne is tapping him on the shoulder, asking him something, but Ryan ignores him. He continues to watch us drive away, and he is furious.

I spend a restless night in bed next to Jackie, my head throbbing despite the pain meds. She's good to her word in being my guardian angel, making sure I don't slip into unconsciousness, waking every few hours to check my breathing. Mary Grace is sleeping in the guest room, and Dusty Rose has bunked down in the living room with a sleeping bag and a spare pillow. I lie between the sheets, floating in a haze of narcotics, listening for strange noises such as Dusty ransacking the house for loose cash. But the only thing I hear from her is resonant snoring.

Despite these indications of a peaceable kingdom, I stare at the ceiling—a prison inmate, agitated, anxious, and tense. The more I think about Seth's lie, or rather his omission of the truth, the angrier I get. And he's not the only one I'm pissed about. For the first time in my life I'm furious with Uncle Benny for deserting me, for leaving me to my own devices. It has always been Benny's guidance—his constant advocacy of me despite my mistakes, his insistence that I find a way to keep the static of my thoughts in check (my own personal Reaping the Grim)—that has kept me balanced. I need to hear his voice again. In my present condition, though, it's like trying to tune in a symphony on a radio with a severed power cord. I have a mad impulse to gather my clothes, sneak out a side door, and drive all night, in any direction, despite my impaired state, just to get out of Dallas.

* * *

Jackie and I wake early next morning to a rhythmic thrumming from the dining room. When we get up to investigate we find Dusty, in her scarlet wig and heels, wielding our vacuum cleaner around the legs of the dining-room table as gently as an archaeologist presiding over an ancient dig. Her sleeping bag and blanket are folded with military precision on the couch.

Dusty has already made coffee and oatmeal for Mary Grace, and she lets us know that if we had something in the refrigerator other than "roots and seeds" she could have made Jackie and me a decent omelet.

Over coffee, Dusty tells us her story: disadvantaged and bullied childhood in Kilgore, Texas; years in the army; dishonorable discharge from the service for kissing and telling; failed romances; attempt to start her own club; more failed romances; then finally the streets. She offers to sing us every Jerome Kern musical. And in exchange for another night indoors, she tells us—just until a friend returns from out of town in a day or two—she'll do all the cooking, cleaning, and looking after Mary Grace.

"Look," she says, "if I had wanted to rob you, I could have already done it. I could have left you for dead in that trap house, but I didn't. It's good karma, baby. Please. Don't make Ms. Dusty Rose beg. Just one more night."

I look at Jackie, who sighs and picks up her coffee cup.

"Honey," Dusty drawls, "it's not like you couldn't find me if I *did* rob you. I'm sort of hard to miss."

The final, deciding word comes from Mary Grace: "She's good people—really! She always helped me find food when I was living at Tent City."

"Okay," Jackie says, throwing a warning look at Dusty Rose. "But if I discover you've rearranged my kitchen, I'm having Betty call the SWAT team on you."

Dusty crosses one finger over her heart and takes Mary Grace's hand into her own sizable paws, patting it reassuringly. A muscular Mary Poppins, with a tan.

I agree that she can stay one more night if she wears a different wig in my presence. That red is too close to Evangeline Roy's.

CHAPTER 14

JANUARY 9, 2014
DR. THEO THEODOSIOU'S OFFICE

The waiting room is all subdued colors and textures, constructed for physical comfort, a quiet sanctuary for the besieged mind: plush armchairs that cradle the back, whispery blue-gray paint on the walls, carpet in subtle Escher-like patterns in monochromatic hues.

Three sessions. I need to get through only three sessions with enough equanimity and cooperation to get back on the force. My heel hammers a rapid staccato on the floor, jiggling the attached leg like a fast-motion drill bit. I check my phone for messages. I fiddle with the zipper on my jacket while nervously watching for the doctor's office door to open. I check for phone messages again, cradling in one hand my still-aching head.

I spent exactly thirty-eight minutes at the station earlier today. Half an hour to write up my incident report of the attack at the trap house, three minutes to have my ass pureed by Maclin (who ignored my questioning about any leads on the murders), and one minute to hand over my SIG Sauer, because God forbid I try to off myself with a city-issued weapon. (Never mind that I have three guns at home; this *is* Texas, after all.)

The sergeant informed me that he had already begun the official suspension proceedings, which would be rescinded only after a new psych eval had been completed. It then took me exactly another four minutes to slink out of the building and into my car. The saving grace in the whole confrontation was Maclin letting me hold on to my badge. It's my glimmer of hope that I'll be granted active-duty status again after the suspension period.

I'm torn between needing to cheerlead the shit out of these sessions in the hope that it will help me regain not only my job but my relationship with Jackie, and wanting to tell everyone— including the redoubtable Dr. Theo—to go fuck themselves. But a little voice inside my head is whispering that maybe the impulse to push away the people who are willing to lend a hand is part of a bigger problem. My father used suspicion like a shield, and the hostile tribalism of his squad as a sword. Asking for help conveyed weakness of character in my Polish Pride family. And anybody who offered it was often met with antagonism. Setting my own pride aside, I have to admit that part of me is grateful, even relieved, that I've been forced into getting help. But in this moment it's a very small part, and one that I'm willing to confess only to myself.

The inner door to the office opens softly, and a tall, bearded man stands on the threshold.

"Betty Rhyzyk?" he asks. There's the slightest accent, honeyed with the sun of some Mediterranean land.

I nod, and he holds out his hand for me to shake. He smiles warmly, his eyes inquisitive, the lips full under a mustache, which, like the beard, is silvered. A handsome man with a gentle, professorial air.

"I'm Dr. Theodosiou. Glad to meet you."

I stand and shake his hand. He motions for me to follow him

into his office at the end of a long hall. There are several chairs and a leather couch next to a large wooden desk.

"Where should I sit?" I ask.

"Anywhere you'd like, Detective," he answers.

I sit in the middle of the couch, wondering if my choice is already bleeding clues onto the report sheet: *The patient impulsively takes over the largest seating area, sits in the middle (showing isolationist tendencies), immediately crosses her arms (indicating reflexive defensiveness)...*

I intentionally place my hands palms down on either side of me, both feet flat on the floor, reminding myself not to nervously jiggle my legs. I've taken the pose of an Egyptian pharaonic statue: mute, unmoving, unyielding, and obsolete.

"How are you today?" he asks. He crosses his legs, balancing a fresh writing pad and a report file on the bent knee and holding an antique pen between long, manicured fingers. I can see that it's not a careless question. His head is tilted, ready to listen, his gaze expectant but calm.

I stare at the file in his lap. "I've been better," I finally say.

"Are you well enough following your injuries yesterday to have this session?"

"Yeah, I think so," I answer.

"Good," he says. "You understand why you're here?"

I meet his gaze. "Yes. So I can get back to work."

"Work is very important to you," he says, pen poised to begin writing. "Would you say it's the most important thing in your life?"

I start to nod my head, but then I remember Jackie. Jackie is the most important thing in my life. But when I open my mouth to speak, I realize I've already revealed my thoughts.

I wait for him to scribble my obsessive devotion to duty on his writing pad, but he remains attentive to me, and to my wordless revelations.

We then go over my chart; the events that led me to his office; and my fractiousness, disobedience, and inappropriate anger directed at colleagues, potential arrestees, and the citizenry in general after my abduction by the Roy family.

"You were hurt very badly," he says. He appears genuinely sympathetic. "How is your leg now?"

"Stiff, sore, a lot of muscle cramps still. It keeps me from running, which is a complete and utter drag."

He regards me silently.

"I used to run a lot," I tell him. "Six or seven miles every day. The doctor's not sure I'll ever be able to do that again."

"That must be very difficult for you," he says.

"You have no idea," I mutter miserably. I reach for the Saint Michael medallion around my neck and unthinkingly pull it toward my mouth. I sense his eyes on me and I freeze before I can nestle the medallion between my teeth.

Dr. Theo smiles and reaches into the collar of his shirt, pulling out a long chain fitted with a large Saint Michael medallion of his own.

"The patron saint of police everywhere," he says. "I started my career as a policeman on Cyprus. Many years ago."

I know I should be comforted by the thought of his being a former cop, but the knowledge makes me slightly wary instead, as though this could be a ploy to build a false camaraderie between us. As in "We're all on the same side here." I'm a little fuzzy on the geography of Cyprus, but the twangy sounds of Greek bouzoukis are playing in my head.

"It's not the original medallion," I say, shaking the chain around my neck. "What I mean is, I used to have one that was worn by my mother and grandmother. It was taken while I was held captive by the Roys."

"Were you close to your mother?"

"At times. Closer than to my father."

He looks at me quizzically.

"My father had a problem with alcohol and anger. And not necessarily in that order. He was a cop too. A homicide detective in Brooklyn. My father and his brother were both cops."

"I see from your file that your brother was a police officer as well, and that he died quite young. Were the two of you close?"

The red-hot defensiveness that had cooled under the gentle questioning and empathetic looks has bubbled up again, threatening to eject itself from my gut into the pristine air of Dr. Theo's well-appointed office. As always, following the reference to my brother, Andrew, there are chaotic, flashing images of a burning building, smoldering corpses, the detritus of human endeavor—furniture, clothing, children's toys—reduced to smoking ash. His pale body on a beach, surrounded by yellow police tape flapping like maddened serpents in the frozen wind from the sea.

I haven't answered his question about my brother, returning the doctor's steady, uncompromising gaze with my practiced, hostile glare. A dread like a yawning shadow begins to build in the four corners of the room, telescoping my vision, and I look down to find my hands tightly clasped together, the knuckles white and straining. My brain inside my skull is an expanding balloon of toxic gas.

"What are you thinking just now?" Dr. Theo asks.

My head snaps up at the intensity of his tone. Beneath his poised, professional air is something else. The metabolized and never-forgotten skills of a seasoned interrogator. A formidable, experienced detective. A cop.

"Nothing," I say.

"That *nothing* has dragon's teeth." He meets my gaze, unblinking, for a few beats. "How long have you been having panic attacks?"

His tone is matter-of-fact, but the walls are beginning to close in.

"Do you need a moment?" he asks. "A glass of water—"

A roar is building inside my head. Dr. Theo's lips are moving. He's talking to me, but I can barely hear the words. He's repeating a phrase that Uncle Benny used to say to me all the time.

"What did you just say?" I demand.

Did he say, "You're stuck in the abyss of your own morass"?

Dr. Theo tilts his head from one side to the other. "What I said was, *It's like getting stuck on a bus, and you've run out of gas.*"

Nervous, strangled laughter bullies its way past my clenched teeth.

"I thought you said something else," I mumble.

"What did you think I said?" he asks. The old interrogator is just there, under the well-polished surface. Taking in every gesture, noting the withheld words fighting against grinding teeth. Seeing everything. Missing nothing.

I give in to the need to cross my arms in front of my chest, but stay mute. He shifts slightly in his chair, removing the pad and the file from his lap and placing them on the desk. He rests both forearms atop his knees, leaning toward me, his hands making elegant gestures as he speaks. "The physical injury you sustained has prevented you from doing the very things that have kept your mind and your body healthy—and your more volatile emotions in check. I can't give you back your leg, but I can help you discharge some of your anger and frustration, your anxiety, so that you can find alternative ways to do so on your own."

"This is beginning to sound like *way* more than three sessions," I say, tucking my chin into my neck.

He opens his hands, smiling encouragingly; the smile the detainer gives the detainee to put them at ease. Then he says the dreaded thing. "It takes as long as it takes…"

My head is a soft-boiled egg caught in a tightening vise. One leg resumes its anxious jiggling. "What exactly does that mean?"

He sits back in his chair, no doubt taking in the full picture of his patient—who is now a mass of tics, grimaces, and agitated breathing. "It means, Detective, that it's up to me to determine when you're ready for active duty again. To decide, with your cooperation, when you are in control of your impulses that are driven by fear, or anger, or an overabundance of anxiety." Regarding me sympathetically, he asks, "Do you feel in control right now?"

"Just watch me," I say, standing abruptly, my knees locking to keep from shaking.

Within a minute I have stormed out the doctor's door, down the hallway, and through the front door. I stride to my car, the buoyancy of decisive action making my bones feel hollow, inflating my muscles with the air of rebellion. I sit behind the wheel and start the engine.

I merge onto the freeway at seventy miles an hour, and for all of two minutes I'm soaring. I'm not sure where I'm going, but wherever it is, when I get there it'll have scorch marks across its back.

A quarter of a mile later an accident between two 18-wheelers turns the highway into a parking lot, bringing every car to a standstill, the flashing lights of the emergency-response vehicles bright enough to illuminate a small village.

The momentary feeling of elation condenses into fight or flight. I pound on the steering wheel, looking for any gap between the immobilized vehicles that will allow me to escape. I want to lean on the horn for nothing more than the satisfaction of making a loud noise. *"Fuuuuuuck!"*

Ahead of me is an old black pickup truck. In bright red paint across the back are crosses and a Jesus fish, along with the inscription 1 COR. 14:34, WOMEN SHALL BE SILENT AND SUBMISSIVE, READ YOUR BIBLE.

Corinthians. The kind of Bible verse that Evangeline would read to me after I'd been bodily chained to a large rock. A Bible verse that has been used to silence, enslave, and subdue women since the Bronze Age.

Peeling my whitened knuckles off the steering wheel, I check both cell phones, personal and work. I've had calls from Jackie, James Earle, and Dr. Theo, plus two calls from Seth. Instead of settling me, their concern works like a crushing weight against my chest, constricting my throat and cutting off the very air I need to breathe.

The car horn behind me is blaring, and I look up to see that the Texas Taliban truck has moved ahead, leaving a gap of several car lengths. The red lettering across the tailgate sets the floaters inside my eyeballs on fire. I put the car in drive and slam my foot onto the accelerator.

The impact of my front bumper crashing into the truck rocks it forward. The collision doesn't obliterate the message, but it crumples the metal enough to obscure it. I've hardly registered the bite of the seat belt across the skin and bones of my chest, or the snap of my head as it recoils on my neck.

The driver hurls himself from the truck to inspect the damage and begins his outraged tirade. He makes his way to my window, screaming and spitting. I reach for my badge and press it against the glass, but it only infuriates him further. Other people are getting out of their vehicles, and it will be mere minutes before one of the cops seeing to the 18-wheelers is summoned to this new accident. In the meantime, I hope the truck driver doesn't pull a gun and serve up some Texas-style justice on me.

I desperately need to talk to a cop who understands what it means to be in the dragon's jaws. With shaking hands I dial Dr. Theo's number on my personal cell phone. After the message I say, in the voice of a twelve-year-old girl with stage fright, "Dr. Theo, this is Detective Rhyzyk..."

I pause, and in the resulting silence before the beep I want to tell him that I am caught in the abyss of my own morass. But I know he will not yet understand what I'm talking about.

So, instead I fill the void by saying, "I think I need to see you again. Soon."

CHAPTER 15

The headache that had hounded me this morning is now the insistent pounding of a ricocheting hammer. I've exiled myself to the backyard deck, where I sit, without cushions, on the hard wooden boards, my feet resting on the riser below, squinting painfully through sunglasses into the late afternoon sun. It's cold and I'm shivering, purposely dressed in too little clothing: baggy shorts, sneakers with no socks, and a thin hoodie. It's self-atonement. I'm an anchoress—complete with shorn hair and a ravaged body with a Catholic icon branded on my right leg—haggard, wounded, withdrawn from the world at large. I can almost hear the Gregorian chanting.

The most important part of my intimate world stands in solemn clusters in the kitchen behind me. They're talking about me, what to "do with" me. I can hear the susurration of their concerned voices ebbing and flowing through the partially open kitchen door. Jackie, James Earle (whose prized car was stolen off the streets of Tent City before anyone could retrieve it), Seth, and Jackie's mother, Anne, are all in attendance. A funeral where the body is still breathing.

Mary Grace had hugged me fiercely, the first one to embrace me after my ride home with Dallas's Finest, her pregnant belly knocking the wind out of me, as though I'd returned home after years lost at sea. She's inside the house, along with Dusty Rose, who is no doubt hovering around the kitchen, perhaps wearing another one of Jackie's mother's aprons, bringing out refreshments for the mourners.

Dusty Rose had brought me comfort of a different kind. Seeing the desolate look on my face, and the bottle of Oxy in my hands, she crept out to the back porch carrying my half-empty bottle of Jameson whiskey and a glass.

She looked pointedly at the pill bottle and said, "You need to give those nasty things to Dusty, or I'm going to show you my impersonation of DeMarcus Ware."

I threw her a blank look and she gave an exasperated breath. "Hello? Tackle for the Dallas Cowboys?"

I surrendered the pills just so she'd go away, which she did after it was clear that I wasn't going to make further conversation with her.

Now there are only a few fingers of dark liquid left in the Jameson bottle, and I pour the rest into the glass. I sip at the fiery liquid, but even this has lost its fragrant appeal. I'd get as much pleasure huffing an ether-soaked rag.

Jackie comes out onto the deck. She sits next to me, her arms wrapped around her shoulders for warmth.

"Why didn't you call me after the crash?" she asks.

"I didn't want to worry you."

"So your coming home in a squad car, with fresh bruises and a story about rear-ending a truck on purpose, is not going to worry me?"

"It wasn't just a truck. It was an assault weapon on wheels."

"The officer said they had to arrest the driver to keep him from attacking you."

I can't keep a wide grin off my face. "Yeah, well. All I said to the guy was I was sorry I'd wrecked his mode of transport for picking up his next twelve-year-old bride."

Jackie sighs and ducks her head. "The officer thinks your car may be totaled."

"I'll pay for the damage—"

"Goddammit, Betty. It's not about the car. I don't care about the car. I don't understand what's going on with you."

"That makes two of us," I say.

She turns to face me. "Do you think you're the only one in this house who ever feels rage? The only one who's ever given in to the temptation for a little vengeful carnage?"

She looks at me with an intensity that threatens to blow my hair back.

"When I was a first-year intern in New York, the hospital's chief of staff was an octogenarian Afrikaner named Hans Ottinger. He called people of color 'bleks.' His nickname was Dr. Hands because he mashed every female intern who walked the halls. When he started on me, I tried the polite approach. When that didn't work, I went to my supervisor. And when *that* didn't work, I almost dislocated his thumb pulling his hand from my ass."

"Good for you—"

She shook her head impatiently. "It only made his advances more insistent. I couldn't sleep, I couldn't eat, I couldn't concentrate. I almost considered giving up my medical career. You don't want to know the horrible fantasies I wished on the man."

"You never told me this before," I say.

"Because—" She breaks off and stares at a spot in the far corner of the yard. "I never wanted you to know what I did to him." She takes a few breaths. "With the help of another intern, I set up a video camera in his office. We broke into a locked office to set it up, and I filmed him putting his hands on me, telling me all he'd do for me if I'd have sex with him. A few days later, at a closed meeting of doctors and surgeons, he played what he thought was a training video. It was the video of him trying to get his hands down my pants. The camera was aimed only waist-high, so you couldn't really identify me. But there was no doubt who the man with the Afrikaner accent was. It caused a big scandal. He resigned and left the hospital."

"Wow, Jackie," I say, smiling. "I'm really impressed."

"But that wasn't the end of it," she says. "I sent a copy to his wife. She left him after thirty years of marriage."

"I still think the old goat deserved it."

"Maybe," she says, staring at her lap. "I'm telling you this because I want you to know that I'm not always the blameless person you've built me up to be. I'm not a saint, and I'm not made of glass. I think…I think you put me in that category to keep from having to be honest with me about what goes on in that head of yours."

Sometimes a revelation of truth hits like a bag of rocks. Other times it's as sharp and exacting as a surgeon's knife. One that cuts deep, but doesn't bleed right away. I can only stare at her in stunned silence.

"Just promise me you won't stop going to therapy," she says.

I swipe my fingers solemnly across my chest. "Cross my heart. And hope to die."

She stands to go back inside. "The first part of that statement gives me comfort. The second part does not."

I hear the squeak of the kitchen door opening, a few hushed

words exchanged by Jackie and someone else, and then the door closes again. Approaching footsteps, and Seth eases down next to me. He picks up the empty Jameson bottle, looks through it, whistles, then sets the bottle down again.

"How're you doing, Riz?" he asks. He's wearing wraparound shades, so I can't fully see his expression.

I pull down my own sunglasses so he can see my black eye. "How the hell do you think I'm doing?"

"Did you really plow into the back of that truck on purpose?" He's grinning, trying to coax me past my black mood, his perfect teeth pearlescent in the lowering sun.

"Did you take drugs from Rivera's body?" I ask him. Jackie had opened the door to some family truth-telling. It was time for me to have the courage to walk through to the other side.

The smile loses some of its wattage.

"What . . . ?" he asks.

"Take off your shades," I order him.

He pulls off the sunglasses, the smile gone now.

"Did . . . you . . . take . . . drugs . . . from . . . the body of . . . Carlos Rivera?" I've turned to face my partner, my nose two inches from his, eyeball-to-eyeball.

"Wait a minute," he says emphatically, one defensive hand raised. "What's this about?"

"One of the strippers at the Spearmint Rhino says she saw you lifting a plastic baggie with some pills inside from Rivera's pocket."

"Which stripper?" he asks, his brow deeply furrowed.

"She called herself Sheela G. She told me that she watched you pocketing a plastic bag filled with drugs."

Seth scoots farther away but maintains eye contact. "I have no idea what you're talking about."

He stands abruptly and faces me. He's not acting confused now. Now he's pissed. "How long have you known me?"

"Just answer the fucking question."

He turns away, shaking his head, arms crossed in front of his chest. "The stripper, was she the one with the dark hair, mole over her lip?"

"That's the one," I say.

He exhales, bows his head for a moment, then sits down beside me again. "That girl was all over me in the parking lot. She got pissed because I told her to fuck off."

"So she made up this story because you wouldn't, what? Take her out? Give her your phone number?"

"She was practically dry-humping me behind the dumpster. I couldn't get rid of her without being very, very blunt."

He reaches out a hand and grasps my arm. "Riz," he says. "Look at me. I did not take drugs from Rivera's body."

His face looks sincere; more than anything I want to believe him. I've known women to literally throw themselves at Seth, even while he was arresting them. But I couldn't readily discount the pills I'd already seen him swallowing like candy. The unanswered calls from the day before. And then there was the unresolved matter of Chuffy Bryant.

"You went dark yesterday," I say. "You didn't answer my phone calls. Wayne told me you were someplace you shouldn't have been."

The comforting hand on my arm is withdrawn. Another exhalation from Seth, filled with emotional distress.

"I was working a job," he says.

"What job?" I ask.

"Maclin asked me to follow through on something. He was the one who directed me away from Tent City. And he asked me not to tell you about it."

That hits hard. Maclin was working to pull me out of the circle even before he took away my badge. I want to ask Seth what the job is, force him to show his loyalty to me. But he doesn't owe me any. I'm officially on suspension, so I have no right to know.

I raise my glass with the thimbleful of whiskey left in it. "Cheers. Good luck with the investigation." I swallow a bit more of the liquor. I sound bitter and pitiful. Which is what I am.

When I can't take his soulful staring anymore, I say, "Bet you haven't seen anyone this dejected since Big Tex burned up at the Texas State Fair."

A hint of a smile returns, and he scoots closer to me so that our legs are touching. "You remember our first case together?"

"The infamous Big Tex operation in south Dallas? How could I forget?"

I'd been with the DPD for a short while, and had met Seth only the morning of the bust.

"You didn't care much for me at first," he says, bumping my shoulder with his.

"Yeah, I thought you were an overconfident ex-jock who thought the world revolved around Texas sports and muscle cars."

"My first words to you were *I've never worked with someone like you before.*"

I smile in spite of myself. "I thought you meant a dyke…"

His eyes widen in feigned innocence. "I only meant someone whose last name I couldn't pronounce."

We laugh and Seth reaches for my glass, polishing off the last of the Jameson. That first day with Seth had been memorable in more ways than one. The dealer we were going to arrest— a guy who bragged to anyone who would listen that his massive python, Big Tex, was a man-eater—opened fire from the front of his house with an AR-15, shooting at half a dozen uniformed cops. Seth and I had snuck into the house through the back door. The weapon fire had been so loud that the dealer never heard us come into the kitchen. Thinking fast, Seth threw a potful of greasy stew that had been boiling on the stove onto the floor and called to the dealer, *"Oye, maricon!"* The dealer came running down the hallway, rifle in hand, slipped and fell on his ass, and we were able to cuff him. After he was loaded into the police van, Seth discovered in a backyard shed the bloody evidence of a dog-fighting ring. Enraged, he and three other cops wrestled the giant, squirming Big Tex from his terrarium and threw it into the van with the dealer.

"Remember what I told the guy?" Seth asks, gleefully.

"'It's a long drive back to booking, motherfucker. You better pray this son-of-a-bitch isn't hungry.'"

We laugh loud enough to bring Jackie and company to the back door, where they stare at us hopefully.

"Riz," Seth says, putting his arm around me. "You believe me, right?" He holds out his other hand for me to shake. "I need you to say you believe me."

And I need to believe in this moment that he is telling me the truth.

"Right now, I'm too tired not to," I tell him.

We shake in an exaggerated gesture of renewed friendship, compadres and blood kin again. He tells me he has to leave. Rather than go through the house, where I'll have to make conversation with people, I walk with Seth through a side entrance to the front, where his car is parked. I watch him drive away, hoping against hope that my doubting him was due to the snakes in my head. *Right at this moment,* I think, *I'd rather be wrestling a giant python myself than continue down this benighted, paranoid path.*

My work phone rings. I don't recognize the number but I answer the call.

"Detective Rhyzyk?" a deeply masculine voice asks.

"Yes," I say warily.

"This is Euell Tilton. We were called to the scene yesterday when some of your colleagues found the body of Carlos Rivera?"

"Right," I say.

"I was wondering if you would have some time to talk to me?"

"Uh, sure," I say reluctantly, hoping the call will be a short one. I turn to face the house and see Jackie watching me through the bay window.

"I was hoping we could meet in person," he says.

"In person?" I ask.

"Yes. I do understand that you're not active on the force right now."

"Okay. I've had a bit of a rough day, though—"

"It's about that body you found in the Trinity," he says.

The body of the young man I had discovered on New Year's Day. The boy with the reddish hair and needle marks in his arms.

"You need more clarification on my statement?" I ask.

"No," he says, pausing. "It's about who the boy was related to."

Jackie has walked out onto the front porch, but she's holding the door open. My invitation to come back inside where there's life, and warmth. Away from whatever it is Detective Tilton is about to reveal.

"You can't tell me over the phone?" I ask.

"I'd rather not," he says. "Can we meet tomorrow?"

I give Jackie the one-minute sign. "I'm without a car right now—"

"That's okay. I'll come to you. Tomorrow morning around nine?"

I give him my address and disconnect. The cold has seeped through to my bones and I feel stiff in every joint, my skin turned to leather, my eyeballs to glass. Jackie puts her arm around my waist as I walk back into the house. She guides me to our bedroom, where she helps me undress and puts me to bed. Immediately I feel the tug toward unconsciousness. Mary Grace and Dusty, who have cleaned up the remnants of the food and drink while gently shushing Anne and James Earle (the latter two still discussing my lapse into insanity), poke their heads through the bedroom door, waking me up to tell me to get some rest.

Jackie lies down next to me, spooning me, hugging me protectively. The weight of the quilt works like a giant hand, pressing me comfortingly into the mattress. Jackie's slender, beaded bracelets—nine rings of gold, representing the number of years we've been together—glow softly against her wrist, and I promise myself there will be a tenth. She murmurs into my ear that her mother and James have finally left, James borrowing Jackie's car until tomorrow morning.

I reassure myself that my partner, Seth, who has always had my back and who has never lied to me, is still my partner. That I have colleagues and family and a girlfriend who care for me. And that I have finally passed through the portals of adulthood by acquiring a shrink. Uncle Benny would have been amused, but I also imagine him telling me that I can at last begin my own Reaping the Grim, banishing the self-destructive trolls nesting in both my ears. Rejoining the human race, if only at a snail's pace.

Falling asleep is like rolling off the narrowest ledge. But it's a fall from a sunlit perch into a steep and slimy well. I dream I'm tied to my bed in the cult compound, nearly naked, spread-eagled in the dark. There are footsteps down the long hallway to my cell. Unhurried, deliberate footfalls. Then there is silence outside my door. The air has turned to a slow poison...

There are people yelling inside the house. The sound of heavy objects breaking. My body's up off the mattress, sitting at rigid attention, even before my mind has engaged with the present, my hand sweeping instinctively under the pillow, searching for the shard of glass I know is not really there. I can hear Dusty swearing, her voice a deep roar of outrage. Something brittle shatters. I clumsily grab for the gun in the nightstand on my side of the bed. Jackie is awake, standing, calling my name.

I run into the hall in a shooter's crouch, knocking into a frightened Mary Grace, backlit by the guest-bedroom lamp. The commotion is coming from the living room. Two bulky shadows slam with great force against the wall, knocking a painting loose. The shadows then fall and roll jarringly onto the floor. The impulse to just start shooting is clawing its way through my eyeballs.

I grope frantically along the wall to find the light switch and flip it on, my gun trained on the heaving bulk on the carpet, but it's Dusty on her back, her arms and legs wrapped like steel bands around a struggling, straining, yelling opponent. The invader, dressed all in black, complete with a ski cap, is a teenager. He's tall but can't be more than sixteen. His face is red with anger — and fear. His yelling is abruptly choked off by Dusty flexing a meaty biceps into his neck.

"What the fuck?" I say, my heart hammering in my chest.

"This one broke in through the kitchen door," says Dusty, barely winded by the impromptu wrestling match. "Princess almost tripped over me trying to get to the family jewels."

"Who the hell are you?" I ask the kid.

He narrows his eyes at me but stops struggling.

"Let him up," I tell Dusty.

As soon as Dusty relaxes her hold on the kid, he bolts. She deftly grabs his ankle, tripping him back onto the floor.

"You try that one more time," I say to the kid, "and Dusty and I are both going to beat the crap out of you." He rolls onto his back. "You got me?"

He nods, but still doesn't look committed to sticking around.

Jackie has walked into the living room, her arm tight around Mary Grace's shoulders.

"Were you the little shit that tried breaking in the other night?" I ask him.

"No cars out front," the kid says. "I thought no one was home."

Realizing my gun is still pointed at him, I relax my stance, shaking my head. "Well, that makes it all okay, I guess."

Jackie brings my phone and I call for a patrol car. She bites her lip distractedly, whispering to me that she forgot to lock the kitchen door after everyone left. The kid's not looking too good now that the flush of exertion is wearing off. He's sweaty and beginning to shiver with withdrawals from something. He ignores me when I ask what he's on.

Two patrolmen pull up within ten minutes, then take their sweet time getting out of the car and sauntering up the empty driveway and into the house. They are familiar with our home invader, even calling him by name: Travis. The flashing lights have brought the neighbors out onto their lawns, and they grumble collectively about personal items being stolen from their homes as well. The patrolmen put the kid in the back of their car, where he stares out the window, wide-eyed and blinking, reduced to looking like a prankster caught toilet-papering the high school.

I stand at the open front door, watching the patrol car disappear down the street. I've been living in fear for so many months—terrified of every night sound, suspicious of those nearest to me, selfishly preoccupied with my own hurts and wants and needs—that I had built a neighborhood teenager's creeping about into a dangerous and immediate threat from the Family.

Dusty Rose, wigless, her face washed clean of all makeup except for extravagant false eyelashes, her athletic body squeezed into a familiar-looking pair of shorts and T-shirt, has already begun righting furniture, collecting the pieces of a broken lamp from the floor. She kneels on the carpet, seeming to feel guilty for the mess, her painted nails fanned apologetically across her chest.

"Are those clothes mine?" I ask her. Dusty grins sheepishly and nods. "Keep 'em," I say. "They look better on you."

I turn to Jackie, my beautiful, devoted, patient Jackie, still hugging Mary Grace for comfort.

"Things are going to be different," I tell her. "I'm going back to therapy as soon as the doctor can fit me in."

The relief on her face makes me want to crawl under what's left of the coffee table, reduced by Travis and Dusty to kindling.

Jackie leads Mary Grace back to bed and I turn off the lights, making sure the locks are secure on all the doors. But I do it out of habit, not from the certain expectation that something deadly is waiting to get in.

Dusty has crawled back inside her sleeping bag. She watches me silently as I cross the living room.

"Thank you," I say, with feeling. I catch and hold her gaze. "Stay as long as you need."

"Oh honey," she says, flapping one hand at me like a victory flag. "You *never* want to say that to a street performer."

* * *

The light is off when I enter the bedroom, but Jackie is still awake and I can sense her eyes on me. From the pocket of my jeans, thrown carelessly over a chair, I extract the dime that I had discovered in my prison room at the Roy house. The dime that I have carried with me the past few months as the promise, the hope, that I would at some point regain my connection to Benny.

The coin feels impossibly small and insubstantial in my fingers. I lay it purposefully on the dresser, next to the other mementos from people long gone. It's through the living that I'll regain my sanity. I crawl in bed with Jackie and pull her warm and pulsing body close to mine.

CHAPTER 16

JANUARY 10, 2014
THE HOUSE

I sit on the steps to the house in sweats and a leather jacket, the front door open, breathing in the cool, moist air of a Texas winter morning, the sky clear and intensely blue. James, hearing about the break-in last night, has come over to make breakfast for everyone, which is exactly what Dusty had planned to do. I can hear them in the kitchen, loudly arguing over the best way to make scrambled eggs.

"Honey, you've got to put milk in with the scramble or it'll go flat," Dusty says.

"No," James says in his scandalized drawl, "it'll burn the eggs—"

"What! You learn to make eggs in the army or something?"

"As a matter of fact I *was* in the army. 'Nam. MP. Two full tours."

"Well, don't get too puffed up about it. Eye-rack, right here, baby. Two full tours of duty my own damn self."

There is a pause in the conversation, sounds of pans being rattled, then Dusty says, "Imagine that. You an MP. I spent some of my finest hours being arrested by MPs..." Loud laughter, and peace reigns again in the kitchen.

I suspect that part of James Earle's good humor lies in the fact that his stolen Crown Vic was found undamaged on the streets of Deep Ellum.

A dark sedan pulls up in front of the house. Euell Tilton gets out, unbuttoning his suit coat, which looks a size too small, his biceps and shoulders bulging at the fabric until I can almost hear the seams letting go.

"Good morning," he says, pulling up his shades to get a better look at me. "How're you feeling?"

"I'm not sure how to answer that. Unless you've got several hours to pick through the debris with me. You know I'm on suspension for two weeks, right?"

"Yeah, I heard about that."

He sits next to me on the steps, trailing an invisible curtain of cologne. It's subtle, a telltale musk, surrounded and beaten into submission with sandalwood.

"I was suspended once for a whole month," he says. "It was not pleasant."

I restrain the urge to ask him what he'd been suspended for. "What'd you do for those thirty days?"

"Drove my wife crazy," he says.

Thinking of Jackie's already-strained patience, I say, "I hear that."

A rumbling noise from the street and a vintage BMW, bright blue on the outside, baby blue on the inside, pulls up to the house. The front door of my house bangs open and Dusty, wearing her heels and red wig, expertly negotiates her way down the stairs, pausing for a few beats to take in the wonder that is Detective Tilton's form.

She waves to the man in the car, then turns to me with one eyebrow raised. "Why is it that some of the men with the flashiest cars live in absolute hellholes? I'm going now, sweetheart. I finally have somewhere else to crash." She bends down and kisses me on the cheek. "You ever need anything, you give ole Dusty Rose a shout. 'Cause if there's anything I know, it's the streets."

She straightens, tugging at the hem of her skirt, and tells Tilton, "I saved her life, you know."

On impulse I get up and follow her to the car, telling Tilton I'll be right back.

"Dusty," I say quietly, "you know a Pearla Simms?"

"Pearla?" she says, grimacing. "Yeah, I know her."

"She's shacking up with an ex-con named Chuffy Bryant. He may be dealing. Would you call me right away if you hear anything about it?"

"Sure, baby," Dusty says, giving one last wave to Tilton. "For you, anything."

Like an Olympic gymnast, she folds herself into the front seat and the BMW roars away.

"Someone you've been helping out?" Tilton asks after I've returned to sit next to him.

"It's a relationship built on mutual trust and mascara. You get the full story of what happened at the trap house?"

He nods. "Bernard Tate filled me in. We've verified that the two dealers shot in Deep Ellum were killed with the same-caliber weapon as Carlos Rivera, and all the dead people in the trap house. A nine-millimeter with a silencer, or some kind of baffle attached to the barrel. We did find a few casings at the trap house. Either it was too dark, or the killer didn't have time to be thorough."

"And the Bible verses left at the scene?"

"The same," he says. "Same paper, same handwriting."

He gives me a moment to take in the information, but I was already certain there would be a connection.

"Any leads on the shooter?" I ask.

"Bernard's been trying to track down the witness to the Deep Ellum shooting."

"You mean the mysterious Gary?"

"Yeah. We're still looking for him. But that's not why I'm here. That body we picked up under the Trinity pedestrian bridge? He's related to someone on your team."

My brain scrambles to come up with an answer before Tilton gives it to me.

"Kevin Ryan," he says, watching my reaction closely. "It was his brother-in-law."

"That was Kevin Ryan's brother-in-law?" I say, shaking my head in surprise. The information doesn't fit the picture of who I know Kevin to be: a churchgoing, pressed-khakis-wearing, conservative kind of guy. And now I learn he's related to an intravenous-drug user I'd found dead under a bridge.

"It's not so surprising that a police officer would have a family member die of drugs," Tilton says. "It was the way he reacted when viewing the body at the morgue."

I remember how I had received the news of my own brother's death. It had rendered me almost catatonic—unable to eat, to work, even to get out of bed.

"What do you mean?" I ask.

"He got angry."

"The response to tragedy can be a funny thing, Detective."

He smiles, taps my leg in a friendly way, and says, "Call me Euell."

His grin is infectious, so I smile back. "Okay, Euell," I say. I tap his leg a bit harder. "Everybody reacts differently."

"Sure," he says, nodding. "I've seen people turn over tables and chairs on hearing that their loved one had passed. But I've never witnessed such quiet rage before. He was Ice Man sitting on top of a rocket booster. Ryan's wife was a mess. She collapsed, was inconsolable. Detective Ryan? He stood over the body for the longest time, just staring. Threw me a look and I thought my eyeballs were going to fry inside their sockets. We ended up taking his wife to the hospital by ambulance."

For a moment I struggle to retrieve her name. Was it Susan? How can I not remember my colleague's wife's name?

"As it turns out, she was a few weeks pregnant," Tilton says. "She had a miscarriage."

I'm floored. I hadn't had a clue. I try to think back over my interactions with Ryan. He looked tired and was a bit aloof, but he showed nothing that would indicate he was mourning the loss of an unborn child. If I wasn't so far inside my own head with my own problems, I would have noticed.

"When I was at the Rhino day before yesterday on that Rivera case," Tilton says, "I talked to Tom Craddock, and he said he didn't know about it either."

So Ryan hadn't told his own partner about the miscarriage.

"You played it very cool," I say. "I never would have known that you and Ryan had met."

"I have a sister—*had* a sister—who OD'd on crack cocaine. In and out of rehab more times than I could count. She finally succumbed to the drugs on her twenty-ninth birthday. Here I was a police officer, and I couldn't protect one of my own. The shame of it ripped my family apart. So I try to be sensitive about revealing other people's family secrets."

A vague memory, made fuzzy by the head injury at the trap house and the subsequent painkillers, resurfaces of my watching

Ryan in the visor mirror as we drove from the hospital for home. He looked angry then too, but the image had been shuffled out of my mind by other, more pressing matters.

"You could have told me this over the phone. Why the need for a visit?"

Tilton reaches into his pants pocket and extracts a package of gum. He offers me a piece; when I decline, he takes his time removing the wrapper and folding the gum into his mouth. "At the morgue, before Mrs. Ryan's collapse, I heard Detective Ryan tell his wife, 'The dealers who did this are going to die.'"

"Kevin's a Boy Scout," I say. "Strictly by the book. He was talking out of his grief."

Tilton purses his lips and shrugs. He's not looking directly at me, but he leans in like a co-conspirator. "According to your partner's CI, Wayne, his friend Gary told him the shooter flashed a badge."

He then studies my face three seconds longer than is comfortable.

"Thing is," Tilton says, rubbing his palms together, "while my family didn't talk about my sister's death, I talked about it a *lot* to my partner. I talked about it with my colleagues. Got drunk, cried, carried on until I got to feeling better. Your team is there for you when nobody else is. Am I right?"

I just look at him, waiting for him to reel it in.

"The reason I came here was out of respect for you," he says. "You got a commendation for bravery from the chief of police following the Roy family affair. What you did to survive was nothing short of remarkable. But sometimes our most difficult job as police comes from the inside: breaking the code of silence. Street chatter now is that dealers are being taken out by cops—or *a* cop," he says. "A little homegrown cleanup crew."

I keep a straight face, but my mind is a collage of recent conversations: Wayne telling me Seth was "someplace he shouldn't be"…Craddock saying someone should get a medal for taking out Rivera…Ryan being so secretive about his family drama. I have to wonder what else they're hiding. I've been the outsider, out of the loop for months. What all have I missed? *Breaking the code of silence,* Tilton had said. This last thought works like an ice pick to the back of my skull.

Tilton gives me another friendly no-harm, no-foul grin. "You might want to have a talk with Detective Ryan. Make sure he's doing okay."

"And then let you know, is that it?" I ask, an edge to my voice. "Who else are you looking at? Kevin Ryan can't be the only cop with a grudge against drug dealers."

He stands, brushing off the seat of his trousers. "You've earned a reputation for being an honest cop—if a bit unconventional." He smiles winningly. "I was hoping for your help. After all, you and I are on the same side, right?"

He holds out his hand for me to shake. "You help me in my investigation, and I might be able to help you get back to active street duty. That's what you want, isn't it?" He gives my hand an extra squeeze. "And to answer your question, we're looking at everyone right now."

I watch him walk to his car.

"Hey," I call. "What's the name of your cologne?"

Tilton grins, and says, "Heat."

He settles himself into his car and drives away.

"Yeah, that sounds about right," I say.

The morning's peace has evaporated. At the fringes of my consciousness I feel chaos rearing its ugly little head again, threatening to derail me into anger and frustration. First I've been isolated from my work, and now I've been made suspicious of my colleagues. For all my good intentions, my house has become Grand Central Station—and the target of a malicious break-in. And despite a passionate respite last night with Jackie, I have a lot of reparations to make to regain her trust. Overshadowing everything, though, has been my paranoia that the Roy family is not finished with me.

It's time to get busy and clear this field of stones.

I pull out my phone and dial Dr. Theo again. After the message beep, I ask him to call me as soon as possible with an appointment date. I tell him I'm ready to work as long as it takes to get back to some semblance of equilibrium, both with my job and with my life partner.

My next call is to Dottie at Slugger Anne's. She has taken in street urchins before, usually those struggling to recover from drugs or alcohol. But she has a big heart (and a spacious house where she lives alone with an ugly cat), and beyond that she owes me for bailing her out of jail so many times. I call her, waking her grumbling from a deep sleep, and within five minutes I've secured a safe place for Mary Grace to get back on her feet.

I sit a while longer on the steps, thinking about my exchange with Tilton. My fear had been that the Bible verses were from the Roys; that like an opportunistic virus they'd been spreading westward from the Pine Curtain—the thick forests of East Texas—to insert themselves into the Dallas drug scene. Possibly, the verses had even been devised as a warning to me, letting me know the Family was in town. But maybe the biblical quotes had been mere distractions, meant to make us think the assassinations were the work of the Family. It's possible it's the Sinaloans. The most painful thing to wrap my mind around is the idea of cops shooting drug dealers.

Finally, I call Seth. It's time to ask the hard questions.

"If you've ever trusted me in your life," I say when he answers after the first ring, "you'd better tell me what Maclin has you working on."

A pause and an intake of breath. Then he says he'll meet me tomorrow and tell me what deep, dark things he's been up to.

CHAPTER 17

JANUARY 11, 2014
NORMA'S CAFÉ

S eth agrees to meet me for breakfast. He shows up twenty minutes late, looking like the wrong end of nowhere but smiling as though he hasn't a care in the world. I had wanted to believe him when he'd told me he hadn't taken any drugs from Rivera's body. But I'd worked narcotics for close to a decade, and I know when someone is stoned. The pupils of his eyes are pinned, and he scratches at his neck and face as though invisible ants are crawling over his flesh. At times his chin dips into the languorous narco-nod I've seen a thousand times. He looks like an overzealous actor in a cautionary ad from the Family Council Against Drugs. All the reassurances he'd given me a few days ago that he could be trusted are fading by the minute.

I stare as he pours a waterfall of sugar into his coffee cup. On his wrist is an expensive-looking dive watch. I'd seen him wearing it, but I've never looked at it closely. It's a famous brand, costing hundreds of dollars.

"Nice watch," I say. "That real?"

Seth twists it to catch the light, and grins. "Pokeno Babe been berry, berry good to me."

"She give you that leather jacket too?" It's new, the leather a buttery lambskin, thin and supple enough to wrap an infant in.

"Jealous much, Riz?" he asks, slurping his coffee. "I tell you what, you're nice to me and I might let you wear it sometime."

"So, what's the sergeant got you working on that you're acting all Secret Agent Man?" I ask.

"Remember Maclin briefing us on this new Sinaloa player, El Cuchillo? The Knife? Yesterday he had me meet with a DEA agent who's been embedded with the Latin Kings. The agent told me that the Latin Kings and MS-13 had a white-flag sit-down to talk about their dealers being taken out."

The news of a sit-down is surprising—like coming across a unicorn galloping down the Tollway. "Takes a lot to get those guys in the same room without taking each other's heads off," I say. "Where'd this meeting take place?"

"South of Parkdale Lake. Scyene Road."

Scyene Road in south Dallas. Not far from Fair Park, it's the second-most-dangerous place in Dallas, right after Hatcher Street only a few blocks away. Where gangs hide in plain sight among the heavily barred family homes, *carnicerias,* liquor stores, and warehouses. The demarcation lines between the players run roughly east to west along Military Parkway, but weekly assassinations constantly redraw the gang lines in blood.

"The agent told me the gangs have had problems in the past with Tango Blast moving into their territories. But the killings in gentrified, mostly white areas of Deep Ellum and at the Rhino strip club are unprecedented. It's been bad for their business across the board."

"They have any idea who the shooter is?"

"Our man Gary's been talking on the street. A lot. He insists it's a cop. But the gangs don't buy it."

"They think it's a new cartel moving in?"

Seth nods. "They think it's the Sinaloans, fronted by our mystery man, El Cuchillo. He of the Ed Gein nightmare boots. If it is the Sinaloans, the Dallas County ME's office is going to be working overtime."

"What about the Bible verses left on scene?" I ask.

There's a pause while Seth checks his cell phone after it pings. He sets the phone back on the table. "The DEA guy thinks it's a red herring. The media made such a big deal of it after your rescue that anyone could have left those verses. There's been no hint of the Roy family in East Texas, let alone in Dallas. The gangs are unanimous in their opinion that the Roys, what's left of them, and their distributors, the Aryan Brotherhood, have been pushed deep into Louisiana. The Bible verses are just a little 'Fuck you' to us cops in general."

"Or to me in particular. Any word on where to find Gary?"

"Still looking. He's scared shitless of the cops right now, but there are only so many places he can hide out. We'll find him."

Seth's phone pings again, and he spends a moment typing a text. He then stands and stretches. "Be back in a minute. Too much coffee."

He heads for the bathroom, leaving his phone on the table. With one eye on the bathroom door, I grab the phone, press in his security code—*1996*, the last year the Cowboys won a Super Bowl—and quickly check his texts. There, at the top of the messages screen, is a text from C—the message is just a question mark—and Seth's response: *Give me 20.*

There are dozens of messages from C: dates, times, street addresses. One of them is the same address for Pearla Simms given to me by Brant, Seth's friend from Vice. And *C* has to be Chuffy Bryant. Seth had sworn he was not using Chuffy as a CI—that the information Chuffy was passing to my partner that night in front of his house was a one-off—but that's clearly not the case. He's been texting C like a hot date.

I slide the phone to Seth's side of the table just as he exits the bathroom. As soon as he sits down again, he grabs it and shoves it back in his pocket. He's rubber-mouthed, sniffing, and scratching at his nose like he's got a bad cold.

"Hey, you know what I was thinking?" he asks. His eyes glow blissfully, like two huge Delft saucers in his chiseled, beaming face. "It's been a while since we had a night out together. Just the two of us. Let's you and me go find some trouble."

It's been only four days since we shared drinks at the Goat.

"Are you high right now?" I ask.

"What?" he says, as though I've just asked if he's from Mars.

I lean forward across the table. "What are you on, partner?"

He stands from the table, zipping up his designer jacket. "I'm here because you asked me to tell you what I was doing for Maclin. I did that—which, as you well know, I didn't have to do, seeing as how you're on suspension. But I'm not going to sit here and continue to reassure you. Either you believe me or you don't." He fishes some bills out of his pocket and drops them on the table. "Correct me if I'm wrong, but aren't you the crazy one crashing into trucks?"

He looks at me for a moment, waiting for me to say something—perhaps to ask him to stay—but I can't speak, choked by anger and worry. He turns to walk out of the restaurant. "Call me when your head's on straight again," he says.

For an instant I consider running after him. But the rise of a new feeling, a deep sadness, roots me to my seat. There's a saying with narco cops that every day on the job is like working in a plague ward; it may not happen today, and it may not happen tomorrow, but at some point you will probably catch the sickness. If the money doesn't get you, the drugs or the hopelessness will. Often it's a trifecta of infection, and you're felled by all three. Sometimes you recover. Sometimes you don't.

My partner, the son of a cotton farmer, wanted nothing more when he joined the force than to do some good, and to see the world from a place other than the back of a hay loader. He's in trouble now, but I know I can't do much to help him unless he's willing to admit he has a problem.

Maybe one of his female admirers *did* give him the watch, and possibly the leather jacket as well. But then again, maybe not. They could be warning signs that he's not just using the product, but moving it as well.

I pay the check and walk out into the brilliant sunshine. Sitting in my car, I turn on the radio and, as Cosmic Coincidences often go, one of Seth's favorite songs comes on. It's an old Eric Burdon and the Animals song, "(Oh Lord) Please Don't Let Me Be Misunderstood." Seth is the closest thing I've had to a brother since Andrew died. My real brother who also worked in Narcotics, and ended up dead because of the slow toxic fallout of the drug war.

I think of the undercover case Seth and I worked together a year ago. We were setting up a cocaine dealer nicknamed *El Serpiente* (The Serpent)—not because he was a ground-hugging lowlife but because he had the reputation of playing Hide the Snake with every woman he came in contact with.

Accustomed to sharing women with his buyers and suppliers, the Serpent decided the deal would not go through until he'd spent some private time with me. I refused. He insisted. I declined once more, this time with a knee to his groin.

The Serpent pulled a six-inch switchblade on me. Before I could react, Seth had placed himself between me and the dealer, saying, "You touch her again and I'll stick that knife down your throat."

The Serpent, taken aback by Seth's composure, demanded, "Why the fuck shouldn't I?"

"Because," Seth hissed, moving to within a hair's breadth of the dealer's face, "she's my sister." He then turned his back on the man and winked at me, his genius for improvisation in the most dangerous conditions putting to shame every other adrenaline-charged cowboy cop and gun-range junkie I'd ever known.

And this hardened dealer, who had once slit the throat of a sixteen-year-old boy suspected of cheating him, backed off.

Following the bust—a record-breaking haul of cocaine in Dallas County for that month—I took to calling Seth "Bro." It was our private joke for weeks. I'd pucker up my lips, making kissy noises and loud protestations of love, which confused the hell out of our team. And the more they were confused, the harder Seth and I would laugh.

But brother or no, if he's playing dirty, there will have to be a reckoning. Eric Burdon's plaintive voice vibrates through the speakers: "I'm just a soul whose intentions are good..."

I turn the radio off and begin the drive home.

CHAPTER 18

Suspension. Two weeks. No pay. That leaves me a lot of time to ponder the imponderable. I wake to aching muscles, tender bruises, and the remnants of a wicked headache. Which may or may not have something to do with downing a Saturday-night triple shot of Jameson right before bedtime. But it's my conversation with Seth at Norma's Café that pains me the most.

I pace around the house until Jackie stands in front of me, offering me my running shoes like a votive sacrifice. She dangles them by their laces, the disused, well-worn bodies swaying on her fingers, droopy as two dead rabbits.

"It's a beautiful day," she says.

"It's cloudy and cold outside," I say petulantly.

She sighs. "It's Sunday. My day off. Either you leave the house, or I have to."

I finally change into my running gear and walk out into the cold air, determined to cover a few miles even if I have to crawl or stagger along the way to finish. I have no clear plan where I'm going. I just need to cover some ground.

The murky sky is an inverted bowl sealing in all the prickly things: the dead grass on the lawns, the rain-starved bushes, the wilted cactus...me.

I pick up the pace to a slow jog. Amazingly—miraculously—both calf muscles feel supple and strong. Jogging feels good. It hasn't felt this good since before the injury. The dry air feels necessary to my lungs, like the finest sandpaper used to buff a shine on rusty objects. I'm careful to pick my steps. A twisted ankle on top of a ruptured Achilles tendon would not be good. Easy does it.

I jog slowly for what must be close to a mile, the fine, powdery frost puffing gently after each footfall. Overhead, a vulture wheels restlessly in endless loops.

I think of the next few weeks, which will be torture without a plan for something productive to do. Besides the mandatory sessions with Dr. Theo, and gym time, I have basically zip, zero, nada to fill my days and keep the spiders out of the old mental attic. I have no departmental resources right now. But then again...I do have valuable street resources. The three things on my mind are determining how bad Seth's drug problem is, uncovering the whereabouts of El Cuchillo, and finding out who, if not the Sinaloans, is killing the street dealers. If it's a cop, as Tilton insinuated, I want to be the first one with a leg up on that information. I believe Seth's CI Wayne, given enough financial incentive, will confide in me, as will Dusty Rose. Mary Grace is now staying with Dottie, and both of them have an ear to the streets. Maybe with a little covert spying I can find out what Pearla Simms knows about Chuffy—and, by extension, about my partner. I may be on suspension, but I'm not deaf, dumb, and blind.

With these rousing thoughts I've picked up the pace, a stupid grin plastered on my face. A new purpose has fueled my muscles, and it feels liberating. *I can do this forever,* I think. *I'm Xena the Warrior Queen.*

Driving toward me is a late-model Nissan, which slows as it gets within a few yards. The driver is an older woman, both hands atop the wheel, her chin pointed forward as if she's carefully studying the road conditions. As the car passes, the driver turns her head and smiles at me. Her teeth are yellowed with age and overuse, her hair a lacquered swirl of hellfire red.

And in the exact moment that my mind has grasped the impossible idea that it could be Evangeline Roy, an invisible Gila monster clamps down on my right leg, its imagined teeth embedded in the muscles and sinews of my injured calf, as though it was bent on tearing the flesh from my bone in massive chunks. I fall hard to the pavement, howling and grasping at my tortured limb, rolling on the sidewalk like something dying.

I yell and swear and yell some more until I'm hoarse, but my spasming muscles won't let me up. My instinct is to crawl to safety, but there's nowhere to hide. I fear the inevitable explosive sound of a gunshot fired in my direction. But the Nissan sails by without stopping, the driver seemingly unaware of my fall. If it was Evangeline, she missed the golden opportunity to kill the wounded beast rolling on the ground.

My fingers gently follow the ridged flesh above my right heel, almost certain I'll find a separation in the tendon, but thankfully it seems to be undamaged. I pray that it's only scar tissue pulling loose. I half-believe that if I examine the tattooed image inked above my right calf I'll find Saint Michael, mouth open, in a silent scream of pain.

I lie on my back, catching my breath, my heart hammering from fear, and stare at the vulture circling overhead. He's reduced his altitude, no doubt hoping I'll stop squirming so he can have an early dinner. I look at the street sign to get my bearings. Trammel Drive. Perfect.

All around me is peaceful, quiet—a suburban neighborhood safe in its cocoon of normalcy. I think of Seth and my other colleagues going about their business out in the Great Wide World, whole and uninjured, and resentment sits on my chest like an anvil. On top of the anvil sits an old fear wearing a red wig.

My phone rings. I think about letting it go to voice mail. But it's Jackie, so I inhale deeply and answer the call.

"I think you need to come get me," I tell her.

Once home again, I sit in a tub of scalding-hot water and Epsom salts. I inhale the steam from the bath until my mind unmoors itself from the day's indignities. Jackie comes to the door and asks if I'm ready for something to eat.

"Give me another half hour, babe," I say. "I just need a little more time to retract my fangs and claws."

She laughs, but says, "I love you anyway."

Yeah, I think, *and Roy of Siegfried fame loved his tigers—and look what happened to him.*

After toweling off, I pull on a pair of fleece-lined sweatpants and a T-shirt and limp barefoot into the study. The hot water has eased the pain in my calf, but the muscles throb angrily and I think I may need to visit the orthopedic surgeon again to confirm, or deny, that I've reinjured the tendon.

I sit at the desk, then pull some blank paper out of the copier and a pencil from a drawer. Dr. Theo has suggested that I start journaling my thoughts before each session: my concerns, doubts, and fears, in the order of their importance in my life. But I was never one for the "Dear Diary" approach—never one to have a decorative little book, under lock and key, into which I poured my yearnings and heart's desires. The closest thing I'd ever gotten to a written confessional was carving my unrequited love with a stick into wet cement on a sidewalk in front of the City Council building in Greenpoint, Brooklyn: *Roberta Del'Angelo, your kisses drive me crazy. I will always, always love you—B.R.*

So I begin to draw a schematic that I can show Dr. Theo— boxes, with interconnecting lines. Inside the boxes at the top, I write the things most troubling me: *Regaining my job status; Seth's potential drug problem; Who's killing dealers?; Relationship with Jackie.* Below the job-status box I write *Relationship with Maclin,* which I have to duplicate under the Seth box, because I can't keep an eye on Seth without being out on the streets. Ditto for *Who's killing dealers?* And ditto again for the Jackie-related box, because if I can't work as a detective—as in "working on the streets detecting things"—I'm going to be a bear (or a tiger) to live with.

Off to one side, as though in quarantine, I draw a double-lined box and write in the letters *E* and *R.* I can't bring myself to write the old witch's name in full. My mind is already distancing itself from accepting the possibility that Evangeline Roy has been keeping an eye on me.

Dissatisfied, I crumple up the paper and start over, redrawing Maclin's box at the top and the other concerns under my sergeant's name. I add a few more cascading items under the *Who's killing dealers?* box: *The Roy family? The Sinaloans? Cops?*

Sitting back, I study the diagram. Two things become clear. I've created the same kind of whiteboard map I would use in a criminal case, with Maclin at the top. Like a crime lord.

And I've put Jackie last in the order of things.

I tear up the second schematic and draw it one last time on

a fresh sheet of paper, putting Jackie's name first and omitting Seth's drug problem. I'm not ready to reveal that bit of information, even to a doctor who has sworn to keep my confessions confidential.

Jackie calls me to come eat and I yell back, "There'd better be red meat on the menu!"

Halfway through dinner my cell phone rings. It's Craddock.

"Hey, I know you're on suspension and all, but I wanted to keep you in the loop about something."

He's speaking in whispers.

I mouth *Sorry* to Jackie and walk into the living room.

"What's up?" I ask.

"We got another dead dealer. Also with the Nuevo Juarez cartel. This one skinned up like the dealer Maclin told us about."

"No gunshot wounds?"

"Died from knife injuries. No gunshots."

"So are we thinking we're dealing with two different killers?"

"Possibly. But get this: DEA thinks they know why the Knife is here in Dallas. Some bright bulb stole a shitload of heroin from the Sinaloans. And the Sinaloans sent their enforcer to get it back."

I hear Jackie removing dishes from the table and disappearing into the kitchen.

"Okay," I say. "Thanks for the heads-up, Tom."

"Listen, let's keep this conversation just between you and me, okay?"

"Sure," I say, and disconnect the call.

I stand looking out the bay window facing the front yard, made a bit brighter by the security light I installed on the front porch. Two different killers, with two different styles. But are they working in cooperation? Or are they from different camps, but both with the same endgame: blunting the competition?

The dining-room light behind me is switched off, and I think Jackie may be going to sleep, but she calls to me.

"You have exactly thirty seconds to get into bed," she says.

I turn around and see Jackie standing in the darkened dining room, completely naked, her skin radiant in the ambient light, her rose tattoo a dark punctuation mark over her clavicle. She doesn't have to tell me twice.

CHAPTER 19

Dusty Rose strides toward me wearing a tight, short skirt and a blond wig, the muscles in her legs tensing impressively like a clenched fist. We're on Lower Greenville and it's crowded, but she ignores the stares and catcalls of passing pedestrians.

"Hey, hey, Bett-ay," she calls to me. She gives me the once-over. She had told me to wear something "festive" for our meet. But after taking in my usual uniform of black jeans and leather jacket, Dusty arches her brow in disapproval.

I do a slow clap in her honor. "Hey, Dusty."

She had called me the previous day, saying she had information about Chuffy Bryant and his girlfriend, Pearla Simms. I was to meet her at the Circus, a club housed in a former metalworking factory, at ten in the evening and she'd fill me in.

"So, what's the story with Chuffy?" I ask.

"I took the proverbial bull by the horns and called that saggy-assed diva myself. To try and find out what Chuffy was up to, you know, like you asked. I had to listen for ten minutes while Pearla bragged on about her new pimp. But I figured it was the least I could do to help you out."

"Is Chuffy dealing?"

"Does a mad dog hump a tree?" she asks. "That crazy bitch offered to have him sell me whatever I wanted. She said, and I quote, 'He's got the best Mexican brown in town.' And plenty of it, from what she told me."

"Pearla's tending bar now?" I ask.

"Slangin' drinks like the windup toy she is."

I follow Dusty into the building.

The Circus is a club I've never been to, but heard plenty about. The space is cavernous, throbbing with loud electronic dance music and bright, strobing lights. And it's packed. We stand for a moment just inside the door, watching an aerialist suspended overhead. She's wearing a flesh-colored bodysuit and dangling from a long chain anchored to the ceiling, the chain looped to form a sort of hammock—all part of the evening's performance, titled "Freaks and Fetishes."

When the good, family-oriented folks of Dallas think about leisure time after the sun goes down, they usually imagine establishments such as Tex-Mex restaurants—ethnic enough to be interesting, but not too exotic. They certainly do not think of a club featuring performers named Amber DeLite and Lilly De-Lish, who dress in glistening latex and spank each other onstage with rubber paddles, simulating sex to the sounds of DJs with self-anointed monikers such as Vag Viral.

Dusty points out Pearla—a tall, willowy figure, slender-hipped, with two thrusting, immovable globes riding high on her chest—serving drinks to customers from behind a long bar.

"Let me get you set up," Dusty shouts in my ear, then strides toward the bar, dodging milling customers like a running back on steroids.

She calls to Pearla and, leaning over the bar, says a few words.

They both look at me. Then Pearla nods, and Dusty returns to where I'm standing.

"You're good to go," Dusty says, giving me a stern look. "Just don't get me into trouble. She doesn't know you're a cop. Yet."

She loses herself in the crowd and I make my way to the bar. I sit on a stool and another female bartender makes a beeline for me. She's raven-haired with plentiful piercings and tattoos, and through her large earlobe gauges I can see the seductive glimmer of Irish whiskey bottles. She looks amply strong, but she's nudged out of the way by Pearla, who leans in and asks, "What can I get for you tonight?"

It's so loud that I'm lipreading more than hearing her voice.

"I'll start with a double Jameson, neat," I shout.

"Neat. You got it." She brings me my drink and lingers in front of me.

We stare at each other for a few seconds, then she bends close and says, "What more can I do for you, baby?"

"My friend Dusty tells me you have party favors."

"What kind of party favors you looking for?"

"What do you have?"

She squints at me, fiddling with an opened pack of cigarettes and a lighter perched next to a tray of wilted limes. "Don't be coy. Tell me plain and tell me quick, 'cause Pearla's real busy tonight."

I motion her closer. "Got any Mexican brown?"

"What're you spending?"

"A lot," I say.

She gives me a lazy smile. "You just sit right there, and I'll fix you up."

Pearla pulls her phone from the waistband of her skirt and taps out a short text.

"Sit tight, baby, help is on the way," she says, moving away to serve the man next to me. I turn my head slightly in his direction and do a quick scan. Compact, swarthy, heavy brows, black hair, jeans, leather jacket. His deep-set eyes shift briefly to mine and it's like looking into a shark's eyes, predatory and unflinching. The club brings in its share of kink, but this guy's hard-core; somebody's bodyguard, or prison-made pimp.

I sip at my drink, the Jameson easing a pleasant burn down into my stomach, and watch the shifting, restless dancers moving to the beat of the music. No doubt Pearla texted Chuffy, and I'm hopeful he'll be eager to hand the drugs over to a prospective client. He won't know me by sight, which works in my favor. Being on suspension, though, I can't arrest him, nor can I make a strategic undercover buy. When he offers the sale, I'll make some excuse to stall him, and slip away. Then one phone call and I can have someone else make the bust.

The ambient lights have grown brighter and all eyes gaze toward the ceiling, where two almost naked aerialists grind together in sensual abandon. When I look down again, I see Chuffy Bryant moving through the crowd, headed for the bar. Chuffy makes eye contact with me and grins expectantly. His gaze flicks over my shoulder and he freezes, the grin vanishing. His eyes widen, then he turns on his heels and pushes his way forcefully back through the crowd.

The guy who'd been sitting next to me brushes roughly past my shoulder and follows Chuffy into the crowd. I'm craning to see where Chuffy's headed, but there are too many people. I quickly stand on the bar stool and, despite protests from bartenders and customers alike, track Chuffy heading for the rear EXIT sign. And waiting beneath the sign is Seth. There's no mistaking my partner for anyone else. A few urgent words are exchanged, and they both enter the black void of the hallway leading to the back door.

The swarthy guy has gotten hung up in the dense crowd, but he presses forward like he's in a rugby maul, finally pushing through to the rear exit as well. Jumping off the stool, I impulsively grab Pearla's cigarette pack and lighter—I need an excuse to go outside—and weave my way through the dancers. By the time I make it to the darkened hallway, all three men have disappeared. Several doors lead to storage or dressing rooms, but I cautiously open the back door and exit the building. The door shuts behind me, and it occurs to me too late that it will lock, automatically barring reentry.

I'm in an alleyway behind the building. Apart from a spotlight over the door, it's dark. I light a cigarette and take a few shallow puffs, trying not to cough, while I listen for sounds of a confrontation. Although it's quieter here, I can still sense the throbbing bass from the dance music inside. There is a flicker of movement and I see a man standing alone a few yards from the door, and he's turned to face me. It's the guy from the bar; he's been searching the alley for something. Most likely Chuffy and Seth. He stares hostilely at me but I casually flick ashes onto the pavement—just a smoker out for some nicotine.

He walks toward the door, head lowered but his eyes on me, and I wish fervently that I had my gun. I start to hold out the pack of cigarettes to him as a harmless, pedestrian gesture. But I think better of it: my hands are beginning to shake.

"You waiting for someone?" he asks. His voice is deep, and heavily accented.

"Me?" I ask. "No. All my friends are inside."

He walks past me and tries the door. It's locked. He's shorter than me—maybe five feet eight or so—but he looks like a street fighter, all tightly wrapped muscle, with scars cutting channels across his eyebrows. I would bet money that he has a weapon—

a gun or a knife, or both—tucked under his coat. He moves close enough for me to smell his cologne. "You shouldn't smoke," he says, his words a mere whisper. "It's going to kill you."

He scans my face, memorizing it, then walks briskly up the alley toward the street.

I take a steadying breath and throw the lit cigarette on the pavement. There's no question now that Seth is tied in with Chuffy's dealing. I want to believe my partner's working him, setting him up for a bust. But my gut tells me that, if he's using the product, his involvement is for his own benefit.

I can forgive a lot from my fellow officers. And I have. I've witnessed more than my share of "bend but don't break" behavior and kept silent. A cop takes a free meal? Hey, you've set yourself up to be bribed at some future date, but you haven't murdered anyone. Take a few dollars from a drug bust? The money's dirty, but who knows what sewer path the dollar bill in *anyone's* wallet has traveled? Besides, you've got four kids and they all need braces. Brother, it's not me going to turn you in for that transgression—just don't expect me to work with you ever again. But you start selling drugs...? The grief I've felt over Seth's diminished state is shoved aside by a sudden, hot anger. I grind the still-glowing cigarette butt out with the toe of my boot.

The guy from the bar looked like cartel. An enforcer. But is he *the* enforcer? El Cuchillo, looking for his competition? The guy felt dangerous despite his soft-spoken words. But there's not enough stature to his menace. Not enough of the seismic heft of a born killer, as Uncle Benny would say.

I throw the cigarettes and lighter into a trash bin and walk down the alley, toward the street, but in the opposite direction of the enforcer.

CHAPTER 20

JANUARY 16, 2014
THE TUNNELS

Wwe sit around the table eating dinner—Jackie, Mary Grace, and I. Actually I'm not doing much sitting. I'm running down my street contacts, people I've used for information in the past, trying to gather news or gossip that might be useful in finding the Knife. Or tracking down the elusive Gary, witness to the dealer shootings. Information that may shorten my period of suspension. Or at least put me on the plus side of the department ledger when I return. I'll take a few bites, the phone will ring, and I'll quickly walk into the other room to finish the conversation.

When I'm not on the phone, I'm staring holes into my plate, trying to figure out how to contact Wayne. If anyone knows how to get in touch with Gary, it will be him. But he hasn't returned my calls—he uses burner phones, so he may have a completely different number by now. I've called all the city homeless shelters on the off chance he'll be bedded down for the night, but no luck. I've even pestered Mary Grace for information on his whereabouts, though I know she's uncomfortable talking about it. She's trying so hard to distance herself from the street.

At some point I'm aware that all conversation has stopped, and that Mary Grace and Jackie are looking at me. I also realize that Mary Grace has just asked me a question.

"What'd you say?" I ask. My tone is impatient, almost accusatory, as though I'm in an interrogation room, not my dining room.

Jackie takes a calming breath. "She asked you if you like the name *Tara* for the baby."

I look at Mary Grace's earnest face and realize with a pang that it truly matters to her what I think.

We had taken her earlier that evening to the OB-GYN for a prenatal checkup. The doctor had given us a tentative due date a month from now, and had assured us that the baby was developing right on target.

Jackie and I had stood on either side of the examining table, holding her hands for comfort while the doctor did the sonogram. Jackie had taken her previously for a medical visit, but Mary Grace was still nervous that her months being homeless might have affected the pregnancy.

When the doctor asked her if she wanted to know the sex of the child, she looked at us with an almost panicked look on her face.

"You don't have to know," Jackie told her, stroking her forehead. "It can be a surprise."

Mary Grace cut her eyes at me and asked, "What do you think?"

In that moment I had felt panicked as well. That she even sought my opinion made me want to simultaneously cry and burst out laughing.

I had squeezed her hand reassuringly. "If it were me, I'd want to know. I hate surprises."

"Me too," she said, smiling and turning to the doctor. "I hate surprises. I want to know."

The doctor had then announced it would be a girl.

Now, her eyes glowing in eager anticipation, Mary Grace is turning to me again for my opinion, this time about the baby's name.

"I like *Tara,*" I say. "*Tara Miller.* Sounds right."

She grins at me, and she looks like nothing so much as a fresh young teenager—her complexion clear, her blond hair tied up in a ponytail—hiding a basketball under her shirt. She goes back to eating her dinner, satisfied, a Mona Lisa smile on her face. *Miller,* I know, is not her real name. She hasn't entrusted us with that information yet. But I'm hoping that with the birth of the baby she'll reveal her true surname. And then I can do some background searches on her family history.

The phone rings again; an unknown number. I let it go to voice mail.

"What's going on?" Jackie asks. "Aren't you on suspension?"

"Thanks for reminding me," I say, spearing my last piece of chicken. "There's a new player in town with the Sinaloa cartel. A very bad guy."

"Aren't they all bad guys?"

"Yeah, but this one sounds like something out of a nightmare. His nickname is El Cuchillo. The Knife."

"The Knife?" Mary Grace says. "Why is he called that?"

I open my mouth, but Jackie shoots me a warning look. "I think we can all use our imaginations on that one," she says through pinched lips.

"All the phone calls tonight," I say, "are my attempts to get some more information on this guy. We've got several dead drug dealers, carved up like pumpkins—"

"Oh for fuck's sake," Jackie snaps, throwing down her napkin.

Mary Grace and I stare openmouthed at her. I've heard five-year-olds who swear more than Jackie.

"What's wrong with you?" she asks me.

Jackie and I will discuss things when we're alone that would make a coroner blanch, but Mary Grace is not a child. She's seventeen and has lived long enough on the streets to know how the world operates. Mary Grace looks downcast, and I curse myself for ruining what should have been a carefree dinner.

"I'm sorry," I say. "Really, I'll tone it down. It's just that I could be out on the street doing some good. But I'm in limbo right now. The more information I get, the sooner this guy will be caught. The right kind of lead could save a lot of lives. I'm frustrated that I can't get my sources to talk to me about what's really going on."

"How ironic," Jackie mutters, jabbing at a lettuce leaf with a little too much force.

"What do you mean?" I ask.

"You being surprised that others would hold secrets."

There's a biting edge to her voice, but it has the bitter tang of truth. Before I can respond, I feel Mary Grace's hand on my arm.

"Can I help?" she asks. "I want to do something for you." She looks at me with her big, vulnerable doe eyes, so filled with gratitude and trust, and I want to kick myself for dragging the dark shadows into our home.

"You can help by washing some dishes," Jackie tells her, gently tugging at her ponytail. "Your days on the street are done." She turns to me. "Don't forget that the visit from the midwife is in a few days."

I give her a blank look.

"For the home birth," she says.

For the...what! Mary Grace is giving birth in the house?

"Hello," she says, exasperation threading her voice. "Earth to Betty. We talked about this at the OB's office today. Remember?"

I open my mouth to respond but my phone rings, and I answer the call. For a few seconds I hear only rough breathing. "Hello?" I say.

"Yeah," the voice wheezes. "It's me, Wayne. You trying to track me down?"

I get up from the table and walk into the living room. "Where are you?"

"I'm headed for the tunnels," he says.

"Which one?"

"Elm Street."

"I'm looking for your friend Gary, and I think you know why."

"Yeah...you and everybody else."

"What does that mean, 'everybody'?" I ask.

"The cops, other dealers. Every swinging dick on the street wants to know who's taking out the competition."

"Do you know where Gary is?" I ask, trying to keep my voice low and calm. Technically Wayne is Seth's CI, but Need and Want have no firm allegiances. "I'll give you fifty bucks, warm clothes, and some food if you tell me where he is tonight. And this is between you and me. No one else has to know you gave me the information. If anybody asks, I'm just helping you out, that's all."

"He'll know I told you." There's a pause, but I can hear his labored breathing. "He's headed for the underground too."

"Listen, has he told you anything at all about Pico Guerto's killer?"

"Yeah, the shooter flashed a badge."

"Okay, I'll be there in half an hour. Don't leave, and keep Gary there with you. I'm not going to detain him. I just want to talk to him."

"Where else are we supposed to go?" he asks, his teeth chattering. "It's really cold outside, man. I'm telling you right now, he's not going to be happy about it. The guy's freaked."

Something occurs to me. "Does anybody else know where Gary is right now?"

A much longer silence.

"Wayne? You still there?" But the call has disconnected, and all I get is dead air.

I grab my coat and car keys from the closet, clipping the holster with my own personal Glock onto my belt. I also pull out a couple of sweatshirts for Wayne, and a flashlight.

When I turn around, Mary Grace hands me an old blanket that she's pulled from the linen closet. "I heard you talking to Wayne. Is it okay to give this to him?"

"Sure," I say, giving her a quick hug. "I'll make sure he gets it."

"I think Wayne is trying to get clean," she says. "He wants to get into a program. You know, to stop doing all the drugs. I told him we could start hanging out again if he quit."

I stroke her cheek and try to smile reassuringly. "You're being a good friend to him, Mary Grace."

Jackie appears in the hallway. "Where are you going?"

"I'll be back soon," I say. "I'm just meeting a contact."

"And for that you need your gun?" Jackie throws up her hands and walks into the kitchen.

"Can I go with you?" Mary Grace whispers.

"Into the tunnels? You crazy? No, my little knocked-up princess, you stay here and keep the shield-maiden from setting fire to the house."

* * *

"The tunnels" is what the street denizens call the underground pedestrian network downtown. The subterranean walkways, connecting the basement levels of office buildings and garages, cover thirty-six city blocks, allowing white-collar workers to buy expensive coffees and reach their SUVs without stepping into the heat of a Dallas summer. Most of the entrances to the network are through private office buildings, but they're closed after office hours. One of the main street entrances is off Thanks-Giving Square, the centerpiece of the small park a spiral-shaped chapel that looks like a giant alabaster seashell stranded on a beach of concrete. When it gets too cold for the homeless to sleep on sidewalks and park benches downtown, they find their way into the tunnels to keep from freezing.

I do a drive-through at a local burger place for food and coffee, enough for Wayne and Gary, then park on the street next to the square. I quickly cross the plaza, clutching the spare blanket, sweatshirts, and food bag tightly to my chest, my breath frosting brightly under the security lamps. A path behind the chapel, and down a wide staircase, leads to the large glass entryway, which is locked. Above the glass doors is a legend meant to be inspiring. But the first letter of the inscription is missing, so it now reads ING UNTO THE LORD A NEW SONG. The letters are raised and metallic, and I wonder if some enterprising thief pried the S loose to hawk for loose change.

Knocking loudly on the thick glass doors with the flashlight, I wait for a security guard to appear, but I see no movement inside the lobby entrance to the network. It's quiet; I'd passed no one on the sidewalk or in the park. It's probably too cold for anyone to be walking around aboveground, but a desperate junkie, insensible to the bitter weather, might risk slinking out of the shadows to mug a lone female. I can hear the muffled rush of traffic from the highway and, from several blocks away, the unexpected sound of a woman's laughter—a high-pitched yelping given volume by nervousness, or alcohol, or both.

I continue to bang on the doors until the guard finally comes to investigate the racket. I show him my badge, and he grudgingly unlocks the door. He looks sleepy and irritated and none too pleased to be roused from whatever little cubbyhole he's settled into for the night.

"What's up?" he asks, yawning into my face.

"I need access to one of the tunnels. Elm Street."

He grimaces, his jowly cheeks petulant. "Oh come on. That got cleared out last week. Besides, my shift ends in forty-five minutes."

He knows full well that if I go into the part of the network closed to the public, he'll have to hang around the connecting door to let me back in. But he also knows that there are a hundred and one ways for the homeless to squeeze back into the tunnels through loose grates, out-of-order elevator shafts, and boarded-over garage doors. No matter how many times the tunnels are evacuated, people find ways to get back in.

"My CI just called me from the square," I tell him.

"Look, you're going to need permission from the city to gain access—"

"You got an old lady waiting for you at home—?" I look at his nameplate, A. GARCIA. "Mr. Garcia, if I have to start contacting people tonight, you're in for a long evening. I'm going to make it my business to keep you here to take a long statement about what you did or did not see tonight. Now, I've got someone waiting for me at home who's already pissed at my leaving after dinner. The sooner I'm in, the sooner I'm out."

Garcia exhales in a short burst of irritation.

"I'll be thirty, forty minutes, tops," I say.

He stares at the blanket I'm carrying. "Looks like you're planning on spending the night down there."

"Just leaving this for my CI."

"You know there's no cell phone service down there."

"I know," I say. "Quick trip. Scout's honor."

He turns and I follow him down the first of two long, sloping corridors that lead to the large triangular lobby directly below Thanks-Giving Square. Our footsteps echo loudly against the concrete walls, our reflections warped into freakish proportions by the glass windows fronting the empty shops and restaurants, some of which have been closed for years. The tiles lining the open spaces are clown-red and acid-yellow, the columns thick and bunker-like. The shop signs are painted in outdated block lettering: LUNCH DAILY SPECIALS $5, HAIRCUTS $10.

Garcia enters a recessed space and punches a code into a keypad on the wall next to a large metal door. The lock is released and he opens the door for me. The weighted door will close and lock behind me once I enter the next series of walkways. The air from the tunnel feels like someone opened an industrial-sized freezer, and it's dark. Not completely black, but lit only by low-wattage emergency lights set into the walls every twenty yards or so.

"You sure you want to go down there by yourself?" he asks.

"You volunteering to go with me?"

Garcia points to his watch. "I'll be back in forty minutes. Be here when I open the door."

I nod, turning on my flashlight, and he closes the door. His flat-footed retreat sounds like muffled gunshots, and for the briefest moment panic constricts my throat. The corridor appears to dead-end about fifty yards away, making the abandoned, vaulted-ceilinged space seem like an ancient tomb, sealed forever below a mountain of rock. I slow my breathing, remembering that cut into the left wall a few yards from the terminus is the entrance to the escalator, immobilized and boarded waist-high with a piece of plywood. The escalator leads down another level to what the street people have named the Elm Street Tunnel.

I step over the plywood, holding on to the sticky, rubberized handrails, and shine my flashlight down to the bottom. I have a moment of vertigo following the thwarted expectation of movement. There will be no emergency lights in this part of the tunnel, which skirts the subbasement of Tower Garage; no lights until the next doorway leading into the adjacent office-building basement a block away. The subterranean lobby on the other side of the doorway is where the homeless gather to shelter from the cold. The lock on the lobby door has been permanently jammed to allow them to come and go. What may not be so easy is to talk to Wayne and Gary without being verbally harassed. Cops are not usually given a warm greeting in Tunnel Town.

I carefully begin descending the escalator, alternately shining the light at my feet and at the corridor that stretches ahead. When I make it to the bottom, I stop and listen while directing the flashlight beam in a widening arc, checking floor to ceiling. The corridor stretches in a straight line into blackness. Despite the cold, I've begun to sweat. I touch the Glock on my hip like a talisman. The last time I was here was over a year ago, with Seth and another undercover, chasing down a small-time dealer who had murdered his girlfriend on suspicion of stealing his meth.

To my left is a door to a storage closet; about ten feet ahead to my right will be another closet door. Another ten feet and there will be a third closet door to my left. It was behind the third door that the dealer had hidden himself. He had heard our approach, and burst from the closet blindly firing his weapon. Seth returned fire and managed to wound him, but not before the dealer had shot and almost killed the other undercover. Following the incident, the city had assured us that new locks had been installed on all three doors. Bracing myself, I test the handles of the first two doors and am relieved to find them both secured. I'm reaching for the handle on the third door when I hear a faint scrabbling sound. The acoustics are weird in the corridor, so it's hard to pinpoint the source of any sound. I freeze for a moment, listening intently for the noise, then sweep the corridor behind me with the flashlight beam.

Two red eyes stare unblinking from the escalator, about six feet from the bottom. It's a rat the size of a Chihuahua, perched on one of the risers. As soon as the beam of light hits him, he scurries back up the escalator and into the darkness.

The noise sounds again and this time I'm certain it's coming from behind the third door. I reach for the handle with one hand, the other on my gun. I grip the handle, and it moves under my fingers. The lock's been broken.

The door opens explosively and something—a figure draped in white—rushes screaming toward me. It barrels into me, knocking me onto the marble floor.

Kostucha…Death in white.

My mouth is open to wail along with the specter, but it rushes down the corridor, into the well of shadows, its piercing shrieks echoing off the concrete walls like artillery fire.

The flashlight, knocked from my hand, has rolled against the opposite wall, the wobbling beam shining enough light onto the fleeing apparition for me to see that it's a woman, short and squat, wrapped in a pale blanket and running blindly for the far end of the tunnel. My heart is pounding an exit through my chest, but it's probably nothing compared with the fear the woman must have experienced listening, in the roiling dark, to my approaching footsteps.

I ease myself up against the wall, my tailbone in agony from the impact, and I'm tempted to haul myself up the escalator and pound on the door until Garcia lets me out again. Somewhere at the far end of the tunnel, a door bangs shut and there is quiet again.

I grope for the flashlight, food, and blanket scattered on the floor, and pull myself to a standing position. Both coffee cups have spilled, making the burgers slightly soggy, but I don't imagine Wayne or Gary will complain much. The base of my spine flares scarlet with pain and my right leg twitches in its own mutinous dance. I point the beam of light ahead and limp to the far end of the tunnel. The door to the lobby area is closed, but I swing it open with little effort.

The lobby, murky and deeply shadowed from the few recessed lights in the ceiling, grows pinpricks of light; the sleeping underground populace holding aloft lighters, or the odd flashlight to see who the intruder is. I turn off my own flashlight and a man's deep voice rumbles out of a blanketed shape the size of a small bunker. "Whaddya want?" he demands.

"I'm trying to find Wayne," I say.

An angry chorus of "Fuck you…Shut up" (and even a few "Got any smokes?") surrounds me. At least two dozen people have taken shelter in this basement. Images of every zombie movie I've ever seen crowd my head—if you run, they'll give chase—so I stand still and wait.

More grumbling, then a woman calls out, "He's over here, sleeping."

The woman, sitting against a far wall, flashes her penlight a

few times, guiding me around the bulky forms restlessly undulating on the floor, trying to recapture some sleep. The odor stirred
up from their collective movements is like cheese ripening under
a heat lamp.

The huddled mound next to the woman stirs. It's Wayne, and
I sit down next to him, handing him the blanket and bag of
food. The smell of the burgers is strong, and the woman continues to stare at me, perhaps hoping I'll have enough food to pass
around.

"For you and Gary," I say, quietly.

Wayne sits up, throwing aside an old sleeping bag. "Thanks,
man."

He tugs on the sweatshirts I've brought, then drapes the blanket around his shoulders with his bare hands. I notice for the first
time that his fingers are long and slender, curiously delicate. I
reach into the pocket of my coat and hand him my gloves as well.
He puts them on and smiles, his teeth—what's left of them—
glinting like Indian corn in the half-light. The right glove sags
where his two middle fingers are missing. He takes a coffee cup
out of the bag and cradles it in both hands.

"The blanket's from Mary Grace," I whisper.

"How's she doing?" he asks.

"She's good. The baby's good. She's due next month."

"Can you tell her I asked after her? I'm glad she's got someone
taking care of her. I tried...but, you know, things being as they
are..."

The misery in his eyes threatens to derail the conversation.
Mary Grace had said he was trying to get clean, but the odds are
against someone surrounded by down-and-out drug users. I make
some soothing noises and pat his arm.

"Wayne," I say, keeping my voice low, "is he here?"

Wayne points at a shape a few feet away. "Hey, Gary," he whispers hoarsely. "Someone here to talk to you."

The figure stirs, sits up, and leans toward us, the smell of stale nicotine assaulting my nose like a swarm of bottle flies.

"Hey, it's Friday night, for Christ's sake," Gary says.

It's Thursday night, but I don't correct him. His voice is shredded from drugs, cigarettes, and booze. Gary's younger than I thought he'd be, but then again he could be seventy and baby-faced.

"I'm trying to sleep here," he moans.

"We need to talk."

"Who're you?" he asks, narrowing his eyes at me.

"A friend of Wayne's."

"Well, Friend of Wayne's, what's in it for me?" he asks, rubbing his face.

"Twenty bucks."

"Go away," he says, gathering his coat around him to lie back down again.

"Okay, fifty bucks," I say.

"She's good people, man," Wayne says, holding out the bag. "She brought us food."

Gary sits up and reaches in the bag, taking one of the burgers. He tears off the wrapping and devours half of it in one bite.

"Got no mayo on it," Gary mumbles. He chews and swallows. "What do you want?"

I have to play this carefully. Whatever happened in the alley where Pico was shot, Gary believes the shooter to be someone with a police badge. And once he knows I'm a cop, the last thing he's going to want to do is talk to me. I take out the fifty dollars and hand it to Gary.

"You got a place to stay, other than the tunnels?" I ask.

"Sure," he says, twisting his mouth unpleasantly. "I got a suite at the Hotel ZaZa, but it's being renovated right now."

"I've gotten Wayne into some shelters—"

"No and no," Gary says, emphatically. "Last time I stayed at a shelter I got rolled for the little money I did have."

"What if I got you a motel room for a couple of nights?" If I can coax him out of the tunnels and into a better, safer place, he might open up to me.

Gary sniggers and gives me a disbelieving look.

"You could take a shower," I say. "Get yourself cleaned up."

His brow crinkles in consideration, and he reaches for the second cup of coffee, pries the lid off, and takes a few sips. "Why're you doing all this?" he asks.

The woman next to Wayne has continued staring at me. Now she points an accusing finger my way. "You're a cop!" she says, loudly. She has recognized me, probably from a former bust.

Gary's hand jerks, spilling his coffee. He sets it down as though it's turned to poison. "You a cop?" he asks. He turns to Wayne. "She a cop?"

There's no more whispering now—and probably two dozen ears straining to hear our conversation.

"Keep your voices down," I warn. "Gary, yes, I'm a cop, but I'm here to help you."

He begins scooting away from me, his eyes wide with alarm.

"Let me help you—" I say.

Gary stands up, stumbling over the people around him in his hurry to get away.

The giant man under the blanket who spoke to me when I entered the lobby has thrown off his cover. He stands ponderously, his arms crossed over his chest, his shadowy bulk blocking the exit. Other men and women have shaken off their coverings, and they begin to stand as well. The grumbling has stopped. It's quiet except for Gary's excited, ragged breathing.

"You need to let him go," the big man warns, and he takes a few steps toward me.

He's at least six-six, with the girth of an elephant and dreadlocks cascading down his shoulders like an ancient battle helmet. I place my hand over my gun.

"I'm a police officer," I say. "And I need to talk to that man."

The silence is total. At least thirty minutes have passed since I made my way through Thanks-Giving Square, and Garcia will be coming soon to open the locked door.

Another man has begun to sneak behind me. The air has thickened with the uneasy expectation of the exhausted unwashed becoming angry, destitute people with little to lose. A lone cop in the tunnels is begging for a little payback from the homeless people who've been harassed, moved along, and arrested for vagrancy for the sole transgression of having nowhere else to go.

Gary says to the crowd, "Jump her, man, what are you waiting for?"

My fingers tighten on my pistol grip. Most of the people in the tunnels are harmless. But some are anything but.

The big man standing before me leans down, his broad, stony face glaring into mine. He blinks a few times.

His head rears back. "Red Betty?" he says. "That you?" He points to his chest. "It's me. The librarian. From Tent City."

"Mountain?" I say, taking my hand from the gun.

"Looks like you finally found Bunsen Gary," Mountain says, holding out a restraining hand to the surrounding multitude. The man sneaking up behind me steps away.

"But, uh, Betty, we have a little problem here," he says, scratching his neck. "We can't let you take him outta here. House rules."

"House rules?" I ask, incredulous. "You know I'm Dallas Police."

"I know," he says. "But you see, for us, this place is sanctuary. And you either have to leave without Gary now, or—" He shakes his head at me.

"Or what?" I ask.

"Or you have to stay with us for the night. Just until morning, when we'll all be on our way. You take Gary, you have to take all of us."

"Mountain, come on—" I say.

"That's the deal, snowflake," Mountain says. "You can leave, but Gary stays."

"I could come back with a shitload of pissed-off cops."

Mountain lowers his chin and folds his hands discreetly in front of his waist like a patient professor. "You could. But I don't think you will."

"Hey," someone in the crowd yells. "I've got my audition in the morning and I need my beauty sleep."

The group snickers and begins finding their places on the floor again. Gary is nowhere to be seen. He's melted into the dark spaces.

Mountain walks me to the exit door. "You okay going back through the tunnels alone?"

"Yes," I tell him. I reach into my pocket and slip him my last forty dollars. "Buy breakfast for some people tomorrow."

He holds the door open for me until he knows my flashlight is working; once I'm halfway down the blackened corridor, he firmly closes the door. I pause for only a second at the still-open closet door. The space inside is filled with shelves and boxes— plenty of places for a person to hide behind.

I walk quickly up the escalator, making as much noise as

possible to scare off any rodents, and leg myself over the plywood barrier. I pull out my phone to check the time. It's been over forty minutes and I race to the end of the vaulted corridor. When I get to the door, I check the handle and, of course, it's locked.

Banging on the door with my fist, I yell, "Hello!"

I listen, my ear to the door, but hear nothing.

Shit, shit, shit!

"Hello, anybody there? Mr. Garcia! I'm here—"

Neither hammering on the door nor rattling its handle brings the guard.

Even if Garcia had left for the night, there'd be someone to take his place. He would have told his replacement there was a cop down in the tunnel. But no sound comes from the other side of the door. As I listen intently, the ambient silence changes—a microscopic shift in the air pressure around my head, making the very molecules in my ears more weighted.

I pivot and shine the flashlight beam back down the corridor, toward the terminal end. The rectangle of blackness to the left, the mouth of the escalator, has changed its shape, as if the vortex of dark has grown an appendage. It's a round form jutting from the opening, but it disappears, as though retreating from the light. The appendage was the size of a human head, peering out from the opening. Watching me.

"Hey," I yell. "I see you."

I turn back to the door and angrily pound on it some more. The anger is a distraction from a growing fear that what's waiting in the corridor behind me is not one of the homeless from the tunnel, but something else.

I pivot a second time, raking light through the empty space. A dark form has stepped over the plywood barrier and is now standing at the far end of the corridor. It's a man, well built and tall, in a bulky jacket and black hoodie pulled tightly around a deeply shadowed or masked face, his arms at his sides. There is a rigid readiness to his stance. Keeping the beam of light directly on the figure, I pull out my phone to make an emergency call. No service available.

I pocket my phone and pull my gun, leveling it at the figure. Where his face should be, there are no features; the man is wearing a ski mask.

"Dallas Police," I say. "You need to get down on the ground. *Now!*"

But the man remains motionless, and I begin to kick at the door behind me with hard heel strikes, in rapid succession. He throws back his head—*is he laughing at me?*—and waves a gloved finger in my direction. Then he turns, stepping back over the barrier, ducking back into the blackness.

The bubble of fear has escaped my reasoning mind—*it's the drug-dealer assassin…it's El Cuchillo…it's one of the Roy family…it's a hallucination*—and I yell and pound on the door until I think the bones in my hand will shatter. The terror that's accompanied my nightmares now inhabits my waking reality. The solid metal gives way as the door is yanked open and I stumble out into the main lobby, crashing against two men.

I'm wild-eyed and breathless, leaning over, hands on knees, to keep from collapsing. Garcia is staring at me with supreme annoyance, and standing behind him, looking concerned, is Uncle Benny.

"Something…someone in the tunnel following me," I gasp. There's a vacuum in my head, and I feel like I'm going to pass out. But one clear thought crystallizes: *It can't be Uncle Benny. Uncle Benny is dead.*

My head snaps up and I see that it's James Earle, not my uncle.

Garcia switches on his flashlight and, with James holding the door open, starts walking cautiously down the corridor.

"You okay?" James asks, grasping my arm as though I'll fall over without the support. He smells comfortingly of beer with a whiskey chaser.

I nod, gulping in air. "What are you doing here?"

"Jackie followed your location on your phone. When she figured out where you were headed, she called me."

"I'm sorry, James. I was meeting a CI. She didn't need to call you."

Brows raised, he takes in my shaky, hobbling, disheveled self and, patting me on the back, rasps, "You could have fooled me."

Garcia walks back into the lobby and swings the door closed with a bang. "There was nothing there."

"Oh yeah?" I say. "There was a man, hooded and masked, who followed me back from the tunnel."

"Well, whoever he is, he's locked in for the night."

But both of us know he'll simply exit the way he came in— through an open grate, a jimmied door, a piece of rotten plywood. I didn't see a flashlight beam, so the guy must have been able to see in the dark like a cat.

"Can we go home now?" James asks. "I need about a few dozen drinks."

"I'm with you there, James," I say.

He looks at me meaningfully, his sad, hound-dog face filled with compassion. "And considering the mood Jackie's in right now, I'd seriously consider taking up smoking too."

CHAPTER 21

It's Saturday and Jackie is packing for a four-day radiology conference in Denver. And she looks positively exuberant about leaving me behind.

I've followed her around all morning—trying to be helpful, trying to make up for her anguish over my expedition through the tunnels two nights ago—but all I've managed to do is annoy her further.

While she showers, I take some toast and coffee on a tray to the bedroom and place it on the bed for her. Earlier she had told me that, when she returns, we're going to need to "talk about some things." When your partner tells you that, it usually means that somebody, often the one being talked to, is going to be asked to relocate.

I can't blame her. Not only did the encounters in the tunnels unnerve me—the screaming woman in the closet, Gary freaking over my being a cop, the shadow man confronting me—but the momentary appearance of Uncle Benny brought back the nightmares I had hoped were retreating.

The unmade bed, with its sweat-drenched, tangled sheets, looks like a battlefield. And not in a good way. Feeling sorry for myself, I pull Jackie's pillow to my face and breathe in her scent: carnations and melted butter. No one else in the world smells like Jackie. The phone in my pocket vibrates and, with a guilty look at the bathroom door, I check the number. It's Dusty Rose. I know I should ignore it, at least until Jackie leaves for the airport. But I answer it anyway.

"Why are you whispering?" she asks.

"I'm not whispering," I say. "Just speaking quietly."

"Pearla wants to talk to you."

The trans bartender at the nightclub who'd set me up to buy drugs from Chuffy.

"She figure out yet I'm a cop?"

"Oh yes, but she finally got tired of Chuffy treating her like a punching bag. She says she's got information about some stolen heroin." Dusty pauses dramatically. "And a dirty cop who's partnered up with her boyfriend. Blond hair, blue eyes, great ass. Sound like anyone you know?"

I think of Seth standing under the EXIT sign in the club and my throat closes up.

"There's just one catch," she says.

Of course the information is going to cost me. "How much?"

"Three hundred."

"What!" I yelp. Being on suspension without pay, and paying people for their information—which so far has advanced my career not one bit—is beginning to pinch my bank account. "No," I say. "I'll give her fifty as a donation to her favorite charity, and I'll bring lunch in a bag."

I hear some muffled conversation—Pearla standing right next to Dusty. "Okay, make it a hundred—and Cane's chicken," Dusty says. "A bucket of twelve, please. And extra napkins. They never give you enough napkins."

We agree to meet at lunchtime, but when she tells me where, I laugh.

"It's the last place anyone would expect to find two ladies such as ourselves, so we won't be disturbed," she drawls. "Bye-bye, baby. We'll talk later about what you can do for old Dusty."

I disconnect and shove the phone back into my pocket just as the bathroom door opens.

Hand on hip, Jackie throws a wilting glance at the charred pieces of bread on the tray, and says, "You are so bad at trying to look innocent."

When I walk her out to her ride to the airport, she gives me a perfunctory hug and hands me a piece of paper. She gets into the car and it drives away.

The piece of paper is from one of her prescription pads. It reads, "Call Dr. Theo—today!! Love, J."

I wave goodbye until the car is out of sight. Then I pull my phone from my pocket and call Craddock.

"Tom," I say, "any more word from the DEA about that stolen heroin?"

I've caught him with his mouth full. He swallows and says, "You know I can't talk to you about this—"

"Just tell me. Do you know how much was taken?"

He pauses, considering the implications. "About twenty keys."

I draw a sharp breath. *Twenty kilos of heroin?* "That would put the value over a million dollars."

"Yeah," he says. "Now you know why the DEA is so hot on this."

"And it's definitely Sinaloan?"

"No question. Maclin's got everybody on this. He wants us to find the Knife before there's more bloodshed. But if he finds out I'm talking to you, my ass will be grass."

"Okay, Tom, thanks. My lips are sealed."

* * *

I sit on the couch trying to wrap my mind around a lot of open-ended questions. People will say that there are no coincidences in law enforcement. But Uncle Benny would have disagreed. Not only are there weird, cosmically skewered coincidences in life, he would have said, but these coincidences can be very dangerous when you're trying to work a case. "Coincidences can kill you," I'd once heard him say.

The Sinaloans had a million dollars' worth of heroin stolen from one of their distributors. Pearla says that Chuffy is dealing stolen heroin with a dirty cop. But it doesn't necessarily mean that Chuffy is peddling the Sinaloan product. How would a two-bit hustler get his hands on over forty pounds of heroin? He probably wouldn't. But a street-savvy cop might be able to.

The other question—a badge-wielding shooter taking out dealers—only clouds my thinking. I've heard nothing from Wayne or Gary for two days. First things first, though: I'll talk to Pearla, then go looking for Gary. Whether what he's saying turns out to be true or not, it'll work in my favor if I'm the one who's tracked him down.

At noon I pass the gates into Fair Park. Across from the Magnolia Lounge near Big Tex Circle is the Old Mill Inn Restaurant. Built in the 1930s, the same decade the park was assembled, the restaurant looks like a Knights of Columbus version of a Bavarian eatery, with a solid brick exterior, a waterwheel, and a fairy-tale bridge. Making the whole package look sullen and run-down are the walls fitted with grab bars for the elderly and the tacky, modern sign out front announcing that the restaurant is currently closed.

The front door is locked, but when I look through one of the windows, I see Dusty waving to me to come around to a side entrance. She opens the door and quickly waves me inside. The place is decorated not in Weimar kitsch but in Disneyland dreck, with a seven-foot statue of Elvis in one corner, neon domestic-beer signs above the bar, and cheap, spindly tables set in front of a massive wood-framed fireplace. The high ceiling is impressively buttressed with WPA-crafted oak beams, the floor laid in what looks to be the original ceramic tiles. *Can I really be the first person,* I wonder, *to want the present owners lashed to their own waterwheel and tortured?*

Dusty takes the large bag of chicken from me, then holds me at arm's length, towering above my nearly six-foot frame thanks to four-inch platform shoes, solemnly giving me the once-over. "Honey, you need to be moisturizing better."

I wave her breath away from my nostrils. "And you need to stop drinking before noon."

Dusty gives me a dismissive gesture and leads me to the back of the restaurant, giving Elvis's crotch a pat as she passes, assuring me it's for good luck.

"Elvis is where we used to keep our pocketbooks safe. He's hollow, but he's *so* good-looking."

We ascend a narrow flight of stairs, her rear end above me swaying like ten pounds of hardening concrete inside a five-pound bag.

"Pearla and I used to work here——" she says.

"Collaborating with the Gestapo?"

She gives me a withering look over her shoulder. "Pearla worked the cash register and I worked in the kitchen. Not in my present incarnation, of course. I make a spectacular Wiener schnitzel."

"I bet you do," I say.

We top the stairs and walk to a party room toward the back of the restaurant. "The place is only open for special events now, but both of us still have working keys. Chuffy worked here too as a dishwasher when he first got out of prison. It's where Pearla met her sterling prince."

She winks at me and opens the door to a small banquet room. Sitting at one of the tables is Pearla, her face made even darker by the bruises circling one eye and one side of her lower jaw.

"Hey, Pearla," I say, sitting down across from her.

She looks at me, eyes wide, one brow raised, daring me to comment on her bruises.

"You okay?" I ask.

She shrugs one shoulder and purses her lips, but the concern in my voice has made her eyes well up.

"I've been better," Pearla says.

"You been to a doctor?" I ask.

She shakes her head.

Dusty says, "Girl, I tried to get her to go, but she says if it's not bleeding or dragging on the floor, it can't be fatal."

Dusty empties the bag of its contents and the two of them attack the chicken, tearing apart the meat with their fingernails.

"What's going on with Chuffy?" I ask.

Pearla points to her blackened eye. "This is what. I've been so good to that man, and this is how he treats me. I made good money for him, and all I wanted was my fair share."

Dusty elbows her and says, "Tell the detective what you told me."

Pearla takes her time wiping the grease from each finger. "You got something for me?"

I take out the hundred dollars and lay it on the table in front of her.

She inhales through pinched nostrils as though I've just insulted her.

"Chuffy's dealing heroin," Pearla says.

"Dusty says it's stolen," I say. "Where'd he get it?"

"From some *Mexicans*, I would think," Pearla says.

I want to reach across the table and throttle her.

"Look," I say, stabbing the table with one finger. "I'm not playing games here. You need to tell me what you know, right now, or I'll take back my hundred and you can walk home. Where did the heroin come from?"

Pearla sighs, and tugs at her wig. "Chuffy told me he found it."

I exhale impatiently. "He just stumbled across it?"

"It was hidden in a back room in a gym where he used to work out."

"What gym?"

"I don't know. Just some boxing gym. He didn't tell me where. He just said it's been closed down."

I take a few breaths and study her. I don't want to ask the next question, but I have to know. "You also told Dusty that Chuffy's partnered with a cop. Do you know who it is?"

"Only by sight. I don't know his name, and I don't want to know. One thing I know for sure: I name a dirty cop and I might as well jump off the Trinity Bridge today, 'cause my life won't be worth a damn thing."

Dusty throws a sympathetic look in my direction. "I hear that."

"Did you know the guy sitting next to me at the bar at the Circus?" I ask. "Dark hair, leather jacket. Tough-looking."

Pearla shakes her head. "I'd never seen him before."

"Did you see Chuffy's reaction to him?"

"No. I only saw you standing on the bar stool and then running into the crowd. I didn't see Chuffy again until I got back to the motel." Pearla points to her eye. "That's when he did this to me."

"I need to stay in touch with you," I tell Pearla. "Where are you staying right now?"

"I had to vacate my apartment," she says. "I was staying at the Alamo Motel with Chuffy. But I'm afraid of what he'll do if I show up there again."

"I just gave you a hundred dollars," I say. "Can you get another motel room for a night or two?"

Dusty gives her friend a censoring look. "She owes me seventy."

"Which only leaves me twenty," Pearla wails.

"It leaves you thirty dollars, Pearla, and you know it." Then, turning to Dusty: "Can't she stay with you?"

"My current mister won't be liking that too much," Dusty says, fluttering her eyelashes. "One of me fills up a lot of space."

"Is there a shelter where you can go?" I ask Pearla.

She shakes her head, sweat streaking her makeup. Tears begin to leak from her eyes and drop from her chin onto the greasy waxed paper holding the remains of her chicken lunch. "You have any idea what will happen to me if I go to the men's shelter?" she asks, her face anguished, devoid now of artifice. Her voice has dropped an octave. "'Cause they sure as hell won't let me into the women's side."

I look at Dusty and she looks at me, catching the look of pity on my face.

"Okay," I say. "I can put you up in a motel for two nights. But that's it, Pearla. You're going to have to call on friends or family after that."

"I thought *you* were my friend," Pearla says with a pleading tone.

"Uh-oh," Dusty says, wagging her head back and forth. "Here comes karma, baby. Swingin' her pocketbook."

I stand up, sweeping the remains of the lunch into the bag. "We're not friends yet, Pearla," I tell her. "You can earn my good-will, though, by keeping me informed of Chuffy's movements."

Pearla rises from her chair, tugging down the hem of her dress and adjusting her wig. "I'm not getting within fifty feet of that pinched-off little prick."

"Fine," I say, leading the way out of the party room. "All I'm saying is, you hear something more about his dealing, you come straight to me—and no one else."

When we've left the restaurant, Dusty walks off, twirling the keys to the borrowed blue BMW, and Pearla jackknifes herself into my car. I drive her to a Comfort Inn, where I pay for a room for two nights with my credit card.

Pearla gives me a bruising hug at the door to her room and says, "You're a good person."

Oh, I'm the Blessed Bronislava all right, I think. *Polish saint of all orphans.*

"You want to thank me?" I warn. "Keep whispering in my ear. I mean it, Pearla—you hear anything and you call me."

When I get to the elevator, Pearla is still standing in the hall-way, platform shoes in one hand, wig in the other.

"And no parties in the room," I tell her.

CHAPTER 22

I go out to the front porch in my bare feet, pick up the Sunday-morning newspaper, and take in the headline: *Vigilante Cop Killing Drug Dealers?*

I look around, but there's no one else on the street. A typical sleepy Sunday morning in the suburbs, belying the fact that a shitstorm of biblical proportions is about to hit the Dallas Police Department. No sooner have I closed the door than my work phone rings. I left it on the dining-room table, and I approach it the same way I would an unidentified snake. It's not going to be Seth or Craddock. Neither is it going to be James Earle or Jackie. They'd be calling on my personal cell.

I look at the number and see that it's DPD North Central Division. I answer the phone and Maclin says, "Did you see the paper this morning?"

"Yes, I just picked it up—"

"Did you do this?" he asks. "Have you been talking to reporters?"

It's not idle curiosity. His voice is choked with anger.

"Absolutely not. I don't know anything about this."

"I've got Euell Tilton and Bernard Tate coming into my office this afternoon. I want you here, in my office, at two o'clock, and I want you to swear on your mother's grave, do a jig, whatever you need to do to convince them that you had nothing to do with this."

"Of course, I'll be there—"

"Did Tilton have a conversation with you about the street rumors that a cop was shooting dealers?"

"Yes—"

"And you didn't think to share that information with me?"

"I'd already been put on suspension—"

"Correct me if I'm wrong, Detective Rhyzyk, but you still have your badge, which means you're still on the force. I demand one thing from my officers, and that is compliance with protocol. You get me? You want to return to street duty? Then you stop all the maverick crap and tell me everything you see, smell, or taste that affects this department. Open fucking book from now on. If not, I'm going to make your life a cold, bloodless, boring hell."

He disconnects and I place the phone back on the table, half expecting it to ring again so Maclin can continue his tirade.

I go back to bed and read the article about the suspected killer cop. The information came from an unnamed source, but one who claims to be with the Dallas Narcotics Division. There's not a lot of substance, only rumors, and the article has been fluffed with a lot of conjecture and the liberal use of terms such as *allegedly* and *possibly* and *believed to be*. I think of every narcotics officer I know, but can't come up with one who would talk to a reporter about an actual, ongoing homicide investigation.

I look at the clock and recall I'd agreed to take Mary Grace to breakfast. She has moved in with Dottie but for some unfathomable reason is eager to spend time with me.

I quickly dress, and leave my house to pick up Mary Grace.

Once I get to Dottie's bungalow, though, I sit brooding in silence for a moment, dreading my upcoming encounter with Maclin. Dottie stands on her porch, coffee mug in hand, watching me. She walks up to my window and raps on it.

When I roll down the window, she says, "I believe from the sour look on your face you saw the paper this morning. What's going on?"

"I have no idea, Dottie. I'm stuck in the abyss of my own morass."

"You believe it's a cop?"

"I don't want to believe it," I say, but shrug.

She leans in closer, her elbows on the doorframe, her gray-green eyes gazing into mine. "You know I can't break the confidence of a fellow recovering drug addict. But if I was to be the blind person leading the blind, I'd say something like, 'Start looking for the killer in your own backyard.'"

For a moment I study her face, well-worn and weathered by hard living. "Are you trying to tell me you know something about this?"

Dottie backs away from the door. "I don't know anything, sweet cheeks. I'm just flapping my jaws."

Mary Grace, looking full-faced and healthy, shuffles from the house as fast as her pregnant belly will allow. She gives Dottie a kiss on the cheek, then throws herself into the car, grinning.

"Hey, Mary Grace," I say, giving her a quick hug. "Looks like you're taking your vitamins and doing your Kegel exercises, or whatever the hell it is you're supposed to be doing with that bowling ball sitting on top of your bladder."

"I did everything but eat today," she says. "And I'm starving!"

"Doesn't Dottie feed you?" I ask, laughing.

"I have a PowerBar—"

Mary Grace rifles through her worn bag, pulling items from its dark interior. Used tissues, a few rumpled bills, and a slick brochure that she places on the console. On the brochure is a photo of a smiling girl, sunlight surrounding her head like a halo. A Bible verse in a banner at the top. The kind of religious brochure handed out to street waifs to entice troubled young teens into a religious institution for a quick meal—and a lasting salvation. But this one sports an emblem. One I've seen before: upswept wings, transected by a sword. The Roy family emblem.

"Where did you get this?" I demand.

Mary Grace startles at my tone. Her mouth full of Power-Bar, she mumbles, "I don't know. Some lady on the street gave it to me."

"What lady?" I've grabbed onto her wrist, and she winces at the pressure.

She swallows and says, "I don't know, just some lady. I was shopping with Dottie and this woman handed it to me."

"What did she look like?" I make myself let go of Mary Grace's arm.

I catch a look at myself in the rearview mirror and a voice in my head cautions, *Calm the fuck down. She doesn't know anything about Evangeline Roy.*

Dottie raps on the driver's window again. "All good in there?" she asks, her brow furrowed disapprovingly.

I give her a quick thumbs-up, and when I turn back to Mary Grace her eyes are filling with tears.

Putting an arm around her, I pull her into a tight hug. "Mary Grace, I am so sorry. I shouldn't have spoken to you like that. You haven't done anything wrong. But it's important that I know who gave this to you."

I hand her a tissue, and she blows her nose. "It was just some grandmother type. She asked me if I'd found Jesus. That I should come to her church. The same thing I've heard a million times before. She seemed nice enough, though. She asked me my name, and I told her."

"What did she look like?" I ask.

She thinks for a minute, then says, "Short, frumpy. Bad skin. Red hair, I think."

I look over my shoulder and see Dottie, her arms crossed, watching us intently as she sips her coffee. I wonder how many space-invader movies—the kind with flesh-eating aliens and apocalyptic endings—start in quiet suburban neighborhoods just like this one. The aliens who assume benign human form and worm their way into the lives of normal, everyday people, the resulting paranoia destroying lives by eroding the trust and goodwill of friends and families. Evangeline has targeted Mary Grace to get to me. She's out there watching.

"Mary Grace, listen to me. I don't want to scare you, but if you see this woman again, I want you to call me immediately. Do you hear me?"

She nods her head that she understands.

"Don't talk to her, don't tell her where you live, just walk away."

"Okay," she says. "Is she a dealer?"

"One of the worst," I say, starting the engine. "Let's get you something to eat now."

Pulling away from the house, I catch Dottie watching us in the rearview mirror. Put a lantern in her hand rather than a coffee cup and she'd look like an aging Cassandra, trying to warn people of coming doom. If only they'd listen.

* * *

When I enter Maclin's office at two o'clock, Euell Tilton and Bernard Tate are already there. They're all seated, three pairs of seasoned eyes focused solely on me. Grim-faced, like Salem witch-trial judges.

There is no third visitor chair in the office, so I'm forced to stand. Maclin looks especially somber. Considered aggressively handsome by most when he first took the job, moving up from homicide detective last year to narcotics sergeant, Maclin has lost considerable luster in only a few months. Hairline receding, waistline expanding. Being away for two weeks, I see what I hadn't seen earlier. Maclin was apparently clueless about the fact that compared with homicide duty (where the duly sworn officers are regimented and orderly in their habits and reportage), under-cover narcotics officers are unregimented, disorderly, and unpredictable, except when it comes to testing the boundaries.

"Did you have a conversation recently with Detective Tilton about some street rumors that a cop was killing the drug dealers?" Maclin asks.

I look at Tilton, but his previous friendly manner has evaporated.

"Detective Tilton visited me at my home shortly after I got suspended," I say. "He shared some street rumors with me."

Maclin crosses his arms in front of his chest. "And you didn't think to share that conversation with me?"

"I didn't give it credence at the time."

"'At the time'—" Tilton says. "Has your opinion changed since then?"

The moment of truth. Do I tell Maclin and Homicide about my foray into the Elm Street Tunnel, and finding Gary? But what would I tell them? There was no discussion, no new information revealed. Gary got scared and ran once he found out I was a cop. Nothing useful to be shared. But I've stayed silent a moment too long.

Tate squints his eyes at me. "Something on your mind, Detective?"

"Nothing I've heard or seen leads me to suspect that a police officer is killing dealers," I say.

"And you didn't speak to any reporters about this?" Tilton asks.

"No," I say.

"Did you speak to anyone else about the conversation we had in front of your house?" he asks.

I meet and hold his gaze. "I did not."

"But you should have told *me,* isn't that right, Detective Rhyzyk?" Maclin says.

"Yes," I say. "I should have come to you. And I would have, if I hadn't already been placed on suspension."

"So you were pissed about it?" Tate asks.

"I wasn't happy about it," I tell him. "But I take my medicine like a big girl. And I didn't go crying in my beer about it to anyone else, either." I turn to Tilton. "My suspension was given with cause, and with conditions. And I'm addressing those issues with my sergeant. Right, Sergeant Maclin?"

Maclin's upper lip twitches, but not like it's about to break into a happy smile. He turns to Tilton. "Are you satisfied now that Detective Rhyzyk did not talk to reporters?"

Tilton looks briefly at me, but nods. Tate only frowns and stares at his shoes.

"Tomorrow morning first thing the chief is going to have a press conference to address this personally," Tilton says. "Network news and print media. There's going to be some hysterics over the thought that if it's not a vigilante cop, a cartel war may be brewing on the streets of Dallas."

"What exactly is he going to say?" Maclin asks.

"He's going to say what's written for him by Public Relations: that Internal Affairs will be working with the captains of Homicide and Narcotics to keep the streets safe and find the killer as soon as possible."

Maclin looks at Tate. "Great—just what we need. Internal Affairs helping us with our investigations."

"Hey, brother," Tate says. "The paper said it was a Narcotics cop doing the talking. This is on you to make it right. But do call us when you catch another stiff."

Tilton and Tate shake hands with Maclin, then leave without another glance at me.

After they go, Maclin points at one of the chairs and says, "Sit."

I comply, and Maclin leans back in his chair, hands laced behind his head. "Helluva way to spend a Sunday. You sure you want to come back to work on the twenty-third?"

"I'm sure. Just curious why you didn't share with Homicide Seth's and my convo with Wayne. The one about his buddy Gary seeing the shooter flash a badge?"

"Because I'm not going to lead them on a wild-goose chase until we verify the source. Do you know where Gary is?"

I weigh my options and say, "No, I do not."

"But you'll tell me the instant you do, right?"

"Absolutely."

"Had your three sessions with Dr. Theodosiou yet?"

"My second was on the sixteenth. Tomorrow morning is my third." I take a breath. "I'll probably keep seeing him after I return to active duty."

"Good for you. And Jackie, too, I would imagine," he says with a smirk. He sits forward, arms on his desk. "Anything you want to share about any of your colleagues in Narcotics?"

My body tenses as I think of my partner, but I just give him a questioning look.

"What are your thoughts on Kevin Ryan?" he asks.

The question surprises me until I remember that Tilton must have talked to Maclin about finding the Trinity River body. "Tilton told you about Kevin's brother-in-law."

"Yeah—and about his reaction at the morgue. Does Detective Ryan seem a little off to you? Wound a little too tight these days?"

"I couldn't say. I haven't been able to spend too much time with him in the field recently, if you know what I mean."

Maclin studies me for a moment. "Enjoy the rest of your stay-cation, and I'll see you back at work on Thursday. But before you get all dewy-eyed about it, I'm keeping you on desk duty for a while."

I open my mouth in protest, but he holds up a censoring hand. "Not one word about it, Detective Rhyzyk. That's the deal. You want to be in this department, you'll ride staplers for a while until I think you're ready to be back on the street. We clear?"

I nod, feeling like I'm about to swallow my own tongue, but before I can escape out the door, he says, "If you see something, say something. And that is not a suggestion."

CHAPTER 23

JANUARY 20, 2014
DR. THEO'S OFFICE

I've taken my place on the couch—dead center with both feet planted firmly on the floor—but this time my arms are not crossed defensively and, as far as I can tell, I'm not scowling. I hope this is considered progress in Dr. Theo's book.

As usual he's dressed simply, but with the elegance of a deposed European count, his gold pen flashing subtly as he takes his notes on the crazy redhead sitting across from him.

He looks up from his notepad and smiles. "How are you feeling?"

"Good," I tell him. "Pretty good."

Except for the painful throbbing and cramping in my right calf. And the returning nightmares.

"Sleeping better?"

"Yep," I say.

There's been no change in his expression, but there it is: the relentless, watchful homunculus that sits behind his eyes. He knows exactly how hard I'm working to appear normal, but he's not showing his hand. Yet.

"You look more rested," he says.

"Being on suspension for a few weeks will do that," I say. "I'll be active duty again in a few days."

"Congratulations. How does that feel?"

"Could be better. I'm riding desk for a while."

"And you're not happy about that." He says it as a statement of fact.

I smile bitterly. "I'd rather be on the streets again."

He nods as though he understands exactly how I feel. "Things good between you and Jackie?"

"Yes, great," I lie. "She's away at a conference for a few days."

"And with your partner, Detective Dutton?"

"Good," I say, maintaining eye contact, my breathing even, determined not to get mired in my partner's illegal activities. Best to just keep talking. "He's made another two successful arrests while I've been twiddling my thumbs."

Dr. Theo is sitting relaxed and silent, waiting for me to resume my supposed open-book policy with him. To distract him from his quiet study of my body language, I give him my journal diagram. He glances at it, not quite suppressing the lift of one Olympian eyebrow. He sets it on the desk and turns his attention back to me.

"The Sinaloans are making an appearance in the Metroplex," I say, hoping that mentioning a dangerous drug cartel will explain my restlessness.

"Are you nervous at all about being active duty again?"

I grin and wag a finger at him. "That sounds like a trick question, Doc. If I say I'm nervous, it may point to my being unprepared for duty. But if I say I'm not, it might signal that I'm too eager and a possible risk to my colleagues."

Dr. Theo grins back at me, and I imagine there are dimples under his neatly trimmed beard. I wonder how many Cypriot perps fell victim to the seemingly casual charms of Officer Theodosiou.

"I'll kill the suspense for you," he says, "by saying that it would be natural to have some nervousness, as well as some excitement. You didn't choose being a detective because you're risk-averse."

"Fair enough. I guess I do sound more like a kid before a birthday party than a sober law-enforcement officer."

"It's good that you're excited," he says. "Many officers counsel with me because they dread their work."

"I dread a lot of things, but my work is not one of them."

"Oh? What kinds of things do you dread?" he asks.

Aaaand away we go... The pleasantries are over. Now for the skull digging. His gaze is directed toward the notepad balanced on his knee, as though the question's not important. But I know better.

"The last time we met," he says, "we talked about your father's drinking, and his violent temper. I don't want to pull you away from your excitement about being on duty again, but I think it's important to look at how handling stress was modeled for you growing up."

"Well, *modeled* is a curiously delicate word for what he did," I say. *Now* I'm scowling. "He didn't *handle* stress, he swung it around like a bullwhip soaked in alcohol."

"How did you protect yourself from your father's rage?"

He pauses for me to continue, but I just shrug.

"My brother, Andrew, and I got good at finding hiding places," I finally say. "We were like mice. We could find the smallest spaces to squeeze into. If we were found, we'd both get a beating."

"You hid as an act of self-preservation. A survival mechanism. You felt your very life was threatened. And sometimes the act of hiding becomes second nature to us, even if the thing we're hiding from is not actually life-threatening."

He looks at me intently, like a safecracker listening for the tumblers to fall into place.

"Andrew was your protector," he says.

"Until he wasn't."

Dr. Theo crosses his legs and waits.

"My father was as dirty as they come," I say. "And he sucked Andrew into it. I lost my brother even before he died."

"How did you escape the corruption?"

"What makes you think I did?" Now I'm scowling *and* defensive.

"I like to give my patients the benefit of the doubt."

"You sure you were a cop?" I ask.

Dr. Theo smiles warmly at me, his weapon of mass disarmament.

"My saving grace was my uncle Benny," I say. "He kept me on the straight and narrow."

"Your father's brother. From what you've told me about his involvement in your life, you must miss his presence quite a bit."

Instinctively I grab hold of my Saint Michael medallion. I think of my startling break with reality as I was leaving the Elm Street Tunnel—my imagining that James Earle had been Uncle Benny. And the feelings of loss I experienced afterward, realizing that it was a false vision. "You have no idea," I mutter.

"Your uncle gave you guidance, advice. What do you think he'd be saying to you now?"

In my second session with Dr. Theo, I had spoken briefly about Benny's role as my guiding light. But what I was careful not to reveal was my uncle's communication with me from the Great Beyond. At least he did before my injury. My goal was to graduate from the good doctor's care, not lock myself into lifelong treatment for being certifiably batshit crazy. Behind Dr. Theo on his desk was a plaque: PRESENT ALWAYS. I knew it was to reassure his patients that he would be ever available to them, but to me it was a caution that without some guarded censorship on my part, I might be present always as a mental patient.

"I have no idea what advice he'd be giving me right now," I say. "Other than some Polish proverb about being your best self. *Bez potrzeby wymówka, gotowe oskarżenie.*"

He looks at me, puzzled.

"A guilty conscience needs no accuser," I translate.

"That's an interesting choice of proverbs," he says. "In Greek we have something similar: *Boreíte na tréxete allá den boreíte na krýpsete.*"

He sets the notepad aside. "You can run, but you can't hide."

I throw my head back and laugh. "Touché."

My laughter soon drains away, the momentary elation replaced by a deep sense of loss—and a sadness so sharp I have to duck my head to mask a sudden welling of tears.

"Because someone has died," he says, "it doesn't necessarily mean their wisdom is gone."

"You mean, 'We'll always have our memories to keep us warm'?"

I know that Dr. Theo knows I'm doing the thing I do so well: papering over my tenderer feelings with a good dose of snark. *Hide-and-seek, bucko.*

He leans back in his chair and looks at me with unsettling directness. "In 1974 I was a young policeman in Cyprus, barely out of the academy. In July of that year we were invaded by the Turks. I was stationed in the capital, Nicosia. They bombed the city before the paratroopers landed. Their primary targets were the National Guard headquarters and the main police station, but they hit several civilian targets as well. We had very little time to evacuate the city, but we did what we could to help the wounded, the frightened, the lost."

He crosses his arms and looks out the window. It's easy to imagine him in a uniform, his classic Greek features and efficient manner imbuing a sense of calm amid the chaos.

"There was this house next to the police station where a family lived, the husband, the wife, and two small children. It had been flattened by the bombing. It seemed impossible that anyone could have survived the collapse of the building. But I called out anyway, asking if anyone was left alive. There were no sounds from the rubble, yet my grandmother told me there was someone left alive, that she could hear one of the children crying. A few other men and I began digging through the debris, and miraculously we were able to save the young girl. The rest had been crushed to death."

His face is clearly lit by the soft winter light from the window, the memory of the tragedy still fresh on his features.

"What incredible luck that your grandmother heard the crying," I say.

He turns to face me, smiling sadly. "My grandmother had been dead for eight years."

"What?" I say, openmouthed. "I don't understand—"

"I'm not a superstitious person, Detective. And I'm not particularly a religious person either. I have two doctorate degrees—one in forensic science and one in psychology. I believe that two plus two equals four, and that the earth revolves around the sun. Yet I heard my dead grandmother's voice as clearly as I'm hearing you today."

"What has this got to do with me?" There are tiny, darting filaments of light in my line of vision.

"In your last session you talked about how important your uncle had been to your sense of emotional balance. You recounted to me the conversation you had had with him over the phone while you were being held captive, and his telling you how to effect your escape using the dime you had found."

"I told you that was a *dream*." My heart is beating so fast that I think I'll pass out.

"Yes, but it worked. It doesn't matter whether it was actually his voice or not. You believed it to be true, and so it was. You needed him. You summoned his essence. Benny died in 2011, yet his wisdom is still with you now, in 2014. You've internalized his voice as a coping mechanism, which is healthy."

"Why are you telling me all this?"

"Because you've been working so hard for me not to see how important his continuing communication is to you."

I turn to look out the window, trying to control my breathing, wondering if I could jump from a second-story window and not break anything. The sky is a welcoming blue. There are no clouds to conceal the onslaught of dangerous things, like planes with bombs or mean drunks in uniform. There are no tunnel monsters in here.

I unclench my fists.

"Betty," he says gently, leaning forward so that I'll meet his gaze.

"You're not crazy," he says, smiling. "We all need our better angels."

He waits a moment for me to respond. When I don't, he reaches for his calendar to make another appointment. "Detective, you will get out of these sessions only what you are willing to contribute to them."

He's said it in an offhand manner, but he's not talking just to hear the sound of his voice.

"I think I saw Evangeline Roy," I blurt out, surprising myself with the revelation.

He looks at me with concern.

"It's possible it wasn't her. Just an old lady with red hair. I was out jogging, and a car passed by—"

He notices me reaching again for the Saint Michael medallion. "But then Mary Grace, the girl that Jackie and I rescued from the street, was approached by a woman matching the same description."

"And you think it was Evangeline Roy?" he asks.

"She gave Mary Grace a religious brochure with the Roy family emblem on it."

"Is the girl in danger?"

"I've warned Mary Grace to call me if she sees her again."

Dr. Theo regards me for a moment. "You care deeply for this girl."

The truth of it burrows through the barrier of my general paranoia like a diamond drill. "Yes, I do. Very much."

He nods at me, encouragingly, and I realize that for the first time I'm relaxed: my breathing deep and steady, my hands resting loosely in my lap, my jaw unclenched. I'm on the verge of revealing to him that I also saw Uncle Benny standing behind Garcia the security guard at the Elm Street Tunnel, but he's pulled the scheduling calendar onto his lap, and I decide I'll tell him then.

"Detective Rhyzyk," he says, filling in the date on an appointment card. "I don't believe you are psychotic, nor do I believe that you are prone to hallucinations or to visions. You are a police officer, trained to observe and react. You've had a bad physical injury and you are still recuperating from a traumatic experience that has caused you great emotional distress and anxiety."

He hands me the appointment card, meeting my gaze. "I would, however, stay vigilant."

CHAPTER 24

To a civilian, desk duty can be described as "modified duty." An officer confined to such detail is still on the force, and draws pay and benefits. A lot of what they do is paperwork: requesting court documents, doing background checks, processing prisoners. But they also drive delivery vehicles, make phone calls for investigating detectives, and file or clear old station documents, among other necessary but tedious tasks. As our illustrious (and very politic) chief of police put it, "Prudence and good order in a police department dictate that at times certain personnel be relieved of their enforcement duties."

An officer can be relieved of enforcement duties for many reasons. Emotional distress, neglect of duty, defiance of superiors, ignoring departmental rules, even criminal behavior can warrant modified service until, and if, that officer is officially cleared and declared fit for active street assignment again. There is no minimum time required. Worse, there is no maximum time spent chained to the desk, sequestered from fellow officers and the public at large. It is strictly up to the powers that be.

To a conscientious officer, especially a detective, desk duty is akin to being in purgatory. A cop would call it being "on cellblock" because it's like languishing in prison. It's a dumping ground, and the perception among fellow cops is that you're a screwup.

Benched, career derailed, destination unknown.

Years ago a fellow Brooklyn detective—a dedicated cop who had the misfortune of tasing a kid who later died from falling and striking his head—committed suicide after being detailed to Fleet Services Division in Queens, which assigned cars to uniformed patrol cops. Proving that, if Brooklyn desk duty was purgatory, admin duty in Queens was hell.

Craddock stops by my desk with a box of donuts, making things only slightly better.

"Cheer up, buttercup," he says.

"You love me?" I ask.

"You know I do!"

"Good. Then shoot me and put me out of my misery."

"Maclin really crawled up your pants, didn't he?"

I grab a donut and almost take off a few fingers at the first joint biting into it.

"You want to do something more important than typing up reports?" he asks.

"Sure, but I'm on top."

The only thing sweeter than the donut I'm eating is watching Craddock blush.

"Har-har," he says, handing me a piece of paper. "Can you run the tags on this? A witness took down the license-plate number on an SUV seen leaving the area of our skinned dealer. Maybe it will lead us to some Sinaloans."

Over Craddock's shoulder I see Kevin Ryan. He looks better, but there's still a haunted look in his eyes and dark circles beneath them. His raw cuticles have been so savaged with worried chewing that he's drawn blood. He unwraps a Band-Aid and covers the tip of one finger. I think of Maclin asking if I thought Ryan was *wound a little too tight these days.* I wave at him and Craddock motions him closer.

"You doing okay, Kev?" I ask.

"I feel bad about you being benched," he says. "Doesn't seem right. We're shorthanded. You're one of the most experienced detectives we've got, yet Maclin seems determined to keep you off the streets. He's hamstringing the entire squad, especially now that all hell's broken loose after the big man's news talk."

The chief's press statement last Monday caused a firestorm among city officials and civilians alike. Advocacy groups were up in arms, announcing publicly in front of City Hall that the Latino community would suffer the most if there was a cartel war going on in south Dallas. And Internal Affairs had swooped in like heat-seeking missiles, assigning everyone in Narcotics a date to be interviewed by their officers. If a cop was killing the dealers, IA was tasked with sniffing him out as soon as possible. Meanwhile the search for the elusive Gary continued, hot and heavy.

"What can I say?" I shrug. "I could have worse than desk duty; I could be in IA."

Kevin gives a humorless little snort. "Well, let me know if there's anything I can do to help you." He turns to walk away.

For all the times I've thought of Kevin as being the weakest member of the team—his lack of experience making it easy for some people to diminish his contributions—I realize he's the only one who's actually offered me help. Donuts are great, but they bring only a momentary release.

"Hey," I call out to Kevin. "Want to get a drink sometime? Catch up?"

He gives me a look I can't quite decipher. "Let's make it lunch," he says, and walks away.

Craddock leans in and says quietly, "You know he gave up drinking, right? He joined a new church. Hard-core fire and brimstone, baby. Kevin doesn't imbibe liquor anymore, as it may lead to something immoral—like dancing."

He laughs and picks up the last chocolate donut.

"Remember the notorious Reverend Hall, the guy who ran for governor a while back?" Craddock asks, brushing crumbs from his tie.

I blink a few times. "Reverend Alan Hall, he of the 'Bible in one hand, gun in the other'?"

"He of the 'Stand your ground over any perceived threat.' Yep, that's the man. He's the pastor of Kevin's congregation." He lets that sink in, then says, "And speaking of 'Stand your ground,' I've spent half a year looking for a Whitworth. It's a Civil War rifle, fires up to a thousand yards, baby. Still operational."

I roll my eyes. "Compensating much, Tom?"

His smile fades, and for a moment he stares down sadly at the remnants of the chocolate donut in his hand. He drops it in the wastebasket and says, "Just killing time, I guess."

Craddock wanders back to his desk and taps listlessly at his keyboard. It seems as though the entire station has succumbed to some creeping, dark funk, and I have to wonder if, like a virus, my own fatalism has infected my colleagues. I turn back to my own computer, thinking about Kevin's recent misfortunes: his brother-in-law's death from a drug overdose, his wife's miscarriage. Extreme tragedy can fuel extreme remedies. Comfort from a place at the edges of conformity. A dire counterweight to inexplicable loss. You want to know how bad the wound is, look at the size of the bandage.

Struggling to remember the Reverend's most-quoted campaign slogan, I do a computer search and quickly find it: *If you do wrong, then be afraid. God did not give rulers a sword for no reason.* The line is taken from Romans, and it's similar to an Old Testament verse, from Deuteronomy, that Evangeline Roy was quite fond of using: *When I sharpen my flashing sword...*

The Roy family's religious brand of vengeful sword-wielding is hardly unique south of the Mason-Dixon Line. And usually the eye-for-an-eye message is taken only as a cautionary allegory. But not always. Hence the bombed women's clinics, the assassinated medical personnel, the abandonment of unmarried pregnant girls to the streets. I make a mental note to keep close tabs on Kevin Ryan, pumping him for more information about the fiery Reverend Hall.

Seth saunters into the station, holding an extra-large take-out coffee. He sprawls in his chair, sorting through messages. His skin is so pale that he looks exsanguinated, a creature of the night, inhabiting all the shadowy places.

If he's seen me, he hasn't given any indication of it. We haven't spoken since our meeting at Norma's. His phone rings and he swivels his chair around so he can answer the call. I stare at his back, usually muscular, toned by hours in the gym. But he's recently lost weight, and his shoulder blades show more visibly through his T-shirt.

Draped across the back of my partner's chair is a black hoodie. Like the one worn by my stalker in the Elm Street Tunnel.

My cell phone buzzes, and when I answer it, a ragged voice screams in my ear. "Someone killed Gary!"

I'm jolted to attention. "Wayne? What do you mean? Who did?"

"I don't know, man," he wails. "It happened in the tunnels last night. Someone down here with us—"

"Where's Gary now?" I ask.

"He's still lying in the dark part of the tunnel, a hole drilled through his head." There's a pause, then the scratching sound of a match being lit, followed by a deep drag on a cigarette. "Nobody heard the shot, but there was somebody down here last night sniffing around. I think it's the shooter. The same guy killing the dealers."

"Wayne," I interrupt, keeping my voice low. "Have you called anyone else?"

There's a surprised intake of air. "You kidding me? Fuck, what if the shooter thinks I know who he is?"

I grip the phone tighter. "Did Gary tell you who it was?"

There's a pause. "He might have said something last night. Before he was killed—"

"Something? What does that mean?"

"What am I going to do?" The hysteria in his voice is building.

"Wayne," I say, forcefully. "Listen to me. Just stay calm."

"Everyone with a phone down here has hit the streets again and called nine-one-one. The place is going to be crawling with cops soon. What should I do?"

I look at the clock. It's not yet ten. "Get out of there," I tell him. "Leave, now. Go to the bus station on Lamar, the front entrance. Just make sure no one follows you. I'm sending someone to get you. His name is James Earle and he drives an old Crown Vic. You can trust him. You're going to stay with him until I can come get you, which won't be for a few hours. Just don't mention to him, or anyone else but me, what Gary told you."

"Your friend a smoker?" he asks plaintively, hacking up what sounds like the rest of his lungs.

"Wayne, you might just be meeting your match."

I disconnect and call James Earle; when he answers the phone yawning, I ask, "Did I wake you?"

"Oh no," he says. "I had to get up to answer the phone anyway."

"What are you doing this morning?"

"Being drafted again, sounds like," he rumbles.

"You know where the bus station is on Lamar?"

"Yes," he says. "Who is it this time—homeless or criminal?"

"My CI, Wayne. Well, technically he's my partner's snitch. I just need to keep him sheltered for a few hours at your house. I'll take him off your hands around noon. That okay?"

"Oh sure. And I guess it goes without saying I'll need to lock up my medicine cabinet?"

"He's a skinny little guy, two fingers on his right hand missing, and he'll be wearing one of my New York Giants sweatshirts."

"So I guess I should leave my Cowboys sweatshirt at home?"

"Thanks, James. I owe you one."

"No," he says, sighing. "You owe me several."

I sit at my desk, piled with reports I've been tasked to do, and think about whether or not I should tell Maclin that Gary's been shot. I gave him my word that I would keep him informed, but I'd really like to talk to Wayne first. I have no idea what Gary told him; how damaging it could be to the department, or how dangerous for me, given that the shooter has been leaving messages seemingly designed to get my attention. Maclin will no doubt hear about it soon enough from his pals in Homicide. But it would probably garner points for me if I tell him first.

Until a few days ago I would have talked to Seth about my dilemma. But my partner has taken a dark turn, extinguishing any trust I might have in him. I don't even know if his dealings with Chuffy connect the dots between the Sinaloans and the dead dealers. The drag on my psyche of all these disparate thoughts makes me want to put my head down on the desk and drift away into unconsciousness.

My dilemma is solved when Maclin comes out of his office and announces to everyone that he's been informed by Homicide that Gary, aka Bunsen Gary, was found dead in the downtown tunnels this morning. Shot in the head and sporting a Bible verse.

Maclin pulls everyone, including me, into the conference room. He waits until we've all settled in and says, "Appearances are that Gary Bukowsky was probably shot with the same kind of handgun used to kill Ernesto Patron, Pico Guerto, and Carlos Rivera, as well as the people in the trap house. So we've got one killer taking out the competition. We're going to let Homicide do their job, but because it's clear that it's all linked to drugs, and because DEA has confirmed that we've got the Sinaloans in town, I think we can all agree that this is pointing in one direction, and we can be a big help to Homicide in this regard. Our focus remains on finding the head of the snake, and in this instance it's El Cuchillo."

Nobody wants to ask the question that must be buzzing inside everyone's head: *What about the whispers that the shooter's a cop?*

As though reading those thoughts, Maclin says, "The rumor that the shooter is a Narcotics officer is just that. A rumor that could have been started by the Sinaloans themselves, looking to make more trouble for us. I'm confident that IA will clear that up very soon."

I catch Ortega frowning, his meaty arms crossed against his chest. He says, "But Gary wasn't a dealer. He was a potential witness to the shooter's ID."

"You sure about his not being a dealer?" Maclin asks.

Ortega shrugs one shoulder. "If he was, it was just enough to keep his own habit fed. The guy was strictly small-time B and E. Why would the cartel waste any time looking for him?"

"And what about the Bible verses?" Craddock asks. "I'm sure that's been on Detective Rhyzyk's mind."

The room gets quiet, and I look at Seth the same moment he looks at me. His expression is unreadable, but his hands are clenched between his knees, the knuckles taut and white.

"The question has crossed my mind a time or two," I say.

Ortega nods and mutters, "*La verdad* with that, *amiga.*"

"There are too many pieces here that don't fit together," I say.

Maclin says, "Isn't that part of your job, Detective? Fitting the pieces together?" He heads for the door, signaling the end of the meeting. "We find the Sinaloans and we'll find the shooter killing the dealers. And then all will be revealed. The who, what, when, and where. Class dismissed."

Seth follows me back to my desk and stands there quietly until everyone is out of earshot.

"I need to talk to you," he says, his voice low and urgent.

"Sure," I say, crossing my arms impatiently. "But make it fast. I'm kind of busy right now."

I'm trying my best to maintain a sufficient level of justifiable anger toward him, but he looks haggard. And, more disturbingly, he looks fearful.

"I don't want to do it at the station," he says. "Can we meet at noon somewhere?"

I think of Wayne, hopefully being picked up at the bus station by James right about now. I'll need my lunch hour to get to James's house, pump Wayne for information, then get back to the station before Maclin can find another excuse to can me permanently.

"I can't do it today," I tell him.

"Then meet me tonight. Please, Riz. It's important."

I swivel in my chair so that my back is turned to him. "I'll let you know later if I can."

I feel him standing behind me for a few seconds before he turns and walks away. And in that moment an unwanted thought crawls its way from some deep recess into my consciousness. I remember my brother, Andrew, calling to me through the locked door of my bedroom, pleading with me to talk to him. But I push that memory out of my mind, like a cannonball from a cannon. My partner's toxic right now. Radioactive. Any proximity to him will lead to my being burned, professionally and personally. For the first time, I'm grateful for desk duty. It gives me an excuse to keep my distance.

Soon after, I get a text from James Earle telling me he waited half an hour at the bus station, but Wayne never showed up.

CHAPTER 25

JANUARY 23, 2014
WHITE ROCK LAKE BIKE PATH

I'm running. It's not fast, and it's not pretty, but I'm running. The path around White Rock Lake is just over nine miles, and I'm circumnavigating it even if I have to crawl most of the way. The tumble I took onto the street the other day was caused by something tearing loose in my right calf. It must have been scar tissue, because the tendon, although still strung tight as a bow-string, remains firm and unbroken.

It's warmed into the fifties, the sun is out, only a little breeze to kiss the brow; perfect weather for a solitary run. *Solitary* being the operative word. I had never realized how exhausting it is to be tied to a desk.

Before leaving the station earlier, I had tried numerous times calling Wayne at his most recent number, but without any luck. It left a sinking feeling in my gut that we'd be having another meeting tomorrow about Wayne being found dead in some back alley. I did manage to track the witness-provided license-plate number to a house in Fort Worth. I passed the information on to Craddock for his follow-up. In thanks, I got his promise for breakfast kolaches tomorrow. If I'm going to eat like Craddock for the next few weeks, I have to make running a habit again.

The lake trail is populated with dog walkers, other runners, and cyclists riding in packs, wearing designer gear and mounted on five-thousand-dollar bikes. When one jerk passes too close for comfort, I fantasize about jamming a stick into the spokes of his bike, upending him headfirst onto the path. I dodge a pair of young moms—blond, perfectly toned, and exquisitely self-aware—pushing expensive strollers.

I pick up the pace, threading my way through a knotted mass of laughing teenagers, the smell of marijuana pungent and clinging to the air like an oily cloud. My thoughts turn uncomfortably to Seth and his plea to talk to him. He doesn't yet know what I know about him. If he tells me what's going on, I give up all deniability. Even if it's only to reveal the truth of his drug use, it will lead to other questions about how and from whom he's getting the product. He would probably tell me that I wouldn't understand. That I couldn't understand the addictive pull of hard narcotics. But in that he would be wrong.

There's a break in the crowd, the path opens up, and I funnel all my energies into my legs. Every bodily process that had struggled to find equilibrium at the beginning of the run—my breathing, my pulse rate, the smaller, deeper muscles rebelling under the tyranny of the stronger, major muscles—now relaxes into the rhythm of synchronous, long-remembered movement. The acid-bright chemicals churned up by muscles under pressure, squeezed forcefully through drowsy glands and beleaguered organs, begin to sharpen all my senses and, like peering through a telescope backward, a clear channel to past memory comes more sharply into focus.

* * *

I'm in Brooklyn, working on my first buy-and-bust as an undercover a few miles from the Cypress Hills projects, the most dangerous place on the borough's east side. It's 2002 and I've been sitting for weeks, night after night, in a bar called the Kiln, letting low-level dealer after bottom-feeding skank hit on me. They'd offer me drugs and drinks and knockoff watches for a quick blowjob or hand job or pony ride in the parking lot out back. The only counterbalance to the weariness of saying no to the dregs day after day was the charged wariness of waiting for the right gangbanger to ask me if I wanted to buy some heroin. But not just any heroin. What I was waiting for was so pure that it had been labeled No Regrets, a sick joke on the users who took too much too fast. The Euclid Avenue gang from Cypress Hills reputedly had cornered the local distribution, which would make them the most powerful and sought-after heroin dealers in Brooklyn—so long as they could hold on to their territory.

Originating in Colombia, No Regrets was brought into the States by Dominicans, who stepped on it a few times and then sold it exclusively to the EA gang. The drug had been showing up in area hospital labs for months, suspended in blood samples drawn from the corpses of the unsuspecting users who had OD'd, unaware of its industrial strength.

I'm wired for sound, but the Narcotics officers listening in to my conversations are blocks away. To park their van any closer to the Kiln would invite a savage knock on the window by some street enforcer—or, far worse, a barrage of nine-millimeter shots through the windshield.

My partner at the time, Tony Esparza, was a Young Turk, wiry, with ceaseless energy; a showboater who was pathologically fear-less. He had worked five years of drug undercover in the worst parts of the Bronx and had crazy eyes. When I was first part-nered with him, I had been warned by an older, more experienced cop who knew my fanatical cleaving to the straight and narrow that Tony was dirty—and that he would demand, as an article of faith, that I take my cut from cash liberated from street deal-ers. For me not to partake would invite trouble. I requested a new partner from the department chief. My request was denied.

While I waited at the Kiln, Tony would come into the bar, posing as my coke dealer. My cover was that I was the daughter of a rich businessman, and that my recreational cocaine use had turned into a full-blown, thousand-dollar-a-week habit. I left ex-travagant tips for the bartender to let me sit in a booth in the back and wait for Tony, who sometimes wouldn't show up for hours. My nervousness at being made was the perfect precipitator of the shiny-faced, shallow-breathing, excitable talk of a true cokehead. I let it be known to the bartender that I had always wanted to graduate to the brown stuff, but that I was afraid of the filler—the trash the heroin was often cut with. I'd heard rumors about a powdered heroin from Colombia that was as pure as a virgin and as soft as a baby's kiss.

One night, after a few weeks of waiting, two black teenagers came into the bar, exchanged a few words with the bartender, and then pimp-rolled their way toward my booth at the back. I mum-bled for the benefit of the wire, "They're here."

The boys were dead-eyed and whippet-thin, each wearing a Gucci hoodie and fifteen-hundred-dollar Balmain jeans, low-riding enough to reveal over their waistbands the grips of two large pistols. Both wore watches that cost more than my car. They smelled of cigarettes and expensive cologne. One boy sat across from me. The other pushed his way into the booth next to me, his thigh crushed insistently against mine.

"What you want, white girl?" the boy across from me asked.

The boy next to me passed his hand in front of my face, making me flinch, but he only pulled a strand of hair away from my eyes. "You've got pretty hair, girl," he said. "Smells good, too."

"Are you the guys with the stuff?" I asked nervously.

The boy across from me laughed, showing two rows of strong, perfect teeth. The laugh was unrestrained, as though he was genuinely delighted with the question.

"Oh, we got stuff for you, white girl. We hear you like the white powder but want to try some brown."

The boy next to me nudged me with his thigh. "You like brown?" he asked, smiling.

He brought out a white paper packet and opened it on the table. Inside was a small amount of beige powder, dull and fine as talcum. With a credit card he separated out an amount the size of a pinhead, then scooped it up with the long nail of his pinkie finger and held it under my nose.

I stopped breathing.

"Do it," he demanded.

The boy across from me said, "If you don't do it, we gonna think the worst of you. You feel me?"

As soon as the two teens had come into the bar, most of the patrons had quickly left. The few who had stayed had migrated closer to the part of the bar nearest the door. The bartender had turned his back to us, polishing and repolishing the same pitted beer glasses. All conversation had stopped.

Tony was in the surveillance van a few blocks away listening to my wire. My eyes flicked nervously to the front entrance. Tony should have already been through the door.

"Wait," I said, trying to smile. "I don't want to do it here. What if I nod off—"

The boy across from me leaned across the table. "That happens, we take care of you."

The boy next to me leaned in close and whispered forcefully in my ear: "My arm gettin' tired. Do it now."

I pinched one nostril closed. The boy's fingernail with the powder slid into the other nostril, and I sniffed hard.

The warmth that spread through me then was like nothing I'd ever experienced before. No amount of alcohol or nicotine or endorphins from a ten-mile run—no sweat-soaked, revenge-fueled sex with the perfect stranger, no controlled dive from a high, lakeside cliff—had ever come close to giving me the euphoria I felt in those few minutes after snorting that heroin. Everything, and nothing, seemed important in that moment. All my cares and anxieties over my work or family, my ambitions and my desires, had crumbled to a fine powder that could be flicked away like dust from a table.

I must have smiled, a rictus of mindless animal pleasure, because the boy across from me said, "Yeah, that's it. You good now, right?"

I wanted to nod to him that he was right, the only right thing in the entire universe, but I couldn't control my movements. My chin fell to my chest, my head too heavy to hold upright. The boy next to me refolded the paper packet and placed it in my hand.

He said, "This worth three hundred dollars. But you keep it. When it's gone, you come see us again and we'll set you up good."

They talked to me about my rich friends, people with money who'd want to get hooked up as well, but I was too stoned to answer them. Finally they got up to leave and I watched them glide away, almost weeping over the beauty of the world. At some point afterward, Tony came in and sat in the spot vacated by the boy with the perfect teeth.

"You didn't make the buy," he said, looking at the packet in my lax fingers. He made an ugly smile. "But you made a score—didn't you, Rhyzyk? Guess you're not Snow White after all."

Tony helped me to his car and drove me home. He labored me up the three flights of stairs to my apartment and levered me onto the bed. I didn't have the strength to stop him when he started undressing me, but something in my eyes, smudged with eyeliner the color of old bruises, made him pause, and he left me to live or die on my own. An hour later I was sicker than I'd ever been in my life, the continuous retching breaking the delicate capillaries in both eyes.

I made it to the briefing with my sergeant the next day, telling him that I'd had food poisoning. My partner and the other detectives on surveillance the previous night never disputed my story. They had their own secrets to keep. I continued to work on the Euclid Avenue gang, making several small buys, until we made our arrests with a ten-thousand-dollar exchange.

I held on to that packet of brown heroin for years. Stashed inside a book, it was there, whispering to me, throughout my mother's struggle with terminal cancer, my father's inevitable death from alcoholism, and the memory and guilt of my brother's suicide. It called to me through all of the duty days filled with the ugliness of need, incessant violence, and the petty, vengeful squabbles within my squad. I had kept the drug close to me for so many years not because it was easy to ignore, but precisely because it had been so hard. For every joke I heard my colleagues tell about junkies—for all their dismissive, pitiless actions and their revulsion toward the addicts they arrested or sent in a meat wagon to the morgue—I knew better than anyone the drug's siren call.

How very, very good it could be, burning away every hurt within the furnace of my body, making the world, for the briefest span of moments, a kind of heaven.

Not even Uncle Benny had known about the packet of heroin tucked away in my apartment. If I'd thrown it away, it would have been because I had to. I couldn't bear to name the power it had over me.

At the thought of Uncle Benny, something deep in my brainpan tingles like the touch of a cauterizing wire. I remember the brief instant I thought I'd seen him outside the tunnel, and I feel a tendril of some gossamer thread, like a spider web, touch the back of my neck. Someone is calling my name. My feet stutter to a stop on the trail, and I turn and look for the person who'd called to me, but see no one else on the path.

Glancing at the pedometer on my watch, I see that I've run most of eight miles around the lake without stumbling, without injury, without any major pain. I walk the last mile and a half, cooling off, my breath rapidly easing to a normal rhythm, buoyant and quietly but joyously exhilarated. It was Uncle Benny's voice I had heard. Of all the uncertainties and doubts in my life, of that I am sure.

CHAPTER 26

JANUARY 24, 2014
THE ALAMO MOTEL

My desk phone rings, but when I answer it all I can hear is someone ugly-crying.

"Who's this?" I ask.

"That bastard's beat me for the last time—" the voice says in between great racking sobs.

"Hold on, hold on," I say. "Is this Pearla?"

"I want that mouth-breathing troglodyte to go *down*! This is the last time Chuffy Bryant lays hands on me—"

"What the hell are you doing hooking up with him again?"

"I got lonely," she says, sniffing. "And you only paid for two nights at the motel. But no sooner I show up at *his* motel than we're arguing, and he punches me in the jaw. He loosened my *motherfucking tooth*!"

"Pearla, you need to calm down if you're going to talk to me."

I listen to thirty seconds of ragged breathing.

"I'm going to tell you something," she says, blowing her nose loudly. "That son of a bitch has got a backpack full of that stolen Mexican powder in his room. You blow the whistle on him this time and he ain't going back to jail for no petty shit. There must be ten thousand dollars of H in that one room, and he says that ain't even all of it."

"Where is he now?"

"At the Alamo Motel down by Fair Park. Room one-oh-six, baby."

I write down the information and promise her I'll send it up the right channels. That the drugs are stolen makes me ponder a connection to the Sinaloans. "Just stay away from the Alamo, Pearla, unless you want to get caught up in the sweep."

After I disconnect, I sit staring at the door to Maclin's office and imagine it burning. But I get up and knock on the door and enter.

"A CI just called me with information about a dealer working out of the Alamo," I say. "He's selling a substantial amount of heroin, and he's at the motel now. Room one-oh-six."

Maclin sighs, but doesn't look impressed. "It's a solid source," I say. "The dealer's Chuffy Bryant. The CI says the heroin is stolen."

Now Maclin looks interested. "Stolen from where?" he asks.

I shrug. "Not sure. But it's a pretty strong coincidence having the Sinaloans looking for some jacked H, don't you think?"

He picks up his phone. "I'll call for a warrant. But you'd better be right about this. Send Craddock and Ryan in here, would you?"

Closing the door, I mutter, "You're welcome."

My phone rings—Pearla again.

"There's one more thing I have to tell you," she says. "That cop I was telling you about? The one doing the deals with Chuffy? He's there too."

She's talking about Seth. My hand grips the phone so tightly that I think I'll crack the case. Kevin Ryan is walking toward me, but I hold up a finger and turn my chair so my back is to him. "You sure?" I ask.

"He was there when I left fifteen minutes ago. I was so upset before that I forgot to tell you."

Frozen in place, I have to remind myself to breathe.

"Hello?" Pearla says. "You still there?"

"Yes. I'll take care of it, Pearla. Just stay away from the motel."

"Don't you worry, I got what I needed from that bastard."

I disconnect and sit perched on the edge of my chair, every muscle straining toward some kind of action. My partner, if he's still there, will be arrested too. Serious jail time. Game over, end of his career. End of his life.

There's a strong impulse to call Seth and warn him to get away from Chuffy Bryant. I start to call him, then disconnect. If he's arrested, how will it look to Internal Affairs that my number showed up on his phone shortly before a drug bust? I already have an interview scheduled with IA in the afternoon regarding the investigation that a cop is involved in the dealer shootings. I look at the clock: eleven thirty, close to lunchtime. I have an hour, maybe a little more, to be gone from the station.

There's a motion over my shoulder. It's Ryan looking to talk to me.

"I did some checking on that OneNation website like you asked me to," he says.

"Oh?" I say, trying to remember the context.

"The Bible verses found on the dealers?"

"Right," I say, standing up, hoping to keep the conversation short.

"There's been no new activity on the website by the Roy family that I can see."

"That's good," I say, reaching for my coat.

"But there's some older posts that I'd like to talk to you about."

"That's great, Kev, thanks. But let's do it later, okay? Maclin wants you and Tom in his office right now. He's getting a warrant for a drug bust."

I head for the station exit before he can detain me further. My knees give out in the stairwell, and I sit, my head in my hands. Maclin has a judge on speed dial, and he'll have a warrant in an hour's time or less, especially once the judge hears the words *possible Sinaloan connection* and that the bust will be at the Alamo Motel. If Seth is still there, he'll go down hard. This is it. This is the one and only time I can come to his rescue.

A bad accident on US 75 forces me to burn more than forty minutes getting to the Alamo Motel, the blood roaring in my ears. At every exit, I weigh returning to the station, but I keep driving until I turn in to the entrance to the motel. A few underdressed pavement princesses lean against the building, smoking and waving dispiritedly to passing cars. I check the parked cars in the front lot, but don't see Seth's truck. I spot it, however, when I drive around to the other side of the motel.

The back lot is almost empty, only a few cars and one SUV— expensive, black, with darkly tinted windows. Its engine is idling, the occupant probably waiting for one of the hookers or his chance to score or sell drugs. The license-plate number seems familiar, so I write it down. The Alamo has been raided so many times by Narcotics and Vice that in law-enforcement circles it's earned the nickname the Take Down Motel. Room 106 is on the ground floor, in the middle of the row of rooms. I put the car in park with the engine on, debating how to extract Seth without letting Chuffy know I'm nearby. If Chuffy does find out, he'll do a runner.

Driving back to the front of the motel, I signal to one of the working girls. She throws down her cigarette and walks to the car, hips swinging in exaggerated thrusts, but laughs when she sees me.

"Oh, it's like that? I charge extra for the ladies," she says, grinning.

"I just need you to knock on a door and ask for a guy named Riot to come out. And bring him out front, to me," I say. "I'll pay you forty bucks for two minutes of work."

She squints her eyes and cocks her head. "Why should I do that? This guy dangerous?"

"Not for you he's not. Just knock on the door and ask for Riot. Say his sister wants to have a word with him, and bring him to me."

"His sister, huh? You a cop?" she asks in a friendly, conversational way.

I put my badge in the glove compartment and hand her twenty dollars, withholding the second bill. "Not right now I'm not. You get the other twenty when you bring him back here."

She palms the twenty and I can almost see the wheels spinning in her head: take the twenty dollars and run, or knock on a door and get twenty more. She turns and disappears around the back of the motel. For the five minutes I wait in the car, I struggle with the growing concern that Seth will not come out, that his ability to improvise in any situation will desert him. Or that he'll know it's me but ignore my summons. I scan the street nervously for patrol cars.

The woman walks back with Seth in tow, his face flushed with anger or alarm or both. I tell him, "Get in the car."

The woman collects her remaining twenty dollars and walks rapidly toward the street, away from the motel.

In the car Seth opens his mouth to talk, but I say, "Very soon there will be cops here to arrest Chuffy Bryant. Maclin's probably already got the warrant, and he's sending Craddock and Ryan down here with some uniforms."

"How did he know we'd be here?" Seth asks.

"I told him. Pearla called me and told me all about the stolen heroin. Looks like Chuffy picked the wrong person to rough up."

"You don't know what's going on."

"Oh, I think I have a pretty good idea."

"You shouldn't have told Maclin."

I'm resisting the urge to punch him. "I'm risking my career— hell, I'm risking *jail time*—by giving you a heads-up." I'm yelling now.

"Would you let me explain?"

"What, that you're an addict? That you stole pills off a dead man—a dead man who was a suspect in a drug investigation? And that you're probably dealing drugs this instant with Chuffy Bryant? Yeah, I saw you with Chuffy at the Circus."

He stares at me, his eyes steadily on mine, and for an instant I think I've got it wrong—that somehow I've missed something important. But then I remember about addicts and their inability to tell the truth.

I put the car in drive, my foot still on the brake. "Neither of us has time to sit and sift through the situation right now. I've told you what's happening. You can stay or go, but if I were you I'd drive away and not look back. This is the last time I do this, Seth."

I stare at him until he climbs out of my car, and I drive away. And I don't look back.

By the time I get back to the station, Craddock and Ryan are at the motel to make the arrest. Maclin signals for me to come into his office.

"That was a damn long lunch break," he scolds.

He has Craddock on the line and puts his phone on speaker.

"You want to tell Detective Rhyzyk what transpired?" he says.

"When we got to the Alamo, the door to one-oh-six was open and we found no suspect, no drugs," Craddock says. I close my eyes and exhale; Seth was not there. But neither was Chuffy, which means he must have been warned off.

"But the place tested positive for traces of heroin," Craddock says. "So somebody had drugs in the room. Also, somebody bled a goodly amount on the carpet."

I move closer to Maclin's phone. "Say that again."

"There's blood on the carpet. Somebody either had a hell of a bloody nose or didn't leave the room willingly."

Could it be Pearla's blood from her beatdown by Chuffy? Or maybe it's Chuffy's—or, worse, Seth's. Pulling my notebook out of my coat, I look at the plate number of the idling SUV in the back parking lot. I know now where I've seen that number before.

"Anyone in the parking lot look suspicious when you got there?" I ask.

"A few parked sedans. Two pickup trucks. All unoccupied. We're running the plates on all of them."

So the black SUV had disappeared by the time Craddock arrived. Maclin's scrutinizing me closely, a tight little smirk on his face. He seems to be enjoying the fact that I'm stuck doing desk duty while the real detectives are out in the field. And that the raid for which I provided information was unsuccessful.

"Okay, Tom, let me know when you've got anything else," Maclin says. "We'll catch him down the road."

For a man who missed out on a potentially important bust, Maclin hasn't even broken a sweat. He's remarkably nonplussed. I would have expected him to crawl down my throat for giving him an unproductive lead and wasting departmental resources. But he dismisses me without further comment, so I go back to my desk to reconfirm what I already know: the SUV

I'd observed at the Alamo Motel is the same vehicle the witness had seen leaving the location of the second Nuevo Juarez dealer found dead. The SUV is registered to an Anna Solario with a Fort Worth address. No prior criminal record. Not even a parking ticket. The car has no liens, title in Solario's name. She also happens to be seventy years old, and unlikely to have chosen a two-ton vehicle to go to the local grocery store. My guess is the car is an "Often Used" Vehicle, derived from OFFTN (Old Friends From The Neighborhood). She herself is not in a crime syndicate, but her name is being used by individuals committing crimes in a "clean" car registered to her. Drill down deep enough into Anna Solario's history and she'll be an aunt, a granny, a wife, a mother to a cartel member. Once the criminals are finished with their business in Dallas, my guess is the car will disappear—and Ms. Solario will declare it stolen and collect on the insurance, buying herself a more sensible car.

Craddock no doubt knows all of this. But what he doesn't know is that I spotted the car at the Alamo as well, and that it was gone by the time he got there. I could tell him I got an anonymous tip from my CI, but I wouldn't be able to corroborate it. And it would be another untruth to add to my many lies by omission. I have to let it go and hope that we catch another break.

I'm so deep into my worry and anger over Seth's disappearance that I don't hear my phone ring. Ortega has to yell at me, "Yo, Rhyzyk—pick up!" It's IA, telling me they're ready for my interview.

Every cop in his or her career will probably be questioned by Internal Affairs at least once. Usually it's in response to a dissatisfied civilian's complaint, but there are many other reasons for an internal investigation, ranging from code infractions to unnecessary use of force to, worst of all, a shooting resulting in a death. Preparedness is everything: for any interview, it's recommended that you know exactly what the investigative team is looking for ahead of time, bring notes, and answer in as few words as possible.

My first time with IA was during my first year of active duty with NYPD. A civilian had filed a complaint against a rude and obstreperous redheaded female cop making an arrest. Panicked, I had called Uncle Benny for his advice. In response he had asked me, "How does a fish get caught? It opens its mouth. Answer truthfully, but say as little as possible."

I'm informed that the interview with Dallas Internal Affairs should take no more than half an hour, given that they're interviewing the entire North Central Narcotics Division. When I walk into the large interview room, two IA officers are waiting for me. Detective Supervisor Burkley, a large, middle-aged man with a military-style haircut, cut to within a millimeter of his scalp; and Detective Adams, a younger man, his pencil poised to take notes, even though the interview will be recorded. Both are in suits, both are hard-eyed and unsmiling. Burkley asks me to sit down and wastes no time questioning me about the reasons for my suspension and assignment to desk duty. That done, they get to the real agenda: the rumors of cops killing drug dealers.

"Detective Rhyzyk," Burkley asks, "are you aware of any rumors of police officers involved in the shooting deaths of drug dealers in the city of Dallas?"

"Yes," I answer.

"How were you made aware of these rumors?" he asks.

"Detective Tilton told me of the rumors on January tenth."

"Where were you when Detective Tilton told you of these rumors?"

"I was at my house."

"Was this before or after you were put on suspension?"

"After," I say.

"Did you discuss these rumors with anyone else?"

"No."

"Did you contact the news media—specifically, any print outlet—about these rumors?"

"No."

Burkley pauses to look through his notes. Imagining the next set of questions, I start to sweat: *Have you heard any law-enforcement officers make threatening statements to any drug dealers? Are you aware of any illegal drug activities among any Dallas police officers?* To which I will have to tell the truth about my colleagues.

But DS Burkley is full of surprises.

He asks, "Have you been involved in any illegal-gambling activities within the state of Texas?"

I look at him, surprised. "No, never."

Gambling for low stakes in someone's home is not illegal in Texas, but betting for high stakes in public spaces is. And though drugs and gambling often go hand in hand, local illegal gambling is handled by Vice.

"You look disturbed by the question," he says.

"Not disturbed. It was just unexpected."

"Are you aware of any officer in your department who's been involved in illegal gambling?" Burkley asks.

"No," I say.

Burkley looks at me closely for a few seconds, then scribbles a few notes. He confers quietly with Adams for a moment, then concludes the interview, telling me I can go.

Several things occur to me as I head back to my desk, legs spongy with stress. I have dodged a bullet in incriminating my fellow officers about statements regarding dead drug dealers, as well as illegal drug use within the department. And it's obvious that IA has a lead on something beyond an internal drug-cartel war. Now illegal gambling has been thrown into the mix. My first thoughts stray to my partner, wondering if Seth might be mixed up in illegal gambling as well.

I walk out of the station at day's end feeling gutted like the proverbial fish, fried over a hot skillet. At some point while I was in the IA interview, Seth had come back to the station. He was filling out a report at his desk, and neither of us acknowledged the other. He appeared whole and unscathed—no scrapes, cuts, or bloody nose—but his expression was wretchedly grim, and overall he looked as bad as I felt. But I didn't stop to ask him any questions about what happened at the motel. I don't want to know.

When I get home, before I even unclip my gun or change clothes, I go straight for the kitchen and the bottle of Jameson. Jackie is somewhere in the house. She's been home from the conference for a few days, but we haven't spoken much. I can hear her talking on the phone, but I don't want to have to make conversation with her just yet. I pour a double shot into a glass and knock back half of it. I want to drown, as quickly as possible, the events of the day. About the time I'm thinking of sneaking out and driving to Dottie's for some serious liquid therapy, the doorbell rings.

"Can you get that?" Jackie yells from the bedroom.

I quickly down the rest of the Jameson, but before I've made it even to the foyer I feel a rush of light-headedness, and I grab for the doorframe to steady myself. I've not eaten all day and the alcohol has burned its way directly into my bloodstream.

The doorbell chimes again, and I growl, "Okay, I'm coming," and fling open the door.

Standing on the front porch is Evangeline Roy.

She smiles and says, "Are you Betty?"

Without thinking, I draw my gun and shout, "Freeze. Don't move!"

The woman screams and cowers, and I see too late that it's not Evangeline Roy but a short, thirtyish-looking woman, her thick arms crossed defensively over her face, her red hair peeking up past her elbows like a frightened cardinal. She shuffles backward until the heels of her shoes wobble uncertainly over the edge of the porch. Then, arms and legs flailing, she topples onto the lawn.

Jackie has run to the door and sees the woman splayed in our yard, me, and my service weapon. I holster the gun with shaking hands.

"Oh my God," she says, running off the porch to help the woman up. She apologizes breathlessly, examining her for injuries.

"What is wrong with you?" Jackie yells at me. "It's the goddamn midwife!"

I had completely forgotten about the home visit. The midwife is still clearly shaken, and she looks at me reproachfully as she stands and brushes herself off. Fortunately she was well padded with a heavy coat and, well, a lot of her own padding.

At that moment, something very near hysteria bubbles up beneath my ribs. The sight of the woman's quivering chin and sensible shoes, making her resemble an overly large toddler, forces a bark of laughter from my mouth. I clap my hand over my lips, but it's no good. The day, and the alcohol, have gotten the better of me, and I howl with laughter. The more I try to contain it, the harder I laugh. Choking and coughing, I stumble back into the house. I can't breathe or speak. I can't even stand anymore. I can only guffaw outlandishly, uncontrollably. Falling on the couch, I'm only vaguely aware of Jackie coming back into the house and standing in front of me.

She waits until I've regained control, then says, "We've lost the midwife—"

"And now from the BBC, it's *Don't Call the Midwife*!" I yelp helplessly, and have to bite my tongue to prevent a new outbreak of unmoored giggling.

Jackie doesn't join in. "She's not coming back, and she may file a complaint."

Tears clouding my eyes, I struggle to regain my composure. Jackie crosses her arms and says, "I think you need to move out until you regain some equilibrium."

CHAPTER 27

I pour a generous amount of Jameson into the plastic cup provided by the front office, kick off my boots, and flop onto the bed.

Flop being the apt word to describe my new digs: two double beds, a small table, two ratty chairs, and an ancient TV set make up the contents of the room. The bathroom is so small I can't sit on the toilet and close the door without taking off my kneecaps. I had already wadded up the bedspread—ornately patterned with flowers in an attempt to hide the abundance of spills and human effluvia that would christen the fabric over the years—and thrown it into one corner. As well, I'd spread a hand towel over the pillow in case the maid hadn't changed the linens since last Christmas. The towel would leave tiny, pointillist pockmarks on my cheek in the morning, but better pillow scars than a staph infection.

I'd rented the room for the week, hopeful that my banishment from home wouldn't last longer than that. In customary self-flagellating style, I don't take the motel room I can afford but the one I think I deserve. Earlier I had texted Jackie my location, hoping she'd see the name of the motel and take pity on me. I sip the Jameson and dial her number.

"Hello," she answers.

"Hey. It's me," I say.

"Hey."

"You doing okay?"

"Yes. I'm fine. You?"

"I'm okay. I called and left a message for Dr. Theo."

"That's good," she says.

There's a long pause and then I say, "Jackie, I'm just so very sorry for everything I've put you through. I love you."

There's another pause.

"God," I say, "I sounded so straight just then, didn't I?"

Normally that would have gotten a laugh, but I hear only breathing.

"I love you too—" she says.

I wait for the *but*.

"But I need some time to not be angry all the time. I don't like who I'm becoming because of it."

"I understand," I say, because that's what you're supposed to say when someone you love tells you they're better when they're not with you. "Is it okay to call you in the morning?" I ask.

"Of course. Get some sleep," she says, and ends the call abruptly.

I finish off the Jameson in one gulp and lie back on the bed, closing my eyes. *Equilibrium,* I murmur to myself. *Equilibrium.* Rolling the syllables past my tongue and into the darkened room. Until a few months ago, all that meant to me was successfully closing a case, having a drink with my partner, running seven miles, then coming home to Jackie to feel her breath on my skin…

There's a knock on the door. The only person who knows where I'm staying is Jackie, and it can't be her because I just talked to her at home. It's also unlikely to be housekeeping because it's not a leap year.

"Who is it?" I ask.

"It's Mary Grace," the muffled voice says. "Jackie told me where you were."

When I open the door, she throws herself against me, hugging me tightly, her big belly knocking the air out of my lungs.

"I feel so bad you got kicked out of your house," she tells me.

"I wasn't really kicked out—"

"What's going on?" she asks.

"Nothing—" I say.

Mary Grace perches on the second bed. "Anything I can do to help?"

"How'd you get here?"

She gives me an exasperated look. "I do know how to take a taxi."

I pull out my cell phone. "Well, I'm calling you another. You're going back to Dottie's."

"Nope," she says, scooting back onto the bed. "I'm staying here for the night. With you. Dottie's great and all, but if I hear one more k. d. lang album I'm going to scream. Besides, I don't want you to be alone tonight."

I call Dottie and tell her Mary Grace is spending the night with me. As soon as I disconnect, there's another knock on the door.

I look at Mary Grace, who shrugs. "Who's there?" I call.

"Me," a familiar voice says.

"Me who?" I ask warily.

"It's Dusty Rose. Let me in."

I open the door halfway. Dusty stands resplendent in a black wig, one hand on her hip, pocketbook dangling from her arm, the other hand holding a blue duffel bag. She's wearing a rabbit-fur coat dyed green, a Russian Cossack hat, and yellow cowboy boots.

"How'd you find me?"

"Well, since you wouldn't answer my calls, I called Jackie, and she told me where you were. You going to do the polite thing and offer me a drink?"

I open the door wider and she brushes past me.

"Oh dear," she says. "The Health Department know about this place?"

She sits on the second bed next to Mary Grace and gives her a hug. I pour some Jameson into the other plastic cup, then give myself a refill.

Dusty demurely crosses her legs and composes her face into a look of concern. "You working undercover, or did you and Jackie have a falling-out?" she asks.

"They had a falling-out," Mary Grace says.

"It's nothing, Dusty. We're just working through some things."

Dusty takes a healthy swig of the whiskey. "Pearla called me today."

Reflexively I tense up, bracing for more bad news. "She did, did she?"

"Mm-hmm. She told me she called you about what Chuffy's been up to. And about that certain someone *who shall remain nameless.*"

I give her a warning look, cutting my eyes to Mary Grace.

"Oh, relax, Ms. Betty, Dusty Rose knows about loyalty. His se-cret is safe with me."

"Whose secret?" Mary Grace asks.

"Nobody's," I tell her. "Besides, the information Pearla gave me didn't do me any good. By the time my colleagues showed up, the motel room was empty. No Chuffy, no anyone else."

"Well, maybe I can do you some good, then." Dusty pulls the duffel bag closer. "This is the bag Pearla took from Chuffy's room this morning."

Don't you worry, Pearla had told me over the phone. *I got what I needed from that bastard.*

"What are you doing with it?" I ask.

"She put it in my trunk when I rescued her today. But I'm holding it for her until she pays me back what she owes me." Dusty puts the plastic cup coyly to her lips and smiles. "She seems in a fever pitch to get it back, too."

"What's in the bag?" Mary Grace asks.

She unzips the bag and rummages through it. "Clothes, shoes, some blue eye shadow I wouldn't put on a pig. And," she says, holding up a set of keys, "these."

She hands me the ring of keys, attached to which is a large plastic tag inscribed *Delano's Boxing Gym.*

"Pearla said Chuffy boosted the stuff from some gym," Dusty says, pointing to the keys. "Well, Delano's was Chuffy's gym when he did his MMA stint. I drove by there on my way here. It's been closed down, some of the windows boarded over. What if it's where he took the stuff?"

Mary Grace, looking from Dusty to me: "What stuff?"

Pearla had also said that what Chuffy had with him in the motel wasn't "even all of it." The rest of the heroin is unlikely to be in the same place where Chuffy first found it, but it's worth telling Craddock about it so he can check it out tomorrow.

Echoing my thoughts, Dusty says, "What if the rest of the stuff is still at Delano's? That would be quite a feather in your cap, wouldn't it? It would get you off desk duty and back on the streets, pronto."

Mary Grace grabs Dusty by the arm. "Will somebody please tell me what you're talking about?"

Dusty pats her hand. "Drugs, baby girl—lots of drugs."

"Don't tell her that," I snap.

Dusty drapes a protective arm over Mary Grace's shoulder. "Listen, she's in the dragon's nest now. She needs to know what's going on."

Mary Grace looks at me, eyes wide. "Anything I can do to help? There's a lot of stuff I know how to do." She smiles conspiratorially. "I know how to pick locks. I can bust a combo lock too."

"Oh really?" I say, making a mental note to ask more questions about Ms. Pregger's past life. "I'm not sure I want to know any more than that."

Dusty has poured herself another large helping of Jameson. "Well, I say since we're all here, let's have a girls' sleepover."

"Oh no," I say. "This is not going to work."

"Officer," Dusty says, holding up her empty cup, "it's going to get icy tonight, and I've had too much to drink to drive."

She puts her arm around Mary Grace again. "How about pizza?" she asks gleefully.

I order a large pepperoni pizza and Dusty finds an old-movie channel. She and Mary Grace eat most of the pizza with their eyes glued to the wavering black-and-white images. The two of them giggle over Barbara Stanwyck pouring a cup of coffee onto a knee-groper's hand.

Mary Grace looks at me, propped up on the other bed feeling sorry for myself, and says, "Things are going to be okay. I'm going to help you."

"You don't have to do anything for me, Mary Grace."

"Hey, that's what family's for."

Her words squeeze my heart like a surgeon's fist, and within the span of a breathtaking moment I've decided no power on earth can dissuade me from letting Mary Grace have her baby in my house. She could give birth to a whole tribe of squirming, slippery newborns and I'd be there as her biggest cheerleader.

"Why can't you just go to the gym and check it out yourself?" Mary Grace asks.

"I'd need a warrant for that," I say.

She looks at me slyly. "What if a civilian did the checking out?"

I wag a monitory finger at her. "You're a dangerous influence, missy. If you want to help, don't encourage my inner pirate."

She giggles, and I ask her, "No further sightings of the woman who gave you the brochure?"

"Not a one," she says. "My life is as boring as oatmeal."

Mary Grace finally falls asleep tucked in the crook of Dusty's muscular arm. Dusty has taken off her wig and is lying on her back, mouth open, gently snoring.

Restless, I want to take a quick run despite the cold, but the whiskey has done its job and I feel the weighted tug of sleep. I turn off the TV and cover Thelma and Louise with a blanket. I quickly brush my teeth, turn up the heat, and crawl into bed.

A relaxed heaviness finally uncoils all my muscles. Wind-driven snowflakes turning to sleet lash the window. I snuggle deeper into the cavelike space beneath my covers, listening to the tiny, rhythmic fingers of rain against the glass.

The storm surge comes in drumming waves, syncopated, almost insectile. The aperture of my waking mind closes, like a camera in between the taking of photographs, and when the lens of awareness comes into focus again I'm cocooned in my old red Toyota, the car heater blowing balmy air in delicious waves. I've got my seat pushed back, my eyes closed, and I'm listening to the radio. I'm waiting for something to happen, but I can't remember what it is. I struggle to open my eyes, the heat making any effort monumental, but finally I turn and look out the driver's window at an empty street. Beyond the street, through the scrim of snow, is a shadowy building, dark except for one brightly lit window on the second floor. It's night—winter in the Loisaidas of Manhattan—and the glow from the apartment spills onto the street. I crane my head to catch any sign of life inside the apartment, but see nothing.

A few sharp raps on the passenger window, yet I see nothing outside but the blackness beyond the storm. Behind me, now, I hear a gentle tapping on the driver's window. The tapping grows more insistent. I don't want to turn and face the window, but I do.

The girl in the yellow pajamas is pressed against the glass—her eyes wide, her hair glistening with snowfall. She pounds her palms urgently on the glass, her mouth working silently. The pounding becomes more frantic, her lips forming words I know I should know.

Then, very clearly, comes Uncle Benny's voice from the back seat: *Betty,* he says. *Sometimes you gotta run **toward** the fire.*

I wake to the sound of my own groaning. I'm sitting up in bed before I've come to full consciousness, momentarily confused by the unfamiliar surroundings. In the bed next to me sprawls Dusty, still asleep, tangled in the blanket. Mary Grace is not beside her. Thinking she's gone to the bathroom, I knock on the door, but it's empty.

An unsettled feeling makes me part the room's window curtain and look out over the parking lot. *Maybe she's gone hunting for a vending machine?* But as I crawl back into bed, I glance at the table where I've put my things: my gun and keys. I turn on the light and see that the keys to both Delano's Gym and my own car are missing.

Roughly shaking Dusty awake, I tell her, "Mary Grace is gone. I think she went to Delano's."

CHAPTER 28

JANUARY 24, 2014
DELANO'S BOXING GYM

We drive to Delano's in the vintage BMW owned by Dusty's current boyfriend, parking on South Lamar in front of the gym, which is housed in an ornate Victorian-style building. Once a prospering neighborhood, the street is now fronted by metalworking shops, trucking firms, liquor stores, and crumbling shotgun houses held up by a thousand coats of paint. A flyer on the wooden door of the gym gives notice that it has been permanently closed. My earlier call to Dottie confirmed what I suspected: Mary Grace had not come back to her house. My empty car parked on the vacant street next to the gym proves that she went to Delano's instead.

An icy rain has begun in earnest, and Dusty reaches over and turns up the heater. I try calling Mary Grace's cell phone one more time, but she doesn't answer.

Dusty points to a second-story window. "There's a light on up there."

The space behind the grimy glass is lit harshly with overhead fluorescent bulbs. But the absence of streetlamps makes the building look like a hulking fortress or prison.

Dusty turns to me. "What in the world was she thinking, coming to a place like this alone, at night?"

"She said she wanted to help me," I say, resisting the urge to bolt out of the car and into the building. A sound begins to build in my ears like the downshifting buzz of a transformer losing power. I have a momentary feeling of disorientation before the electrifying feeling of déjà vu. It is winter, and I am in a car, on a street, in front of an old Victorian building. A stand-alone building like the one in lower Manhattan, blown into a raging fireball.

Loisaidas… The girl in the yellow pajamas…

"Stay here," I tell Dusty. "Give me fifteen or twenty minutes to find Mary Grace. If I'm not out by then or I don't answer my phone, call nine-one-one."

"You sure you don't want me to come in with you?" she asks, pulling a pistol out of her purse. "Hey, don't give me that look. I was in the army, remember?"

"Yes, I'm sure. Stay here. Just keep a sharp eye out, and call me if anyone pulls up front."

I get out of the car, my feet sliding on the ice on the worn asphalt, and pick my way carefully across the street. I climb the few steps to the front door and try the handle. It's unlocked—Mary Grace using Chuffy's gym keys—and the door opens with some gentle pushing. Unholstering the SIG Sauer, I step into the foyer.

The electricity is still on because the entrance area is dimly lit by a few remaining bulbs. The space is empty except for a large corkboard on one wall with notices and flyers pinned in an avalanche of paper announcing old fights and forgotten challenges. There are doors to other rooms, a coat-check concession, and a maintenance closet. The foyer leads to a set of double doors opening into a cavernous arena, also poorly lit—and filled with deep shadows. The ceilings must be thirty feet high, with second-floor viewing balconies on all four sides.

The building is quiet and cold, the age-old stink of sweat, resin, and cigars attesting to the long-ago press of feverish, combative men, clustered in tribal knots.

Folding wooden chairs, new before the Second World War, are scattered haphazardly throughout the room. Piles of debris—fast-food bags, soda cans, fallen plaster from the decaying ceiling—lie in clumps against the chairs and along the skirt of the elevated center ring, as though blown there by a high wind. There have been no boxing matches in this room in a long time. Startled, I realize a man is standing motionless in the middle of the ring, wearing a high-crown Western hat, a shearling coat, and cowboy boots. He shows no surprise at my entry and says nothing to me. There is no sign of Mary Grace.

A jab of metal against the back of my head—the unmistakable press of a gun barrel against my skull—and a man behind me says, "Bend down and put the gun on the floor. If you move the wrong way, I will shoot you."

The man with the gun is practiced at stealth. He had made no sound as he came through the doors behind me. I remind myself to breathe. If he had meant me to kill me right away, I would be dead already.

The man in the ring tilts his head expectantly, as though making a mental bet on what action I will take. I do what the man behind me has demanded and place the gun at my feet. He kicks the gun away and searches my pockets, taking my phones, turning them off, then throwing them carelessly on the floor. He keeps my badge.

Studying his face, I realize that this is the guy at the Circus bar who chased Chuffy Bryant into the alley.

He moves behind me again and taps his gun roughly against

the back of my head, prodding me to move forward, toward the ring. Once I am standing close to the ropes, the man in the ring walks to the edge so that his boots are directly in my line of sight. The leather is smooth and exotic-looking, the color of tea-stained parchment, with a scorpion engraved in the hide of the left boot and a skull encased in thorns in the right. The silver tips are polished to a mirrored shine.

"Detective Rhyzyk," the man says. His voice is heavily accented, deeply resonant, but surprisingly soft. A lover's voice whispered through a bedroom door.

"Alfonso Ruiz Zena," I say, my eyes moving upward past the elaborately tooled belt—studded with carved silver disks and fitted with turquoise—to meet his gaze.

El Cuchillo's face is predatory, the brow bones and chin angled and sharp, the skin beneath his cheeks deeply hollowed and pocked. If the Knife is surprised that I know his true identity, he doesn't show it.

My focus is drawn to the canvas floor behind him. It's splattered with fresh blood. My expression changes, and I go rigid.

"No," he says. "The young woman is alive. And what a gift it will be for you to keep her that way."

Zena moves to the corner to my right, slips deftly through the ropes, and descends the ring steps. He unfolds two chairs and says, "Sit down, Detective."

I sit, and he pulls the other one close to me. He takes off his coat, draping it across the back of the chair. He wears a shoulder holster and, clipped to his belt, a carved leather sheath, slender and eight inches long, a bone-handled knife fitted snugly inside. Our knees touch when he sits down facing me. He removes his hat, smoothing back his hair, black and coarse as a horse's mane, with one hand.

My eyes are pulled to a glistening patch on the floor next to the ring, where a wash of blood is smeared like a trail to the back of the arena, disappearing under a now-closed door.

"Detective," Zena says, mildly, "please do not be distracted by anything other than what I need to know from you. Your friend's life will depend upon it. As will yours." He shifts in his chair, leaning toward me. "We have searched the entire gym, but we have not found what was taken from me."

"Where is she?" I ask, forcing myself to meet his gaze.

He looks at me unblinking for a moment, then nods to the man with the gun. The gunman pulls out a phone and calls someone, mumbling a few words of Spanish.

Zena settles back in his chair, studying me. His movements are deliberate, spare, fluid, like a dancer's. I glance at his hands, the fingers long and tapered; where the fingernails meet the cuticle, they are crusted with something dark that was once red.

"I have been very interested in you," he says. "The Roy family, yes? You were taken by them and tortured. But you escaped, by your wits. By your courage."

His gaze captures and holds mine. "You killed a man," he says. "With a large knife."

My mouth is parchment-dry. "It was a bayonet," I croak.

"A what?"

"A Civil War bayonet."

A twitch ripples across his lips. "You are a very interesting person, Detective. I've also heard on the street that you have a large—" He pauses and looks to his gunman. *"Como se dice 'adorno'?"*

"Adornment," the gunman says.

"Adornment," Zena repeats. "On your right leg. The Angel of Vengeance. San Miguel. I would love to see it."

Involuntarily I glance at his boots with their monstrous designs, then force myself to look him in the face again. "To do that," I say, my intestines turning to water, "you're going to need a bigger pair of—*Como se dice* 'boots' *en español?*"

There is another twitch of the lips, but the eyes are as dead as ball bearings.

The door in the back of the arena opens—the door with the trail of blood—and another man, holding on to Mary Grace's arm, walks her toward us a few feet and then stops. Reflexively I start to stand, but the gunman puts a hand on my shoulder, forcing me down. Her face is milk-pale, her eyes wide and filled with tears, but she doesn't look injured—only terrified. She opens her mouth to speak but manages only a groan. The man turns around and leads her stumbling back through the rear exit. The door closes again.

"Now, Detective," Zena says. "Do you know where my heroin is?"

"No," I say. "I figured out that the heroin was taken from the gym. But I have no idea where it is now."

"Why did your friend come here, then?"

"She overheard me talking about it. I didn't tell her to come here."

Zena gives me a doubting look.

"Hey," I say, "I don't know where your drugs are. If I knew, I'd tell you. It's not worth losing our lives for something that will be back on the street in a week from some other source."

"Unfortunately, that is precisely the point," he says. "Some other source robbing me of over a million dollars. It's not a loss I will take lightly. So, I will ask you one last time. Where are my drugs?"

"I don't know. Why don't you ask Chuffy Bryant? Isn't he the one who stole them in the first place?"

Something in Zena's expression shifts, hardens. I want to keep him talking as long as possible.

"Is that the reason for the dead Nuevo Juarez dealers?" I ask. "You were trying to find out who had the heroin?"

"That is what led me here, to Dallas," he says.

"And what about the other dealers, the ones you shot?"

"Ah, that was something completely different. It had more to do with clearing the streets. I did not shoot them. But I will tell you something," he says, leaning close enough for me to feel his breath on my face. "The person who shot them is someone very close to you. Someone who, in cleaning up his own mess, was making sure that you would feel the weight of your past mistakes."

"Is it a cop?" I ask.

For the first time there's a glint of satisfaction in his eyes, and he says, "Yes, Detective Rhyzyk, it is."

He stands, putting on his coat. He nods to his gunman and says, *"Llevala arriba con la otra."*

The gunman motions with his pistol for me to stand, and we walk toward the rear exit, following the trail of blood, now drying in rusty swaths. My eyes search for anything I can use for defense, or as a barrier between me and the two men. I calculate the odds of making a grab for Zena's weapon, using him as a human shield, running. But Zena appears to be all sinew and muscle, and the gunman behind me, as though sensing the rising tension in my body, mutters, *"No intentes nada!"*

"I used to box as a young man in Culiacán," Zena says, gesturing to the upper galleries as though to an audience. "Bare-knuckle fights in the Barrio de San Luis where I grew up. But it was not for pride. No. At first it was simply to eat. And then it became something else."

His voice carries no emotional weight. It's mild, matter-of-fact, as though giving a tour of a shoe factory. *Or a boot factory,* my mind screams irrationally. One he's given a hundred times before. We approach the back door and he pauses. I lock my knees to keep my thighs from quivering.

"Do you know that in Mexico it is common for the fighters to hide razor blades between their knuckles?" he tells me. "You can injure a man in the ring while his blood is up, and he will bleed out before he even realizes that he's been cut. That is the persuasion of anger, the pull of revenge. When you're calm," he says, opening the door and motioning politely for me to pass through, "you feel every pass of the blade."

Behind the boxing arena is a narrow hallway, paint peeling from the walls in wide patches, with a switchback staircase rising to the second floor. The blood trail on the floor leads to an open cleaning closet, lit by one bare light bulb suspended from the ceiling. Propped against the closet wall is what's left of Chuffy Bryant, head bowed to his chest, his shirt ripped open, his chest a mass of oozing red. Something tubular and glistening spills from his abdomen, resting in his lap like a crimson snake that has crawled from his belly.

My legs buckle and Zena grabs my arm, moving me rapidly up the stairs, the gunman following close behind. Waiting outside a door at the top of the stairs is the second gunman. A grime-encrusted skylight overhead filters sickly light onto the objects placed at the man's feet: two red plastic cans—the kind that hold gasoline—and some piles of rags.

The second gunman opens the door and I'm pushed inside a large room with a worn massage table, a few benches, and a row of six flimsy metal lockers, tilted backward against one wall. Mary Grace stands. I go to her and hug her shaking body to mine, trying to calm her. She holds me so tightly I can hardly breathe.

Zena walks into the room while his men guard the door. "It seems that Mr. Bryant had more endurance than I could have guessed."

For all his sneakiness and bullying, the little bastard was tough. "He died before he could tell you where he took the heroin, didn't he?" I ask.

Zena nods. "But it's not a complete loss. Fortunately, the previous owner left quite a lot of gasoline in the basement. Apparently he meant to burn everything down for the insurance money."

He takes a knife from his back pocket—not the knife in the sheath at his waist, but a large pocketknife with a folding blade—and I shove Mary Grace behind me. Begging will do no good. Neither will reasoning, or bargaining: I have nothing to bargain with. I take a wider stance, preparing to launch myself at Zena.

But he places the open blade on the massage table with deliberate, almost delicate slowness. "I have respect for you, Detective," he says. Then, apologetically: "But you have seen my face, and I can't let you go."

"So you're just going to shoot us? A cop and a pregnant woman?" My voice is shredded, pinched, as though a metal wire is tightening around my throat.

"No," Zena says, his eyes luminous, expectant. "I'm not going to shoot you. The knife is for you to use."

He steps closer, his voice growing softer, as if relating an intimate secret. *"Las mujeres embarazadas sangran muy rapido."* He touches the side of his throat with his slender fingers. *"Cortar profundamente en la garganta. Acqui. La cuchilla es muy filosa. Ella no sentira dolor. Entiendes?"*

Zena knows I understand him because my mouth opens as if to scream.

He turns, walks out of the room, and closes the door. There is the rattle of keys and the turning of the lock on the door. I can hear and smell the gasoline being poured on the landing outside the door, over the rags, and at the top of the stairs. A moment later there's a *whoosh!*, then footsteps retreating down the stairs.

Mary Grace's face is ashen, her breathing erratic. But if she had understood what the Knife said to me about the purpose of the blade lying open on the table nearby, she would have been panicking.

A pregnant woman bleeds very quickly...cut the throat deeply...the knife is sharp...she won't feel pain.

Zena felt no need to tell me how to use the knife on myself.

I rush to the door and touch the wood. It's not warm yet—the door is solid oak—but it soon will be. The old dry-pine floorboards will catch quickly. Then the fire in the hallway will race along the wood to the walls, and once the walls catch there will be flashover, with nothing to keep us from burning alive in the room. We have less than ten minutes to evacuate.

Grabbing the massage table, I heave it over to the window and stand on top of it. I try opening the window, but it's been sealed shut. Even with the glass broken out, the bars over the window look solid and bolted fast to the exterior brick, and there is no fire escape if we were to somehow knock out the metal bars.

Mary Grace cries out and points. Thick smoke curls under the door, and I change my mind about breaking through the glass. Yanking off one heavily soled boot, I leap back onto the table, turn my head away, and shatter the glass. The inrushing air will diffuse the smoke, but it will also draw the flames.

I turn, desperately scanning the room for an exit or a way to keep the fire at bay until the fire trucks arrive—which, even if Dusty calls 911 now, will probably not be for another twenty minutes. Thick pipes—steam or water—run up the wall, but the paint is chipped and stained with rust. If I can disconnect or rupture a water pipe at a weak point where it's oxidized, it could flood the floorboards, keeping them from igniting, at least for a little while. I need a crowbar or a large wrench—anything solid enough to break through the metal.

Jumping down from the table, I run to the lockers, rocking them back to an upright position, and start flinging open the doors. Most of them are empty. A few contain pieces of tattered clothing, jump ropes, fraying boxing gloves. Nothing that could be used to smash open the pipes.

Loud crackling noises are coming from the hallway on the other side of the door. The studs behind the drywall are beginning to catch fire and buckle. The updraft from the stairwell is feeding the flames, and an explosion of glass signals the skylight shattering. The flames will quickly climb higher, chasing the oxygen, which will pour smoke out over the roof, signaling to the outside world that Delano's Gym is burning.

But within a few moments the fire, newly fed and whipped into frenzied motion, will spread outward, eating its way through the walls and into our room.

I touch the door with the back of my hand. It's hot, and beginning to swell and splinter. The walls on either side of the door are bubbling, as though hundreds of insects are burrowing below the paint and plaster. I look helplessly at Mary Grace, who is holding her shirt over her mouth, trying to filter out the acrid smoke.

Hoping to forestall the fire, I try to drag the locker unit in front of the door. It's not heavy, just awkward to move.

"Help me!" I yell to Mary Grace. The two of us wrestle it in front of the door.

The heat is too intense for us to stand near the walls, which have begun to bulge and turn dark and sooty in spots, as though blistering with a black plague. The walls are smoking. It will be only minutes before the fire eats through the wood.

We back away from the lockers, their doors open like gaping mouths, and I feel Mary Grace slide into the crook of my shoulder. Cradling her belly with both hands, she stares at me with naked terror—and, much worse, a dawning understanding that she will be burned alive. I look at the knife on the massage table, the open blade pointing toward us, and my arms instinctively pull her tighter, burying her face against my chest. My heart feels like an exploding grenade inside my rib cage.

I close my eyes and, when I open them again, I see what the lockers had hidden: a raised wooden platform, in the middle of which is a circular hinged lid about three feet across.

It has to be...

I drag Mary Grace, choking and coughing, to the platform with me and tug desperately at the lid's bar handle with one hand. It doesn't budge. I jump onto the platform. Using both hands and the strength of my legs, I pull on the handle until the lid springs open, knocking me backward and cracking my head against the wall.

It's an old laundry chute. Used for decades, then abandoned when the gym fell on hard times. I peer into the dark shaft, which might or might not be a straight drop thirty feet down to the first-floor laundry room. A fall that will kill or maim anyone lacking a soft place to land.

The contents of the lockers—clothes, gloves, jump ropes—are beginning to steam from the fire raging on the other side of the door. A flame licks its way through the top of the door, like a dog testing the air with its tongue. The blackened spots on the walls dissolve first into circular yellow masses, then orange, and finally red. The fire has broken through, and flames race upward toward the ceiling. Flames surround the lockers.

But the ropes...

I lunge for the jump ropes inside one of the lockers, but the heat is a wall that can dissolve hair off the scalp and skin from the bone. Pulling my coat over my head, I drag myself along the floor, crab style. I make three tries before my hand closes around the coils of ropes, and I yank them toward me. The backs of my hands touch the metal frame; they sizzle like meat on a grill, and chunks of flesh evaporate.

I roll away, my lungs screaming, hair smoking. The taste of blood is in my mouth.

Mary Grace has moved toward the window, her arms raised defensively in front of her face. With fevered eyes she watches me tie the ropes together with sheet-bend knots, my burned hands clumsy with the stiffened fibers. They are long enough—three nine- or ten-foot ropes—but they are old and brittle, the hemp braiding frayed. Mary Grace stands unmoving, her gaze fixed on the approaching fire, as I wind a section of the rope around her chest and tie it under her arms, but I have to drag her over to the opening of the chute. Her fear has paralyzed her. I shake her roughly, then grab her face with both hands.

"You're going down that chute or you're going to die," I yell.

The crack of the wood is deafening, the heat crushing. She shakes her head wildly.

"I won't drop you, Mary Grace," I scream at her. "Trust me."

I lift her awkwardly onto the platform, praying that the chute is wide enough all the way down. I wind the free end of the rope around the pipes as a pulley, anchoring it around my hips. Taking up the slack in the rope, I brace my feet against the wall and plead, "Now, Mary Grace. It's got to be now."

She straightens her legs and, instead of easing herself in, she jumps, feetfirst, like falling into a well. Her plummeting weight yanks me forward and I crash face-first into the pipes. Mary Grace screams as the tether jerks her to a stop, but I've held on to the rope and slowly pay it out, lowering her toward the first floor as rapidly as I can.

I turn my face away from the heat, even as the hairs curl on my arms and the skin begins to blister on my legs beneath my jeans. The smoke, thick and caustic, has been rushing past my face like a dark river, threatening to suffocate me before I can be incinerated where I stand.

The smoke abruptly reverses course as clean air from outside is pulled in through the window. The massive flames pouring in from the outer hallway retreat, as if sucked up by a powerful vacuum.

Gusts of rising storm winds racing over the skylight are pulling the fire backward, into the stairwell. But the reprieve will be short. As soon as the winds abate, the flames will expand again with a vengeance.

The rope is payed out as far as it will go, but the far end is fully weighted. Its load is still suspended somewhere above the floor.

"Mary Grace," I yell, the effort making my vision blur. "Can you hear me?"

There's no answer. The roar of the fire has turned to the screaming of a jet engine ascending, full throttle, up through the roof of the building. The sound of distorting, bending metal cracks and echoes as loudly as cannon fire. Cold wind rushes inward, dragging with it errant snowflakes stained dark by soot and ash.

I struggle to tie the end of the rope to the pipes, my burned hands as red and raw as roadkill.

"Mary Grace!" I scream, thrusting my face into the chute.

Still no answer.

"Are you close to the bottom?"

I close my eyes against the silence, and pray. "Is there fire down there?" I finally croak.

I have to descend *now,* but remembering the knife, I snatch it from the table, closing and pocketing the blade. I perch on the platform, dangling my legs into the darkened chute.

The shrieking jet engine on the stairwell has stalled, and a growing bass rumble shakes the building. A superheated stream of smoke and ash explodes through the walls just as I drop into the chute—holding on to the rope with both hands as ribbons of flame flash over the opening where my head had been a few seconds before. The wooden platform above me is smoking, catching fire, as will the rope keeping me suspended in my small enclosure, thirty feet above the ground.

I'm counting the seconds, descending about a foot a second, supported by my feet wrapped around the rope. At the count of fifteen, the rope's fibers in the room above begin to disintegrate with the heat, and I can feel the line splitting, jerking, getting ready to give way completely.

I loosen my grip and slide the rest of the way down the shaft, grimacing in pain, the rope burning through the palms of my hands, eating through flesh like acid. I slide free of the chute, my feet a few yards off the ground, and find Mary Grace dangling loose-limbed and groaning beneath me. I manage to drop to the floor without smashing her in the head with my boots.

I grapple her lax form to me with one arm and reach up with the knife to cut the rope. But it shudders and breaks and she falls heavily against me, knocking me over, the smoldering length of the rope falling like an afterthought. I drag her away from the open end of the laundry chute, down which burning bits of debris and belching smoke are beginning to drift. The fire overhead is a roaring, obliterating furnace. An avalanche of crashing sounds coming from the adjacent exhibition area signals that part of the second story is starting to collapse. I wrap my arms around Mary Grace, looking for injuries, and she yelps when I hold her too tightly.

"I think I broke some ribs," she pants.

Her pants are soaked from the crotch down, and with renewed panic I think that maybe her water has broken a month too early.

"We have to get out of the building," I say. "Can you move?"

She nods, and with difficulty I pull her to her feet. The space — once a laundry room, but long used for storage and maintenance supplies — is filling with smoke. The fire bellows in the main boxing arena like a starving beast.

There is an exit door. It's made of metal and locked with a large Master combination lock. I pull on the lock but it won't budge, the hasp firmly attached to the door.

I scream in frustration, searching frantically for anything to break the lock — two wrenches, a hammer, whatever. There's nothing at hand but old cleaning supplies and rags. I turn back to Mary Grace, ready to use my body as a battering ram. But she is standing calmly at the door, methodically spinning the dial on the lock with one hand, the forefinger of her other hand stuck through the metal clamp, applying constant and practiced pressure. She makes a few passes — left, right, left — and the lock releases. She takes the lock from the locking eye, twists the doorknob, and swings the door open to the outside.

She turns to me—this tiny pregnant teenager with the fake last name, her face blackened with greasy, tear-stained soot—and crows, "Told you I could bust a combo lock!"

I rush to her and lead her out of the burning building into a cold winter night.

CHAPTER 29

Q: How do you know you're in front of a Polish firing squad?

A: The guys with the guns are standing around you in a circle.

The joke here is not completely ridiculous in my case, because besides taking aim at me for unwittingly running afoul of one of the cruelest enforcers in the Sinaloa cartel—not to mention barely escaping from a building that burned to the ground—the men in the hospital examining room are taking potshots at one another; marking territory, claiming jurisdiction, demanding answers.

Standing in a semicircle around the examining table are Maclin, Craddock, DEA Special Agent in Charge Donald Haslett, and three of his field agents, as well as the fire chief and two arson investigators.

They all look like they're at the beginning of a particularly morose dance recital: arms crossed in front of their chests, chins down, hooded eyes scrutinizing me, swaying restlessly from foot to foot. They glare, they grunt, they grind their teeth. What they don't do is tell me how Mary Grace is doing.

The fact that Dusty had already called 911 right about the

time we were shinnying down the laundry chute allowed police and EMT to arrive at the gym shortly after we exited the building, injured and exhausted. Mary Grace and I had been taken to the hospital in the same ambulance. I sat next to her as she lay on a stretcher, holding her hand with my own mangled ones and murmuring encouragement. Dusty drove to the hospital in her boyfriend's BMW, chasing after us like a bright blue comet's tail.

Mary Grace had been assured by the emergency techs that her placenta had not leaked, only her bladder. (Frightening a pregnant woman by dropping her down a dark hole will do that.) But after being processed through the emergency room, she was quickly moved to another floor for continued observation, and I had been given no further updates. Dusty agreed to leave only after I promised her I'd call with any developments.

An hour later and I'm still on the table, my hands heavily bandaged with layers of gauze, the tips of my fingers exposed but swollen to the size of Vienna sausages. I have heat blisters on my legs, second- and third-degree burns on the backs of both hands, open wounds on each palm, burns and abrasions on my arms and neck, and welts on my inner thighs from the slide down the ropes. After my face was wiped clean of grime, I was told I'd have a large bruise on my left cheek as well. The attending doctor then gave me the one piece of good news: I hadn't cracked my maxillary bone when I did that face-plant into the pipes.

The painkillers have made me woozy and my body feels like it's gone through a meat grinder, but I've recounted the story to the best of my ability. When I got to the part about being locked in a room and using a laundry chute and three jump ropes to escape, the fire chief—last name Brzezinski, a solid, older man with good Polish blood clogging his arteries—looked at his guys and whistled under his breath. He turned to Maclin and said, "Jesus Christ, you don't want her after this, we'll take her."

Before leaving with his men, the chief tells me he'll be in touch to collect a formal statement confirming that the fire was arson.

"Do you have any idea where Chuffy Bryant would have taken the drugs?" Haslett asks.

I shake my head wearily. "Unless he told someone else, the only person who would know for sure is now dead, gutted like a fish."

Haslett turns to one of his guys. "We'll need to get a sketch artist down here right away so she can get to work on a likeness of the Knife and the two gunmen."

"Hold on," Maclin says. "Detective Rhyzyk has been through quite an ordeal."

"Which she signed up for," Haslett says, turning to me. "Right, Detective? I mean capturing drug dealers is what you do."

Like a barrier, Maclin stands in front of him. "Do you smell that, Agent Haslett? That wafting odor of charred flesh and singed hair? That aroma is emanating from one of my officers, who at great risk rescued a civilian. A pregnant civilian. This can wait until the morning."

"Zena is here, in the States, right now," Haslett insists. "He's on the most-wanted list for both the DEA and the Bureau. Every minute counts. He leaves for Mexico, we won't know where to *begin* to look for him—"

I lie back on the examining table as the two men argue, contemplating closing my eyes for just a moment. Through a semiconscious fog I hear Haslett say, "She's the only person in U.S. law enforcement who's seen Zena's face and lived to tell about it."

But his voice has taken on the urgent tone and timbre of Uncle Benny's voice, the way he'd spoken to me in my dream of the girl in the yellow pajamas: *Sometimes you gotta run toward the fire.*

Which I had done: I'd run toward the flames to grab the ropes, giving us a chance to escape. Benny's in the room with me now, bending down, whispering in my ear, *Where does a man go when he wants to feel safe?*

"He goes home," I mumble, my eyes opening to the bright lights in the examining room.

"What?" Maclin asks.

I sit up too abruptly and grab the side of the examining table to keep from falling to the floor. "Barrio de San Luis," I say to Haslett. "He told me that was his hometown. Culiacán. He was a boxer there."

"Son of a bitch," Maclin says.

Haslett looks at his nearest agent. "Did we know that?"

The younger agent shakes his head. "We do now," he says.

"One more thing," I say, pulling the knife out of the pocket of my jeans, which lie rumpled on a nearby chair. "You'll find two sets of prints on this: mine and Zena's."

Fifteen minutes later the doctor comes in to release me, informing me that my friend is waiting for me on the floor where they're treating Mary Grace: "A Dr. Walden," he says.

I'm so doped up it takes me a second to realize he's talking about Jackie.

Everyone but Craddock has left, and he waits for me in the hall while I get dressed. I'm offered a wheelchair but wave it off, leaning instead on Craddock's comfortable bulk as I hobble to the elevator.

"Thanks for hanging around," I say.

"Hey, it's the least I can do. Want me to drive you home?"

The drugs, the fallout from being terrified, and my injuries—

along with the realization that home for me now is the Fiesta Motel—overwhelm me, and my knees start to sag. Craddock steers me to a bench and I collapse, my head resting against the wall.

"I'll be all right in a minute," I tell him. "Look, I can get one of the nurses to wheel me upstairs. You should go home."

"I don't mind waiting. If you can walk out of a burning building, I can miss eating dinner."

Craddock's phone rings. "It's Seth. He's called about a dozen times. Wants to know how you're doing."

Zena had told me the man shooting the dealers was "someone very close" to me. Someone trying to clean up a "mess" he had created—and tear me down in the process. The closest person to me who's in a world of trouble is my partner. I shake my head and say, "No."

"What's going on with you two?" he asks, putting the phone back in his pocket. "I thought you were like family."

That's exactly the problem, I want to say to him. A family where you stew in unspoken resentments and keep each other's toxic secrets; a family where you declaim clannish fealty to outsiders but turn a cold shoulder to your brother's private agony. Or illegal activities.

I let my head sag onto Craddock's shoulder. "I'm seriously fucked up," I tell him.

"How do you say that in Polish?" he asks.

"*Zwariowany.*"

"Sounds like a Polish Christmas cookie."

His reference to food makes me smile.

"This has been a tough time for all of us," Craddock says. "We've all had some terrible losses: you with your injury, Kevin losing his brother-in-law, his wife having the miscarriage. It's something you never get over, losing a child. It's been eight years since my wife and I lost our daughter, Angie, to drugs."

I sit up again. "I'm so sorry, Tom. I had no idea."

"I don't really talk about it. It's the reason I went into Narcotics, but—"

I wait quietly for him to finish his thought.

"It didn't turn out the way I expected." He turns and looks at me, the pain of his daughter's death fresh in his mind. "I guess I thought there'd be some closure by locking away the scumbags who sell drugs to kids. But there's no closure—no resolution. Only an endless supply of drugs and the shitbirds who deal them. My wife tells me it's turned me cynical." He smiles sadly and pats his stomach. "Not cynical, I tell her—just cylindrical."

I give his arm a squeeze because I don't trust my voice not to break.

"You asked me if I was compensating for something. You know, buying all the guns. It got me thinking about my hobby. I've hunted since I was a boy, collected guns my whole life. All those weapons didn't keep Angie safe, but it's what I know, what I'm certain of. And these past years have handed me a lot of empty hours to fill."

We sit quietly for a moment, staring ahead into the darkened hospital corridor.

"Come on," he finally says, pulling me up. "I'll take you to Mary Grace's floor, and then I think I'll go home."

We ride the elevator up a few floors and I step out of the car, insisting that I can find my way alone.

The poorly lit elevator casts deep shadows on Craddock's face, puffy from overwork, bad food, and not enough sleep. "I'll tell you one thing," he says, holding the elevator door open. "I completely understand Kevin's rage."

"But you don't think he'd kill someone in cold blood, do you?"

"Kevin? No way. It takes a special kind of arrogance to kill someone up close and personal like that."

"Or desperation," I say. "Zena told me the shooter was someone close to me who was trying to clean up his own mess. Someone who wanted me to 'feel the weight' of my 'past mistakes.'"

The elevator door has started dinging in protest. "Well, good thing you've got the best detectives in Dallas to help you. Now go home. Get some rest."

The door closes and I find my way to Mary Grace's room. I lean against the doorframe watching her sleep, an oxygen mask over her face, her belly gently expanding and contracting with every breath. Jackie has been sitting with her, and she gives me the update: one fractured rib, which will probably affect the labor, multiple bruises, and a few first-degree burns. The baby, due in four weeks, seems fine.

Jackie stands next to me. I can feel her gaze on me, scorching the places the fire hasn't reached. "She kept asking for you," she says. "She blames herself for what happened."

Weariness is crushing my bones into powder, and all I can manage is a whisper: "She thought she was helping me."

Jackie weaves her arm through mine and says, "Come on. You need some rest."

I look at her pleadingly. "Back to the Fiesta Motel?"

"No," she says, putting her arm around my waist. "I'm taking you home."

CHAPTER 30

Red Hot Betty. That's my new nickname with my colleagues."

Dr. Theo smiles at me. "I've heard worse. How are you feeling now?"

I hold up my bandaged hands. "Useless. Humiliated during bathroom breaks."

"How's the pain level?" he asks.

"Not as extreme as it should be."

He looks at me quizzically. "You believe you should be suffering more pain?"

I stare at my boots—the same ones that survived the fire. They still smell like a campfire pit after a hard rain, and probably always will. I had recounted to Dr. Theo the events leading up to the fire: my assignment to desk duty and my banishment to the Fiesta Motel; my face-to-face with the Knife; Chuffy's violent death. It didn't seem possible that only a week had passed since my last therapy visit. Viewed in a stream of consciousness, the recent events seemed like an insurmountable tidal wave.

Doc, we're going to need a bigger boat.

"I've been keeping secrets from the people I care about," I say.

"Anything you want to share with me now?" he asks, like a priest preparing to give his congregant greater scrutiny inside the confessional.

I take a breath as if to speak, but end up shaking my head. Even now I can't talk about what I know, and what I suspect, about my partner. "I'm not ready. Not yet."

"Are these secrets putting you in danger?" he asks.

"Only of making me more of an asshole than I already am."

"Ah," he says, with a mock frown. "That, I'm afraid, is beyond my field of expertise."

Dr. Theo studies me for a moment, then says, "Last time you were here, you spoke about your family. About how it was normal—expected, even—to keep secrets. You said it was a sign of loyalty, professionally and personally. Can you tell me more about the relationship you had with your brother, Andrew?"

"My brother was always there for me when we were kids."

"You said he was your protector. Against your father's anger, his emotional instability."

"And when my brother needed me the most, I wasn't there for him."

"What would you have done differently?"

"I would have listened—counseled him to get help."

"And do you think that by doing so you could have eradicated his own guilt over his corrupt actions?"

"I'll never know for sure. But at least I could have tried."

"What about your own guilt?" he asks.

The question pierces me to the core. The weight of the possibility that I could have stopped Andrew from killing himself makes breathing difficult. "I pushed him away," I whisper.

He leans forward, gesturing expressively with his hands. "Have you ever thought that keeping your brother at arm's length, once you discovered his true character, was necessary to your emotional survival? That in order to keep your equilibrium and integrity intact, you had to in effect push him away—and that *not* to do so would have put your own safety at risk?"

I look at him in surprise. My brother had always been a heroic figure in my eyes, pulled into the swamp of corruption by forces he couldn't fully control. But, of course, he had made the choices he made without a gun to his head.

"A drowning person often pulls under the very person trying to save them," he says.

I think of my brother's chosen form of self-destruction: a short swim in the frigid Atlantic Ocean. And I remember what Uncle Benny had told me when Andrew's body was pulled from the water. He had looked at me with blinding grief and anger in his eyes and said, "Complete and utter selfishness. Took everything that was good with him, and left you behind to pick up the pieces."

"I heard my uncle Benny's voice in a dream a few nights ago," I say to Dr. Theo. "He gave me instructions about what to do to escape the fire, before the fire had even happened."

Dr. Theo sits quietly, waiting.

"Then, when I was in the hospital emergency room, I drifted off for a moment and heard his voice again, reminding me what the Knife had told me about his hometown. I think it was important information for the Feds. And, I...I thought I saw him waiting for me the night I escaped the Elm Street Tunnel."

A secretive grin plays around Dr. Theo's lips.

"What?" I ask.

"I think this is the surest sign of healing so far."

"You don't think it makes me more nuts? Hearing voices? Seeing things that aren't there?"

He puts his head back and recites, "'A person needs a little madness, or else they never dare cut the rope and be free.'"

"Freud?"

"Kazantzakis. A Greek writer." He pulls the pad and pen back into his lap. "I believe that you may be coming closer to cutting the rope of guilt as regards your brother."

The talk of cutting "the rope" drags me back to the fire, dangling helplessly in the laundry chute, waiting for the flames to engulf me.

"What is it?" Dr. Theo asks. When I don't answer right away, he says, "Detective, you're swimming away from the shore at this moment."

"Before El Cuchillo set the fire," I say, "he told me that the shooter — the person killing the drug dealers on the streets — was 'someone very close' to me, and a cop. Someone who was leaving the Bible verses on the scene to make me 'feel the weight' of my own mistakes."

Dr. Theo takes a few beats to study me. "What mistakes do you think he was talking about?"

"I've made so many, I couldn't even begin to guess."

He leans over his desk, picks up a piece of paper, and holds it out to me. It's the diagram of names I had given him during my last visit.

"Your next homework assignment. On this list are the people closest to you. Study it. The killer may be here."

I reach for the paper with my swollen fingers, but he doesn't let go right away.

"It takes courage to see what you don't want to see," he tells me.

The two names that jump off the paper first are Evangeline Roy and my partner, Seth Dutton. But only one is in law enforcement.

I fold the paper and slip it in my pocket. "One would think you'd been a cop in a past life."

He smiles, handing me a card for our next appointment. "Once a cop, always a cop—isn't that right, Detective?"

"So I've been told," I say.

CHAPTER 31

I sit hunched over my desk, my injured hands throbbing like mad, and study the schematic I had drawn for Dr. Theo. Like when I work a homicide case, I want to eliminate all of the suspects who have good alibis or no motive to commit murder. The Knife had confirmed the shooter was a cop, so I scratch off *Jackie* and *Evangeline* right away. It seems ridiculous to suspect James Earle, but he had been a military policeman, so I write his name down. Then, remembering that he was with Mary Grace at the time I was in the trap house with the dead drug dealers, I immediately cross his name off the list.

That leaves Seth, Craddock, Ryan, and Maclin. The day that Carlos Rivera was shot at the Spearmint Rhino, Craddock was in the station early, sharing donuts with me. But Ryan had come in late, looking pale and asking a lot of questions about a potential witness to Pico Guerto's shooting. I'd also seen the look of intense anger on his face following the attack on me at the trap house. He might have a motive to seek revenge on the dealers because his brother-in-law died of an overdose. The pastor of his new church is Reverend Hall, a revenge hound if ever there was one. With true zealots, the distance from evangelical zeal to self-justifying violence is about as narrow as a communion wafer, and just as brittle. Even Sergeant Maclin had asked me if I thought Ryan was wound too tight lately.

I'm fully aware that I'm building a case against Ryan because, more than anything else in the world, I don't want the shooter to be my partner. Crossing Craddock's name off the list, I swivel around in my chair, my brain on fire.

"Hey, Tom," I call. "Where's Kevin?"

Craddock shrugs. "He just left for lunch. You can catch him if you hurry—"

Grabbing my coat, I run for the exit closest to the parking lot, and spot Ryan just as he's getting into his car.

"Hey, Kevin," I say breathlessly, jogging up to him. "You got some time for me?"

He startles, and gives me a cautious look. "I was going somewhere—"

"That's fine," I say, getting into the passenger seat. "We can talk on the way."

He pauses for a moment. He's impatient, but he's also more than irritated at the intrusion. I keep my face a friendly mask.

"What do you want to talk about?" he asks.

"You doing okay these days?"

He inhales like a swimmer about to take a long dive, the muscles in his face tightening.

"You look like you're not getting too much sleep," I say. "Like something's really bothering you. Anything you want to share with me?"

He bites his lip and stares out the window.

"I'm worried about you, Kev. You come in late, you leave early. You're distracted—and worse, you're angry. All the time."

He laughs bitterly. "Says the person who's been on suspension for her anger issues."

"Yeah, that's fair. I've got my own demons to wrestle with. It's why I know a demon when I see it."

"How's this for demons: I just buried my brother-in-law, who died from a drug overdose. I'm kept up most nights by the sound of my wife crying because she's had a miscarriage. I'm behind on my mortgage, and I don't know if I want to be a cop anymore."

"That's a lot to deal with."

"You think?"

Time to go fishing. "Makes you want to hit back," I say.

His expression hardens. "You have no idea."

"You talking to your pastor about it?"

He gives me a look I can't decipher. "Reverend Hall? Yeah, I've talked to him."

"What did he say?"

"You don't want to know."

Is this a dismissal—a way to forestall this line of questioning? Or is this a warning? I look at his tight grip on the steering wheel, his forehead sweaty.

"Why were you late to the station the day that Carlos Rivera was shot?" I ask. The question sounds casual, but he gives me a sharp look.

He starts the engine and puts it in gear.

"Where are we going?" I ask. The garage is empty—no one to see that I'm in a car being driven by Ryan—and I can only hope that Craddock remembers our brief exchange about his partner.

He backs the car out of the parking space and roars out of the garage.

* * *

It's colder and wetter outside than on the New Year's Day when I'd found the body of Kevin Ryan's brother-in-law. The clouds are moving low and fast with the biting wind, so we sit in the car facing the Continental pedestrian bridge with the engine running. Ryan stares through the windshield for a while, his skin tinged blue in the murky light.

"I come here a lot, often in the morning," he says. "It's why I've been late to work. I think about what more I could have done to save him."

"Some people can't be saved," I say. "No matter what we do."

"That's what Karen tells me." He turns to me. "I'm just glad it was you who found him."

"Wish I'd known who he was," I say. "I would have stayed with him until you and Karen could have come to the ME's office."

His gaze is pulled to a lone figure on the bridge. A man walking his dog.

"He looked so broken," he says. "He was just a kid. And now he's gone."

"I heard you were beyond angry at the morgue." *Ice Man sitting on top of a rocket booster* was how Euell Tilton had put it.

His brow wrinkles and he blinks a few times, as though processing something beyond his understanding. I was tense, in full defensive mode, when we first parked here. But no sense of danger emanates from Ryan now. Only a profound sadness.

"I was…enraged. Haven't had a moment's peace since then." He brushes a hand over his face, flattening the creases in his forehead. "Remember the conversation we had last fall about us not doing much good as law enforcement?"

The last time Ryan and I had been at Norma's diner, before I'd been kidnapped by the Roys, he had told me that he was thinking of transferring out of the department; that it had seemed to him that all our efforts were futile next to the never-ending supply of illegal drugs. Many cops transfer out after three or four years of working narcotics. The strain of always losing is just too crippling.

"Standing over his body in the morgue brought all the feelings of helplessness back," he says. "What a senseless waste it all was. Then Karen lost the baby—"

His voice trails off and I wait in silence for him to continue.

"I can't even begin to tell you the dark thoughts I was having."

"Kevin—" I begin.

"No, it's true. I've got all these things crowding my head."

"Have you talked to Tom?" I ask.

He shakes his head. "Tom's my partner. I can't burden him with my personal problems." He grins without mirth. "I did talk to Reverend Hall about it, though. You know what he told me? He said it was God's punishment for my brother-in-law being an addict. According to my pastor, he was at that moment burning in hell."

"Oh shit, Kevin," I say, shaking my head. "I'm sorry."

"Remember when you asked me to check on the OneNation website? Well, I did. And guess who showed up in a photo taken a few years ago at one of their guns-and-grits picnics?"

"Reverend Hall?"

"Yep. There'd been no activity on the site in a long time. And no whisper of the Roy family. But there was Alan Hall draped in an American flag, an AR-15 in one hand and a nine-mil pistol in the other. I'm done with him and his 'church.'"

"What can I do to help?" I ask.

"Buy me a drink sometime," he says.

*   *   *

Back at my desk, I draw a line through *Kevin Ryan*. Before I can put a circle around Seth's name, however, my personal cell phone rings. Gingerly, trying not to snag the bandages on my hand, I pull the phone out of my pocket.

"Hey, it's me. Wayne," the voice says. "I really need to talk to you."

CHAPTER 32

Adair's Saloon on Commerce Street, within spitting distance of U.S. 75 and Good Latimer, is a popular honkytonk known for its hamburgers, one-dollar beer, and live music. I had come here several times with Seth, and we'd spent the evening drinking and happily shouting to each other over the ear-splitting decibels of slide guitar and monosyllabic country wailing. It was evening, but with band flyers covering every inch of the front window it was hard to tell how many people were inside.

I park, pull up the collar of my jacket, and start looking for Wayne. I hear my name being called and see him standing in the parking lot across the street, in front of a mural of a cowboy being unseated by a bucking bronc. The lot is filled with cars, and one lone ice-cream truck that seems to be doing a brisk business despite the cold.

"What happened to your hands?" Wayne asks.

"Long story," I say, impatiently. "Where have you been?"

Wayne is still wearing the hooded sweatshirts I'd given him, as well as my gloves, but he's shivering with cold—and fear. He shrugs. "Been hiding, man. Here and there. Trying to stay alive."

"Why didn't you wait for my friend at the bus station the other day? I was beginning to think you'd gone the way of Gary."

"I got spooked. Too many undercovers hanging out in front of the station."

"Have you eaten anything recently?"

He shakes his head, and I cross the street to Adair's. I order two hamburgers and a coffee to go. When I return with the food, we hunker down behind an SUV, which blocks the worst of the wind.

When Wayne finishes eating, I say, "Talk to me."

"After Gary got killed, I got really scared. Scared me straight."

He pulls a coin out of his pocket and shows me. "Desire chip, man. I'm eleven days sober. Last drink and drugs was the night you found me in the Elm Street Tunnel. And if you think it's easy staying clean while hiding on the streets, you're crazier than I am." He puts the coin back in his pocket. "I'm doing it for Mary Grace."

"If you're doing it for anyone but yourself, Wayne, it's not going to work."

"I know. It's just thinking of her gives me some hope, you know?"

I nod. "I know."

"Part of the program is making amends. Clearing the slate." He looks around carefully. "There's something I need to tell you about Gary."

"I'm listening."

"The shooter? Gary said he knew him. He recognized him because the guy had busted him on a B and E. It was a long time ago, but Gary never forgot a face. It's what made him so good at a con. The guy had aged some, but it was the same cop who'd booked him."

I'm shivering right along with Wayne now. I want to get up

and walk away, or tell him to take it to someone else. But I can't. I have to hear this.

"Who's the cop, Wayne?" I ask.

"I don't know," he says.

The breath I'm holding is released in an explosive white mist. "What do you mean, *I don't know*?"

"I mean that Gary only told me he recognized the guy. He never told me his name. That's why I'm so fucking wound up. I don't know who the guy is."

I put my head in my hands. "You're going to give me a heart attack."

"Can't you check Gary's arrest records?" he asks.

I look at him—this skinny little tweaker missing two fingers and even more teeth, trying to maintain sobriety against a culture bent on keeping him permanently addicted to anything, and everything—and I say, "Yes, I can." I hand him all the cash in my pockets. "You got someplace safe to stay?"

"Yeah, I'm sticking close to Mountain these days." He smiles weakly. "He's acting as my bodyguard."

"Want me to drive you somewhere?"

"Take me to my NA meeting? My sponsor, Dottie, says ninety days, ninety meetings."

"Wait a minute," I say. "Your sponsor's name is Dottie? Wild gray hair, wears cowboy boots all the time?"

Dottie, the cautionary Cassandra who'd been hinting at hearing recovery confessions about a killer?

Wayne nods.

"Son of a bitch," I say.

"She scares the hell out of me," he confides.

"Wayne, Dottie scares the hell out of everybody."

We get up to walk to my car, and Wayne points to the ice-cream truck, currently serving two college-aged kids. "No never-mind from me, man, but they're selling meth and weed out of there like a house on fire."

I drop Wayne off at his NA meeting. I watch him walk into the building with a bunch of haggard yet hopeful citizens, followed a few minutes later by the owner of Slugger Anne's Bar, the Wild Wild West's matron of honor, Dottie. I then call James Earle and tell him everything about my partner: his drug use, his stealing drugs from a dead man, and my suspicions that he's been selling drugs either for, or in competition with, the Sinaloans. I tell him about Wayne's confession of Gary Bukowsky seeing the shooter, and that the killer is probably a cop.

I summon up the image of the figure in the black hoodie and the ski mask, trying to match the taunting man I'd seen with Seth's proportions. "I think the shooter may be the guy I saw in the Elm Street Tunnel that night," I tell James. "And pulling Gary's arrest warrants should tell me who he is."

There's a long silence on the other end. Finally an intake of air, and James says, "You have to take this to your sergeant. You can't carry this alone anymore. Speak up, and let the chips fall where they may."

"What if I'm wrong?" I ask.

"That's what we have judges and juries for, Red. You're just the delivery system. Go home. Be with Jackie, then tomorrow morning do the right thing."

"Thanks, James. Just don't—"

"Wild dogs couldn't drag from me what you've just confided. Your secrets are safe with me."

CHAPTER 33

I stand at Maclin's open doorway, waiting for him to notice me and invite me inside. Brow furrowed, a sheen of sweat along his hairline, he's staring at something in one of his desk drawers as though deciphering pagan runes. He looks more than tired; he looks ill.

He's finally aware of my presence and his head jerks up as he closes the drawer. "What do you want, Rhyzyk?"

"I really need to talk to you—"

"I can't talk to you right now. I've got a meeting in less than ten minutes."

"Then I'll make it short." I walk into his office and close the door.

"Did you not hear me? I can't talk to you right now."

He's red in the face, trying mightily to resist raising his voice. So much for the concern he showed in the hospital after the fire. The way Maclin tried to buy me some recovery time against the prodding of Special Agent Haslett had given me hope that his animosity for me was thawing. His expression at this moment says different.

I sit in the chair in front of the desk. "I've got information about what Gary Bukowsky saw in the alley the day Pico Guerto was killed."

Maclin's still angry, but he also wants to hear what I have to say. He impatiently motions me to continue.

"Before Gary was shot, he told one of my CIs that he recognized the shooter."

His eyelids go to half-mast and he stares at me expressionless for a moment, his jaw flexing. "What do you mean *recognized the shooter*? He knew the guy?"

"It was a cop," I say.

"Who was it?" he asks.

"Someone who had arrested him a few years back."

Maclin's hands, resting on the desk, clench in anticipation. "What's this cop's name?"

"That's the thing. Gary told my CI the cop had arrested him on a B and E, but he didn't reveal the cop's name."

There's a rap at the door. "Just a minute," Maclin barks, maintaining eye contact with me. "You think you know who it is, don't you?"

"Maybe."

"Who?"

Seth's name burns on my tongue like acid. "I'm not going to venture a guess. Better we know for sure."

"You tell anyone about this?" he asks.

"I've told no one else in the department," I say, which is technically true; James Earle is outside the department.

He looks at me doubtfully and opens his mouth to say something. But the rap comes again, this time more insistently. Maclin stands and points a finger at me. "You do not tell anyone— *anyone*— what you told me. You hear? Not until I can prove or disprove it. Any more rumors of this kind will blow up the entire department."

"Sergeant Maclin," says a voice outside the door.

"Coming!" Maclin yells. He's standing toe-to-toe with me. "I will personally check Gary's arrest records, and you'll be the first to know."

"I can check—"

"Right now you're still on desk duty, and I don't want you doing anything this morning beyond pulling tags. Are we clear?" Maclin asks, his breath in my face.

"Crystal clear," I tell him.

"You did good bringing this to me," he says in a more conciliatory tone. "This may be the thing that puts you back on the street again."

Maclin opens the door to the two Internal Affairs officers who had interviewed me: D.S. Burkley and Detective Adams.

I nod to the detectives as I leave the office. They go inside and close the door.

Craddock and Ryan are both standing by my desk, Craddock upending the last of a small bag of peanuts into his mouth. "Well, that didn't look warm and fuzzy," he says.

"You can say that again." I hitch a thumb at Maclin's closed door. "What's all that about? I thought they already interviewed him."

"They did," Craddock says, licking the salt off his fingers. "It's his second interview with them."

"He appears not to be happy about it," Ryan says.

"He making book somewhere?" I say jokingly, and then I remember Euell Tilton saying that Maclin would bet on anything that moved. Maybe Maclin's not as squeaky-clean as he would like his colleagues to believe? It would explain his foul mood.

Actually, the thought of him having a down-low vice makes me feel better about him. Marginally.

"I hope they give him an upper and a lower GI while they're at it," I mutter.

Craddock and Ryan go back to their desks and I sit at mine, stewing. If my partner turns out to be the shooter, would I be able to make the arrest? Look him in the eye and read him his Miranda rights? I'd heard Uncle Benny say once that the hardest part of the job is putting the cuffs on one of your own.

My phone rings and Dusty asks, "How you doin', Red Hot Betty?"

"Well, my clothes have stopped smoking. What's up?"

"Pearla's left town." She gives a sharp, victorious laugh. "I just put her on a bus. She was so mad at me for bringing you Chuffy's keys that she stopped talking to me. Until she realized I was the only one who'd give her bus fare back to New Orleans. She did tell me something interesting about your partner, though."

"Oh?" I say, swiveling my chair around to note who's in the station at that moment. Seth, as usual, is out on the streets.

"Pearla told me that he tracked her down and leaned on her hard about where the rest of the heroin was."

The knot in my stomach hardens. "What did she tell him?"

"What *could* she tell him? That she had no idea where it was. Chuffy never told her, and now Chuffy's dead."

"Yeah, well, we may never know now. Look, Dusty, I've got to go—"

"One more thing. Pearla said your partner told her that her life might be in danger if she stayed in Dallas. That the cartel would be looking for her. Scared her so bad, she was wearing men's clothes when she met me to get her bus fare. Truth be told, she looks better in pants."

We say our goodbyes and I disconnect the call.

This is bullshit, I think. Sitting frozen at my desk, tracing stolen cars while the world burns down around me. After another fifteen minutes the door to Maclin's office opens and the two IA detectives leave. In the civilian world, investigators appearing jubilant usually indicate there's a fire beneath the smoke. But these guys look grim and solemn—which in the world of Internal Affairs means they've got a bead on someone and they're closing in. Good for IA's solve rates, bad for the department. It's perversely satisfying to know that I'm not the only one having a bad day.

Maclin closes his door and I go looking for Craddock. He's not at his desk, and his coat's not on the back of his chair.

"Where's Craddock?" I ask Ryan.

"Ulcer's acting up again, I think. He took the rest of the day off. Is there something you need?"

Searching out Craddock to be reassured was an impulsive move, fueled by the agony of not knowing. I sigh resignedly and start to walk away.

"Hey," Ryan calls, motioning me back. "What's wrong?"

I hesitate, every muscle tense, wrapped in the barbed wire of worry and frustration. He takes my arm and I let him guide me into the break room.

"Look," he says, "anyone with eyes can see the way Maclin's been riding you. I know it's been tough, but something else is really eating at you. You reached out to me. Now it's my turn. What's going on?"

I begin to shake my head, crossing my arms in front of my chest. It's a daily reflex, this defensiveness. I've been paranoid for so long over lingering doubts about everyone in my department that my self-imposed isolation has hardened into a lobster shell.

"Do you remember what you told me after that high school party raid last year?" he asks.

He'd been working undercover at St. Borromeo, a Catholic high school, getting invited to all the rich-kid parties where drugs were as accessible as candy. There had been a sexual free-for-all at the party that was raided, and when the undercovers broke in for the arrests, Kevin had been stripped down to his underwear, a girl with her face in his lap. He'd been mortified—afraid that his churchgoing girlfriend, now wife, would find out. The guys had teased him mercilessly about it until I shut them down, threatening to tell their wives and girlfriends all their own dirty little secrets.

"Do you remember what you told me?" he asks.

In spite of myself, I grin.

"You told me you would personally crack the head of any guy who breathed a word of it. And that wild horses couldn't drag it from you."

I think of James Earle making nearly the exact same promise to me. The Brotherhood of Secrets.

I take a breath. "I need a records search done, but I can't do it on my computer. I don't want anyone to know it's me doing the searching."

"I'll do it. What do you need?"

"Gary Bukowsky's arrest records," I say quietly.

"Bunsen Gary?" he asks, surprised.

"He was arrested on a B and E a few years ago. I don't know how far back you'll have to go, but I need to know who the arresting officer was."

He nods. "I've got a bunch of reports to file first, so it'll take me some time to pull the arrest records."

"There's one more thing. When you find the name of the officer, I need you to tell me, and only me. Can you do that?"

"Sure," he says.

"No matter who it is."

He frowns, but before he can ask any more questions, I pat him on the arm, thank him, and walk back to my desk.

When my shift ends at five thirty, Maclin's door is still shut. Getting ready to leave, I knock and he calls me in.

"Before you ask," he says, "I'm still searching. Go home. But keep your phone close at hand. I'll let you know as soon as I have a name. It should be soon."

I turn to go.

"And, Detective," he says. "Not a word to anyone until we know who we're dealing with."

I pass Ryan's desk as I walk toward the exit. He's staring at his computer screen, frowning in concentration. The shadows on his face have resurrected the appearance of a man not only agonized by current events, but confounded by them as well. He looks up and, for the briefest moment, his anger shows. Then his expression morphs into a reassuring smile.

"I'm starting your search now," he says. "Where're you headed?"

"Home," I say. "And a long run."

I walk to the garage and get in my car. My hands are shaking, and I grip the steering wheel hard to steady them. It won't be long now.

As soon as I get to the house, I change into my running gear, give Jackie a quick kiss, and bolt out the door. It's above freezing, so there's no ice, and I'm running before I leave the front porch.

Grateful for the cold air clearing my head, I fit my cap more snugly over my forehead and lean into the wind. It's already dark, and the route I'm taking has few streetlights. But I want to get to White Rock Lake. I need some easy paths, framed with something more calming than houses with winter-dead yards and left-over Christmas decorations. It'll be Valentine's Day before some Texans remove their wilting laurels and twinkly lights.

I take Lawther Road south, toward the entrance to the lake. I run about half a mile before I'm aware of the car following me, headlights on, slowed to crawling speed. There are no sidewalks, only packed dirt and bushes on either side of the narrow road. Thinking—hoping—that the driver is merely concerned I'll veer out onto the pavement, I move closer toward the bushes and wave the car ahead. The car picks up speed and pulls alongside me. I can't see the driver, but it's a muscle car, the engine thrumming loudly. Running alone in the dark without a weapon now seems like the most foolish decision I've made in at least a week. The car stops and the driver's door opens. Seth steps from the driver's seat.

"Riz," he says.

"Go away," I tell him, maintaining my steady pace.

"I'm sorry—"

"Don't talk to me," I say. My heart is hammering, but I continue running.

I hear the car door slam and the engine rev. He pulls alongside me again and lowers the passenger window.

"Riz, you have to talk to me," he says.

"I don't have to do shit," I say, picking up the pace. I'm running at a near-sprint.

The car roars past, gaining speed. It turns at a sharp angle in front of me, braking hard. The door flies open and Seth is out of the car, walking in my direction. On full alert, I back up. My heel catches on a root and I almost go down. I turn and run in the opposite direction.

"It was me who called the paper," he yells.

"What?" I say, doing a 180.

"I was the anonymous source saying the shooter was a cop."

"Why would you do that?"

"To pressure whoever was killing the dealers," he says, walking toward me.

"So you're saying it wasn't you?"

"How can you ask me that?" He sounds sincerely hurt, but I back up an equal number of steps.

"You fucking kidding me?" I ask. "After using and probably moving drugs stolen from the Sinaloans? Chuffy and Gary both murdered, plus the dealers shot in the streets? Leaning on Pearla to leave town? Connect the dots, partner. I did."

He's near enough now to see the expression on my face. A realization like a wasp sting draws him up short. "You're afraid of me."

My only thought in that moment is wondering if I can vault the bushes lining the road—or at least plow through them to make my escape. He puts up his hands in a placating gesture.

"Riz," he says. "I knew the drugs were stolen from the cartel. Chuffy told me he'd stolen them, but the dumb bastard had no idea the Knife would come looking for him. I was using my position with Chuffy to work a line to the Knife. I knew the Sinaloans would eventually come looking for him."

"And almost got me incinerated in the process. Your association with Chuffy didn't do *him* much good."

"He was taken the day you pulled me out of the Alamo Motel—"

"Oh, so it's my fault Chuffy got his intestines aerated?"

"No, Riz—that's not what I'm saying."

"And using the product was all a part of your elaborate setup as well."

"I'm not going to lie to you, Riz: I've got a serious problem. I know that. But it has nothing to do with doing my job."

"And what's that?"

"Taking down El Cuchillo, as well as the shooter. They're related, but not the same."

"Who's the shooter, then?"

"I can't tell you. Not yet."

"That's what I thought," I say bitterly. "Look, I can't believe anything you have to say to me right now. If you can't trust me, I can't trust you. It's as simple as that. So I'm done talking. The shitstorm is about to get real—and I don't want to be anywhere near you when the fallout happens. You got it?"

I turn my back on him a final time and run toward home. I hear the car engine rev, but the sound diminishes as it heads in the opposite direction.

It's hard to find my way home in the dark; my eyes are too misted to see what's right in front of me. For once I let the anger recede, and the loss washes over me—not in gentle, coursing swells, but with the crushing force of a rogue wave, bruising and suffocating. I find a tree for support and lean against it as I mourn, loudly and unashamedly, for what I've lost, and what may never be reclaimed.

CHAPTER 34

JANUARY 28, 2014
BELLA VISTA

I've turned onto my street, winded and slowing to a walking pace, when my cell phone rings. It's Maclin. I take a steadying breath and answer, my voice hoarse from my crying jag.

"Where are you?" he asks.

"I'm just returning from a run. On my street now."

"I'm in front of your place. I'll wait."

I break into a jog again and, as I approach my house, I see a dark sedan parked directly across the street.

The driver's window rolls down and Maclin calls, "Detective, get in."

I get into the front passenger seat, my lungs still heaving from the run. As soon as my door is closed, Maclin puts the car in drive and pulls away from the house.

"Where are we going?" I ask.

"I need to show you something. I found the name of the officer who arrested Gary Bukowsky." He gives me a meaningful look. "You're not going to like it."

"Who is it?"

"It was Craddock," he says.

"What?" Of all the names I was expecting, Tom's was not one. It's like a brick to the head. I think of his cheerful, jowly face and can't reconcile the image with the thought that he's a cold-blooded killer. "But that doesn't make sense," I say. "He was at the station the morning that Carlos Rivera was killed."

"Yeah, but Craddock was the one setting him up for the buy-and-bust. He could have lured him there earlier in the morning."

I search my memory for the details of that day. My attention was focused primarily on my partner and his stealing drugs from a dead man. I wasn't paying much attention to Craddock. "I don't think the timing matches up," I say, uncertainly.

"And yet, there it is," Maclin says.

I look out the window and try to remember anything Craddock might have said or done to support Gary's claim that the cop who arrested him was the shooter. In terms of an obvious motive, Craddock seemed more sad than angry when he told me about his daughter dying of an overdose. But he did make statements that the dead dealers, in effect, got what they deserved. And he left the station early today. Did he know he was being scrutinized?

"Where's Craddock now?" I ask.

"That's what we're going to find out," Maclin says.

"So where are we going?"

"We're meeting someone who can corroborate the story. A CI who sold him an unlicensed handgun."

I'm still shaking my head in disbelief. Maclin is driving south on Abrams, picking up speed.

"You have your gun on you?" he asks.

"No, I don't take it when I go running—"

I look at Maclin, and the way he's now gripping the wheel as though he'll snap it off at the base. He's nervous and sweating profusely, his jaw working as his teeth grind together. This has really shaken him. As though acknowledging my searching looks, Maclin says, "I know you like Tom. I do too. But we have to follow in the direction that the information is leading us."

My cell phone dings and I pull it from my jacket. It's a text from Kevin Ryan.

The text jumps from the screen like an emergency flare: *Maclin was the arresting officer! What do you want me to do?*

My head snaps in wild alarm toward Maclin at the same moment he takes a hard left onto a side street, knocking me against the passenger door, and pulls roughly to the curb.

"Turn off your phone," he says. He's still holding the wheel with his right hand, but in his left hand is his SIG Sauer, the barrel held steady over his crooked elbow and pointed at me. I turn off the phone.

"Throw it onto the back seat," he says. "Now!"

For a moment I consider slamming it into Maclin's head, but there is no remorse or pity on his face, only feral expectation. I believe in that moment he would like any excuse to kill me.

"I will shoot you and dump your body right here," he says, spittle flecking his lips. "Keep both hands on the dashboard, where I can see them. You twitch and you're dead."

I toss the phone onto the back seat. "What now?" I ask, putting my hands on the dash.

"Now we tie up some loose ends," he says.

He drives through the quiet streets of Lakewood and I realize we're headed toward White Rock Lake. Jackie can track my movements on her phone, but I had cut my run short after the incident with Seth. I'm often gone for hours when I'm really stressed, and it may be a long while before she checks her phone for my whereabouts.

"What's going on, Maclin?" I demand. "Why are you doing this?"

He looks at me, his eyes bloodshot, his mouth pulled into a scowl. "You couldn't just do your job and stay out of matters that didn't concern you," he mutters, angrily. "All you had to do was shut the fuck up and do what you were told."

"Is that why you kept me chained to a desk? On suspension? And here I was thinking you were concerned about my well-being."

He grimaces. "You think I gave a good goddamn about your mental health? Even being put on suspension, you had to go sticking your nose into it. What happens next is all on you."

Seth had told me that the shooter was not the same as the Sinaloans, but that the two were related. "What's IA got on you?" I ask.

Maclin's right hand slaps me viciously across the face, and returns to its two o'clock position on the wheel within seconds. "Shut the fuck up. I've had to listen to the smart-ass crap coming out of your mouth for months. Not another word."

I taste blood where a tooth has nicked the tender inside of my lip. The car makes several turns, the last one onto Lawther, circling the lake.

The grassy areas and parking lots are empty and dark. I tense, waiting for Maclin to turn in toward the dilapidated White Rock Boathouse, abandoned at this hour, or to slow down as we pass the overgrown areas fronting the lake. The marshy inlets, choked with towering cattails and brush, would conceal a body for days.

But he drives along the lake until he turns up a narrow street leading to a large mansion facing the water. A bronze placard on the iron fence reads BELLA VISTA. The half-acre front yard slopes up to a two-story antebellum monstrosity, and he pulls into the private driveway and parks.

"Get out," he tells me.

He orders me to walk around to the side of the house. We enter a walkway canopied with an arbor. Like a dark tunnel. I remember the hooded man who had taunted me in the underground terminus.

"You were the one in the Elm Street Tunnel," I say.

Maclin shoves me from behind to keep walking. He says, "It was worth the effort of searching for Gary just to see the fear on your face."

When we emerge from the arbor, motion-sensing security lights blaze in sequence, blinding me for an instant.

"Keep moving," Maclin says.

Behind the house is a full acre of private property, the winter-rye grass a neon green. In the near distance are what look to be a small barn and riding paddock. True wealth in Dallas is measured not only by lot size and dwelling footage, but by how much yardage you have to board your million-dollar horses.

Maclin jams the barrel of the gun in my shoulder blade and points toward the barn.

"Open the door," he tells me, and I slide the double panels apart and step inside. There are only two stalls that I can see. A horse, his neck arched over the latched gate in the nearest stall, stares at us expectantly with wide, unblinking eyes. Standing next to the horse is the dark-haired man I'd first seen at the Circus bar; the man who'd held a gun on me at Delano's Gym. The same gun he's holding now.

The gate to the second stall swings open and the horse within walks out calmly, following a man holding a rope, which is secured loosely around the horse's neck. The man's face is angled like chipped granite under the light of the barn's incandescent bulbs. He's holding a long, narrow knife in his other hand, and wearing boots imprinted with intricate designs—patterns that differ from the ones he wore the last time I saw him. El Cuchillo looks at me and then points the tip of the blade to a place a few feet away, signaling where he wants me to stand.

I have the urge to bolt and run, but the man with the boots has read my body language: "Please, Detective," he says in warning.

I manage to move a few steps forward, trying to keep both the cartel gunman and Maclin in my peripheral vision.

Alfonso Ruiz Zena stares at me for a moment. Then, as though resigning himself to some unspoken decision, he takes a deep breath and returns his attention to the horse. He wraps one arm over the horse's neck and, with his knife hand, places the flat side of the blade over the pulsing, tender area of the main artery, just below the jawline. The horse snorts softly, his eyes heavy-lidded, his body relaxed.

"I have always loved horses," he tells me. "But the thing about horses is they are very stupid. Trusting, but stupid. The opposite of some people, I think."

He looks at me in a calculating way. The blade points at me like a finger. "I think you are not stupid. How did you escape the fire?"

It takes a few breaths to find my voice. "I wove a ladder from my hair," I say, clenching my hands into fists. "Like Rapunzel. Then I just climbed down."

His lips stretch into something that is nothing like a smile.

I hear Maclin say, "I told you she had a smart fuckin' mouth."

"No," Zena says to me, without acknowledging Maclin. "You lean into the fear. You are afraid, but you fight." He taps the flat of his blade against the side of his head. "I know this well." He throws a hooded glance at Maclin. "Others do not."

"What is this place?" I ask. The setting—the mansion, the well-manicured grounds—makes the encounter surreal, as though some alternate universe had spilled black, toxic sludge over the rarefied world of old Dallas money.

"Until a few hours ago it belonged to a competitor of mine," Zena says. "He was a banker of sorts, laundering money for the Nuevo Juarez cartel. I thought perhaps he would know where my heroin was. But it seems he did not."

"He's dead," I say, my lips barely moving.

"Yes," he says, as though it's of no consequence. "You've seen much death too, I think." The blade points at me, then passes through the air like a conductor's baton. "I see death all around you."

"*Kostucha,*" I whisper. *Death in white.*

He nods as if he understands.

"We also have a name for death," he says. He returns the blade of the knife to the horse's neck, the sharp edge against the pelt. "La Pelona."

He slowly scrapes the knife along the horse's neck in gentle upward motions. It shaves glossy hair cleanly off the hide, exposing the dark flesh underneath.

"Death for us comes as a woman," he says. The scraping sound of the knife against the pelt is loud in the otherwise silent barn, the hair falling in wisps to the ground. "Perhaps you understand this better than anyone."

I can hear Maclin stirring. He's restless, afraid. Eager to be gone from whatever is about to happen. "We need to finish this up," Maclin says.

"Did you know about your sergeant?" Zena asks me.

I shake my head. All my limbs are trembling uncontrollably. I'm beyond speaking now. I can only follow the path of the blade against the horse's neck.

"Your sergeant has a bad gambling addiction, Detective. He was deeply in debt to some very dangerous people."

A scarlet line has appeared in the horse's flesh; one tiny ribbon of oozing red, seeping upward like a miniature spring. There is no movement from the horse except a slight ripple of muscle. The muscles in my own injured leg—the leg with the tattoo—begin a painful cramping.

"I offered your sergeant a way out of his problem," Zena says. "For every Nuevo Juarez player he took off the street, I paid off part of his debt. And if he found my heroin, I would pay the entire amount: one hundred thousand dollars." Zena dispassionately studies the blood swelling from the newly made wound, which slowly trickles down the horse's neck. One droplet spatters to the ground, and I stare at it glistening under the lights.

So Maclin had been the shooter. Not Craddock or Ryan or my partner. I turn my head to look at Maclin and see what I should have all along. I recall the chart I'd made for Dr. Theo with Maclin's name uppermost, *the same kind of whiteboard map I would use in a criminal case,* with the crime boss at the top of the pyramid. Who better to cover up a murder than a homicide cop? And how better to finance one's vices than to be a sergeant in a narcotics squad, with access to almost limitless, often-unaccountable, resources of cash? Internal Affairs had been on to him, but they hadn't yet connected everything.

Maclin looks at me with unmasked hatred. As Uncle Benny had told me, one of my most unattractive qualities is running things to ground. I had put pressure on Maclin without knowing the full measure of his corruption, or knowing how far he would go to undermine my confidence in my professional abilities, in my team, in my own sanity. Leaving the Bible verses on the dead bodies was just an added, vicious jab directed at me.

"But I'm still without my heroin," Zena says. "And the sergeant left a witness too long alive." He sighs and pats the horse in a perversely friendly fashion. "My time here has come to an end."

He leads the horse back into the stall and closes the gate. Then he stands before me, his hands relaxed at his sides, the long knife blade crusted with a thin line of the horse's blood. He raises the knife and touches the tip of the blade to the notch at the base of my throat.

"Your sergeant has failed. What if I make you the same offer I made him? One hundred thousand dollars."

"Wait a fucking minute," Maclin says, his vocal cords shredded with tension and fear. "I'll find the drugs. I just need a little more time—"

I feel the sharp, biting sting of the metal between my collarbones. The blade has punctured the skin, and I sense the warm trickle of my own blood running delicately down onto my chest. I want to cry out, but a memory of Uncle Benny settles over me like a warm towel. I'm sitting in a hospital room next to his bed. He's dying of cancer and I'm holding his emaciated hand in both of mine. I ask him if he's afraid. He grins and says, "If you can leave this planet with the grease of hard work on your hands and a clean rep, you've lived a good life."

The entirety of the world has telescoped itself onto the brutal features of the man standing in front of me. His lips part expectantly, showing the strong white teeth of a predator. With the adrenaline rush of terror, the overhead lights seem to flare as my pupils dilate, etching a corona of light around El Cuchillo's head. The resemblance to Paul Krasnow, my brother's old partner, is uncanny. My brother, my ever-faithful protector at home, had slipped so quickly into the sucking pit of corruption. How easy it would be to nod a simple *Yes,* if only to save my life. Worse than

betraying me, Andrew had betrayed the best part of himself—
and he had died rather than live with it.

Uncle Benny's voice whispers in my ear: *Don't get caught in the
abyss of your own morass.*

One hundred thousand dollars, the Knife has offered. A nod of
the head and you can live.

I fill my lungs with air and say, "No."

In a voice tinged with hysteria, Maclin bellows, "What are you
waiting for?"

Zena looks from me to his gunman and makes a slight, af-
firming movement of his head. There is the explosive sound of a
gunshot and I jump, but there is no pain. The horses scream in
their stalls and I see, at the edge of my vision, Maclin falling to
the ground, clutching his chest. The gunman walks closer to him
and fires twice more, into Maclin's head. He thrashes briefly, then
there's no more movement.

Both my hands have gone instinctively to grasp the Saint
Michael medallion around my neck. I meet and hold Zena's gaze,
bracing for a second volley of shots that will crush my spine. Or
the quick, silver slash of his knife across my throat.

Instead, he carefully returns the long knife to the sheath hanging from his belt and says, "*Con dinero baile el perro.* You understand this?"

"Everyone has his price," I translate.

"Except you, it would seem," he says. "But do not excuse my
actions for kindness, Detective. I have my reasons." He motions
to his gunman, and they slip quietly through the sliding panels,
leaving me alone with the body of my former sergeant.

With trembling legs I ease myself down to the ground, onto my
hands and knees, and press my forehead against the cold cement.
When the worst of the quaking has stopped, I crawl to one of the

stalls, as far away as possible from the spreading circle of blood leaking from Maclin's head. I sit with my back against the gate, inhaling the richly sweet smell of hay and horses. I think I should retrieve my phone from Maclin's car, place some kind of bandage over the still-seeping gash at my throat. But the thought of movement is too much to bear, so I sit, hugging my knees tightly to my chest. It seems a long time before I hear the shrill sound of sirens approaching.

CHAPTER 35

I lie in my bed—the bed I share with Jackie in our home—and listen to the sounds of pans being rattled in the kitchen. The fragrance of freshly brewed coffee and something yeasty baking in the oven fill the bedroom. I throw off the covers and sit up carefully.

Padding into the bathroom, I stand in front of the mirror, peel back the bandage that Jackie had applied at the base of my throat, and examine the inch-long nick between my collarbones. It could have been made by a surgeon's scalpel, so thin it is. But the skin around the wound is red and angry-looking this morning, and I'm certain I'll carry a scar there for the rest of my life.

I don't know all the reasons why the Knife spared my life. It seems impossible to think he hadn't killed me because I couldn't be bribed, or because I had merely survived the fire. Instinctively I believe it was a point of pride for him that because he wasn't able to bribe me this time, he would try again at some point in the distant future. He said *I have my reasons,* but it's pointless today to try to guess what those reasons could be.

Jackie appears at the bathroom door holding a steaming mug of coffee. She hands me the mug and kisses me. The doorbell rings, followed by a hard knocking at the front door.

Jackie makes a face. "It's the local news," she says.

I set the mug down and hold Jackie close. "Let's ignore them," I whisper into her ear.

The knocking comes again, this time more persistently.

She pulls away from me. She has a look on her face that I've often seen when she testifies in court as an expert medical witness on a child-abuse case: serenely angry, dangerously focused, with majestic intent.

"I've given them two warnings already," she says.

I follow her into the kitchen, where she goes out the back door and moves to the side of the house. Walking to the living room, mug in hand, I stand at the large bay window wearing only my shorts and a T-shirt. I'm spotted by the news crews dotting the front lawn like carrion birds.

"Detective Rhyzyk," a female reporter yells. She gets as close to the window as she can without trampling the hedges in the front garden, and says, "Can we just ask you a couple of questions about your sergeant being killed last night? Were you injured? How did you escape the killers?"

At that moment Jackie comes from the side of the house, striding across the front lawn holding a garden hose. She takes a wide stance, like a swordsman about to do battle, and turns the nozzle on full blast. The first wall of water hits the female reporter climbing through the bushes; she shrieks and tries unsuccessfully to protect her salon-straightened hair. When she's thoroughly doused, Jackie turns the hose on the other reporters and cameramen. They scatter back toward the street, cursing furiously.

Jackie turns off the hose and calls out cheerfully, "Have a nice day."

When she comes back into the house, using the front door this time, her color is attractively high, and she's grinning a Cheshire Cat smile. She tells me defiantly, "Just because I'm a vegetarian doesn't mean I don't know how to kick some ass too."

We are left blissfully alone for another hour, enjoying our breakfast in peace, until the doorbell rings again. But this time it's Brant, Seth's friend from Vice.

I take him into the office and close the door. He positions his chair close to mine and sits facing me, making sure I'm listening carefully, his expression serious.

"I wanted you to know that Maclin had been under investigation for big-money gambling for quite some time," he says. "We had some undercovers following him to illegal gambling sites, and we were monitoring his online gaming as well. IA was doing their part from the intra-office, procedural side. We'd had a tracker installed in his car, and that's how we were able to find you last night at White Rock Lake. Jackie had seen you get into Maclin's car after your run. When your cell phone went dead, she got worried and contacted Tom Craddock. As well, Kevin Ryan discovered that it was Maclin who had arrested Gary Bukowsky, and immediately called IA. So you had a lot of people looking for you."

He pauses for a moment, and adds, "Including Seth."

"Yeah, well, we had a bit of a confrontation last night," I say.

"Seth has been working with us, Betty. We had the illegal-gambling angle, but your partner was the one who, through Chuffy Bryant and the stolen heroin, helped tie Maclin to the Sinaloans. The Feds were in on it too, as well as the DEA. He didn't tell you about it because you'd been on suspension and restricted duty, and he was told not to—not by us, but by the Feds. Believe me, he wanted to."

I sit quietly, taking it all in. Brant leans closer to me and says,

"Look, I know he's got a problem with drugs. A big problem. And he's going to need all the friends he can get to put himself straight again."

When I finally walk Brant to the door, he gives me a brief hug, and says, "He needs you, Riz."

The rest of the day I spend with Jackie, doing simple domestic things. The joy of the quotidian. At four o'clock the doorbell rings once more, signaling a special-delivery package. It's a small box addressed to me in handwritten, block letters. I peel back the brown paper and remove the lid of the box. Inside is a layer of cotton, which I also remove. Underneath the cotton is a worn and pitted Saint Michael medallion on a chain. The medallion worn by three generations of Rhyzyk women, taken from me by the Roy family months ago, and which I thought I'd never see again.

I read the note aloud to a wide-eyed, startled Jackie: "Vengeance is mine, thus sayeth the Lord. But I will help Him see it done, and soon.—Evangeline Roy."

My hands are remarkably steady as I set the box down on the dining-room table. After all the anxious wondering and waiting—*Will she or won't she appear in my life again?*—I've finally gotten confirmation that I'm not crazy to have been worried and vigilant after seeing an abundance of redheaded crones around town.

I walk into the bedroom, holding the medallion tightly in my hand, willing the heat from my body to exorcise the bad juju infused into the metal by the Roys. I slip the chain holding the original Saint Michael around my neck, letting it rest heavily over the medallion Jackie had given me. The old and the new, like a connective thread joining the past and the present. It lies protectively against my sternum, under the wound given to me by the Knife, like a newly found breastplate to an incomplete suit of armor. I reach for the dime I had placed on the dresser so many weeks ago, and slip it into my pocket as a talisman.

I'll burn the note from Evangeline to ashes. She's given me fair warning that she's not finished with me yet.

CHAPTER 36

FEBRUARY 4, 2014
FUEL CITY CAR WASH AND TACO STAND

Oczyszczenie pola kamieni. "Clearing the field of stones." It's what Uncle Benny would have said needed to be done before anything vital could grow; as true for nurturing potatoes as it is for nurturing people.

Or as James Earle might put it: "Making amends." James, I discovered, has offered Wayne a room in his home so long as he keeps going to 12-step meetings and stays clean and sober. Surprisingly, or maybe not so much, James has started going to meetings as well. He tells me he'll see how it goes. No promises. Just one day at a time. I like to picture the two of them standing among their fellow recovering addicts, happily swilling gallons of coffee, surrounded by a bank of cigarette smoke.

For me, making amends includes a lot of people. First and foremost, it means making it right with Jackie again. I'm back in the house full-time, but I know I'm on probation. I've agreed to go to couples counseling. Unfortunately it can't be with Dr. Theo, who will continue to meet with me, one-on-one, for a while. I had teased him that it was just as well: Jackie wouldn't be the pushover I had been in therapy. He'd laughed and said he wished more of his patients could be like me.

"Stimulating?" I had asked.

"Let's just leave it at *challenging*," he had answered.

Do people inevitably become what they do? That's what I had pondered in my last session with Dr. Theo. Homicide detectives deal in solving murder cases—day in, day out. Does that proximity to unnatural death eventually warp some basic, intrinsic goodness? Or are people drawn to the thing they do because it reflects some essential part of themselves that is dark, angry, less than humane?

And what did it say about me that I was a decade into a career fighting a losing battle to put away dangerous poison peddlers, when ten more were waiting to replace them? Dr. Theo told me he thought it was a little bit of both—and that, if it could be taken as any comfort, the fact that I was asking the questions proved I hadn't fallen completely off the beam.

I find I'm looking forward to my future sessions with him. I'd like to think that this newfound eagerness for headshrinking is a sign of a more lasting recovery.

But questions of my sanity (or the sanity of the world in general) aside, I was back at work, fully reinstated, within forty-eight hours of Maclin's death. And within twenty-four hours of returning to the station, I had figured out where the missing heroin was.

I have to give some of the credit to Tom Craddock. I was having breakfast at Norma's Café with Craddock and Ryan, hashing over the Sinaloans' missing heroin, trying to figure out where it could be hidden, when Tom, who knows all things Elvis, started humming "Love Me Tender" along with the background music. A realization like a bag of cement hit me over the head: the only place besides the Alamo Motel where Chuffy and Pearla shared a common history (and keys) was the Old Mill Inn Restaurant at Fair Park, where they had worked—Pearla at the cash register, Chuffy over the kitchen grill. The restaurant had been searched in a perfunctory way, as every place associated with Chuffy had been. But no one had thought to look in the oversized hollow statue of Elvis—the place where Pearla and Dusty had kept their pocketbooks safe. Inside the King was almost all of the two kilos of Mexican heroin, stolen from El Cuchillo and the Sinaloa cartel.

Chuffy Bryant was a despicable human being. But he had more courage, or maybe stubbornness, than most anyone else tangling with the Knife. Despite unimaginable pain, he never did tell his torturer where he'd hidden the drugs.

Solving that particular case has pushed my name forward again for a sergeant's badge. Ryan had told me, "Three times a charm": first Verne Taylor, then Marshall Maclin, now me. But Craddock shook his head doubtfully at the news: "Uh-uh, Red Hot Betty— three on a match would not be a healthy life choice."

The search for the Knife continues, here and across the border. After leaving the Bella Vista mansion on White Rock Lake, he disappeared like smoke into the atmosphere. But now, at least, there is a sketch of his face, a set of fingerprints, and the known whereabouts of his hometown. Even if he is killed or captured, which is bound to happen sooner or later, there will be more like him to fill his nightmarish boots.

I think about all the people who have lost loved ones to drugs. Craddock losing his daughter. Ryan his brother-in-law. Euell Tilton his sister.

And then there's my partner, whom I haven't spoken to since the night of Maclin's death. I have amends to make to Seth Dutton as well. I don't know if he'll get clean and sober, but I judged him harshly, believing that the man who is the closest thing I'll ever have again to a brother could have been responsible for cold-blooded murder.

I have driven down the Tollway to Riverfront Street, passing beyond the twin oil tanks marking the entrance to Fuel City. I pull into the parking lot—guarded, as always, by the rusted oil derrick and the life-sized bronze buffalo statue. The lot is nearly full, but I find a space next to the old-fashioned phone booth. Like the buffalo, it's a thing of the past—relegated to the nostalgia of things that were but are no more on this fourth day of February 2014, the anniversary of my brother Andrew's death.

In the distance I see my partner waiting for me. He's sitting at a picnic table, close to the pen holding the longhorn steer cropping the thin grass with weathered lips. I touch both of the Saint Michael medallions around my neck for luck; I also touch the dime that I carry in the pocket of my jeans, a reminder that Uncle Benny is with me again.

I will tell my partner of things that are attached to life. That Mary Grace will be having her baby in our house in a few weeks. And that she has decided on the baby's name: Elizabeth.

I'll tell him that I'm running again, daily. That the nighttime terrors have stopped, even as the knowledge that Evangeline Roy and El Cuchillo are both still alive and fueled with vengeance sometimes sits on my chest like a heavy stone. I'll tell him that I miss him, and that I'm more sorry than I can ever say, and that I need him. What more can I do?

I get out of my car and walk toward Seth. He stands from the table to greet me. He enfolds me in a tight hug, and his arms feel good.

ACKNOWLEDGMENTS

A world of gratitude to my agent, Julie Barer, who, more than a decade ago, took a chance on an unpublished writer, and now— wonder of wonders—we're launching our fifth book out into the world! Heartfelt thanks also to my editor, Joshua Kendall, who, with patience and a "killer's" instinct for the necessary elements of exciting, contemporary crime fiction, guided me through some rocky places to find the true path of the story.

My thanks also to Brant Hickman, Plano Police Department (Ret.), for his humor and true-life stories, hard won over thirty years of service in law enforcement; Theo and Lorin Theodosiou for their wisdom and warm company; David Hale Smith for challenging me to write crime fiction in the first place; Daniel Hale for his unwavering support; Dave and Mitzi Nix for their West Texas savvy; and Joe Lansdale for his friendship and generous advocacy.

I would not have succeeded without the continuing support of Mulholland Books and Little, Brown and Company: Michael Pietsch, Reagan Arthur, Pamela Brown, Emily Giglierano, Sabrina Callahan, Ben Allen, and Nicky Guerreiro.

There are many aspects to bringing a book to publication, but none more important than the copyeditors who dedicatedly, and painstakingly, polish the final manuscript. Many thanks to

ACKNOWLEDGMENTS

Pamela Marshall and Allan Fallow for their contributions in bringing this book to completion.

To my family and friends who have supported me through the many ups and downs while writing *The Burn,* bless you all. And, finally, Jim David, you are forever and always my sunshine.

ABOUT THE AUTHOR

Kathleen Kent is the author of the Edgar Award–nominated *The Dime*, as well as three bestselling historical novels: *The Heretic's Daughter, The Traitor's Wife,* and *The Outcasts*. She lives in Dallas.

MULHOLLAND BOOKS

You won't be able to put down these Mulholland books.

LONE JACK TRAIL *by Owen Laukkanen*

TROUBLED BLOOD *by Robert Galbraith*

THE BOOK OF LAMPS AND BANNERS *by Elizabeth Hand*

BLOOD GROVE *by Walter Mosley*

SMOKE *by Joe Ide*

LIGHTSEEKERS *by Femi Kayode*

YOU'LL THANK ME FOR THIS *by Nina Siegal*

HEAVEN'S A LIE *by Wallace Stroby*

A MAN NAMED DOLL *by Jonathan Ames*

THE OTHERS *by Sarah Blau*

Visit mulhollandbooks.com for
your daily suspense fix.